PRAISE FOR THE LADY

"[A] history mystery in fine Vict[orian style].... [This] spirited debut mixes classic country-house mystery with a liberal dash of historical romance."
—*New York Times* bestselling author Julia Spencer-Fleming

"Riveting.... Huber deftly weaves together an original premise, an enigmatic heroine, and a compelling Highland setting."
—*New York Times* bestselling author Deanna Raybourn

"[A] fascinating heroine.... A thoroughly enjoyable read!"
—*USA Today* bestselling author Victoria Thompson

"Romance, suspense, mystery . . . add up to a fine read."
—*Kirkus Reviews*

"Gripping.... Fans of C. S. Harris's Regency mysteries will be pleased."
—*Publishers Weekly*

"[Huber] designs her heroine as a woman who straddles the line between eighteenth-century behavior and twenty-first-century independence."
—New York Journal of Books

"[A] must read.... One of those rare books that will both shock and please readers."
—Fresh Fiction

"Anyone who enjoys historical mysteries, atmospheric settings, and strong female investigators should have Huber on their automatic buy list."
—Criminal Element

"One of the best historical mysteries that I have read this year."
—Cozy Mystery Book Reviews

Titles by Anna Lee Huber

THE ANATOMIST'S WIFE
MORTAL ARTS
A GRAVE MATTER
A STUDY IN DEATH
A PRESSING ENGAGEMENT
(an enovella)
AS DEATH DRAWS NEAR
A BRUSH WITH SHADOWS
AN ARTLESS DEMISE
A STROKE OF MALICE
A WICKED CONCEIT
A PERILOUS PERSPECTIVE
A FATAL ILLUSION
A DECEPTIVE COMPOSITION
A TARNISHED CANVAS

A Tarnished Canvas

ANNA LEE HUBER

BERKLEY PRIME CRIME
New York

BERKLEY PRIME CRIME
Published by Berkley
An imprint of Penguin Random House LLC
1745 Broadway, New York, NY 10019
penguinrandomhouse.com

Copyright © 2025 by Anna Aycock
Penguin Random House values and supports copyright. Copyright fuels creativity, encourages diverse voices, promotes free speech, and creates a vibrant culture. Thank you for buying an authorized edition of this book and for complying with copyright laws by not reproducing, scanning, or distributing any part of it in any form without permission. You are supporting writers and allowing Penguin Random House to continue to publish books for every reader. Please note that no part of this book may be used or reproduced in any manner for the purpose of training artificial intelligence technologies or systems.

BERKLEY and the BERKLEY & B colophon are registered trademarks and BERKLEY PRIME CRIME is a trademark of
Penguin Random House LLC.

Library of Congress Cataloging-in-Publication Data

Names: Huber, Anna Lee, author.
Title: A tarnished canvas / Anna Lee Huber.
Description: First edition. | New York: Berkley Prime Crime, 2025.
Identifiers: LCCN 2024059712 (print) | LCCN 2024059713 (ebook) |
ISBN 9780593639436 (trade paperback) | ISBN 9780593639443 (ebook)
Subjects: LCGFT: Detective and mystery fiction. | Novels.
Classification: LCC PS3608.U238 T37 2025 (print) |
LCC PS3608.U238 (ebook) | DDC 813/.6—dc23/eng/20241227
LC record available at https://lccn.loc.gov/2024059712
LC ebook record available at https://lccn.loc.gov/2024059713

First Edition: June 2025

Printed in the United States of America
1st Printing

The authorized representative in the EU for product safety and compliance is Penguin Random House Ireland, Morrison Chambers, 32 Nassau Street, Dublin D02 YH68, Ireland, https://eu-contact.penguin.ie.

*For my in-laws—Tony and Jima.
In gratitude for all of your love and support
and for raising such a stellar son.*

A Tarnished Canvas

CHAPTER 1

Virtue itself turns vice, being misapplied.
—WILLIAM SHAKESPEARE

MARCH 1833
EDINBURGH, SCOTLAND

I could count on one hand the number of times I'd witnessed a gentleman hanging out of a window, and most of those had been the result of some foolish wager. I trusted my husband's current predicament wasn't due to such idiocy. Though one could never be sure.

Regardless, it was a precarious enough position to give me heart palpitations when I ventured into the nursery to discover whether the odd thwacking sound I'd been hearing was coming from within. It had been loud enough and repetitive enough to pull me from my concentration on the latest portrait I was finishing in my studio at the opposite end of the corridor. I'd dropped the brush I'd been wielding into a jar of linseed oil and set aside my palette, picking up an old paint-splattered rag to wipe off my hands as I went in search of the source of the noise. The sight that had met my eyes upon opening the nursery door had silenced my query before I could even utter it.

Mrs. Mackay, our nanny, stood holding my eleven-month-old daughter as they both stared wide-eyed in the direction of the window. If their expressions hadn't been sufficient to alert me, then Mrs. Mackay's uncharacteristic silence would have. It seemed the only time the good-natured nurse wasn't talking was when she or her charge was asleep.

From this angle, all I could see was Gage's lower extremities spread wide to anchor himself against the frame as he leaned perilously far out the window. I gasped and hastened forward even as the thwacking noise which had drawn me to the nursery in the first place continued.

"What are you doing?" I demanded, wanting to grab hold of him, but fearful that my touch might inadvertently cause his already unstable grip to slip.

"Just trying . . . to dislodge . . . this branch," he communicated between grunts, even as he wielded some sort of boat hook or fireplace poker, thrusting it outward, presumably toward the offending bunch of twigs. It thwacked against the stone edifice of our town house on Albyn Place, ringing with a more metallic clang than I'd been able to detect at a farther distance. His left elbow, I noted, was braced heavily against the stone ledge, and I could only pray the masonry held.

"Just a little . . . farther," he groaned, hooking his right leg around the frame and inching his left hip out.

I lurched forward, grasping onto his pelvis, propriety be dashed.

"Almost . . . there." He gave one last lunge like a fencer, before exclaiming in apparent victory.

A small crowd which had gathered below backed away as the branch tumbled toward the pavement. "Apologies," Gage called with a lift of the poker.

I tugged at the waist of his trousers, eager to have him back inside the window before he issued any other proclamations. "Mind your head," I urged as he ducked under the sash, slithering back into the room.

Once he was through the aperture with his feet planted firmly on the floor, he straightened, closing the window with a satisfied snick. Flush with victory, he pivoted to face us, still brandishing the poker like a saber.

"What were you *thinking*?" I snapped; my hand pressed to my chest as I sought to slow my racing heart.

"Well, I was . . ." His words petered out as he seemed to note all of our goggle-eyed expressions for the first time. He slowly lowered the poker to his side as he sought to explain. "Mrs. Mackay told me a tree branch had become wedged in the corner of the ledge. It must have blown there during the storm two days ago. That it kept tapping the corner of the far windowpane over the stairwell whenever the wind blew." His gaze flickered toward our daughter, still cradled in the nanny's arms. "That it was disturbing Emma."

That might have been so, but I was quite certain Mrs. Mackay hadn't informed him of this so that he would take it upon himself to immediately remedy the situation by dangling out the window with a fireplace poker. She'd undoubtedly expected him to order our butler to arrange for the nuisance to be taken care of in a safer and more dignified manner.

However, I didn't say any of this. I didn't need to. I could tell from Gage's sheepish expression that he'd already realized this.

Instead, I inhaled a steadying breath and turned to Mrs. Mackay. "Time for a nap?"

"Aye," the nanny confirmed.

Though whether our daughter would settle after the excitement of the past few minutes was anybody's guess.

I offered Emma a reassuring smile and moved close to press a kiss to her cherubic cheek, her golden curls tickling the bridge of my nose.

"It's nearly time for tea," I told my husband as I moved toward the door. "Give me a few minutes to clean up. Then I'll join you in the drawing room."

Where we could continue our discussion of his startling behavior in private.

I hadn't intended to stop painting yet, but Gage's reckless conduct concerned me. I'd known he was feeling a bit at loose ends, but his near obliviousness to the danger he'd just put himself in suggested a problem that ran deeper than mere boredom.

After ensuring my pigments and supplies were sealed and secured, I scraped and cleaned my palette and hung my smock on the hook by the door. The room was cool from the March chill, but I made no move to close the cracked window, knowing the air needed to circulate about the room to not only help the paint dry but also clear some of the caustic fumes. Then I closed and locked the studio door—a precaution I'd first begun taking when I'd lived with my sister and her family after my first husband's death. I'd feared that my nephew or one of my nieces, or a member of the staff, might enter and unwittingly poison themselves from handling some of the toxic substances that comprised my pigments. Now that I had a child of my own, as well as a staff to care for, I'd decided it was best to continue the safeguard.

After a swift detour to the washroom to ensure no stray streaks of paint marked my features, I made my way down to the drawing room. I found my husband, Sebastian Gage, standing before the large window flanked by sage green damask drapes which overlooked Albyn Place, his hands clasped behind his back. He had put his deep blue frock coat back on and repaired his tousled golden hair, presenting a respectable appearance again. Truth be told, I preferred him a bit disheveled, a bit undone. Perhaps because he was so rarely less than perfectly put together, and only in private. But not when that disheveling was the result of him dangling out a window.

He turned as I entered, crossing to meet me before the walnut sofa upholstered in daffodil silk. "Kiera, I apologize," he said as he grasped hold of my hands. His pale blue gaze was earnest. "I never meant to cause you or Emma or Mrs. Mackay alarm." He lifted a hand to rub the back of his neck. "To be honest, I'm not entirely sure what I was thinking."

I coaxed him to sit, though I didn't immediately speak, as Jeffers, our butler, had entered with the tea tray. Ever efficient, he must have been waiting for me to arrive. He set the tray on the low table centered on the Axminster carpet before the sofa and then, sensing we desired privacy, withdrew without a word.

"I am," I declared once the door was shut behind him.

Gage appeared slightly startled by this pronouncement.

"You've been at sixes and sevens for weeks," I continued as I began to pour our tea. "Wandering the house, at a loss for something to do." I noticed a smudge of yellow ochre I'd missed on the underside of my right wrist as I added a dash of cream to his cup. "I take it Lady Pinmore's stolen brooch proved to be not much of a challenge."

For the better part of the last decade, Gage had acted as a gentleman inquiry agent, often alongside his father, conducting investigations for those who found themselves in precarious or difficult circumstances, or in need of more delicate assistance than what could be provided by the police or men like the Bow Street Runners in London. I'd been assisting him in this regard since nearly the moment we'd met, as I'd been implicated in a crime that had befallen a fellow house-party guest. Since then, we'd unmasked a number of murderers, recovered missing artifacts and heirlooms, and foiled half a dozen dastardly plots.

However, I didn't actively take part in every inquiry he undertook. There were instances when my involvement was both unneeded and my interest unpiqued, as I also had my art and daughter to occupy my time. In fact, it had been several months since I'd done more than confer with my husband on the cases he was working on, which had admittedly been few.

Gage's mouth compressed with derision. "Because it was never stolen. She'd merely lent it to her daughter-in-law and forgotten."

"Oh, dear," I replied in dismay as I passed him his teacup, an attempt to mask the amusement quivering in my breast.

Apparently I wasn't successful, for Gage scowled in irritation. "It isn't funny."

"Oh, come now," I countered soothingly, no longer bothering to suppress my smile. "You must admit, it is a little bit. Her ladyship was so very certain one of her scurrilous nephews had taken it."

I'd not been party to his interview with Lady Pinmore, but I'd overheard this strident accusation in her raised voice through the drawing room door.

Gage's expression softened as he appeared to at least consider my point, waiting until I'd brought my own cup to my lips before replying. "That, or one of Edinburgh's criminal gangs."

I sputtered, nearly choking on my tea.

His eyebrows arched. "Perhaps even Bonnie Brock Kincaid himself."

"You're jesting?" I finally managed to respond.

"No, indeed," he answered before taking a sip of his tea.

I frowned at the absurdity of the suggestion. "As if Bonnie Brock would bestir himself or his gang for such a paltry haul."

"Try politely explaining that to a viscountess," he muttered dryly.

As head of Edinburgh's largest gang, Bonnie Brock Kincaid was not only a formidable criminal but also our reluctant ally and friend. I couldn't describe him as anything less. Not after a year ago when he'd saved me and Gage from where we'd been trapped inside the farthest depths of the dank and dark vaults built within the arches of the South Bridge. Not only had we been locked inside a storage chamber, but Gage had also suffered a head injury from our abductors, our lantern had snuffed out, and I had gone into labor. If not for Bonnie Brock, Emma would have been born within the vaults, and it was unlikely any of us would have made it out alive. That is, *if* we'd ever even been found. The very thought still made me quaver.

"Speaking of Kincaid, I haven't seen him . . ." he glanced over his shoulder in the direction of the window ". . . or any of his lackeys in some time."

"I haven't either," I confessed. Though that didn't mean the rogue wasn't still keeping us under surveillance. Perhaps this crop of men was simply better at concealing themselves. Or perhaps he'd given up on the enterprise entirely. We'd long lamented his stubborn persistence in having us watched while we were in Edinburgh, but I had to admit it caused an odd pang in my chest now to think that we weren't. One I had no desire to examine more closely.

"Maybe he finally recognized what a waste of time and resources it is," Gage said, echoing my thoughts. "For it's doubtful he's suddenly decided to take our desires into consideration."

"Maybe," I conceded, wanting to change the subject. "What of Sergeant Maclean? Have you heard anything from him?"

Seeing the deep furrows that creased his brow, I wished I could retract the question.

"No." Gage frowned into his cup. "He's maintaining his distance."

Sergeant Braden Maclean was an officer for the recently established Edinburgh City Police. The former pugilist had worked with us on a number of occasions, even bringing inquiries to Gage's attention that he believed my husband could assist him with. However, a year ago some heated words had been exchanged, and aspersions were made that could not so easily be taken back. Gage and I had soon after been exonerated, and Maclean had made an apology, but matters had not been the same since.

I studied Gage's profile, wishing there was something I could say or do to restore their relationship. But then I also sympathized with Sergeant Maclean's position. He had a wife and children to support, and his superintendent had not looked on us with much favor a year ago, placing great pressure on Maclean to sever his ties with us. I couldn't imagine that had changed in the past twelve months.

The trouble was that Gage wasn't accustomed to so much leisure. He preferred to remain active—conducting inquiries, managing his properties, riding his horse, even building furniture. But currently there were no pressing investigations, his properties were in good order, the weather over the past few weeks had been dismal and not conducive to outdoor pursuits, and the place where he most indulged in his woodworking hobby stood a short distance from the city at the estate of a friend who was currently in London. While Mr. Knighton, no doubt, wouldn't have minded him using it in his absence, I could tell Gage felt awkward doing so, and the blustery weather certainly didn't motivate him to make the trek. I knew he had made more frequent visits to the Royal Academy to engage in bouts under the tutelage of George Roland, the fencing master there. But there were only so many hours a day he could spend at the fencing *salle*.

I felt a twinge of guilt regarding all the hours I'd been spending in my art studio preparing for my upcoming exhibition, knowing that otherwise we might have spent it together and with Emma. A less honorable gentleman might be driven to alleviate his boredom in less noble pursuits, frequenting gambling dens, cockfights, brothels, and the like. There were plenty of examples of such men throughout Edinburgh and London, as a gentleman was not supposed to sully his hands with work. Gage's activities as an inquiry agent and with woodworking already pushed the boundaries of gentility. Not that I cared. After all, my hands were almost always tainted with oils and pigments. But I was more aware than most of the expectations of society and the implications for those who refused to obey protocol.

Gage drained his cup and leaned forward to set it on the low table, shaking his head in answer to my query whether he'd like some more. "How are your paintings progressing?" he asked, sinking back and turning to face me more fully, his arm draped along the back of the sofa.

"Well," I replied reservedly, never certain exactly how to answer such a question. Art was so subjective. I never knew how close a portrait was to being finished until it was. To an outsider, this might seem facetious, but I could spend weeks or sometimes months tweaking an ostensibly completed painting. Even then, I wasn't always entirely satisfied.

"Do you think it's time to begin searching for a venue?"

I reached out to set my own cup on the table, playing for time. "Probably."

"You sound hesitant."

I looked up to find him regarding me curiously. "Yes. No," I stammered, and then squeezed my eyes shut in frustration. "I mean, yes, it's probably time. But now that it's come . . ." I lowered my gaze to my lap, where I'd begun pleating the lavender fabric of my skirt, struggling to voice my worries. "Maybe this isn't such a good idea."

"What do you mean? Of course it is."

"But this won't be like any normal portrait unveiling or even an exhibit at the Royal Academy of Arts. It's just me and my paintings. Paintings that haven't even been *commissioned*."

As such, they weren't of aristocrats, wealthy industrialists, and society figures desirous of another likeness to adorn their walls. In my case, one painted by the infamous Lady Darby. No, these portraits were of the everyday people always around us. Those who were unlikely to ever have their images captured in oil and pigment. The poor, the downtrodden, the financially and politically oppressed. The people we most needed to see and yet who were constantly overlooked. This was my way of shining a light on them, and I knew the members of the elite would not thank me for it.

Gage leaned forward to grasp hold of my hand. "Kiera." He waited for me to look at him before continuing, his voice gentle with concern. "I thought this was what you wanted?"

"It is. But . . ."

"But what?" he prodded when I left the sentence dangling too long, unable to force the rest of the words past my lips.

What if the portraits don't make a difference? What if they are no good?

There was a rap on the drawing room door, and I drew a softly startled breath, grateful for the reprieve. I forced a smile, shaking my head. "Never mind." Then, before Gage could press the issue, I called out for the person to enter.

"This just arrived for you, my lady," Jeffers announced, crossing the room to hand me a box. It was of the size that normally held documents.

I thanked him as he bowed and departed.

"Were you expecting something?" Gage asked as I scrutinized the smooth grain of the wooden lid.

"No, but perhaps it's for Emma's birthday."

Our daughter would be turning one in just a few weeks' time, and we had planned a celebration to mark the occasion. Guests would begin arriving in a week or two, including my brother, Trevor, and Gage's half brother, Lord Henry Kerr. Gage's father—Emma's only living grandparent—couldn't make the trip from London, as long journeys still aggravated the wound in his leg where he'd been shot the previous summer. Lord Gage had promised to make it up to his only grandchild when we returned to his estate in Warwickshire in May, where work should nearly be completed on the former dower house, which we intended to make our country residence. But I wouldn't have been surprised if Emma's grandfather had arranged for a gift to be delivered here to mark the occasion. He doted on her so.

However, there were no markings on the package to indicate the sender or receiver, let alone our address. As such, it must have been delivered directly from a shop.

Intrigued, I lifted the lid, expecting to find a garment or toy inside. Instead, I discovered a small book accompanied by an embossed invitation. Gage leaned closer to read the card with me as I pulled it from the box.

Catalogue of the Extensive, Genuine, and Highly Valuable Collection of Pictures, late the Property of the Hon. John Clerk of Eldin, one of the Senators of the College of Justice . . . which will be Unreservedly sold by Auction

by Messrs. Thomas Winstanley & Sons (of Liverpool), at
No. 16, Picardy Place, Edinburgh, on Thursday the 14th
of March 1833, and thirteen following days.

"An auction," Gage remarked somewhat unnecessarily as I passed him the invitation so that I could remove the catalog beneath.

It was bound by marbled boards with a spine tooled in gilt. Clearly no expense had been spared, indicating the collection must be valuable indeed. I had, of course, heard of Lord Eldin's death the previous spring, and I'd heard speculation about the upcoming auction of his effects, but I'd been so consumed in recent weeks with my own art that I'd not given anyone else's much thought.

I'd certainly not expected to be issued an actual invitation to the auction. Not that one was required. The auctioneer merely sent them to individuals whom they already knew to be collectors in hopes of enticing them to attend. Though it seemed I must be a late addition to their list, as the auction began the next day. This didn't give me much time to peruse the prospective artwork at leisure.

Opening the catalog, I discovered a list of the artists whose various works were up for auction. Several names immediately leapt out at me, making my heart quicken with excitement. Raphael. Titian. Tintoretto. Veronese. Dürer. Rembrandt. Van Dyck. Rubens. The folded frontispiece even boasted an engraving of Titian's *Adoration of the Magi*.

And the auction didn't just boast pictures, but also prints and drawings by artists like Dürer, Leonardo da Vinci, and Michelangelo, as well as an extensive collection of the Adam brothers' architectural drawings, in addition to articles of virtu: ancient china, bronzes, terra-cottas, jewelry, and even Roman and Greek coins. It was certain to draw an eclectic mix of collectors. I had read speculations that the collection of architectural drawings was particularly exceptional, for the celebrated Adam brothers had been Lord Eldin's uncles.

"I take it your interest is piqued."

I looked up from the pages of the catalog I'd begun flipping through to find Gage watching me. A glint of amusement lit his eyes.

"How can it not be?" I admitted sheepishly, realizing I'd been all but ignoring him.

Fortunately, he didn't seem to take offense, instead chuckling as he draped his arm around me to draw me closer. He pressed a kiss to my temple, speaking into my hair. "Sometimes I wonder whether you love me or art more."

Hearing the teasing note in his voice, I bantered back. "Must I choose?"

He narrowed his eyes playfully and I leaned away, laughing. Only to be pulled back into his embrace, my lips sealed in a searing kiss. If he'd meant to remind me how much I adored him, it was entirely unnecessary, but nevertheless, much appreciated. Especially when it demonstrated just what an effect all the extra fencing and training was having on his physique.

When he pulled away, bending over to fetch the catalog from where it had tumbled from my grasp to the floor, I almost protested. As it was, it took me several seconds to unscramble my wits. But then again, Gage's kisses had always had that influence on me, and well he knew it. His smug smile made that clear as he passed me the catalog.

"Now, tell me what paintings you wish to bid on."

Well, two could play at that game, I decided, snapping the listing closed and pushing to my feet. "There's something I'd like to show you upstairs first," I told him, backing away from him, still clasping the catalog before me.

His eyes fastened on me intently, and I knew if I was closer,

I would be able to see that his pupils had dilated. "Is that so?" he drawled, rising almost lazily to follow me.

I shrugged with feigned nonchalance. "Unless you're too fatigued from your heroics earlier," I murmured, waltzing away from him toward the door. Before I could even open it, he was at my back, hurrying me through and drawing a smirk to my lips.

CHAPTER 2

Though the auction began the following day, I opted to wait until the second day to attend. For one, I had a project which needed my attention and could not be abandoned for so long. Not if I was to achieve the effect I'd been attempting. For another, I wanted time to consider the catalog and its contents.

Gage questioned this decision, for there were two Titians being auctioned on the first day and he knew I was an admirer. But I already owned a Titian that I believed to be far superior to the two up for bidding that day. It had been bequeathed to me by Gage's grandfather along with about a dozen other paintings which had formerly graced the walls of his manor at the edge of Dartmoor. They were currently being stored at Lord Gage's Warwickshire estate, waiting to be hung at the former dower house once it was completed.

No. 16 Picardy Place was located east of the Queen Street Gardens at the edge of Edinburgh's New Town, practically in the shadow of Calton Hill. It boasted much the same edifice as all the other Georgian town houses north of the city, but as soon as one stepped through the door, there the similarities ended. Oh, I supposed the floor plan was much the same, but whatever furniture had originally filled the home had been pushed to the edges or removed to make way for Lord Eldin's collection now up for auction. Though at least some of it must have been displayed here during his lordship's lifetime, as well as in his consulting room, where he practiced law, and at his small country estate.

Gage and I might have walked the several blocks to the auction, but the damp weather continued, so we elected to take the carriage instead. As such, we arrived with plenty of time to browse before the bidding began. The entry hall was larger than most, offering ample space for new arrivals to congregate out of the rain while they waited for one of the staff members to collect their outer garments. I wasn't certain whether the two men were employees of Thomas Winstanley & Sons or retainers of the late Lord Eldin, but they worked with quiet efficiency, even as a gentleman with bushy side whiskers scowled at them from across the room.

"Who do you suppose that is?" I murmured softly to Gage.

He didn't appear to be an employee of the auctioneers. Or if he was, not a very welcoming one. I could only imagine his presence would be off-putting to all but the most determined bidders.

"Probably a relative," he replied. "I heard Lord Eldin had something like five brothers and sisters."

"Six, actually," a voice behind us proclaimed. "And yes, that's his brother William. Inherited his estate."

We turned to look at the gentleman, who was smiling rather remorselessly for eavesdropping. He boasted a head full of pale brown hair now going to gray.

"Apologies. But I couldn't help but overhear."

Of course, he could have, but neither Gage nor I corrected him on that point as it would be fruitless. In any case, he had provided the answer that neither of us knew.

"Allow me to introduce myself. Sir James Riddell, at your service," he declared with a bow of his head and a flourish. I'd thought his pout was some sort of artifice, but now I could tell he simply possessed full lips.

"Sebastian Gage," my husband replied, shaking his hand before nodding to me. "And this is my wife . . ."

"Ah, yes," Sir James replied before Gage could finish. "Everyone knows Lady Darby."

This was yet another false statement, or at least not an entirely correct one. Many people knew *of* me, thanks to my late husband and my somewhat scandalous reputation, but that didn't mean they *knew* me. Not by any stretch of the imagination. Though Sir James didn't appear mean-spirited, merely intrigued by my presence.

"Please, call me Mrs. Gage," I requested, offering him my hand and hoping he wouldn't ignore my wishes as so many members of society did. By courtesy, if not right, I was often still addressed by the title granted to me during my first marriage to Sir Anthony Darby because my first husband outranked my second. However, I had no desire to be reminded of my time with the cruel anatomist, nor to maintain the name which had linked me to him.

"Of course," Sir James agreed, a curious glint in his eyes as he clasped my fingers, offering a brief nod.

"Are you a collector, or were you a friend of the deceased?" I asked as we reached the front of the line and the footman took my hat and fern green mantle, revealing the softer mint green shade of my gown underneath.

"Both." He passed over his own outer garments to the staff

with a smile, displaying nary a twinge at the reminder of the loss of his friend. But then again, Lord Eldin had died the previous May, so I supposed there had been time to adjust to his absence.

"I'm not sure anyone has seen his entire collection," he remarked avidly as we moved deeper into the house. "He was a bit . . . defensive of it." A small frown marred his brow as if that had not been the exact word he was looking for. "Wouldn't have considered parting with even a coin while he was still alive," he tried to explain. "I can only imagine he's turning in his grave to see it all dismantled now."

This last remark was clearly aimed at Lord Eldin's brother, who turned his scowl on Sir James. But despite the barbs contained in this statement, Sir James didn't seem to hold any genuine animosity toward William Clerk as he offered him a jaunty smile, which he then turned on us. "If you'll excuse me."

"Curious fellow," I murmured as he hastened off.

Gage didn't respond to this remark, but I could tell that he agreed. "Now, where to first?" he asked as we paused to consider our surroundings.

The room to the right was open, as was the room at the back, though Sir James had moved directly toward the staircase. I had just opened my mouth to suggest we might do the same when I caught the eye of a young man who seemed to know what he was about.

"Good afternoon," he declared with a congenial smile. His gaze dipped to the catalog I held in my hand. "Are you here for the auction?" He broke off at the end of the last word, inhaling sharply. "Oh, my! Your ladyship, I didn't recognize you at first. What an honor!" He pressed a hand to his chest. "I've had the privilege of viewing a number of your portraits, and if I may be so bold to say, they are exquisite."

I blushed, both at his praise and the attention he was

drawing. It wasn't often that a person's excitement to meet me was directed toward my artwork rather than my reputation. "Thank you," I answered, though I wasn't certain he heard me as he rushed into speech again, albeit with a lower tone, almost as if confiding a secret.

"And I hear rumbles that you're working on something new. Something extraordinary." His dark eyes were alight with interest beneath his mop of dark curls. "Now, that is something I would love to see." He grinned with such artlessness and awaited my answer with such eagerness that he put me in mind of a puppy anxious to be let outside for a run about.

I hardly knew how to answer him. I was about to ask where he'd heard such rumbles when he stumbled into speech yet again.

"But my apologies." His expression turned sheepish. "You're here for the auction, not to listen to *me* blather on. I'm Barnard Rimmer, Mr. Winstanley's assistant."

"Not one of his sons?" Gage asked.

Mr. Rimmer gave a huff of laughter. "No. They are back in Liverpool managing matters there."

I'd forgotten the firm of auctioneers and art dealers was based in England, and I wondered at the choice. No doubt there were firms located nearer, either within Edinburgh or the surrounding area.

"As I understand it, Lord Eldin chose Mr. Winstanley to conduct the auction himself and stipulated as much in his will," Mr. Rimmer said, almost as if he'd read my thoughts. But perhaps it was a common enough question.

Nevertheless, this seemed to contradict Sir James's remark about Lord Eldin turning in his grave to see his collection sold off. Which assertion was true?

"Is there anything in particular you're interested in acquiring?" he asked, eyeing the catalog I held. "As expected, the

Titians, Tintorettos, and Rubenses garnered great interest yesterday, as well as the Wilkie sketch. And several people have expressed interest in the Adam brothers' architectural drawings." His gaze cut toward William Clerk, who had pulled aside one of the footmen to have a word. "That is, if they go up for auction."

"Is there some doubt?" I asked.

He straightened, as if realizing he'd spoken out of turn. "Just a small family dispute. Now, where can I direct you?"

Family indeed, for Lord Eldin's mother had been the sister of the Adam brothers. As such, William Clerk or another of his brothers and sisters or cousins might wish to keep the drawings in the family.

"I think we'd just like to browse for now," Gage answered for us when I failed to reply.

"Of course," Mr. Rimmer said. "Some of the paintings, and the china, bronzes, terra-cottas, and other items of virtu are located in the dining room." He gestured to the room on the left and then behind him. "And breakfast room. The prints and drawings and other paintings are located upstairs, where the auction will take place, as well as the coins, jewelry, and various sundries."

"Then the paintings up for auction tomorrow are also on display?" I queried.

"Many of them." He eyed me keenly. "Is there one in particular you wished to examine?"

"The Van der Neer landscape."

His eyebrows arched gently. "I should have known you would choose by the eye and not the name."

Spoken in another voice, this might have been an insult, but it was clear Mr. Rimmer meant it as a compliment. He was a genuine art lover, then. This would seem to be a requirement for such a profession, but such was not always the case. In fact, the patriarchal title of the business suggested it was not. Just because the father admired art did not necessitate the sons would, regardless of their inheritance.

"Rimmer," an older gentleman with spectacles said, hastening toward him. He paused to address us briefly before directing the younger man. "Excuse us. I need you upstairs."

"Of course, Mr. Winstanley." He glanced toward us. "Have you been introduced yet to *Lady Darby* and Mr. Gage?"

Mr. Rimmer had leaned heavily on my title, but if his employer recognized it, he gave no indication. "A pleasure to meet you," the auctioneer replied perfunctorily. "The auction will begin momentarily." He pivoted on his heel as he muttered. "*Now*, Rimmer."

Mr. Rimmer offered us a tight smile. "If you'll excuse me," he said, before following Mr. Winstanley toward the staircase.

Neither Gage nor I spoke as the two men disappeared around the corner, but I suspected my husband was also contemplating the auctioneer's impatience. The auction itself wasn't slated to begin for another twenty minutes, and people continued to arrive, crowding into the entry hall behind us. The volume of voices had risen, forcing Gage to lean toward me to be heard.

"Where to?"

I realized Mr. Rimmer had been interrupted before he could direct me to the location of the Van der Neer. "Let's wander through the rooms on this level before making our way upstairs."

He guided me into the dining room, and we made a circuit of the tables displaying many of the items of virtu which would be up for bidding during the latter days of the fourteen-day auction. Much of it was undoubtedly fine and possibly of some historical significance, but I was in no way an expert in such things and, to be truthful, largely uninterested.

"I wonder if Mr. Knighton will be sorry to have missed the auction," I told Gage as we returned to the entry hall to venture back toward the breakfast room. The door to the room adjoining them, usually a study, was locked, preventing us from making a circuit of the rooms as designed. "Given he's somewhat of an expert in antiquities." Or so I'd learned during a recent inquiry. Gage had consulted with him upon occasion on the subject.

"Yes, but he's more concerned with stonework—busts and statues and such," he replied, nodding in passing to an acquaintance. "Though the coins and casts might be of some interest."

The breakfast room was filled with many of the same items, but I was able to locate the landscape I sought. The catalog had merely described Van der Neer's painting as "a view in Holland with figures," and I was disappointed to discover it was not one of his night compositions, with the scene atmospherically lit by moonlight. But it was an excellent wintry landscape, nonetheless, with skaters on a frozen canal and the first glimmerings of sunset in the clouds. I was determined to bid on it the following day.

We joined the stream of people climbing the stairs. A healthy number of people were congregating in the drawing rooms in anticipation of the auction. I estimated there to have been well over a hundred, all told. Probably closer to 150. As such, it was difficult to navigate with any ease throughout the space. Many had already claimed seats in the back drawing room where the actual bidding would take place, but there were also several dozen clustered around the artwork displayed in the front drawing room which was to be put on the block that day. Happily, the pieces were arranged in the order in which they would go up for bidding, and we joined the queue so that I might examine the pieces I'd found of most interest in ascending order.

"Holbein. Now, here's an artist you should have in your collection," I heard someone murmur over my shoulder as I examined the pair of portraits. "Painted kings and queens and more. Look. Even Lady Darby is interested."

Except I'd just decided the paintings weren't worth the additional cost Holbein's name being attached to them would demand. Truth be told, they were in dubious condition, and I suspected at some point an overzealous conservator might have altered the composition. But I said nothing of this to the men and woman behind me. Though I did wonder who the gentleman with the broad, shiny forehead was, as he was obviously advising the couple accompanying him on which artworks they should bid on. Whoever he was, I found his counsel questionable.

However, moving on to the other pieces, I discovered he wasn't the only one who had marked my presence and interest. No one was showing the least bit of attention to the Bracklencamp painting of an old woman with a chafing dish until I sidled up to it. Likewise, the Geddes portrait of a lady with a bird. And when I ignored the two inferior Van Dycks, it seemed to pull people away from them. Perhaps I should have been pleased my expertise in this area was being acknowledged, albeit indirectly, but I found myself annoyed. Continuing through the room, I felt compelled to give each painting the same glancing interest, lest I tip my hand to the others I was intrigued by.

We finished just as the gavel fell to announce the opening of the auction and a Michau landscape was placed on the easel at the front of the back drawing room near the hearth. Finding the space packed with bodies both standing and seated, we opted to hover in the entrance to a smaller drawing room at the rear of the staircase. From there, we could still observe the proceedings without wading into the fray. We would have to arrive earlier the next day if we hoped to claim a space closer to the front.

Mr. Winstanley stood on a stand to the left of the fireplace with a clerk seated at a small table next to him, taking notes on the proceedings. The auctioneer certainly possessed the commanding presence necessary for such a role, directing the auction with quick, concise words and movements. Mr. Rimmer and another gentleman with sandy close-cut hair appeared to be in charge of the paintings—setting them into place on the easel and then removing them to a partitioned area where I supposed the winning bidders went to pay for and claim them.

There being a dozen or more lots before the first piece of artwork I intended to bid for, I soon lost interest, wandering deeper into the room to scrutinize the drawers of coins, jewelry, snuffboxes, daggers, pistols, and other small, portable miscellany set within glass-topped cabinets. A young man wearing a pin on his coat lapel that signified he was an employee of Thomas Winstanley & Sons stood next to the door leading to the staircase, no doubt there to answer questions as well as discourage any light fingers. I offered him a polite smile as I passed him, bending close to examine a pearl-handled penknife and a bloodstone locket set in gold, before moving on to a small case which contained four silver coins nestled within the larger cabinet.

"But when will a vote be held?" a deep voice to my right muttered in frustration.

"Patience," the gentleman with him counseled. "The club's next meetin' is no' for another fortnight."

"But canna a special meetin' be called?"

"No' on such short notice. No' for somethin' like this."

"Balderdash!" the man exclaimed. "I've waited long enough, Jamieson."

I'd continued my examination of the drawers, attempting

to ignore their conversation, but at this display of temper I couldn't help but look up and mark them. The angry fellow glared down at his companion from his superior height, his face flushed and medium brown hair in need of a comb. He resisted all attempts by the older man dressed in black he'd called Jamieson to calm him.

"I ken weel 'twas Eldin who blocked my membership," he declared loudly, drawing even more interest from those around him. He poked the white-haired Jamieson sharply in the chest with his finger. "The blackguard! Weel, he's been dead and in the ground for nigh on ten months noo. And I'm tired o' waitin'."

"Come noo, Innes. There's no cause for that," interrupted another gentleman, punctiliously dressed in a dark brown tweed coat, waistcoat, and trousers.

"You stay oot o' this, Smith," Innes growled, storming from the room and knocking his shoulder into mine in the process.

I gasped, but he paused barely long enough to utter an apology before continuing on his way. I scowled at his back, rubbing my shoulder where it smarted.

"Are ye injured, madam?" the gentleman in black asked. Now that I could see the manner in which his white cravat was tied and paired with his sober black attire, I could tell that Jamieson was most likely a clergyman. Possibly a retired one, judging from his age.

"No," I replied. "Just a little sore."

"Kiera," Gage murmured anxiously, having been drawn to my side.

"There's no cause for concern," I hastened to reassure him. "Truly."

"I really must apologize for Mr. Innes's rudeness." Reverend Jamieson sighed and shook his head. "I dinna ken what came over him."

"Greed, pure and simple," Mr. Smith scoffed before returning to the auction.

I could hear Mr. Winstanley's resonant voice announcing the next lot.

Reverend Jamieson didn't dispute this assertion, nor did he seek to explain further, forcing me to ask questions.

"What club is he so eager to join?"

"The Bannatyne Club." He arched his chin proudly. "'Tis a publication society aimed at printin' rare works o' Scottish relevance. 'Twas founded by Sir Walter Scott, among others." A pleat formed in his brow. "Includin' Lord Eldin."

Who for one reason or another had blocked Mr. Innes's membership. Or so Innes believed. Though it wasn't immediately apparent to me why he was so anxious to join. Unless he had a text of Scottish interest he wished them to publish. Or the club did more than print rare books.

I peered up at Gage to see if he might know, but his focus appeared to be directed at me.

Jamieson began to back away. "I shall let ye return tae the auction," he said with a little bow.

Gage nodded to him. "Do you wish to stay?" he murmured, shepherding me toward the auction room.

"Yes, of course."

Gage appeared as if he might argue, but then thought better of it.

A swift glance at my catalog told me there were still three lots before the Cipriani I was intent on possibly acquiring. That is, if the price wasn't driven too high. The landscape of a scene from *The Tempest* must have hung in the smoking room or some similar noxious environment, for it required some careful cleaning, though I suspected a lovely piece lay beneath.

Disinterested in the pictures that came before, my mind began to wander back to Innes's outburst and the Bannatyne

Club. I knew there were any number of gentlemen's clubs located in Edinburgh and London, not just the more famous ones like White's, Brooks's, and Boodle's, but I'd never heard of the Bannatyne Club. In and of itself, that was not odd. I'd probably not heard of half the clubs in existence. Still, I was curious.

"What do you know of the Bannatyne Club?" I asked my husband, pitching my voice just loud enough that hopefully he might hear it but no one nearby would mark it.

He didn't turn to acknowledge me, keeping his gaze focused on the proceedings before us, but I could tell by the slight pursing of his lips that he'd heard me and whatever he knew was not complimentary. In fact, it might be downright scandalous.

"That bad?" I prodded when fifteen or twenty seconds passed and still he hadn't answered.

"No, just . . ." His lips pressed together, as if he was reluctant to speak. "I've heard some of their revelry-making can get out of hand. Word is the deceased even broke his nose after he fell down a staircase during one of their whisky punch–soaked meetings."

Now I understood that Gage's reticence was less about the club's activities, for nearly every gathering of gentlemen was bound to boast a flowing bowl of some kind of spirit-laden punch, and more to do with a desire not to speak ill of the dead, in his own home, no less, during the auction of his collection. Nevertheless, it did rather cast Lord Eldin and his intimates in a different light. I knew of him only as a solicitor and a Lord of Session, as well as apparently an art collector. I supposed the image of him as a judge on the bench imbued him with a rather more sober demeanor than perhaps he'd possessed.

Whatever the case, the notion of such venerable gentlemen

indulging in drunken revels so extreme they resulted in injury did not make a favorable impression on me, no matter how august the personalities involved. By no means was I a prude or a teetotaler, but there was such a thing as moderation. But then again, having viewed the breadth of Lord Eldin's eclectic collection, moderation didn't seem to be something he'd aspired to in any area of his life.

CHAPTER 3

If possible, the third day of the auction of Lord Eldin's collection seemed even more heavily attended than the day before. The back drawing room in particular groaned with people crowded in a space that was meant to accommodate about a third of those present. Gage and I had arrived early enough to claim a place on the south side of the back drawing room nearer to the easel, but we'd had to be content with standing. For once, I was grateful for the wide gigot sleeves which I despised, yet were so fashionable, because they afforded at least a little more space between me and the gentleman next to me.

My and Gage's efforts the previous day had met with mixed results. I had lost the Cipriani as well as Mignard's picture imitating a painting of the Holy Family by Raphael to bidders who were clearly ignorant of their genuine value, for they'd overpaid. But I *had* managed to secure the Guido painting of *A Magdalen in Adoration*, but I suspected this was only because others were reserving their funds to bid on the Rubens, Raphael, and Titian pieces that followed.

Given my frustration with the auction the day before, I was determined not to lose the Van der Neer landscape today. It was unlikely anyone else was as interested in the painting as I was, and I hoped my failure to participate in the bidding over what many others had viewed to be the previous day's most coveted pieces would discourage others from contesting me based solely on my reputation. In this instance, at least, it would be better if they believed me uninformed.

The manner in which Gage opened and closed his pocket watch multiple times told me the auction was beginning later than advertised. I couldn't blame him for his impatience. It was growing stuffy in the room with so many bodies packed together, and some of our fellow bidders had not bathed as punctiliously as we had. I remained close to Gage's side, turning my head periodically to inhale a breath of his freshly laundered indigo blue frock coat and starched cravat. He smiled in commiseration the third time I did it, evidently recognizing my ploy.

The room seemed to breathe a collective sigh as Mr. Winstanley and his clerk made their way through the crowd toward their posts. Mr. Rimmer and the sandy-haired fellow followed close behind, wearing protective gloves as they utilized the space which had been roped off for them to carry the artwork back and forth from the front room. The Van der Neer was one of the last dozen of the sixty or so pictures to be auctioned that day, so I settled in, resigned to the wait.

However, I was surprised by how swiftly I became swept up in the excitement of the bidding. Standing in the midst of the crowd rather than on its periphery, it was far easier to be drawn into the drama that seemed intrinsic to the process. The room hummed with speculation as each picture was carried through the door and positioned on the easel. Then Mr.

Winstanley would describe the piece and its merits. I believed some of these to be exaggerated, but then, of course, the auctioneer's job was to attain the highest possible bid.

As he called for the opening bid, it always began with the same cool calculation, as those interested in the lot didn't wish to appear *too* invested in acquiring it. But the voices and tension would rise as the bids climbed higher, revealing exactly what the bidders had initially sought to conceal. Eventually, the supplicants would dwindle down to two and then one, and with the final bid the gavel would fall with a sharp bang that startled the senses even when one was expecting it. The winner would struggle to conceal his smile just as the losers would thinly veil their discontent with haughty reserve. However, there was little time to either bask or sulk before the next lot was presented and the process began all over again.

I observed the proceedings with as much detachment as I could, but my feet hurt, and the warmth of the room was beginning to make me perspire. My mouth was dry, and I wished for a drink of water to at least make the wait bearable, but I knew if we moved from this spot, we would never return to it. I'd hoped the crowd would thin as the pictures were auctioned off one by one, but at the halfway point there seemed to be even more bidders and spectators squeezed into the space than at the beginning.

Then the auctioneer's assistants carried in a Teniers painting which generated excitement. It was composed of a trio of boorish men with a fourth in the background, all amusing themselves outside a tavern. Though Teniers was not to my taste, I had to admit that the picture was representative of the Flemish Baroque artist's best work. Mr. Winstanley also claimed the piece had been one of Lord Eldin's particular favorites, which, if true, I felt revealed more about the late owner than perhaps he realized.

The bidding opened and swiftly climbed, with numbers being proclaimed from different parts of the room. "Sixty guineas," someone called out, and was acknowledged by the auctioneer. But before another word could be uttered, a terrible crash rent the air. Like those nearby, Gage and I glanced about us in confusion, trying to ascertain the source of the disturbance. Had some shelving fallen? Or maybe some paintings had been overturned in the next room.

Only when a harsh creaking noise began and the floor began to undulate alarmingly beneath our feet did I realize what was happening. By then, it was too late.

My heart lodged in my throat as a thick cloud of dust rose up around us. Then the floor dropped out from beneath me, and I plunged downward.

Terror coursed through my veins and screams echoed in my ears, possibly my own. I was blinded by the debris which permeated the air, seeming to swallow me whole. It filled my nose and coated my tongue.

Though the fall could not have lasted more than a few seconds, it seemed much longer. When I landed, it was hard, jarring every bone in my body. I didn't attempt to move at first, too riddled with pain and shock. I simply lay in the midst of the rubble of wood, plaster, and bindings, sprinkled with broken furniture, artwork, and bodies, struggling to breathe through the miasma of lime and dust. I didn't dare open my eyes, as I felt the fine particles of debris stinging my skin almost like tiny insects.

As the cascade of wreckage settled, I slowly began to take stock of myself and my surroundings. My lower back ached dreadfully where it had borne the brunt of my landing. I hissed in a breath as I moved my left arm, feeling a trickle of blood run down its length from some scrape, but the small amount of the rivulet led me to believe it wasn't serious.

I'd lost hold of Gage's arm as the floor collapsed, and I couldn't feel him beside me now. Fear jarred me back to full consciousness as I blinked open my eyes, squinting into the cloud of dust.

"Sebastian," I called weakly, as I struggled to sit upright. I heard fabric ripping as one of my sleeves was torn away, having become caught on something. I coughed before crying louder. "Sebastian!"

"Here."

I felt a hand grope for mine and turned to see Gage slowly crawling toward me. "Oh, thank God," I exclaimed, reaching out to embrace him. The feel of his arms around me made tears threaten. Or perhaps it was merely the lime and dust. Either way, now was not the time to give in to a spate of weeping. Not when we were still far from safe.

"Are you hurt?" I asked, moving my hands over his torso.

"No." He coughed. "Nothing serious anyway. What of you?"

"No."

Of course, I was well aware that neither of us could know this for sure. We could very well have damaged something internally, or a worrying injury could manifest later. But we both understood what the other meant. We weren't wounded in any way that would prevent us from escaping of our volition.

Another cough shook my frame, adding my hoarse barks to the chorus of rasps, wheezes, hacks, and groans surrounding us. I could barely see Gage though he was no more than two inches from me, but I could tell that we were both covered in thick powder. It coated our hair and exposed skin, as well as the torn and shredded clothing still contriving to cover us. We discovered the others who had fallen through the floor were in a similar state. Moving gingerly, we made our way through the rubble toward the voices calling out for assistance in extricating themselves, but we soon discovered we had greater worries.

It was becoming increasingly more difficult to breathe in the miasma. The lime and dust were quite literally choking us, and if we didn't escape soon, we could very well succumb to suffocation. However, the doors to the apartment in which we'd fallen, which I judged to be the study below the back drawing room, appeared to either be locked or blocked by debris.

The tone of everyone's voices rose in fright and distress as the precariousness of our situation became clear. I feared for a moment that panic might take hold, within myself as well as others. It took all I had to restrain the terror rampaging through me, making my heart pound within my chest and my desperation for air even greater. I closed my eyes against the grit now coating my corneas, telling myself to think of Emma. If I had any hope of making it home to my daughter, I had to remain calm.

Blinking open my eyes, I was relieved to perceive several individuals urging others to remain composed as well, counseling patience. The pounding and hammering and raised voices heard coming from outside the door, indicating the efforts to free us, undoubtedly helped. It was only a matter of time now.

Slowly, I resumed my progress through the rubble in the direction Gage had gone, moving just a few feet before I nearly collided with him. He was bent over, helping to shift a chest of drawers which had fallen on top of someone. Once it was moved, I crawled closer, seeing what could be done for the man. He was covered in dust and debris like the rest of us, but it was not difficult to spot the large contusion on his forehead bleeding freely. A large fragment of hearthstone lay on the floor beside him, and I feared this was what had struck him. What horrendous luck!

Scrutinizing the man's features as best I could, I realized I knew him. This was the man in brown tweed that Mr. Innes had addressed as Smith when he'd interrupted his argument with Reverend Jamieson the previous day.

Before I could say anything, a mighty thwack coming from behind us drew all our attention. Particularly since it was followed by the crackle of splintering wood. Similar noises were coming from the opposite side of the room, where the other door was also being broken down.

"Help me to lift him," Gage told another man standing over the injured Mr. Smith.

"Oh, move me easily," Smith groaned faintly. "I am very much hurt."

"Dinna worry," the other man said. "We've got ye."

Maybe so, but I feared that Mr. Smith's contusion and whatever other wounds he'd suffered were too severe. As it was, he appeared to be barely conscious.

I followed the men as they picked their way through the rubble toward the now open door, wheezing and hacking with each step. As I neared the door, several pairs of strong arms reached out to steady me and guide me through. Once on the other side, I took a deep breath of sweet fresh air and promptly dissolved into a coughing fit which nearly brought me to my knees.

"Young lady, you should sit," an elderly gentleman urged me.

"No . . . I'm . . . well," I assured him, pointing in the direction Gage had gone. "My . . . husband."

He frowned but did not stop me when I crossed the dining room toward where Gage now stood, his head swiveling left and right as if searching for something. When he caught sight of me, he hastened forward to draw me to him.

"Mr. Smith?" I rasped.

He turned me toward the far wall where he'd deposited Mr. Smith onto a couch. A man bent over him, and Gage explained. "A physician is attending him."

Though he didn't say so, I could tell from my husband's grim expression that he believed Mr. Smith wasn't long for this world either.

I pivoted to survey the other victims, wondering how many others had been gravely injured or killed. We made a ghastly sight coated in dust and lime, our clothes torn and tattered and in some instances shredded from the debris. One man was calling for a blanket or coat of some kind to shield a woman whose gown had been ripped apart. I crossed my arms over my chest, covering myself lest the split seams along my shoulders and bodice give way.

I scarcely recognized those nearest me, begrimed as we were, but we all seemed to be sporting similar expressions of pensive shock. The filth undoubtedly masked many bruises and contusions, but there were few who were not streaked with blood in at least one place or another by a scrape or puncture. I was startled as Gage's coat sleeve fell away to see that his fine linen shirt beneath was soaked red at his biceps.

"Sebastian," I gasped, grasping for his arm.

But he shook his head, asserting, "It isn't serious."

Perhaps not, but I would insist it be seen to nonetheless. Though it needn't be here. The physicians and surgeons present were rightly tending to those with more severe injuries. As for those of us who had been able to walk away from the catastrophe, there was no reason we couldn't leave to return to our own abodes and send for our physicians to attend to us there. It would certainly relieve the strain and congestion here, particularly as we were still coughing and struggling to clear our lungs.

Gage appeared to have realized this as well, for he began to shepherd me toward the entrance hall. Still dazed from everything that had happened, I cast one last glance behind me, wondering if I should be committing it all to memory. But surely the floor collapse had been an accident. A terrible, awful accident. Though I doubted that fact would be much of a comfort to Mr. Smith's family should the worst happen.

In the end, I was too weary and stunned to do more than allow myself to be propelled from the house and past the phalanx of observers who stood along the pavement outside, having been alerted to the calamity within. The cool air had a bite to it, especially without our coats and with our clothing in tatters, but in all the tumult, we weren't about to turn around to retrieve them. I realized then that I must have also dropped my reticule. That, or it had been ripped from my arm by the falling debris. I shivered, and Gage tightened the protective arm he'd draped around me—the one that wasn't bloodied—and hustled me down the line of carriages, searching for our coachman and conveyance.

Most of the scene was but a blur to my overtaxed senses, but I noticed the cluster of city police in gray greatcoats standing to the right of the stairs. Apparently, someone had summoned them, or else they'd come of their own volition. None of them made an impression on me except the brawny bear of a man with a crooked nose. Even then, I had to blink several times before it fully penetrated my consciousness that I was looking at Sergeant Maclean. Though stoic as always, his countenance was not without compassion. I suspected Gage had seen him, too, but he didn't pause to speak with him, instead straightening as he spotted Joe and our town coach.

In short order, I was bundled inside as Gage urged Joe to return us to Albyn Place as quickly as possible. I sank gratefully back against the squabs, tipping my head to the side to lean it on Gage's shoulder as he joined me, merging my dirt with his. The carriage would be filthy once we emerged from it, but there was nothing to be done about that now. I felt grateful he'd taken control, for my mind refused to focus.

Left to my own devices, I would probably still be standing immobile in the late Lord Eldin's dining room, my gaze fixed on the splinters of wood that had fallen to the floor when they'd broken down the door to extract us, while my mind filtered through the same ream of sensations. The heat of the room. The press of the crowd. The pound of the gavel. The floor giving way. The cloud of dust engulfing me, filling my lungs.

I gulped a breath, half afraid I couldn't, and gripped Gage's arm tighter between my hands.

CHAPTER 4

"I dinna like it," Bree McEvoy, my maid, declared as I straightened, catching my breath after my last bout of coughing. "I dinna like it at all."

"Dr. Graham said the coughing is good for me, remember," I replied, pressing a hand to my chest. "That it's necessary to clear as much of the grime I inhaled from my lungs as possible."

"Maybe so. But I can tell hoo much it pains ye." She reached for the bottle on the table nearby. "Won't ye take some o' the elixir he left?"

I shook my head, struggling to restrain another cough. "Not until tomorrow. As he *instructed*."

"Aye," Bree grumbled, setting the bottle back before she resumed her ministrations to my hair, pulling the brush through my damp chestnut brown locks with long, sure strokes.

A roaring fire crackled in the hearth a short distance from

where I perched on an ottoman, allowing the heat to dry my thick tresses. Several moments passed with naught but the tick of the clock and the soft scrape of the brush against my hair to break the silence, though I suspected my maid was only biding her time, waiting to voice her next whinge. Regardless, the warmth of the fire and the soothing repetition of my maid's ministrations were lulling me into a welcome stupor, especially after the events of the past few hours had been spinning around and around in my head. I allowed my shoulders to droop and my back to bow.

"Mayhap ye should lie down, m'lady," she murmured in concern.

"No," I answered drowsily. "I need to stay upright as long as possible." Another recommendation made by Dr. Graham. "But if my hair is dry enough, I will gladly move to the settee."

She helped me shift to the piece of furniture upholstered in robin's-egg blue fabric, draping a shawl around my shoulders and a rug over my lap. I sighed contentedly as I settled deeper into the corner.

"Tea?" Bree inquired, already crossing toward the bellpull.

"Yes. And then I'd like to see Emma."

I'd wanted to see my daughter the moment we returned home, but I'd been afraid my mangled and soiled appearance would frighten her. So I'd forced myself to wait until Dr. Graham had been summoned to examine me and Bree had helped me bathe away every last remnant of the floor collapse while my tattered gown and undergarments were swept away. I had little hope of their being salvaged, but in the past Bree had proved to be quite a miracle worker at repairing stained and damaged clothing. A skill that came in remarkably handy considering my and Gage's proclivities. As such, I knew better than to assume the garments were irredeemable.

Beyond a number of minor cuts and contusions, I had survived relatively unscathed. Though Dr. Graham had warned me to take it easy the next few days and to send for him if I developed any new symptoms or my cough worsened. Gage had not escaped quite so easily. The laceration on his left arm had required cleaning and a handful of stitches. However, he was still fortunate that, under the circumstances, he'd not suffered worse.

Word had reached us a short time after returning home that Mr. Smith had succumbed to his injuries. Apparently, Alexander Smith had been a banker by trade, but other than that, we knew little about him. I asked our butler, Jeffers, to find out what he could about the man, so that if he had a family I might send along our condolences. It would only be a matter of time before we learned of the fate of any other victims, I suspected, but I asked Jeffers to inquire about any serious injuries from the calamity as well.

I closed my eyes, listening to Bree bustle about the bedchamber, straightening things that didn't require straightening. I knew this was her way of grappling with the anxiety my returning home in such a state had caused her. Like me, she found it easier to confront strong emotions by keeping herself busy. Unfortunately, I was too exhausted to do more than sit, and too much movement sent me into a spasm of coughing. I would have ordered Bree to sit, but her fretful hovering would have annoyed me.

When Gage had purchased our town house just before our wedding two years ago, he'd ordered the master bedchamber decorated in various shades of blue, knowing it was my favorite color. From the walls and drapes to the furniture upholstery and the plush counterpane covering the large four-poster bed, all of it was dyed a different shade of blue pulled from the pattern of the carpet underfoot and accented with ivory. Most of the furniture was constructed of a warm oak, including the fireplace mantel, and the tile surrounding the hearth, which had been specially imported from Holland, also exhibited flecks of blue glaze. It was my favorite chamber in all the world, including my art studios, and I'd requested that our bedchamber in the dower house at Lord Gage's estate be decorated in a similar manner.

Though it was common among society for husbands and wives to sleep in separate bedchambers, Gage and I preferred to share the same bed. As such, the adjoining bedroom was merely used by Gage for his ablutions and to dress. Even now, I could hear the low rumble of his voice and an occasional cough as he conferred with his valet, Anderley. A short time later, there was a brief rap against the connecting door before Gage entered. Finding me clothed and settled comfortably, he left the door open a crack, inviting Anderley to join us once he'd finished his tasks.

Gage's golden curls were still damp from his bath, and his cravat was tied loosely around his neck beneath his merlot red dressing gown. I wondered if the laceration which had required stitches might be paining him, but he gave no indication of it. Instead, he paused before the low tea table to gaze down at me, a gentle smile softening his features.

"You look as if you were but a breath away from slumber."

"Just resting my eyes. I can only imagine mine are as red and bloodshot as yours."

Dr. Graham had said it might be several days before our corneas recovered from the irritation all the flecks of debris had caused them.

Gage sank into the chair opposite, hooking the ottoman I'd sat on before the hearth with one of his long legs and drawing it toward him so that he could prop his feet up. "You rang for tea?" he asked Bree.

She ceased her fidgeting with the contents littering the surface of the dressing table and turned to face him. "Aye."

Gage nodded, settling deeper into the chair, but I could tell Bree had something else she wished to say. Her cheeks were flushed, a not uncommon occurrence given her coloring. A few strawberry blond curls brushed the sides of her softly freckled face, having escaped her efforts to tame them in the heat of the bath she'd assisted me with. Her hands were clasped tightly before her, holding herself in check, but I could see the agitation sparkling in her whisky brown eyes.

"'Twas an accident?" The words burst from her mouth just as Anderley appeared in the open doorway.

Gage looked up at her in surprise.

"The floor collapsin' like it did," she clarified as Anderley crossed the room to stand next to her. "'Twas a mishap?"

"Undoubtedly," Gage replied before glancing at me. "I don't see how it could be anything else." He searched Bree's fretful features. "Do you think differently?"

"Nay. 'Tis just . . ." Deep furrows formed in her brow. "Ye have the verriest luck."

So consumed was she by apprehension that she didn't pull away as she normally did when Anderley reached for her hands in front of us.

Though their relationship had endured more than its fair share of challenges, I'd been relieved to see over the past few months that they seemed to have found a more even keel. Though I couldn't help but wonder how much that had to do with the fact we hadn't taken on any major inquiries. After all, cases like Lady Pinmore's missing brooch weren't exactly strenuous or life-threatening. If Gage had enlisted his valet's assistance, it would have been to do little more than gently probe members of the staff or tradesmen, people whom he felt would confide more to Anderley.

Anderley was certainly an engaging fellow. With his coal black hair and brown eyes, he served as a dark foil to Gage's golden good looks. He was tall and charming, and he possessed a pleasing voice and a twinkle in his eyes that many found disarming. Luckily, he was also steady and fiercely loyal to Gage and Bree, and consequently me, otherwise the aforementioned might have gotten him into trouble.

"We were more fortunate than many," I pointed out. "Definitely than poor Mr. Smith."

Gage's voice was solemn. "Any word on the other wounded?"

"Not yet."

He nodded, his gaze drifting toward the crackling fire.

"Hoo could such a thing have happened?" Bree demanded to know after a few moments of silence, evidently still struggling to reconcile with it all.

"Careless workmanship most likely," Anderley suggested. "Some of the homes at that end of New Town were built at a staggering pace." He tipped his head toward the eastern wall. "Or so Murdoch next door claims. Says the builders must have neglected something. It wouldn't be the first time it's happened. Remember the incident in Kirkcaldy."

I gave a small gasp. "I'd forgotten about that."

About half a decade earlier in Kirkcaldy—a small village lying almost due north of Edinburgh across the Firth of Forth—a section of the gallery of a church had collapsed as its congregants gathered for the evening service one Sunday.

"How many people were wounded that day?" Bree asked.

"If I recall rightly, more than two dozen were killed and countless were injured," I answered.

Bree blanched.

"Yes, but as I understand it, most of the victims were claimed during the panic to escape when people became wedged in the turn of the staircase." Gage scraped his hand back through his still-damp hair. "We're fortunate everyone remained calm during the incident today, or else the outcome might have been far worse."

He was right. We had been very fortunate. For I'd felt the tenor of the crowd shifting toward panic more than once, and yet thanks to the coolheaded response of several individuals who had counseled patience, the agitation had been contained.

There was a rap on the door, heralding the arrival of the tea, I believed. Until it was whisked open before Bree could take more than two steps toward it and my sister rushed in.

"Oh, thank heavens," Alana exclaimed on catching sight of me.

"Lord and Lady Cromarty," Jeffers intoned somewhat belatedly from the doorway as my brother-in-law, Philip, crossed the threshold at a somewhat slower pace. Though I didn't blame our butler for his inability to deter Alana. My sister was a force to be reckoned with.

"When I heard about the floor collapse during the auction of the late Lord Eldin's effects and learned you were *there*, I feared the worst." She plopped down onto the end of the settee by my feet in a flurry of flounces, her eyes narrowing accusingly. "Why didn't you send word?"

Normally such an indictment from my often-overbearing sister would have rankled, but I was too weary to be riled. In any case, it was obvious the prospect of my being harmed was what had truly overset her. As my older sister, she'd been looking after me my entire life. Particularly after our mother died when I was but eight years old. Now seeing that I was alive and unscathed, she was seeking to mitigate her alarm by provoking me.

"We've only just been examined by Dr. Graham and finished bathing the dust and debris away," I answered evenly, my voice still rough from the particles I'd inhaled.

Alana reached out her hand to grip mine where it rested in my lap. Her deep lapis-lazuli blue eyes, the same shade as mine, ached with worry. "How severe is it?"

"Nothing that won't heal in a few days' time," I assured her. My gaze shifted to my husband. "I believe the worst we suffered was a laceration to Gage's arm."

Bree caught my eye then as she and Anderley retreated toward the adjoining bedchamber door. "Emma?" she mouthed, asking if I still wished her to bring me my daughter. I nodded.

The tea arrived, and Jeffers took the tray from the maid and carried it into the chamber to set it on the low tea table. "I'll fetch two more cups," he informed me, catching my eye. I could tell there was more he wished to say—perhaps about the other victims—but that would have to wait until later.

As Jeffers departed, Philip sank into the second armchair. "Terrible calamity," he said as he adjusted the tails of his coat. "I heard there's been at least one death."

"Yes, a banker named Alexander Smith," Gage replied.

Philip shook his head sadly, and I noticed the silver at the temples of his brown hair had become more pronounced, though he'd only recently turned six and thirty. Not that it detracted from his good looks. I had always suspected my brother-in-law would age well, simply growing more dignified in appearance. A fact that would aid him if he ever made a bid for a cabinet position or even prime minister one day. As the Earl of Cromarty, he was already an active member of the House of Lords. But for now, I knew he didn't wish to spend any more time away from his wife and four children than he had to.

Jeffers returned with two more cups, asking if we required anything else.

"No. Thank you, Jeffers," I said, dismissing him when I would have rather asked him to stay, but Alana was already agitated enough. She didn't need to hear about anyone else's injuries.

"Shall I pour?" she asked me, already moving to the edge of the settee to do so.

"Please."

I took a moment to appraise her dress. Alana was nothing if not stylish and always impeccably attired at the height of fashion. However, I couldn't help but feel that fashion—that mercurial term—was growing rather more and more ridiculous. With each year, the width of the sleeves at the shoulder continued to grow, now tripling the breadth of space a lady occupied, but then narrowed abruptly from the elbow to wrist. Admittedly, the pattern of her gown's fabric was lovely, consisting of a series of wavy cornflower blue stripes interspersed with fern green leaves and cherry blossom pink dots. However, the scallop-edged epaulettes over the shoulders and high-necked collar, all fashioned of the same white lace as the bodice, seemed excessive, as did the large gold brooch fashioned at the throat. They put me in mind of wings, as if Alana was a great swan, waiting to take flight.

I strongly suspected my sister would not appreciate the analogy.

"I presume it was an accident," Philip was saying to Gage.

"More than likely," Gage replied, his voice even rougher than mine. "Though one that should never have happened."

Philip nodded in understanding. "Negligence on the builders' part. The laws are hopelessly antiquated when it comes to the construction of new domiciles, let alone the upkeep of older ones. Especially when the house's construction is contracted by an individual and is therefore under their inspection and approval. One would think that would make the home superior to those built merely on speculation, but sometimes the individual is persuaded to cut costs or in their own ignorance allows improper methods and inferior materials to be employed." He sighed. "It is something that may need to be raised in Parliament if it is not addressed by the cities and burghs."

Alana handed both men their cups before carefully passing me mine. "Then you both . . . fell through the floor?" Her eyes were wide as she struggled to voice the query.

I had been doing rather well not to dwell on the event and the tumult of emotions roiling inside me. But confronted with my sister's earnest concern and the gentle touch of her hand against my leg, they bubbled a little closer to the surface.

My gaze shifted to meet Gage's, and I was forced to swallow, lest I choke on my response. "Yes."

"That must have been . . . terrifying." Words seemed to fail Alana again.

Much as they failed me. "It was," I whispered.

She lurched forward suddenly, wrapping her arms around me. It was all I could do to move my cup aside so as not to spill my tea all over her pristine white lace. "I'm so glad you weren't severely injured."

I returned her embrace awkwardly with one arm, struggling not to burst into tears. When I felt my teacup being lifted from my hand, I looked up to see that Gage had taken it from me, allowing me to clasp my other arm around Alana's trim waist and lower my head so that it was buried in the fabric across her shoulder. There was plenty of it.

She smelled of roses and the same French perfume our mother had always worn. All at once, I was four and twenty again, hiding away at Philip's Highland estate, cowering from the world and the repercussions from the scandal that had erupted after my first husband's death and the revelation that I had drawn the anatomical sketches for the definitive anatomy textbook he was working on, though not by choice. By the time I'd realized Sir Anthony Darby's intentions in asking for my hand in marriage—so that he could force me to create detailed renderings of his dissections, claiming them as his own rather than share credit with a male illustrator—it was too late. The only trouble was that Sir Anthony's anatomist colleagues had known that he was a notoriously poor draftsman. As such, they'd deduced rather quickly when the unfinished manuscript was passed into their hands upon Sir Anthony's death my role as the illustrator.

Not only had the other surgeons expressed their shock and horror that a gentlewoman had dared take part in such a gruesome undertaking, but they'd also dragged me before a magistrate, accusing me of unnatural tendencies and suggesting I was guilty of all sorts of heinous crimes. When the press and populace had found out, I'd been slandered and vilified, labeled another Burke and Hare—two criminals from Edinburgh who had murdered people from the street and sold their bodies to the anatomists for dissection at their private medical schools—though I was nothing of the sort. No one had been interested in hearing the truth. They had all still been too terrified by the idea that there were other Burkes and Hares at work in various cities across Britain.

If not for Philip and Alana, and my brother, Trevor, I would have undoubtedly found myself imprisoned in a lunatic asylum, just as Sir Anthony had threatened dozens of times if I did not cooperate. My family had secured my release and sheltered me while I struggled to heal and the scandal of my involvement with my late husband's unsavory work died down. They had saved me, in more ways than one.

Most of the time, that all seemed a long time ago, though just four years had passed since Sir Anthony's death. It had been two and a half years since I'd met Gage and set on the path of this new life. I was not that cowering, withdrawn, terrorized woman anymore. But there were still moments, like now, when I wished I could shrink behind my sister's skirts. Or in this case, even her sleeves would be enough to conceal me.

Neither of our eyes were dry when she pulled away. Gage and Philip were both ready with handkerchiefs. I dabbed at my eyes and opened my mouth to say something, but the words caught in my throat as I was overcome by a cough. I clasped the handkerchief over my mouth, leaning forward as I tried to get my barking under control.

Alana rubbed my back and helped me ease upright once my hacking had subsided. Then Gage passed me my tea as they both urged me to drink.

"The physician said I should recover within a few days," I assured Alana hoarsely, seeing her concerned expression.

"You must have inhaled a lot of dust." Philip's voice was soft with compassion.

"We all did," I said.

There was another soft rap on the door, and I turned eagerly to see Mrs. Mackay entering with Emma.

"She's fresh from her bath," she said, perhaps to explain the delay.

I passed my teacup to Alana and reached out for my daughter. She came to me easily, burrowing against my chest. It was nearly her bedtime, and sleepiness already weighed heavy on her, for she eyed her aunt and uncle guardedly. I brushed her damp curls back from her face and pressed a kiss to her sweet-smelling forehead. Tears briefly burned my eyes, threatening to fall again as I was overwhelmed by a swelling of love for my child, but I blinked them back. Cradling her close, I uttered a silent prayer of thankfulness that I was still there to hold her.

Alana leaned forward to offer Emma a gentle smile as Mrs. Mackay slipped away. "My, how big you're getting! I saw you but a week ago, and yet I swear you've grown another inch," she cooed as Gage asked Philip something about the upcoming parliamentary session.

"Aye, we'll have to return to London soon," Philip answered. "As soon as the roads improve from the winter thaw and spring rains."

"But not before Emma's birthday," Alana assured us.

"There are several bills for which Lord Grey and the Whigs will need my support. And we'll be nearer to Berkshire to fetch Malcolm when he's finished with his latest school term."

"You must be anxious to see him," I said to my sister, knowing how difficult the past year had been for her, sending her eldest child away to school for the first time.

"I am," she confessed. "And so are his younger sisters and brother. Especially Jamie. Who, I should warn you, is quite excited for Emma's party. I'm afraid he also thinks it's for him." She shared a chagrined look with Philip. "Quite insists on it, in fact, no matter how many times we correct him."

I chuckled at my two-year-old nephew. "Well, his birthday is only one day before, so I suppose that's hard to understand." I peered down at my daughter's sweet face, who was silently watching and listening. "I'm sure Emma won't mind sharing."

Upon hearing her name, she tilted her chin so that she could look up at me.

"Do you?"

She merely blinked her wide blue eyes with their long lashes.

The others laughed, uncertain what this response indicated, but I understood that it meant she was close to dropping off to sleep.

"I'm afraid I need to tend to Emma," I told them.

Many ladies hired wet nurses to see to their infants' needs until they were nearly two, but a growing number of women among society were choosing to nurse their children themselves.

I was among them. Just as Alana had tended to her children. So I knew she and Philip would comprehend.

"Of course," Alana replied immediately. "We should be going anyway." She reached out her hand to clasp mine once more. "I'm just so relieved your injuries aren't worse. I will call again in a few days."

"I'd like that," I murmured.

Then with a final squeeze of my fingers, she pushed to her feet to stand next to her husband.

Philip cast a warm smile at me. "Take care, Kiera." He offered Gage his hand. "Send for us if you need anything."

"We will," Gage assured him, escorting them toward the door while I began to coax Emma to open her drooping eyes with soft kisses and tickles.

CHAPTER 5

Gage arranged to have our dinner delivered to our bedchamber on trays as soon as Mrs. Mackay had collected Emma and taken her off to bed.

"Now, if only Jeffers will return to tell us what he's learned," I remarked as I scrutinized the meal before me. Braised beef stew with red currant jelly. It was simple fare, but hearty and comforting. Perfect for just such a night, particularly with the occasional gust of wind splattering rain against the windows.

"He will be bringing dessert," Gage replied in amusement.

I looked up with a grateful smile. "You've thought of everything, then, haven't you?"

"Everything but a swifter way to shift this tray so that I can press a kiss to my lovely wife's lips."

"Later," I said with a coy arch to my eyebrows as I lifted a bite of the stew to my mouth. It was warm and rich and perfectly seasoned. Mrs. Grady wasn't afraid to liberally add spices—a fact I was grateful for. Sir Anthony's cook had simply boiled everything to death and called it done.

I paused as I began to spoon a second bite, realizing Gage was still looking at me with a tender glint in his eyes.

"I love your hair down," he remarked.

My cheeks flushed with pleasure at his compliment, but I was also hard-pressed not to stifle a surge of mirth. "Oh, I know."

He tilted his head and smiled. "Why do you say it like that?"

I shrugged one shoulder, taking another bite rather than explain.

As was typical, Bree braided my hair each night before bed so that the long chestnut brown locks wouldn't become tangled. Except that, more often than not, she spent several minutes the following morning picking out snarls from my hair because Gage had removed the ribbon from my braid and unbound my tresses so that he could bury his fingers in it. However, I had no intention of explaining this to my husband. Not when Bree would have found the notion terribly embarrassing. If he hadn't figured it out on his own, I wasn't about to enlighten him.

Fortunately, Gage allowed the matter to drop, perhaps thinking I was the one who was embarrassed. For the next several minutes, we both became absorbed in our own meals. But not so distracted that I failed to note the manner in which my husband lifted his left arm periodically, flexing the biceps.

"Is your laceration causing you pain?" I asked in concern.

His brow pleated. "I'm not sure if *pained* is the right word, but it's certainly irksome."

"Did Dr. Graham leave you anything for the discomfort?"

He grimaced. "He suggested laudanum, but I think I'd rather imbibe a dram of whisky or two."

I didn't blame him. I was not enamored of the opium derivative either. The whisky might not dull the pain quite as effectively, but it would taste better and hopefully allow him to rest.

Ever the consummate butler, Jeffers appeared to have anticipated this, for he brought Gage a glass of Matheson single malt from the distillery that Philip owned, along with slices of lemon cake with crème Chantilly on top—my favorite. Mrs. Grady must have made it specially.

Her kindness made a lump form in my throat. The long day and the unpleasantness at the auction had left me more emotional than normal. It took me several moments before I could utter the words to ask Jeffers to pass my thanks along to our cook.

The compassion glinting in his eyes as he nodded was almost enough to undo me.

I didn't know whether Gage sensed this or he'd simply decided to take the reins of the conversation, for I kept my gaze fixed on my dessert, but he invited Jeffers to have a seat in the other chair before taking a swallow of his whisky. The butler sat with the same absolute correctness he did everything. In fact, I didn't think I'd ever seen him with even a single hair out of place.

"Were you able to uncover anything?" Gage asked.

"I was," he intoned in his distinguished voice. "Mr. Smith did, indeed, have a family. A wife and multiple children, and perhaps a few grandchildren. I am awaiting confirmation. He was an esteemed partner of the banking firm of Smith and Kinnear, and his house is located in Moray Place."

"How dreadful," I murmured, offering up a silent prayer for the family.

"I shall endeavor to discover the house number, as I assume you wish to send your condolences," he offered after a brief pause.

"Yes, please do."

Moray Place was practically around the corner, so I might even pay my respects in person. However, that would have to wait until I was in more of a fit state to do so.

Gage rolled his shoulder again, making me wonder if in addition to the laceration in his arm he'd jarred the joint when he'd landed. "What of any other victims?"

"No other deaths have been reported, but there were a number of injuries serious enough to require attention. Mr. Thomson, the musician and publisher, received a sharp blow to his chest. A Mr. Lorimer fractured his arm, an accountant called Belches is suffering from a number of cracked ribs and contusions, and a young lad broke his leg."

I hadn't seen any boys among the crowd, but I supposed there might have been a few. Perhaps they'd operated as runners, either for the auctioneers or one of the merchants or professionals bidding on the pictures.

Jeffers clasped his hands before him. "From what I've been able to ascertain, while there have been a number of severe injuries, none of them are expected to prove fatal."

Gage paused in bringing his whisky to his lips. "That's . . . rather astonishing, considering how many people fell through the floor."

And that amount of rubble and debris that had fallen around us. And below us and above us.

"It's a minor miracle," I agreed. Though I had no doubt Jeffers's information was correct. The best butlers were always well informed. And Jeffers was certainly among the best.

It was why Gage had committed the vulgar offense—at least among polite society—of poaching him from Lord

Drummond following our inquiry into the death of the baron's second wife. Though it should be said, Jeffers required very little convincing, as he'd already decided to leave Lord Drummond's employ. His lack of fondness for and failure to kowtow to Lord Gage had also been a point in his favor, since at the time my father-in-law had treated me with thinly veiled contempt and scarcely rubbed along any better with his own son. We had since healed that rift, but Jeffers's loyalty to us would always be appreciated.

"The city police are also saying so," he added evenly.

"Then . . . they're investigating?" I asked, eyeing him closely, for I was uncertain what this meant.

"It could be merely a formality." Gage tilted his glass toward the firelight, swirling the amber spirits within that the Scots considered the water of life. At least, that was what the Gaelic term for whisky—*uisge beatha*—meant. It was what Philip still preferred to call it—among family and close friends, that is—revealing his Highlands roots. But I could tell that Gage's narrow-eyed scrutiny had less to do with the quality of his drink than the consideration he was giving to the police's actions. "After all, a man did die and numerous more were injured. Not to mention the property damage. They have to at least ensure nothing criminal occurred."

"There's also the matter of the property left behind," Jeffers said. "Not only the artwork, but also what dropped from people's pockets or was torn from their person as they fell."

I nodded in understanding. My reticule and hat were among the items tangled in the wreckage. Gage's hat must have also been left behind, I realized, for he'd been bareheaded when we'd left the premises. Who knew how many other things had been lost during the calamity and everyone's urgency to escape. There could be a small fortune scattered amid the debris.

Jeffers straightened. "Word is that the city police are guarding the scene from those who might be tempted to pick through the rubble and risk injuring themselves in the process."

I'd not considered that. It would undoubtedly seem an attractive haul to those unscrupulous or desperate enough. And there were sadly a great many of the latter living in Edinburgh, particularly in the squalid and overcrowded tenements of Old Town, or worse, the dank and dark pseudo-underground world of the South Bridge Vaults.

Jeffers cleared his throat. "Speaking of which, Mr. Kincaid came to the servants' door asking for you."

I blinked in confusion for a few moments, struggling at first to apprehend whom he meant. When I realized he was referring to Bonnie Brock, my eyes widened in shock. "He's here?!"

"He *was*," Jeffers clarified.

"You sent him away?" Gage's expression had darkened with displeasure. "Good."

Jeffers nodded in confirmation, his lips taut with disapproval. "Though he didn't go without difficulty. I was only able to convince him after swearing an oath that her ladyship was unharmed."

I was slightly taken aback and uncertain how to feel about such a pronouncement. It had been so long since I'd seen Bonnie Brock, and yet I owed him much. My life and Gage's and Emma's, in fact. Our relationship with the blackguard had always been complicated. Especially mine. A criminal he might be, but it seemed wrong to turn him away without an explanation. But I should have known he would never be deterred so easily.

"And he's threatened to call again tomorrow morning." Jeffers's voice had lowered sternly. "Says he'll continue to do so until her ladyship agrees to see him."

Gage took no pains to hide his displeasure, but then he sighed resignedly. "I knew it was too much to hope we were rid of the man." His gaze lifted to meet mine. "No matter that good turn he did us."

Saving our lives from such a horrible fate in the vaults was rather more than a good turn, but Gage and Bonnie Brock's interactions had always been contentious. Bonnie Brock did delight in poking the bear, so to speak. He loved nothing more than to make my husband snap and growl.

"If he merely wishes to see for himself that I'm uninjured, then I imagine the interview won't take long," I consoled him.

Though once the suggestion was made, I did begin to wonder if perhaps there was another reason for Bonnie Brock's insistence on seeing me. After all, he had eyes and ears all over the city. If anyone had learned something dubious about the floor collapse at Lord Eldin's former home, it would be him.

But then just as swiftly, I discarded the notion. It had been an accident, plain and simple. To suggest otherwise was ridiculous.

Gage exhaled another long-suffering sigh. "I suppose there's nothing for it. We'll have to receive him." He tossed back the remainder of his whisky and then gritted his teeth, either from the burn of the spirits or the prospect of seeing Bonnie Brock. Perhaps both. "But that doesn't mean I'll like it."

"Of course not. Heaven forfend."

Gage looked up at me sharply, as if uncertain whether I was taunting him. When I merely stared back at him innocently as I savored another bite of my lemon cake, he narrowed his eyes, unconvinced.

Jeffers coughed into his fist, smothering what I strongly suspected had been laughter. My husband seemed to agree, for he turned his glare on the butler, whom I grinned at remorselessly, feeling absurdly proud that I'd amused our stalwart majordomo.

"Will there be anything else?" Jeffers asked, preparing to rise to his feet and demonstrating yet again his shrewdness in knowing when it was best to retreat.

"No. That will be all," I told him before Gage could say otherwise. "But please let us know if you hear anything else."

He agreed, bowing formally before departing.

I turned to find Gage eyeing us both, as if we were conspiring against him. "You don't want your cake?" His dessert sat untouched on the tea table next to his now empty glass.

"No. But you're welcome to it."

I considered it, for Mrs. Grady's lemon cake was difficult to resist, but then I shook my head, allowing it to loll back against the settee. "I'm sore enough without adding a stomachache to my list of complaints." A cough suddenly shook my frame, and Gage stood to remove my tray from my lap, lest I overset it. However, when he reached for me as if he might pick me up, I protested. "No, darling. You'll tear your stitches."

"Well worth it to have you in my arms," he countered, displaying his legendary charm. The glimmer in his eyes and the softening of his features told me the whisky was at least having some effect in dulling his pain.

But I was having none of it. "You can have me in your arms once we're both in bed, but I can transport myself there, thank you very much."

He chuckled, offering me his hand instead to help pull me to my feet. "Far be it from me to argue with a lady."

I failed to completely stifle a groan as my back and right leg objected to my movement.

"You never did get your painting," he said as we hobbled toward the bed.

"No, but it hardly seems worth mentioning considering all

that's happened. And it might have been damaged in the collapse."

"True. But if it wasn't, they will still need to auction it at some point. Perhaps you should write to that auctioneer's assistant we met and let him know you're still interested."

"Mr. Rimmer? Yes, I suppose I could do that. And ask after his health as well. He must have fallen with the rest of us," I realized, for the floor of nearly the entire southern half of the back drawing room had collapsed and the last time I'd seen him he'd been standing next to the easel displaying the Teniers picture.

As I removed my dressing gown and climbed up into bed, I thought back over all the other people we had met or exchanged greetings with at the auction yesterday and today, wondering how they had fared. And what of Mr. Smith's friend Reverend Jamieson? Had he attended today? Was he aware of his friend's passing? Was Mr. Innes—the fellow they'd quarreled with? If they'd been close associates, I hoped yesterday's words of anger weren't the last they'd spoken to each other.

Gage returned to the hearth, dampening the fire and then extinguishing the braces of candles set about the room before undressing. I heard the soft thud of each of his garments landing on the floor and smiled, grateful as always that I wasn't the one who had to clean up after him. Slowly, he crawled under the covers and lay down beside me, but neither of us made a move to take the other in our arms. For my part, I was too sore to move.

A few moments passed, and then I felt his hand brush mine. "Perhaps we could just lie side by side touching," he suggested in a stilted voice that suggested he was stifling a cough.

In answer, I turned my hand over to cradle his. "What a

pair we make," I attempted to jest, also struggling not to wheeze.

"Better than the alternative."

With this statement, Gage lost his battle, eliciting a great barking cough. One that set me to coughing as well. It was some time before we both subsided, and for a few long moments there was nothing but the sound of our labored breathing.

Then his hand suddenly gripped mine tighter. "When the floor dropped, and your arm slipped from mine . . ." The sound of him swallowing was an audible click, and then I heard the rustle of my husband's hair against his pillow as he turned toward me. "I thought . . . I thought . . ."

"I know," I whispered, turning to peer at his shadowed features. In the flickering firelight, he was naught but smudges of gold, sienna, and umber, but occasionally the glow was bright enough to reveal the glint of his pale eyes. The agony and residual terror matched my own.

"I'm so glad we didn't lose you," he murmured in a broken voice.

Ignoring the ache in my bones, I rolled toward him as he did likewise, meeting me halfway. The joining of our lips was brief, but fervent, and as much giving comfort as seeking it. For all the times that I had been in danger, for all the times I'd risked death in the course of our inquiries, this was only the second time I had actually felt on the brink of it, just one step from the other side. The first time, I had been drowning and nearly insensible. But this time I had been fully aware. Fully aware of what I faced, and that Sebastian was also facing it.

How indefinite life could be. How fickle and changeable and mutable. And like the flame of a candle, so easily snuffed out.

These were things I knew, things I'd encountered before.

My first husband had been an anatomist, for heaven's sake. His research had required him to dissect the recently deceased for the betterment of the living. I had aided him in that for a time. And now I used the skills I'd learned from him, wittingly or not, to aid my second husband in the effort to bring justice to those who had been murdered—deliberately taken from this world before their time. Even conceptually, the idea of death had never frightened me, for I believed in Our Lord and Savior and His resurrection and an eternal afterlife in heaven.

Yet, somehow, today was different.

I knew the simplest explanation was that I was now a mother. It was no coincidence that the first thing I'd thought of when the moment of crisis had come was my daughter. It terrified me to think of leaving her before she'd grown. Before she'd even taken her first steps. Who would be there to love her, to protect her, to teach her all the things a mother should?

I couldn't help but think of my own mother. How frightened she must have been to know she was dying. It gave me new appreciation for the amethyst pendant she had gifted me for protection. Not that an object could ever actually hold such magical powers to safeguard someone, but I knew that it was imbued with all her love and desire for my safety, and that was enough.

But had I died today, Emma wouldn't have even retained a memory of me, let alone the assurance that I'd loved her. It was a nearly unbearable realization, and it had cut me to the quick. However, I didn't think all my rattled nerves could be laid at its feet.

I wondered if my husband's thoughts ran similar to my own, but I was too sore and weary to put them into words. I suspected he was, too, and he had the benefit of the whisky to lull him. His breathing slowed and evened out, leading me to believe he'd settled into slumber. It was only after I'd rolled over, trying to find a more comfortable position, that I realized he hadn't when he reached out to pull me back into the spoon formed by his long, warm body. His arm held me fast to him, and not wanting to jostle his stitches, I settled, eventually drifting off to sleep.

CHAPTER 6

I wasn't concerned at first when Bonnie Brock didn't pay us a call the following morning as he'd threatened to. After all, the scoundrel did prefer to keep us off guard, usually appearing when we least expected him. I even wondered if he might be attending service somewhere, as we would normally be doing on a Sunday morning. Instead, we slept late and enjoyed a leisurely breakfast in bed with Emma. It was true, she didn't seem to appreciate our bruises and scrapes, but Gage and I were both more than willing to endure the discomfort her feet and elbows and head caused us just to hear her laughter and absorb her snuggles.

Our coughing upon first rising had been horrible, as our lungs seemed to seek to expel everything that had settled in them overnight, but once the worst was over, my chest felt less tight. Even so, I allowed Bree to dose us with the tincture Dr. Graham had left for us, much to her relief. Anderley also cleaned the area around the sutures in Gage's arm and changed the dressing. Any sign of angry redness and we were supposed to send for the surgeon, but thus far it was healing nicely. Though when Gage finally confessed how sore the entire appendage was—for, indeed, he was doing a dreadful job of concealing it—we convinced him to at least wear a sling to cradle it and ease some of the discomfort.

Around midday, we rose to dress and prepare ourselves for the day, correctly guessing we were going to be inundated with callers. Some we genuinely welcomed, for they were friends and acquaintances we trusted were sincerely anxious for our well-being. Others were little more than curious gawkers, feigning concern in order to collect the latest gossip.

If I'd had a choice, I would have barred entrance to them. I'd been subjected to enough captious interlopers and malicious scandalmongering earlier in my life. I had no desire to face it now. But sometimes one had to endure the presence of others in order to avoid the appearance of slighting them and risking greater scrutiny and criticism later. Such were the social constructs of polite society, and the irony of the term, for in my experience, it was anything but polite. There were always people eager to find fault with others, and my awkwardness and "unnatural" tendencies had made me an easy target.

Of course, it was also those same "unnatural" tendencies that made me a fascination to others, and a highly sought-after portrait artist. In the months following my first inquiry with Gage, my paintings had suddenly become desirable, and I'd been offered numerous commissions to capture various members of society and the wealthier merchant class on canvas. However, a year ago I'd decided to decline them all, instead focusing on the paintings for my upcoming exhibition.

Contrarily, this only seemed to make people even more impatient to commission me to paint a portrait for them. That day alone, I was pressed no less than three times. A fact that did not please me but irritated me and made me even more anxious about what was to come. For I was certain these same people would not appreciate the collection I intended to show. In truth, they would very likely be offended.

Feeling unequal to the task of receiving yet another round of well-wishers, I pleaded fatigue and retreated from the drawing room, leaving Gage to contend with them. But rather than climbing the stairs to our bedchamber, I slipped into the servants' staircase and descended to the morning room. I'd noted through the windows that the sun was shining this afternoon, and I'd decided that what I needed most was to feel its warm rays upon my face. Pushing open the French doors, I stepped out onto the raised terrace, closing the doors softly behind me.

Inhaling deeply, I welcomed the scents of freshly turned earth and green things returning to life. The gardeners had been at work out here the previous week, readying the beds for spring. Here and there, small green shoots could be seen peeking from the soil. In a few weeks, the daffodils, irises, and hyacinths would bloom in brilliant yellows, blues, and purples, and in another two months the white trellises would be covered with pastel roses. For now, there was only the tantalizing promise of what was to come.

I lifted my gaze to the robin's-egg blue sky, its expanse swept with mare's tail clouds. It all somehow seemed more vivid to me today, more brilliant than I could recall. This undoubtedly had something to do with my brush with death, but I didn't want to think of that now. I merely wanted to enjoy the simple beauty all around me, even in the intricate wearing of the pale stone of the walls and buildings and the glint of the black railings.

I couldn't exactly say that I was surprised when I lowered my gaze and discovered I was no longer alone. Truthfully, somewhere deep inside me I thought I'd almost anticipated his arrival, but I didn't say so, deciding a somewhat predictable Bonnie Brock was better than an erratic one. In fact, I didn't say anything at all.

He was lurking in the doorway to the carriage house and stables, and I waited until he realized I was not going to come to him. Gage would already be vexed when he discovered the rogue had approached me on his own. There was no need to make it worse by speaking to him at a distance from the house. At least here, my husband could believe that a member of our staff would hear me if I called for help.

Bonnie Brock detached himself from where he'd been leaning cross-armed and cross-legged against the doorframe to swagger across the stone walk which led from the carriage house to where I stood on the terrace. As usual, he was dressed finely but informally, his greatcoat open to reveal the silver-and-blue brocade of his waistcoat and the fine linen of his shirt, which gaped at the throat, for he rarely wore a cravat. The streaks of red woven through his tawny hair glinted in the sunlight. I noted it was cut shorter than usual, though it still hung longer than was fashionable about his face, concealing the wicked scar that I knew ran from his hairline down across his temple to his left ear. It and the ridge of scar tissue along his crooked nose stood out sharply white against the flush of his skin when he was angry. There was no doubt he was bristling with weapons, though I couldn't spot any. At least, not until a gust of chill wind blew aside the left placket of his coat to reveal the hilt of some sort of dagger. Perhaps a Highland dirk.

"Quite the display o' concerned friends," he drawled in his deep brogue as he drew nearer, revealing his annoyance at my failure to come to him, no doubt.

I pulled the ends of my Indian silk shawl tighter around me, wishing I'd thought to grab a pelisse. While fashionable, the short, puffed sleeves of my smoke blue gown were not warm. But then again, I hadn't expected to be outside for more than a few minutes.

"You know better than that," I told him softly, refusing to be baited.

He climbed the two steps of the terrace to my level, and while he was not overly tall, I still had to look up to meet his gaze. "Aye," he acceded, briefly turning his head to survey our surroundings. As the leader of Edinburgh's largest gang, he always had to be vigilant. Much of the city might view him as a Robin Hood–like hero, but there was always someone eager to see him dead or imprisoned, be it the city police or a rival criminal. I had read that most of the members of his chief rival gang had been detained several months ago, including the leader, but that didn't mean there weren't others eager to take their place and Bonnie Brock's.

His shoulders were as broad as ever, and his waist as trim, but his complexion seemed somewhat pale, and I sensed an underlying weariness to his movements. I couldn't help but wonder if he'd recently been ill or if there was another reason for his pallor.

"How is Maggie?" I asked, having anticipated he might bring his sister with him. I had helped the girl out of a number of patches of trouble in the past, and I knew Bonnie Brock held a soft spot for her. She was perhaps his most dangerous vulnerability, and so he often kept her close. But today she was nowhere to be seen.

"As stubborn as always," he groused, and I couldn't withhold a flicker of a smile. One that he saw. "Aye. I blame ye."

"Me?" I retorted, pressing a hand to my chest.

"Aye. Ye've been a terrible influence on her. Ye bloodthirsty wench." This last had become somewhat of a term of endearment, though it had not begun that way.

"Oh, no. I can't take credit. Maggie was already stubborn long before she met me. She comes by that honestly."

"Even so."

Considering his gruff demeanor, I wondered if Maggie was still stepping out with the young man she'd begun to fancy the previous spring, however I elected not to ask. Not when my last memory of the fellow was not a good one.

"How's the wee bairn?" Bonnie Brock murmured as he shifted from one foot to the other, looking more uncertain than I was accustomed to seeing him.

"Emma is doing well." I smiled at the thought of my daughter. "She's turning one in less than a fortnight, if you can believe it."

"Aye."

The word was heavy with meaning, and the smile slipped from my face, for I doubted either of us would ever forget that terrifying night which had ended with such great joy. At least, for me and Gage. Bonnie Brock's path had been less smooth. Not only had he still been a wanted man, but he'd learned his half brother, the legitimate son of his father, had been the person who—with the help of Bonnie Brock's rivals—had set about to destroy him and nearly killed me and Gage and our daughter in the process. Bonnie Brock had been confronting the repercussions ever since.

I felt an unexpected pulse of guilt to have left him to wrangle with all of that on his own. But then, we'd already risked more than enough to help bring the truth to light, and it wasn't as if we were going to assist him to rebuild his criminal enterprises. In the past, we might have been reluctant allies with the devil out of necessity, but that didn't mean we weren't cognizant of some of the offenses he'd committed and just what he was capable of. Nevertheless, I hoped he had someone to speak to about his half brother's animosity, someone in whom to confide.

"She's the spittin' image o' her father," he observed, seemingly offhandedly.

He'd seen Emma, then, out and about with us or on walks with her nanny. Something I should have expected. "Yes."

He rubbed a hand over the stubble shadowing his jaw as he glanced toward the house. "Ye ken, I had pale curls when I was a bairn, too."

I narrowed my eyes at this remark. For one of the spurious claims his half brother had made in his book about him was the implication that he might be the father of my child. Yet Bonnie Brock knew full well that we had never lain together. He'd tried to kiss me once, but I'd put a stop to that. Normally he saved such taunts for when Gage was present, so I could only surmise that this was his way of regaining his footing after the past few moments of discomfort. The roguish glint in his gold-green eyes seemed to suggest it had worked, but I wasn't about to leave it at that.

"You forget, I've seen your mother's journal and her sketches of you. I'm aware of what a beautiful baby you were."

The laughter faded from his eyes, shifting to something much more menacing. For his mother's journal was a very private thing, and I'd correctly deduced he wouldn't appreciate being called "beautiful," no matter his sobriquet. But I simply arched a single eyebrow in return, letting him know I was far from intimidated and that if he sought to provoke me, then two could play at that game.

It seemed to be the right tack, setting us on more even ground rather than each of us focusing on how the other had seen us at our most vulnerable. Bonnie Brock when his world had been unraveling and he'd feared his sister was kidnapped, and me in the throes of advanced labor as he'd carried me from the depths of the vaults.

"I've come tae warn ye," he stated without preamble, finally coming to the real reason for his visit.

"To warn me?" I repeated in surprise.

"Aye." He peered around him again. "I ken ye quarreled wi' Mean Maclean. Because o' me. So I dinna ken if he'll share any o' this wi' ye. But there's somethin' no' right aboot the incident at Picardy Place."

"You mean, something that suggests it wasn't an accident?" I asked, trying to understand. "But how . . . ?"

"They've called in a number o' men—builders, architects, and the like—and the rumbles I've heard are no' encouragin'."

"But . . . the rumbles would hardly be encouraging even in the case that the original builder had used inferior materials or unsound building methods."

He shook his head. "Nay, lass. They're talkin' o' tamperin' and sabotage."

This momentarily shocked me into silence. "Then . . . not an accident." The notion horrified me.

Bonnie Brock's mouth flattened into a grim smirk. "Though they seem intent on keepin' that quiet for noo."

I didn't know what to say. The idea that someone had tampered with the structure in some way to make the floor collapse as it did . . . well, it was simply appalling! I found myself reliving the moment the ground had dropped out from beneath me, recalling the terrified screams of all the people who had fallen with me, their stunned faces smeared with blood and debris as we stumbled away from it. And someone had done that deliberately? But why? Why would someone do such a thing?

"I just thought ye should ken," Bonnie Brock explained. "Since ye were there." He eyed me almost warily, and I realized I hadn't spoken in some time.

"Yes," I finally replied on an exhale, having held my breath.

"Yes, we were." I blinked, tightening my grip on my shawl as I considered his words more closely. "But surely . . . we weren't the target."

However, I could tell from Bonnie Brock's expression that he wasn't as convinced of this.

I waited, hoping he had more to share, to support why he thought Gage and I might have been the intended victims. But then, perhaps the explanation was obvious. After all, we were inquiry agents who had helped to apprehend more than a few murderers, as well as thieves, forgers, body snatchers, and any other number of petty criminals. Furthermore, we were also friends, of a sort, with Bonnie Brock. Those were more than enough reasons someone might wish us ill.

"Thank you for telling us," I murmured, intent on sharing what he'd said with Gage as soon as possible.

As if summoned by the thought, my husband stepped through the French doors just as Bonnie Brock was nodding in acknowledgment. To say that Gage looked displeased was stating the matter mildly. I wasn't sure if I'd ever seen his brow so thunderous. But Bonnie Brock cut him off before he could give voice to his anger.

"Dinna gnash yer teeth. I was just leavin'." His gaze dipped to Gage's arm still cradled in its sling, and I braced for some disparaging remark, but his brow merely furrowed as he turned back to me. "Yer wife can fill ye in on what I had tae say."

With this, he descended the steps and retreated across the garden to the carriage house. Neither Gage nor I spoke until he'd disappeared from sight, the door closing behind him.

"Did you know he would be out here?" Gage demanded. "I thought you were resting."

I scowled at him, before turning toward the French doors. "Let's adjourn to somewhere more private, shall we?"

His mouth clamped shut around whatever words he was

about to utter as he followed me into the morning room. As it was the room where we also ate breakfast, there was a round pedestal table and a Hepplewhite sideboard, but also a double settee tucked into the one corner. From its vantage you could view the garden through the low window. I closed the door to the chamber before settling on the settee, spreading my smoke blue skirts wide as Gage began to fume, pacing back and forth in the tight space.

"Kiera, I have asked you repeatedly not to speak with that blackguard alone. He may have saved us from those vaults, but he's still not to be trusted. I . . ."

I held up my hand, cutting him off, for I'd had quite enough. "Sebastian, don't you dare vent your spleen on me just because you were denied your chance to tear into Bonnie Brock." I glanced toward the door. "Or is it those supercilious gawkers you're so put out with?" I dipped my head toward his arm. "I'm sure that isn't helping your temper either."

He stood still, frowning down at me in all but confirmation.

"Now, to answer your question. No, I did not know he would be there. I simply needed some air, and when I stepped out, he appeared."

"You should have . . ."

"There was no staff nearby." I raised my voice to speak over him. "And I wasn't about to shout for someone and alert all our callers to what was going on." I glared up at him. "And before you suggest it, I had absolutely no intention of turning and running away from him. I'm no coward, and he's not some leper to be shunned or a monster to be feared." I gestured toward the French doors. "I stood sensibly by the house, so that someone could hear me if I *did* require assistance, and made him come to me. I do believe that was more than adequate," I challenged, arching my chin upward.

Gage's expression remained stubbornly affronted for a few moments longer before he relented with a weary sigh, sinking down onto the settee beside me. He scraped his fingers back through his hair using his uninjured arm. "You're right. It is." He turned to me, his pale blue eyes stark with regret. "I apologize. But when I saw Kincaid . . ." He heaved another sigh, shaking his head.

I pressed my hand to his where it now rested against his knee, able to guess what he couldn't put into words. Gently, I touched his chin, turning his face toward me. Dark circles ringed his eyes, and I could see brackets of pain about his mouth. "Your arm is aching terribly, isn't it?"

He looked as if he was about to argue, but instead nodded reluctantly. "And when I cough . . ." His chest moved up and down as he stifled a wheeze and then gritted his teeth. "It makes it worse."

"Perhaps you *should* take that laudanum and lie down for a time."

"Maybe so." His agreement to take something he hated revealed the extent of his pain. "But first, tell me what Kincaid told you."

I relayed his words as swiftly and succinctly as possible, not wanting him to change his mind about the laudanum. However, he didn't react with the amount of alarm I was expecting, and I told him so.

"Did you question Kincaid about the source of this information?"

"Well, no," I stammered. "There wasn't time, and I didn't think he would share it with me anyway." I studied his unhappy expression. "Why? You think he's lying? He's never shared false information with us before."

"Perhaps not lying, but misinformed or . . . misinterpreted." He shook his head, clasping my hand. "It must have been an accident, Kiera. I simply don't see how it could have been deliberate. Sabotaging the integrity of the structure of a building like that . . . it's difficult."

"But not impossible."

"No." He drew the word out uncertainly. "But highly, *highly* unlikely. Kincaid simply must have misunderstood."

My husband's certainty gave me pause. "You really think so?"

"I do."

"Then . . . it was an accident."

"Yes." His hand squeezed mine. "A horrible, terrible accident, but an accident nonetheless."

I nodded slowly, unable to summon the same confidence that he had. I should have known Gage would sense my reticence.

"Kincaid probably saw it as an excuse to call on you again, and he leapt at the chance before fully comprehending matters."

This made a certain amount of sense to me. Just a few days prior, hadn't I wished for just such a reason to ensure that Bonnie Brock was well? Perhaps he had harbored a similar desire. One that monitoring me from afar could not abate.

Gage lifted the hand of his uninjured arm to brush aside a stray hair that had fallen over my eye. "Whatever the case, I'm sure the matter will be made clear soon enough."

I returned his faint smile, hoping he was right. The alternative was simply too awful.

But just then, there were more pressing matters. Namely getting my husband settled comfortably in bed and dosed with laudanum.

"Come," I urged him, both relieved and concerned when he complied.

"Don't send for Dr. Graham," Gage requested, deducing the direction of my thoughts. "I will be well enough once I rest."

When I didn't immediately agree, he pulled me tighter to

his side. "If you're worried, just stay with me. Then you'll know what I'm saying is true."

I eyed him askance, opening the door to the morning room. "Is this your way of convincing me to rest, too?"

"I never said you had to rest," he protested, but then continued in a woeful voice. "Though I do slumber more deeply with you by my side. I'm afraid I've simply grown accustomed to your presence. It soothes me."

I chuckled, knowing when I'd been bested. For how could I resist such persuasion? In any case, I'd already intended to lie down for a short time after I looked in on Emma.

He tilted his head toward mine. "Shall I say more?"

"No. That was quite sufficient wheedling," I teased. "Just don't complain when I steal all the covers."

"After the laudanum, I'm unlikely to care about much of anything, let alone whether I'm covered or not."

CHAPTER 7

Gage proved to be correct about at least one thing. After taking the laudanum, he slept for nearly sixteen hours. So deep was his slumber that a number of times I held a mirror beneath his nose, waiting for it to fog with his exhalations just to ensure he was still breathing sufficiently. After all, there were plenty of instances of people taking too large a dose of an opiate—especially one as seemingly mundane as laudanum—and never awakening.

I, on the other hand, slept rather fitfully. No doubt because of my worry for my husband, but also because of my own aches and pains. I might have taken a dose of laudanum as well, but I thought at least one of us should remain cognizant enough to be roused. I was also still nursing Emma three times a day, and I was uncertain how it might affect her.

However, Gage seemed none the worse for his dose. In truth, he looked much improved. Gone were the dark circles around his eyes and brackets of pain, and his laceration seemed to be knitting nicely.

These were things I could be grateful for while still envying his restfulness as I sat at the breakfast table cradling a cup of coffee rather than my normal cup of warm chocolate and listened to him read from the *Caledonian Mercury*. Just as I could be glad of the article's contents even as I resented Gage's cheeriness at being correct.

It stated plainly that the incident at the auction had been a calamitous accident, before describing in great detail the events preceding, during, and following the floor collapse. It reported that some eighty to one hundred people had fallen when the floor gave way and listed some of those present, as well as a number of those injured, and of course, Mr. Smith's death. The reporters at the *Caledonian Mercury* had even gone so far as to state what they believed to be the cause—a joist with a knot in it extending nearly through its entirety just three or four feet from where it was inserted into the wall. As it had been the lone joist holding up that portion of the floor, when it had given way under the pressure, there had been nothing to prevent the collapse. Clearly this was an oversight on the builders' part. Not only should the beam have been constructed of better materials, but there also should have been a second joist.

Gage seemed to believe this was confirmation that the collapse had, indeed, been an accident. And it undoubtedly was. But I also couldn't help but note that just because this was what the newspapers were reporting, didn't make it the truth. After all, when the scandal had broken at the discovery that I had assisted Sir Anthony with his medical research, some of the newspapers and broadsheets had not bothered to ascertain any of the facts, preferring instead to trade in gossip and innuendo and spread atrocious lies about me—whatever would sell the most papers. Even in regard to our most recent brush with the press here in Edinburgh concerning the publication of the book and subsequent play about Bonnie Brock, several of the newspapers had skirted very near the edge of libel concerning my and Gage's involvement.

However, I didn't point this out to Gage. Nor did I remind him that Bonnie Brock had said the police and officials were eager to keep the truth concealed. Because despite the skepticism I still harbored, I wanted the *Caledonian Mercury*'s report to be true. I *wanted* the collapse to be the fault of poor materials and building practices. And I was too cross to debate the matter with any sort of equitable temper.

I had planned to spend the day in my studio, but I found I was still too sore and out of sorts. This meant I was falling behind on the completion date I'd set for myself, but it could not be helped. Not when my very bones ached from the jarring they'd taken two days prior.

So instead, I settled in the corner of one of the sofas with pistachio green upholstery set before the hearth in our library, which Gage also used as his study. He'd confessed he'd had some correspondence and other estate matters to see to, so I'd elected to join him there. I might have decided to lie back down, but the idea of spending any more time tossing and turning in discomfort in our bed held no appeal.

The sofa cushions being plush, I was comfortable enough, though I read very little from the book resting in my lap that I'd pulled from one of the oak shelves covering nearly three entire walls of the chamber. I was too preoccupied by everything that had happened, my thoughts seeming to drift. Periodically, Gage would direct his concerned gaze my way, but I pretended not to see. Just as I pretended not to notice when occasionally he rolled his shoulder, testing the tenderness of the joint.

A gentle rain was falling outside the tall windows, and between that and the soft crackle of the fire, I was soon lulled into a sort of stupor. Though initially not one deep enough that I couldn't appreciate how I must mirror the portrait I'd painted of my niece Philipa that now hung above the fireplace. In it, she was curled up in a chair fast asleep, a book opened in her lap and her head pillowed on Earl Grey—my former gray cat, whom I'd gifted to my nieces and nephews upon my marriage to Gage and departure from their home. The mouser gazed out of the painting like a prince humoring his subjects.

However, as my torpor deepened, I briefly wondered if Bree had mixed something else into the willow-bark tea she'd insisted on bringing me for my aches—something sedating or at least calming. Because of it, I wasn't sure how long I'd dozed, or if I'd fallen asleep at all, when Jeffers rapped on the library door.

Gage quietly bade him enter.

Jeffers took in the scene at one glance, lowering his voice so that I could barely hear him. "Sergeant Maclean is at the door. He requests a moment of your and her ladyship's time."

At this pronouncement, I straightened to alertness, noting the lingering surprise that had transformed my husband's features. However, when he glanced at me, I knew what answer he was going to give. "Perhaps another time . . . ," he began at the same time I urged, "Show him up."

Gage's mouth creased with doubt. "Are you certain, darling? You were just resting quite peacefully."

"Yes," I replied adamantly, swinging my legs over the side of the sofa so that I was seated more properly. "Perhaps you can stifle your curiosity, but I can't." When he still looked as if he might argue, I added, "I'm afraid it's quite hopeless. I won't be able to sleep a wink until it's satisfied. So we might as well discover what he wants."

I couldn't be confident, but I thought I detected a flicker of amusement in Jeffers's dark eyes.

Gage's reaction was more skeptical, but he nodded to our butler. "Show him up."

He bowed his head and departed, closing the door behind him.

"Are you sure about this?" my husband asked as he rose from his chair and rounded his oak desk.

"Yes." I didn't bother to conceal my aggravation. "Sergeant Maclean hasn't called on us since Emma was born. I'd like to know what spurred him to change his mind." I arched my eyebrows. "And you would, too."

He frowned but didn't deny it. "It might not be what you think," he cautioned.

"Of course," I conceded, having already told myself not to jump to conclusions. It wasn't hard, because I could already think of half a dozen reasons other than the floor collapse Maclean was paying us a visit, and I was certain there were at least half a dozen more. "But we won't know that until we speak with him."

At the sound of approaching footsteps, Gage turned toward the door, a flicker of apprehension passing over his features. Though I could hardly credit it, for my husband was normally so self-assured and confident, I began to wonder if he might be anxious about seeing Maclean again. Perhaps that had been part of the reason behind his hesitation, not just his protectiveness of me. Before I could ask him about it or even offer him reassurance, the door opened to admit Jeffers and then Sergeant Maclean.

The police sergeant was as brawny and imposing as ever, filling the entrance with the breadth of his shoulders. He bore the traces of his former career as a pugilist in his crooked nose and scabbed and scarred knuckles, the joints perpetually swollen from past—and present—scuffles. He moved with great care, conscious of the amount of space he took up, surveying us and the room in one swift look as Gage greeted him.

"Good morning, Sergeant. To what do we owe the pleasure?"

He stepped forward, lifting his arm to reveal two garments draped over it. "These were left behind at Lord Eldin's residence. I believe they're yours."

"Why, yes," Gage replied, moving to take his greatcoat and my mantle from him. "We left a number of things behind. As I've heard, many people did," he added with a glance at Maclean.

"Aye." The single word was heavy with implied meaning, though he didn't elaborate.

"Shall I take those for you, sir?" Jeffers offered.

Gage passed the garments to him while continuing to address our guest. "Was that all?"

"Um, er, nay." Maclean cleared his throat, rocking back on his heels. "I also wondered if I might have a moment o' yer time."

My husband turned toward me as if to ask for permission, even though he already knew my answer.

"Tea, please," I told Jeffers, who nodded and retreated from the room, closing the door behind him.

Gage gestured for Maclean to join us near the hearth. "You've been part of the investigation at Picardy Place, then?" he queried as he took a seat next to me on the sofa, allowing Maclean to sit in the adjacent wingback chair. "We read the article this morning in the *Caledonian Mercury*."

"Aye, weel." Maclean rubbed a finger under his nose. "The papers have been kent tae jump tae conclusions."

Gage and I turned to look at each other.

"What do you mean?" I asked carefully, seeing no reason

why Maclean would wish to diminish the validity of the article.

Maclean scrutinized us both, as if trying to come to an important decision. Or perhaps he was merely struggling to overcome the awkwardness between us where once upon a time there had been none. After all, he must have already determined to confide in us if he was here. Unless he'd planned only to ask us questions about the incident. But then why the veiled comment about the press? And why the sudden reticence to speak?

Gage and I waited patiently for him to continue, though I could tell that my husband was as aware of the tension in the air as I was, for his leg lightly jostled up and down, vibrating the cushion beneath me.

Maclean finally exhaled a long juddering breath before glancing significantly toward the door. "What I'm aboot to tell ye is sensitive, ye ken?" His mouth compressed into a taut line, accepting our silence as acquiescence. "Ye read aboot the knot in the joist, aye? Weel, while that is true in a sense, evidence is also beginnin' tae mount that the beam was tampered wi', compromisin' the integrity o' the structure."

"Tampered with how?" Gage asked as the unsettling knowledge that what Bonnie Brock had told me was correct resonated through me.

"The beam was sawed from the existin' knot tae nearly the other side. A sliver was left connected, presumably in the hopes that it would crack under pressure and cause the floor tae collapse."

I pressed my hand to my mouth. "Dear God."

Even though this was not the first time I'd heard the allegation, having it confirmed struck me sharply in the solar plexus anew.

Maclean's gaze, when it fastened on me, was not without

compassion, though as a rule his features did not reveal much in the way of emotion.

"But that's . . . that's madness!" Gage stammered. "The culprit—whoever he is—might have killed dozens of people!"

"Aye," Maclean stated patiently in his bass rumble, allowing us a few more moments to come to terms with this revelation, believing it was the first time we'd heard it. I didn't dare tell him Bonnie Brock had stolen a march on him, so to speak.

"But how certain are you?" I asked, finally finding my voice.

He grimaced. "I'm here, are'na I?"

I supposed that was answer enough. Gage seemed to agree.

"What can we do to help?" he queried, leaning forward to rest his elbows on his knees. But this appeared to bother his injured arm, and so he sat upright again.

A soft rap on the door preceded Jeffers's entrance with the tea tray. We paused until he'd set it on the sideboard and bowed in retreat once again. I stood to pour while Maclean continued.

"As ye ken, there were a number o' privileged people in the room, and that does tend tae make the nobs take more o' an interest."

There was an edge to his tone. One I couldn't fault him for. Gage and I had noted the partiality of justice. Those with wealth and influence tended to have it swing in their favor when they'd been the ones wronged, while it looked the other way when the opposite was true. It was the reason I'd shifted the focus of my portraits, the reason I was pursuing this exhibition.

"Especially when the high-rankin' officials who've been informed o' the facts begin clamorin' for answers," Maclean continued rancorously.

"I see. Which is why you've come to us."

Gage sounded terse, and I glanced over my shoulder to see that his posture was stiff with affront. Across from him, Maclean began to withdraw behind his granite features. I hastened to finish preparing their tea before their pride allowed the discussion to dissolve into a quarrel.

"It's been *suggested* that yer assistance might prove beneficial in this instance," Maclean replied crisply, clearly quoting one of those officials or perhaps his own superintendent.

"And I suppose this time we're above suspicion since we're among the victims."

This was obviously a reference to the brief time a year earlier when we'd been considered suspects in the murder of the publisher who'd printed *The King of Grassmarket*, the book about Bonnie Brock. Given the circumstances, our inclusion on the list of possible suspects was justifiable. However, Maclean's uncharitable remarks about me had not been, though he'd apologized. Regardless, that was all in the past and needed to be put firmly behind us if we were to move forward.

"Here we are," I declared blithely, moving first toward Maclean. "Now, you'll have to tell me if my memory has failed me, but I do believe I recall correctly from the times we met at Mrs. Duffy's Tea Room that you only take one lump of sugar in your tea."

He gingerly accepted the saucer I passed into his large hands. I'd also made sure to add a selection of Mrs. Grady's biscuits and small cakes. "Aye. Thank ye."

Then I turned to Gage to pass him his tea, arching my brows in gentle scolding. "Darling."

He frowned in response but remained silent.

"What else have you uncovered so far?" I asked Maclean as I returned to the sideboard to fix my own cup of tea. "Other than the tampered joist, that is." It was certainly an unusual turn to find myself being the one forced to wheedle information rather than Gage. Normally, he was the interrogator, for he had charm in spades, and I had a habit of saying the wrong thing. Though, admittedly, sometimes my gracelessness and abruptness had its usefulness.

"Weel, it appears the culprit, or culprits, gained access tae the house in the hours after the auctioneer and most o' his staff had left for the day."

"Did they not have a guard at the house?" Gage queried in disbelief.

Maclean seemed to share his disapproval. "Nay. Winstanley claimed the house and each individual room containin' any auction items was locked, and that had always proved more than adequate in the past." He scowled. "Didna like us suggestin' otherwise."

"Perhaps one of his employees is involved?" Gage proposed as I rejoined them. "Either as a central party or even a witless accomplice who was bribed."

"I admit, that 'twas my first thought also. But the truth is, I dinna think it would have been all that difficult tae break intae the house wi'oot bein' caught." He turned to me just as I was taking a sip of tea. "Kincaid and his men no doubt could've done it."

This was unfortunate timing for such a statement, for I nearly choked on the hot beverage.

"No' that I'm accusin' them," he hastened to add, clearly recalling as I had that Bonnie Brock was at the center of our last disagreement. "Can't see what would be in it for him, especially since nothin' was stolen."

"You're certain?" Gage asked, patting my back.

I waved him off, for his thumps were not helping.

Maclean eyed me in concern as I continued to cough, though less vociferously. "So the auctioneer claims. But perhaps ye could take a look."

Given my reputation as an artist, it made some sense that he was making the request of me. After all, I'd uncovered art forgeries in the past. There was also the fact we were familiar with the auction and its content, though I suddenly realized I'd lost my auction catalog among the rubble when the floor had collapsed, but the auctioneer, no doubt, had one to spare. At least, I hoped that was why Maclean was still looking at me, and not because I'd given away the other reason for my reaction to his Bonnie Brock comment. That the rogue had paid us a visit just the day before to apprise me of the developments at Picardy Place.

"Of course," I replied hoarsely.

"It would be good to examine the entire scene and speak with Mr. Winstanley and his staff, and anyone else involved," Gage chimed in to say, but then checked himself. "That is . . . if they know. And if you're officially asking for our assistance?"

The two men squared off, each scrutinizing the other, though this time I knew better than to interrupt. For all that Maclean was a great hulk of a man, that wasn't the only reason he excelled at his job. He was also intelligent. And part of that intelligence was in accepting when it was best to defer to another's expertise.

Whatever passed unspoken between them appeared to be satisfactory to both, for Gage's shoulders relaxed even before Maclean spoke. "Aye. They ken. Could hardly keep it from them or Mr. Clerk. And aye. I'd like yer help." His gaze shifted to me. "If ye're up for it."

I nodded.

"Then if you've the time noo . . . ?"

I took one last sip of my tea before setting it aside, my recent fatigue forgotten at the prospect of answers. "I'll just fetch my redingote."

CHAPTER 8

Given the rain, our carriage was summoned to carry us the short distance to Lord Eldin's former home. We might have taken a hackney cab, as it seemed Maclean had since he'd not dripped all over our rugs, but our carriage was more convenient and infinitely more comfortable, even with Maclean occupying the seat across from us.

"The house is bein' secured by a pair o' constables at all hours," he explained as our coachman urged the horses forward, confirming what we'd already learned from Jeffers. "We dinna want someone else disturbin' the scene or stealin' the valuables."

"Were there a great deal of personal items left behind?" I asked quietly.

Maclean turned from the window where he'd been looking out at Queen Street Gardens. "Aye," he answered, speaking as softly as I had, displaying some understanding that this was not going to be an impartial viewing, at least on our part.

Gage, meanwhile, seemed lost in his own contemplations, frowning at the squabs beyond the sergeant's left shoulder. "The most puzzling question—the one which seems to me to be at the heart of all this—is who was the culprit's target? Who was their intended victim?" He paused before voicing a more troubling suggestion. "Or wasn't there one?" He turned to Maclean and then me as if one of us might hold the answer, but I was as baffled as he was.

"Seems a rather . . . convoluted way tae go aboot killin' someone," Maclean agreed.

"And heartless," I interjected forcefully. "After all, they must have known that more than their intended target would be hurt."

"To that point, how could they have known their intended victim would even be injured?" Gage queried. "That they would be standing on that portion of the floor when it collapsed. Or was it simply a reckless shot in the dark?"

I clenched my hands in my lap, telling myself not to become emotional, to consider all of this logically. "There was one victim who died." I glanced up at Maclean. "There was just one?"

"So far," he replied in a voice that was far from reassuring.

"However, it seems faulty in a situation like this to presume that the one person who succumbed was actually the person intended to. Though I suppose the possibility can't be entirely ruled out."

"No." Gage's brow furrowed. "But at this juncture, it seems no one else who attended the auction Saturday, or any of the days prior, can be ruled out either."

"Noo ye apprehend the right fankle I've stumbled intae, and why I need yer help," Maclean groused.

We came to a stop in Picardy Place. A small crowd of people who were apparently anxious to see the sight of such a tragedy was still gathered outside its door. I'd learned well how gruesome and macabre the populace of London and Edinburgh could be. Had they not lined up by the thousands to view the murderous Burke's anatomized corpse? Had they not picked clean even the bark on the tree in the garden outside Bishop and Williams's home in Bethnal Green, London, eager for any sort of morbid souvenir? Their interest here would be no different, though perhaps less rabid as the newspapers had reported the calamity had been an accident.

As such, I doubted Maclean's superiors would want us to be seen by so many people entering the building, given our reputation as inquiry agents of some renown. The last thing they needed was speculations being made about our presence, particularly if the people making the speculations were newspapermen.

"Perhaps we should enter through the mews?" I suggested.

"Too late for that," Maclean remarked as the crowd's interest shifted toward our fine black-lacquered conveyance. It might not display a noble coat of arms, but its quality certainly marked us as people of distinction.

Gage agreed. "If we drive away now, it will only draw more attention. Best to brazen it out."

"We were victims," I pointed out.

"Aye, and we've had a few o' those stop by." From the look on Maclean's face, I deduced their visits hadn't exactly been welcome. They'd no doubt been demanding answers. Imperiously.

"Let's go," Gage urged, as our footman had lowered the step and now stood waiting with an umbrella.

There was nothing for it but for me to exit first, as I was closest to the door. I accepted Peter's hand to help me down, doing my best to appear solemn—tragic even—behind the half veil of the aubergine plaid bonnet Bree had fortuitously selected for me. I was quickly followed by Gage, who took my arm and the umbrella from Peter and escorted me across the pavement and up the steps into Lord Eldin's former home. Maclean followed close behind us.

We were ushered inside without objection, Maclean's colleagues with the Edinburgh City Police presumably being aware of his errand. That or they were too overawed by Gage to object. The two footmen who had attended to the people arriving for the auction were no longer present, and I remembered that I'd wondered who had employed them—the auctioneer or Lord Eldin's brother. I said as much to Maclean.

"I was told that Mr. Clerk hired them for the duration o' the auction at the suggestion o' Mr. Winstanley. Mr. Winstanley has repeatedly made it clear that his auction house isna responsible for the security o' the items or any private homes where an auction might be held, merely facilitatin' the sales and ensurin' the items are handled properly while doin' so." Maclean had lowered his voice, I supposed so that the auctioneer and his staff wouldn't overhear.

It wasn't difficult to understand why Mr. Winstanley wished to emphasize this point. I could even appreciate why his business was structured as such. If the valuable art and treasures he was auctioning had been stored on his own premises, matters might have been different. He could have ensured the safekeeping of the items. But each private home would prove an unknown quantity, and being responsible for securing the contents would infinitely increase his expenditures and liability.

"Then Mr. Clerk was responsible for the security of the building and its contents?" Gage deduced, matching Maclean's tone.

"It appears so, as he's inherited the town house. But he's no' willin' tae accept liability either. Apparently, he trusted his brother's home was built correctly."

"As any normal person would," I felt compelled to say in Lord Eldin's brother's defense. I scrutinized the nearly pristine stucco of the entrance hall's ceiling. "It's a relatively new construction, at a respectable address, and his lordship doesn't appear to have spared any expense in its design."

"Aye," Maclean conceded. "However, Mr. Clerk didna bother tae read the auctioneer's contract, and he insists nothin' was mentioned verbally aboot his bein' responsible for security, while Mr. Winstanley claims the opposite."

Gage set his hat on a side table and began to unbutton his greatcoat. "There were no witnesses to this alleged conversation?"

"Nay. Though the contract does verra clearly lay oot the terms."

"Have you seen a copy of Lord Eldin's will?" I asked, electing to leave on my hazelnut-colored redingote.

Both men turned to me in apparent confusion, and I realized that this query required an explanation.

"It's merely that I wondered who selected Thomas Winstanley and Sons as the auctioneers. They do seem a bit of an unusual choice given they're based in Liverpool. In fact, we heard contradicting information at the auction about why they were selected. Someone—I believe it was one of Winstanley's assistants—told us that Lord Eldin had chosen the firm himself and stipulated as much in his will, while a friend of his lordship suggested he must be turning in his grave to see his collection sold off."

Gage tilted his head in contemplation. "I hadn't caught that discrepancy, but you're right. We did hear contradictory claims."

"I havena seen the will." Maclean's eyes narrowed. "Though perhaps I shall have tae ask for it if we dinna get a plain answer from Mr. Clerk on the matter." He began to lead us toward the doorway on the right which led to the dining room.

"The collection and all of Lord Eldin's other effects," Gage said. "Who inherits those? Mr. Clerk?"

"Partially," the sergeant replied over his shoulder. "He inherits the effects from the houses, but the pictures and other collections, as weel as any proceeds from their sale, are tae be shared by all o' his lordship's brothers and sisters."

Maclean didn't hesitate at the entrance to the dining room, but I found myself more reluctant to cross the threshold into the chamber that adjoined the space where the floor had collapsed. I peered through the opening to discover the room was even more crowded with objects than before, presumably because some of the artwork and other objects had been removed from the floor above. From all reports, only the painting being auctioned at the time of the collapse had been damaged, the rest of the collection having been stored in the other rooms, so there was still a great deal of art and antiquities in the building. Canvases leaned against the wall six deep in some places, while smaller drawings and engravings jostled for space on the various tables with china, bronzes, terra-cottas, and other items of virtu. My gaze skimmed over the couch pushed against the far wall where Mr. Smith had expired shortly after we'd departed the house that awful day. The cushions were now laden with casts.

Maclean, who had carried on into the room, suddenly realized we weren't following and turned to look at me. Compassion glinted in his eyes, and that combined with Gage's warm hand pressed to the small of my back caused a knot to form in my throat. One I ruthlessly swallowed, blinking my eyes in refusal to give way to maudlin emotion. I forced myself to take a single step forward and then another toward the constable who was stationed next to the entryway through which we'd escaped once the door had been broken down.

"Why dinna ye take a wee break," Maclean told the man.

The policeman didn't object, but he did eye us curiously as he departed.

"It seems 'twas fortunate a carpenter happened tae be passin' by when the floor collapsed and heard the upheaval and the cries for help. He's the one who broke open this door and directed the others hoo tae break doon the other. A physician who was here said he likely saved many lives wi' his quickness, as the air inside was suffocatin' wi' debris." Maclean was speaking more than usual, and I strongly suspected he'd launched into this recitation to allow me time to acclimate to the spectacle in the chamber beyond.

It was indeed a horrific sight. Piles of rubbish—broken joists and rafters, and fragments of flooring—filled the space, all coated in a layer of the lime and dust that had settled. Here and there, buried amid the wreckage, appeared furniture—a bookcase or the end of a sofa. A desk near the middle of the room was littered with the remnants of a lamp. In contrast, the far end of the room, above which the floor was still intact, appeared nearly untouched except for a fine coating of white dust.

Seeing the state of the room, I was struck anew by what a miracle it was that more people had not been seriously injured or killed. The carpet had not been rolled up in this room, which I recalled was the study, and that had cushioned some of our falls, but it didn't explain all of it. Though the physician Maclean spoke of had undoubtedly been right. If the doors had not been broken down so promptly, many victims might have succumbed to suffocation.

A fact Gage agreed with. "I can attest to that," he told Maclean, standing solemnly at my side as we surveyed the rubble. I followed his gaze toward the ceiling, where a massive, jagged hole allowed us to peer up into the chamber above. "Is it safe to enter?"

The sergeant made a sound that was far from confident, causing us to look at him in question. "The room's been searched, but late yesterday another small section o' the ceilin' fell in. So we've been instructed tae stay oot until the chamber can be shored up."

Gage nodded, for neither of us was going to argue against such a caution. "How did the culprit access the joist to tamper with it?"

Maclean stepped closer, pointing toward the end wall at approximately the midway point of the hole. "We believe they cut a hole in the ceilin' o' the study tae access the joist. Which no one noticed because . . ."

"The study was locked," I said along with him, having just recalled.

"Aye," Maclean confirmed.

"Then the culprit must be someone who knows something about building construction," Gage speculated, leaning his injured shoulder unconsciously against the doorframe, but then straightening again.

I swiveled to study the ceiling of the dining room. "That's an excellent point." It wasn't everyone who would know how to go about sabotaging a floor joist. I certainly wouldn't.

"Aye, but many would at least have some idea o' hoo tae go aboot it," Maclean cautioned. "And we dinna ken what their original intentions were." He scratched his chin, rustling the dark bristles. "Maybe they merely had some vague notion o' damagin' the structure but stumbled across that knot that already existed in the beam and made use o' it. We just dinna ken. No' yet. And before ye ask hoo they reached the ceilin' . . ." He pointed toward a pile of broken wood. "We found the remnants o' a ladder beneath the rubble from above."

Gage nodded. "Then whatever damage was done, it must have been shortly before the incident. Otherwise, wouldn't someone have noticed both the ladder and the hole in the plaster? Or did they never enter the study?"

I frowned. "Yes. Why was it kept locked?"

"Mr. Clerk insisted upon it. 'Tis where a number o' his brother's important papers were kept. He also stored several furnishings there he didna wish damaged durin' the auction." He dipped his head toward the clutter behind us. "But the auctioneer also deposited a few o' the more valuable pictures wi'in 'til they could be put up for bid. The last time anyone admits tae enterin' the chamber was the evenin' before the incident, and both o' Mr. Winstanley's assistants swear nothin' was oot o' place."

"So the tampering must have occurred overnight or the following morning before anyone arrived."

"Or at least before the doors were opened to patrons." Gage amended my statement. "It is possible that someone slipped into the study while others were in the building and sabotaged the joist without anyone realizing. Though their chances of escaping discovery decrease dramatically. Even so, we should ascertain whether anyone saw someone entering or leaving the study that day."

"Furtively," Maclean warned, reminding us we weren't supposed to reveal that the collapse wasn't accidental.

Gage's brow tightened with annoyance. "We might not be able to control the fact that our reputations precede us, but you know perfectly well that we're always circumspect."

The sergeant's grunted reply was neither confirmation nor denial, but I spoke before Gage could presume either way.

"What of the footmen?" I asked, glancing back through the doorway that led into the entry hall. "I suppose you've already questioned them."

"Aye. Mr. Clerk's solicitor directed us tae the employment

agency he used tae hire them. My men are trackin' them doon noo."

The sound of creaking overhead made my pulse jump as my gaze jerked up toward the ceiling warily.

"'Tis footsteps," Maclean assured me, having noted my reaction. "The auctioneer and his assistants are still storin' some items upstairs in the front drawin' room and rear adjoinin' chamber."

"And it's safe?" I demanded to know.

Maclean used a measured tone. "Aye. The only floor compromised was the one o'er the back drawin' room."

I nodded, though residual alarm still flooded my veins, making me want to flee. Maclean led us back to the entry hall and then turned right toward the staircase. However, Gage halted midstride before we'd reached the first riser. I peered around his shoulder to see why.

The petticoat table against the wall was piled high with various articles—hats, reticules, umbrellas, walking sticks, a pair of silver spectacles, a pencil case, and even a tattered black veil which had undoubtedly been torn from one of the other unfortunate female victims. There were also a number of crumpled and torn copies of the auction catalog, discarded just as I'd dropped mine.

"Are these from . . . ?" Gage's voice faltered midsentence.

Maclean turned to see what he was referring to and then rejoined us. "Aye. Least what we'd gathered from amidst the debris before we were ordered tae stop 'til the structure could be reassessed. The more valuable items were taken tae the police house for safekeepin'."

"Such as?" Gage seemed to ask idly as he lifted one of the hats.

"Pocketbooks, watches, a couple of snuffboxes." He paused to watch Gage lift another similar-looking hat. "If any o' those things are yours, you're free tae take them."

None of the bonnets looked like the chapeau I'd been wearing that day, but as my husband continued to sort through the headwear, I spotted my beaded reticule. A peek inside showed that my fan, coin purse, handkerchief, and small etuis fitted with writing implements were still tucked within.

Gage eventually located his hat, but discovering it crushed, the top torn, he dropped it back on the table. "I'm afraid this is bound for the rubbish bin."

I tried not to blanch at the damage, reminding myself it must have occurred after it was knocked from his head, but it was still a tangible representation of how much worse our injuries could have been. How much worse they could have been for the eighty or more people who had fallen. How much worse they *had* been for Mr. Smith.

CHAPTER 9

I snatched up one of the rumpled catalogs and grasped hold of Gage's arm as we turned once more toward the steps. As we climbed, we could hear voices—one slightly higher and bickering, and the other lower and placating. As we rounded the turn in the staircase, I could see that the peevish one belonged to the auctioneer, Mr. Winstanley. The entire matter had undoubtedly been a nightmare for the gentleman, and he was clearly struggling to stifle his vexation if the manner in which he was speaking to the young assistant we'd met the second day of the auction was any indication.

"You ensured they wore gloves," Mr. Winstanley demanded.

"Yes," Mr. Rimmer answered calmly.

"Because I don't want their grubby handprints all over the frames. You remember what happened to that Lawrence in Stockport."

"I moved most of the pictures myself, particularly the more valuable ones."

"The Titian?"

"And the Rubens and Rembrandt."

"Good. Good," Mr. Winstanley repeated, but he still seemed agitated.

However, his assistant was no longer giving him his undivided attention, as he'd seen us mounting the stairs. His dark eyes flared wide for a moment, but that was the only indication of his surprise. "Lady Darby. Mr. Gage." He nodded to us and then Maclean. "Sergeant."

Winstanley on the other hand merely glanced at us dismissively before scowling at the police officer. "Have I not answered all your questions? My men and I have work to be done."

"Just a few more," Maclean replied, unruffled by his querulousness. He gestured to us. "Ye ken her ladyship and Mr. Gage."

"We met briefly." His manner was stiff, but he understood it would not do to insult us. Though I intuited that had more to do with our potential as clients and bidders than anything to do with our role as investigators.

"They will be assistin' wi' the inquiry."

Winstanley's gaze sharpened even as Mr. Rimmer darted a glance at him out of the corner of his eye, though I couldn't tell the precise motivation behind either reaction.

"As such, they naturally have some questions o' their own." Maclean watched the two men closely. "Such as, who hired ye as the auctioneer?"

A pulse of what appeared to be annoyance tightened Mr. Winstanley's jaw as he arched his chin. "Lord Eldin himself. He engaged my services approximately five years ago when he was suffering from a bout of ill health. He had done his research, and he wanted to work with an auctioneering firm with the reputation to ensure that his substantial collection was handled with the utmost care."

A loud thump came from the front drawing room, as if someone had dropped or overset something, and seemed to belie this statement. He grimaced, and I could tell he was repressing strong words. Rimmer pivoted toward the noise, but Mr. Winstanley reached out to forestall him before he could move off in that direction, no doubt to scold the offenders.

"He stipulated as such in his will?" I asked the auctioneer.

"Yes." Mr. Winstanley sniffed. "Or Mr. Clerk would have undoubtedly dispensed with our services."

The inflection of Gage's voice deepened with incredulity. "He wished to keep the collection?"

"He *wished* to rid himself of it however he saw fit."

I turned to see what Maclean thought of this. "I was under the impression that the collection had been bequeathed to all of Lord Eldin's brothers and sisters jointly."

The auctioneer dismissed this with a shake of his balding head. "All I know is that Mr. Clerk has been acting as the family's representative. I do not concern myself with what they discuss among themselves."

It was unclear what he meant to imply with these statements. Was he insinuating that Mr. Clerk would have dealt unfairly with his family had the collection been left for him to distribute as he wanted? Or was he simply casting aspersions on the man's business and artistic acumen?

"As it was, I had to spend considerably more time and effort readying this house and the collection for the auction than should have been required," Mr. Winstanley groused. "Mr. Clerk refused to see the necessity in altering the house in any way, or in removing the cats that were living here—*six* of them, mind you. He's fortunate they didn't damage anything of value." His thin lips compressed in disapproval. "In the end, I had to insist that Lord Eldin's solicitor hire cleaners and furniture movers and the like."

I supposed that explained some of the delay in the auction occurring nearly a year after Lord Eldin's death, but I was curious. "How long did it take you to prepare the collection for sale?"

Mr. Winstanley looked to his apprentice, a crease marring his brow. "There were a number of pictures and items of virtu that required cleaning and repair. But nothing beyond the usual."

Mr. Rimmer didn't object to this assessment, but after these remarks and the ones he himself had made the second day of the auction when we'd met, I began to wonder if the younger man was not the one better trained in the art-dealer side of the business. At least, in terms of the restoration and valuation of the art itself. Perhaps this also explained how he'd known about the paintings I was currently working on. I'd not yet had a chance to ask him.

"Then Mr. Clerk was upset by the auction?" Maclean interjected, returning us to the matter at hand.

Mr. Winstanley's glower was answer enough. "Though he had no reason to be. Everything has been handled with the utmost professionalism, and he stands to turn a tidy profit once it's finished. Even despite the fact the auction will now have to be conducted at a different location."

I wondered if Mr. Clerk might actually turn an even bigger profit given the notoriety surrounding the auction. If they all might. This might be seen as a motive, but an unlikely one in my estimation. There were far more guaranteed and less destructive ways to court notoriety, if that was the goal.

"Was Mr. Clerk here the day of the collapse?" Gage asked.

I searched my memory, trying to recall whether I'd seen him.

"No. And it was the first day he'd missed," Mr. Winstanley said darkly.

It had been only the third day of the auction, so I didn't see how any sort of pattern could have been established or that suspicion could arise from the breaking of it.

"Mr. Clerk is a court clerk," Maclean informed us before we could ask. "And we've confirmed he was employed that day."

"You were both there," I remarked, turning back to the auctioneer and his assistant. They had both been in the back drawing room when the calamity occurred. I scrutinized their faces for any evidence of injury. "How did you fare?"

Mr. Winstanley cleared his throat. "I was standing near where the floor collapsed but did not go down."

I looked to Mr. Rimmer, who appeared somewhat nonplussed by my interest. "I . . . I narrowly escaped going over. I managed to grasp hold of the crossbars on the grate over the fireplace and scale the chimney. Some gentlemen extended a plank of wood so that I could cross to the more stable floor."

"What of the rest of your staff?" Gage glanced toward the entrance to the room where coins had been displayed and then the one leading to the front drawing room. Noises could be heard coming from both. Meanwhile the door leading to the back drawing room directly in front of us had been sealed with a board hammered across it from one side of the frame to the other. I found it mildly alarming to know that if I opened it, I would be staring down into the pit where the floor had given way. "Were they all accounted for that day?"

"Yes." Mr. Rimmer glanced at his employer, but Mr. Winstanley seemed content to allow him to answer this question. "They all reported here that morning and, as far as I know, were positioned where they were supposed to be, ready to assist and answer questions. That is, until the floor collapsed. Then it became more imperative to help the victims."

Gage nodded in understanding. "Are they all here today?"

"All but Matthew Fletcher, Mr. Winstanley's other assistant. His hand was sliced open the day before and became infected, and he suffered a number of contusions in the fall." This seemed to distress Mr. Rimmer, for he scraped a hand back through his dark curls and then glanced at the auctioneer again. "Mr. Winstanley insisted he rest for another day before returning to work."

This spoke well of Mr. Winstanley, especially when he didn't seek to expound on this kindness.

"We'll want to speak with them all. But first, the study downstairs." Gage looked intently from one man to the other. "Who was the last person to enter it?"

"Mr. Fletcher and I," Mr. Rimmer replied. "We removed about a dozen paintings we'd stored there. Carried them up to the front drawing room for the next day's auction, made sure everything was prepared as usual, and then locked all the doors and left."

"So you were the last people to leave?"

"Yes. And . . . the first to arrive the next morning." The hesitation in his voice and the glimmer of wariness in his eyes told me he wasn't entirely ignorant of why we were asking these questions or the suspicion that might fall on him.

"You and Mr. Fletcher arrived together?" Gage clarified.

"Yes."

"As was customary," Mr. Winstanley added, lest we take issue with this.

Gage acknowledged this with a dip of his head before turning back to the assistant. "And you didn't notice anything out of the ordinary about the study?"

"No, sir."

"Nor did you see anyone enter or leave the study the following day?"

"No, sir."

"Would you have?"

Mr. Rimmer opened his mouth to answer, but then paused,

seeming to give the matter greater consideration. "I suppose I can't say for sure. I do move about quite a bit, up and down the stairs and in and out of the rooms. And during the auction I'm needed upstairs." He frowned. "But the only keys to the room are in my and Mr. Winstanley's possession."

"And Mr. Clerk's." Mr. Winstanley had removed his spectacles to clean them with a pristine handkerchief he'd pulled from his pocket. He flicked a glance at us, arching his pale gray eyebrows. "He holds a set of keys to every door in the house. It is *his* house after all. He can come and go as he likes."

I supposed the auctioneer's continued and determined denunciation of Mr. Clerk was understandable, both personally and professionally. Not only had they evidently taken a disliking to each other, but the reputation of Thomas Winstanley & Sons was at stake. And no matter how belabored his finger-pointing had become, he wasn't wrong.

"Yes, we'll be speaking to Mr. Clerk," Gage assured him. "Now, if you could call all of your staff together, we'd like to speak with them. But first, can you think of anyone in particular who might have wished to either harm someone at the auction or perhaps undermine its success? A rival auctioneer, for example. Or maybe a disgruntled collector or former employee."

Mr. Winstanley was visibly uncomfortable with this question, fidgeting once again with his spectacles and then the fall of his frock coat. What wasn't clear was whether this was because he disliked the idea of being the intended target for such a malicious act or because he had something to hide. "Well, of course, there are other firms who begrudge me my success, but I cannot imagine any of them going to such lengths to sabotage me. It sounds preposterous!"

It did, at that. But then every avenue we'd considered thus far seemed preposterous.

He conferred with Mr. Rimmer. "We have no former employees living in the near vicinity, that I'm aware of."

The assistant concurred.

"And the notion of an earnest collector—disgruntled or not—willfully risking damage to pieces of art out of spite . . ." He shook his head. "I can't conceive of it."

He was right. Anyone who was a serious enough collector that they might have taken offense at some past action would never have hazarded harming the art itself. As such, I dismissed that possibility out of hand.

"Then there's a strong likelihood the reason for the sabotage lies in either a grudge against Lord Eldin or with one of the attendees," I ruminated. "But hundreds of people must have moved in and out of this house just in those three days." More than two hundred had likely been in the building at the time of the floor collapse alone. "I don't suppose you kept any sort of record of who was here?" I directed this question to Mr. Rimmer, though I suspected I already knew the answer. After all, there had been no registration sheet, no footmen barring entrance to only those with invitations.

"I'm afraid not." He grimaced before turning to Gage and Maclean. "Shall I gather the staff, then?"

"Yes, please," Gage replied. "Perhaps in the back room."

Mr. Rimmer hurried off to do so as I tapped the catalog I'd retrieved from the table downstairs against my leg. A thought stirred just as Mr. Winstanley was attempting to take his leave.

"If you require nothing else from me . . ."

"The catalogs." I lifted the rumpled one I clutched in illustration. "You must have created a list of people to whom they were sent." It would be far from definitive. There would be people on the list who hadn't attended, and others who hadn't received a catalog who had, as an invitation hadn't been required. But it would be a start. "May we see it?"

"Of course. I'll have it delivered to your home," Mr. Winstanley replied impatiently. In that moment, I suspected he would agree to just about anything to escape. "Now, if that's all, I do have other matters to see to."

If Gage or Maclean were ruffled by his terseness, they didn't show it, allowing him to depart without a word.

In short order, the six other men comprising the auctioneer's staff were arrayed before us in the small parlor off the back drawing room. Here the coins, jewelry, weapons, and other valuable objects were still situated in their various display cases, though the space was now also cluttered with crates and boxes of items that had already been prepared for transport. The six men ranged in age from their early twenties to a grizzled but distinguished sixty. The oldest fellow and another in his thirties acted as clerks, while the other four took on various tasks. I recognized the auburn-haired lad, for he'd been stationed in the parlor during the second day of the auction.

Gage and Maclean began to question them while I lingered near the doorway with Mr. Rimmer. Maclean had spoken to most of them before, but once Gage had established the basics such as their names and positions, he began to ask them more pertinent queries, such as whether they'd witnessed anything suspicious or if they'd seen anyone entering or leaving the study. Most of their answers were stilted and uninformative, and my thoughts began to drift to the man beside me.

As far as we knew, Mr. Rimmer and the other assistant, Mr. Fletcher, were the people with the most opportunity to tamper with the joist. Thus far, Mr. Rimmer had struck me as open and ingenuous, and I wasn't aware of his possessing any motive to commit such an act, but I decided it would behoove me to get to know him a little better. Then I could corroborate anything he told me later with Mr. Fletcher.

"How long have you worked for Mr. Winstanley?" I murmured, so as not to distract the others.

"Almost three years," he replied. "Before that I was at Cambridge and then abroad in Italy for a time."

I turned to him in interest. "Studying art?"

His eyes gleamed with the recognition that he was speaking to another true art enthusiast. "That's where I met one of Mr. Winstanley's sons, and we became friends. He convinced me to apply for the position which had opened at his family's firm of art dealers and auctioneers."

It seemed my initial assessment of Mr. Rimmer was fairly accurate. He was a gentleman, but one from a family of limited wealth and little consequence. Though undoubtedly there was some sort of title within his lineage, he was far removed from it. Educated as a gentleman, he'd probably been intended for the military or the church, the usual bastions of younger sons, but his interest in art had motivated him to diverge from this path. I wondered if his family had been affronted by his choice, or if they were far enough removed from nobility so as to not have the liberty of being offended by the notion of a profession. For his sake, I hoped it was the latter.

I clasped my hands before me and surveyed the other men. "What of the rest of the staff? Have they been in Mr. Winstanley's employ for long?"

He crossed his arms as he pondered the question. "I'd say Sullivan has been with us the least amount of time, but still eighteen months or more. Price and Bray perhaps fifteen years, and the others somewhere in between. Except King." He nodded at the older clerk. "He's worked for Mr. Winstanley for thirty-three years. Almost since the beginning."

"What about Mr. Fletcher?" I looked for any indication of how he felt about the coworker with whom he shared a title, but he answered matter-of-factly, tilting his head in thought.

"Perhaps five? Yes. He'd already been with Mr. Winstanley for two years when I began."

I wondered if this had caused any upset. Though it was doubtful a bruised pride had led Mr. Fletcher to sabotage the ceiling so that it collapsed with his standing over it, injuring himself in the process. However, the other employees had escaped harm.

"Do you trust them?"

As before, Mr. Rimmer considered the query before rushing to answer. "I do," he said, but I could hear a caveat in his voice. He huffed a laugh in acknowledgment of the misleading nature of his response. "I do, but admittedly I also don't know some of them well. For the most part they're agreeable and hardworking, and many of them have families back in Liverpool. So perhaps I simply *want* them to be trustworthy." His expression turned sheepish. "Or perhaps I'm overcomplicating the matter."

I suspected Sergeant Maclean would say so, but I appreciated the distinction, and I recognized that for Mr. Rimmer trust was not immediately given but hard-won.

"What about you? Do you have a family back in Liverpool?" He was old enough to have a wife and a young child or two, but I suspected he didn't. He seemed too dedicated to his work, and though I couldn't possibly know this, I sensed he would be the type of devoted husband and father who wouldn't want to remain apart from them long.

He smiled, revealing a dimple in his right cheek. One to match the dimple in his chin. "No. I haven't yet met the lady to tempt me."

Something about the tone of his voice and the way he looked at me made me flush, unaccustomed to such open admiration from men other than my husband. Though I strongly suspected that any admiration on Mr. Rimmer's part was directed at my art rather than my person.

"You mentioned hearing rumbles about my recent portraits," I broached carefully, having wanted to ask about this since he brought them up. He turned to me eagerly, as if anticipating something, but his shoulders slumped at my softly worded "How?"

"There is always discussion among dealers and such about new pieces," he explained with a shrug. "Particularly if those paintings have not been commissioned."

And therefore might earn the dealer something for the sale. I could read between the lines.

His eyebrows arched. "Word is, you haven't accepted a new portrait commission in over a year. That you've turned down dozens of offers." His dark gaze searched mine. "And yet, rumor is you're painting more than ever."

I didn't confirm or deny this, slightly uncomfortable with the idea that people had been discussing such things about me without my being aware.

"Speculation is that you're preparing an exhibition of your own." His voice lowered. "That soon you'll be looking for a broker."

I knew what he was about to say, what he was about to offer, and I wasn't certain how to respond. Yes, it was time to begin seeking out a broker and a venue for the exhibition, something I found incredibly anxiety inducing. One hoped for an advocate who would support one's work with such passion and excitement. But as had already been established, these portraits were very different from the usual artistic fare. The thought of showing them to someone, of watching that passion and excitement possibly dwindle and die, made my chest tight.

Before Mr. Rimmer could say anything more, Gage interrupted.

"Mrs. Gage, might I have a moment?"

"Of course." I glanced distractedly toward Mr. Rimmer before crossing the parlor. Most of the auctioneer's other employees had been dismissed, but the red-haired fellow Mr. Rimmer had called Sullivan remained along with Sergeant Maclean.

"Mr. Sullivan here . . ." Gage nodded to the stiff-backed fellow ". . . was just reminding me of the dispute you and he both witnessed in this room on the second day of the auction."

"Why, yes," I replied. "I thought of it earlier but hadn't yet had a chance to bring it up. One of the men involved was Mr. Smith."

Maclean straightened to alertness. "The banker who was killed?"

"The same. Though he wasn't part of the initial dispute, but rather interjected at the end."

"Tell us about it," Gage urged.

I looked to Mr. Sullivan, seeing that he was waiting for me to speak first. "A man named Innes was apparently impatient to join the Bannatyne Club and upset that a special meeting wouldn't be called to vote on his membership. He was arguing with a reverend about it until Mr. Smith stepped in. Then he . . . he accused Lord Eldin of having blocked his membership while he was alive."

Maclean frowned. "The Bannatyne Club, huh?" The way he spoke its name made me suspect he was aware of its reputation as more than just a publication society. "And hoo did Smith factor intae the altercation?"

"He merely urged Innes to temper his outburst."

"And hoo did Innes respond?"

"He told him to mind his own business before barreling out of the room."

"And straight into Mrs. Gage," Sullivan expounded when I failed to, though I suspected he wished he hadn't when he paled at Maclean's reaction. The sergeant's face did rather resemble a snarling dog's.

"He apologized," I felt compelled to add in his defense, perhaps to mitigate Maclean's ire.

Gage was also angry, though he concealed this better as he conferred with Maclean. "We should speak to this Mr. Innes. And the reverend involved in the quarrel as well."

I agreed, though I had little confidence in Innes being the culprit. For certain, he'd been angry and anxious for the vote about his membership to be called, but I couldn't see how sabotaging the structural integrity of Lord Eldin's home was the next logical step in either taking revenge or hastening the outcome he wanted. No, I still believed that Mr. Smith's death had been naught but a bit of particularly rotten luck.

Maclean scraped a hand over his shadowed jaw, turning to Mr. Sullivan. "Do ye have anything else tae add tae what Mrs. Gage has told us?"

"No, sir."

"Then ye can go," he told him in dismissal.

Mr. Sullivan didn't need to be told twice, beating a hasty retreat.

CHAPTER 10

I progressed slowly through the back parlor and then the front drawing room, checking the collection against the catalog as best I could. But with some items having already been packed away for transport and many others having been haphazardly shifted to different spaces, there was no way I could be certain everything was accounted for. The best we could do was trust that Mr. Winstanley and Mr. Rimmer had been speaking truthfully when they'd asserted nothing was missing or stolen. Gage and Sergeant Maclean remained with me as I sorted through the items on the upper level, presumably for my security, and I listened as they overviewed the investigating the police had already done.

Maclean and some of the other officers had already spoken with the people in the neighboring buildings, asking if they'd noticed anything out of the ordinary, especially during the night when no one should have been at Lord Eldin's former residence. This had been done prior to the story being published in the *Caledonian Mercury* claiming the collapse was accidental, but even then, they'd had to tread with care so as to not alarm anyone. Yet no one had reported anything suspicious, and now it was too late to put out a broader request, asking for anyone with pertinent information to come forward. Not without revealing the newspaper's allegations to be faulty and possibly inspiring panic.

I could acknowledge the need to maintain calm, but I also found their logic somewhat flawed. For there were still a great number of people fearful for a different reason. A fear the *Caledonian Mercury* and other newspapers had espoused, cautioning those who lived in the "City of Palaces" which comprised the New Town to have the upper floors of their homes inspected before hosting any dances or large routs to ensure the timbers were sufficiently robust to withstand such heavy use. Men of the appropriate expertise would be kept busy for some time examining all the homes in question. However, if these same people had been made aware that the joist in question had also been tampered with, the alarm might not be so pronounced and the urgency for inspectors so great.

"Was any sort of saw found on the premises?" Gage queried as I sorted through the drawings stacked in a crate. "One that would be capable of cutting the beam as it was."

"Aye. In a closet off the kitchen," Maclean replied.

"That's an odd place to find such a hefty tool."

"'Twould normally be kept in a gardener's shed or the like," he agreed. "But there's also nothin' tae prove it was the implement used. 'Tis merely possible it's the blade in question."

"And anyone might have stowed it there once the cutting was done. It wouldn't be hard to slip down the service stairs to the ground floor, stash it in the nearest closet, and slip back upstairs again." There was a lull in their conversation, and when Gage spoke, it was clear he'd been contemplating the matter. "It would take a great deal of strength to wield a saw like that effectively over your head. I'm not sure I could even do so with any ease."

"Not with your arm still healing from that laceration, you couldn't," I warned, lest he take it upon himself to attempt it.

I could hear amusement in Maclean's voice as I moved on to a box of prints. "I take yer point. No' just anyone could do it. And almost certainly no' a lady."

I didn't dispute this. Which wasn't to say there weren't women capable of the described feat, but it was unlikely they would go unnoticed. I tilted my head, examining a print allegedly by Dürer as a thought occurred to me. "Unless they weren't working alone."

When neither man replied, I glanced over my shoulder at them. "There's nothing to say two men—or two women, or a man and a woman—didn't work together." I resumed my scrutiny of the inventory. "Though I suppose that would require two ladders, and only one was found. Unless they removed the second." I frowned at the image of St. Jerome with a lion. "But I suppose that raises a whole different set of possibly unnecessary questions. Why remove one and not the other? Were they almost caught? Or was it to another purpose? Are there even any other ladders on the premises?"

"Aye," he surprised me by answering. "In the gardener's shed."

"Then perhaps we should take a look at it," Gage suggested.

"We'll do so when I show ye the rear entrance. Are ye finished here?" Maclean asked me as I straightened from the last crate.

"Yes."

I followed the men back to the ground level, beginning my assessment of the inventory in the breakfast parlor while Gage and Maclean checked all the exterior doors and the doors to the study for evidence of tampering. The constables had since returned to their posts outside the two entrances to the study, and they looked on in interest. The study doors themselves were broken and shattered from the tools used to force them open, making their inspection all the more difficult. It would be easy to confuse the marks left by our rescuers for those that might have been left by someone picking the lock.

As the sergeant and my husband made their way belowstairs to examine the servants' entrance and gardener's shed, I moved to the dining room. I didn't know where Mr. Winstanley and his employees had all gone—perhaps belowstairs as well—but I was grateful to be left to my own devices. It was awkward enough to have the constables as an audience.

I worked with particular care given the crowded state of the chamber and the unwieldy size of some of the paintings. As with the other rooms, I recognized the impossibility of ensuring all the unsold and uncollected pieces from the auction were accounted for, but I could tell the principal pictures were there. I wished for better lighting to examine them more closely, my skin tingling and my heart rate accelerating with the pleasure of being in such close proximity to so much masterful artwork. Having recognized a fellow aficionado, I wondered if Mr. Rimmer felt this every time he examined a new collection. The thrill of potential discovery must have been the most exhilarating part of his job.

As if summoned by the thought, he appeared by my side as I was taking in the Van der Neer I'd hoped to bid on at a closer angle.

"Exquisite, isn't it?" he murmured.

"Yes," I stated without equivocation.

We stood silently for some minutes simply enjoying the skill and beauty of the painting, the play of light and shadow, and the delicate brushwork. Though Gage and my brother and sister and various friends tried to appreciate art as I did, they could never truly see it the same way. My husband's valet, Anderley, possessed the ability, but we did not often rub shoulders in the places such art was exhibited except for at private country houses, and then usually only during investigations.

"I'll ensure you're notified when this piece is to go up on the block," Mr. Rimmer informed me as I returned the painting to its original position.

"Thank you," I said, for I would genuinely have liked to own it.

He cleared his throat, drawing my attention as he glanced warily toward the door. At first, I thought he was about to broach the subject of my impending art exhibition again, and I found myself wishing Gage would provide another interruption. But when he began to speak in a hushed voice, I discovered he had another matter on his mind entirely. "I didn't know how to say this before, but there is one matter I think you should be aware of. While it's true that Mr. Clerk's grievance with us is largely due to his brother's will and the manner designated for the disposition of his assets, there is one set of pieces that the entire family is loath to part with."

"The Adam brothers' architectural drawings?" I guessed, having remembered the remark Mr. Rimmer let slip the first time we'd met that they might not go up for auction. He'd described the problem as a family dispute.

He didn't seem surprised I'd deduced as much and, in fact, seemed relieved not to be the one to have to make the matter plain. "You already know, then, that Lord Eldin's mother was the sister of the Adam brothers."

I nodded. "It makes sense that someone within the family—a brother or sister or cousin—might wish to keep the drawings."

Robert Adam; his older brother, John; and his younger brother, James, had been the preeminent British architects of the late eighteenth century, designing and remodeling both the exteriors and interiors of countless public buildings, churches, and private homes and estates for the upper echelons of society. Their neoclassical style had made an indelible mark on the country, and particularly on Edinburgh, as the brothers were Scottish.

"I don't dispute that. But..." He frowned. "I do wonder to what lengths they might go to make sure of it." His gaze was troubled. "I haven't seen Lord Eldin's will, but I've heard Mr. Winstanley discussing it with his lordship's solicitor, and there is no ambiguity in the matter. Lord Eldin wanted the drawings sold along with the rest of his collection."

I understood what he was trying to convey. If it was unlikely William Clerk and his brothers and sisters would prevail legally, what might they do in order to triumph by other means?

"Except the Adam brothers' drawings are still accounted for." I'd just seen them in several boxes in the corner of this room. "So I fail to see what goal they could have hoped to accomplish by sabotaging the joist."

"Yes, but perhaps their ultimate goal wasn't to obtain them illicitly, but rather to discredit Mr. Winstanley's firm. To weaken his legal standing and cast doubt on Lord Eldin's will being of sound judgment." My skepticism must have been evident, for Mr. Rimmer grimaced. "I didn't say it was rational, simply something worth keeping in mind when you speak to Mr. Clerk."

The sound of Gage's and Sergeant Maclean's voices raised in conference reached our ears, and Mr. Rimmer excused himself, nodding to the two men as he waited for them to enter the room before he left. My husband looked to me in question, but I shook my head, indicating that what Mr. Rimmer had shared with me could wait for later.

"Were any of the locks picked?" I asked instead, curious about their findings.

Gage propped his hands on his hips, glancing mindfully at the constables still listening. "It's difficult to say."

But Maclean seemed to have no qualms about his men overhearing. "There are any number o' scratches and small gouges on each o' the doors near the locks, especially the door at the rear o' the house, but none that tell us whether 'twas from the lock bein' forced rather than the normal wear and tear on such a mechanism from clumsy fingers."

"If it was picked, it was done skillfully," my husband concluded.

I could tell he was dissatisfied with this fact, but there was nothing more to be done. "And the gardener's shed?"

Maclean rubbed his jaw. "Aye. Holds a ladder. But it doesna appear tae have been moved in some time."

Gage concurred. "Not in the last week, in any case."

I gathered up my things, including my tattered copy of the auction catalog. "Then the cut must have been made by a strong man."

At least that was something. Though it didn't rule out as many suspects as we might have liked given the fact any number of them could have been working with a burly accomplice.

"You need to return home for Emma," Gage said, observing my movements. It was more of a statement than a question, for he must have realized it was time I saw to our daughter's needs. Past time, in fact, if the familiar heaviness in my chest was any indication.

"I ken you're both still recoverin' from yer ordeal," Maclean stated with a side-eyed look in my direction.

The initial excitement of his revelation about the joist having long subsided, I'd been struggling not to reveal the growing discomfort and fatigue dragging at my body, making each step more tiring than the last. Evidently, this effort had been unsuccessful, and my increasingly haggard appearance was the reason the sergeant would no longer meet my eye. It was that or Gage's veiled reference to my breastfeeding our daughter. But Maclean had several children of his own, and he and his wife were not of the class that might have passed off their infants to a nursemaid. Given this, it seemed doubtful he was squeamish about such a necessity of life, and if he ever had been, from what I'd heard about his wife, she wouldn't have allowed such nonsense for long.

He tugged down on the belt covering his gray greatcoat. "So I'll call on ye in the morn, and we can confer then."

Gage agreed. "In the meantime, I'd like permission to speak with some of the trusted members of our staff. As I'm sure you're aware, they often assist us with our inquiries and have proved to be invaluable and discreet. They may be able to help in ways we can't."

Maclean's jaw worked as he considered his request. "Often 'tis the servants who ken all the best gossip, isna' that right?"

The old adage was often quoted for a reason.

He nodded. "Aye. Just be sure they step wi' care."

Following luncheon, Gage swiftly informed Bree, Anderley, Jeffers, and Mrs. Mackay about the revelations and discoveries made that morning while I nursed Emma and put her down for her nap. The nanny looked to me in silent query as I joined them all in the library.

"She's asleep," I murmured to her even as Gage continued addressing a question put to him by his valet. Truth be told, Emma had fallen asleep a quarter of an hour ago, but I'd lingered, wanting to gaze down at her precious slumbering face and smell her sweet baby scent. Time was passing too fast, and soon my darling girl would be one. I wanted to capture these moments and seal them in my memory before it was too late.

"I left the door to the nursery ajar, so we'll be able to hear her when she wakes," I added, and Mrs. Mackay nodded, turning back to my husband.

My gaze drifted from face to face, curious how they'd taken the news. Jeffers sat tall and straight to my left in a ladder-back chair that had been dragged over from the table near the window, his expression as placid and proper as ever except the liveliness of his eyes, taking everything in. Bree perched opposite me on the matching sofa, her hands clasped, and her mouth crimped as if she was still trying to reconcile everything she'd heard. Next to her, Anderley listened avidly to what Gage had to say, leaning slightly toward him, as if ready to spring up at his first request. Gage had claimed the single wingback armchair. The same chair I'd painted Philipa having fallen asleep in for the portrait above the hearth. Though his voice and movements were animated, I noted how his left arm remained at his side, telling me it still twinged enough not to be used normally.

Of those gathered, only Lettuce Mackay—sitting beside me—seemed entirely unmoved, but then it took a great deal to rattle her. She was the oldest person present, and I wondered if her unflappable nature was born of experience and the travails of her position. After all, she had worked as a nursery maid and nanny for nigh on fifty years, raising multiple generations of children for wealthy families throughout Scotland. I had come to rely on her steadiness and confidence, sometimes feeling I was in her charge as much as Emma was.

My sister had initially expressed some concern about our nanny's age when she'd learned whom I'd hired, but I had known from the instant we'd met Mrs. Mackay that she was the right woman for the job. She might have been well past sixty, with wrinkles and gently sagging skin and silver hair tucked beneath her cap, but she brimmed with energy, and she'd expressed a desire to travel, to see other parts of Britain and possibly Europe, which complemented our household's somewhat nomadic existence. Most of the women we'd interviewed had not seemed enthused by this notion, believing they would remain in Edinburgh or a country house with their charges while we ventured about as we wished. I understood this was the way many aristocratic families operated, as often the parents had very little to do with the raising of their offspring, but I had no intention of leaving my children behind. So Mrs. Mackay's desire for adventure coupled with her experience had seemed a godsend. I'd not regretted for one moment hiring her.

Having finished his response to Anderley, Gage turned to me, letting me know that everyone was now on the same page. "We will have to proceed with care," Gage informed us all. "While Sergeant Maclean has requested our assistance, he is adamant that the truth about the joist not become public knowledge. At least, not until there is a better grasp of the matter and the motives and players involved. He wishes to stave off any panic."

"But . . . I still dinna understand." Bree's brow was knitted with concern. "They're *certain* 'twasn't an accident?"

"Well . . ." Gage's gaze met mine, and I could tell he was recalling how he'd assured her of the exact opposite just two days prior. "We didn't get a chance to examine the joist with our own eyes as the chamber's ceiling had been deemed too unsteady for further exploration until it has been shored up, but they had a number of experts scrutinize the matter, and it was they who brought it to the city police's attention." One corner of his mouth curled wryly. "And I feel quite confident in stating that Sergeant Maclean would not have brought the matter to our attention if he wasn't absolutely sure."

"Aye, but . . . it doesna make sense," Bree insisted with a shake of her head. "Why would someone cause a floor tae collapse under a hundred people just tae kill one man? Seems a foolish . . ." her eyes darted to me ". . . and *reckless* way tae go aboot it. Why, he might o' killed dozens o' people!"

"Yes, but we don't know that Mr. Smith was the target," Anderley pointed out. "In fact, it seems doubtful he was. Unless the killer was tremendously lucky."

"No, I agree." Gage leaned to the side, propping his chin in his right hand. "The notion that the one person who was killed was the one intended to be seems all but impossible. Particularly as nothing we've learned thus far about this Mr. Smith draws suspicion." He looked to Jeffers. "Unless you've uncovered something?"

"From everything I've been able to glean, Mr. Smith was an upstanding citizen, well loved by his family and his clients. But I can continue to gather information."

Gage nodded. "Yes, do. Discreetly. We don't want to cause his family any more pain than necessary if he was merely an innocent bystander." He turned to me. "Though we should still speak to this Mr. Innes fellow he argued with to see what he knows."

"But Bree's point is still valid," I argued, having seen her mouth clamp in frustration. "It *was* a foolish and reckless plan to sabotage the joist if their intended victim was but one person. There are dozens of more effective ways to go about it."

"Then perhaps there wasna' just one intended victim," Mrs. Mackay said. "Maybe their reasons for committin' such a scurrilous act were broader."

It was worth considering. It would address some of the difficulties that I, like Bree, was having in believing that someone could commit such a heinous and irrational act. Perhaps it added credibility to the notion that it may have been an act of sabotage against the auctioneer.

"Ye mean like if someone wanted to halt the auction?" Bree queried, thinking along the same lines.

"Or perhaps harm the people, in general, who were bidding?" Anderley added.

Silence fell as we all contemplated this.

"Lord Eldin was a Lord of Session for a time," Jeffers reminded us. His chair creaked as he crossed one leg over the other. "Perhaps some sort of criminal or plaintiff was after revenge and, not being able to have it on the man directly, decided to take it on his reputation, or his memory, if you will. After all, this floor collapse at the auction of his art collection is likely the thing people will associate with him most after those who knew him personally have died."

"That's an astute observation," Gage agreed, seeming much struck by this. "Though I don't think such a motive can be limited to only criminals and plaintiffs he might have crossed."

"Even a friend or family member might possess such a desire," Anderley said.

I arched my eyebrows. "Or someone disgruntled that their membership into a club had been blocked by the man in question."

Gage recognized what I was referring to. "I agree, that is a sounder reason for Mr. Innes to be involved than the idea that he was targeting Mr. Smith specifically. Perhaps we should try to learn more about this Bannatyne Club."

Mrs. Mackay nodded sagely. "They are kent for their rather notorious revelries." My surprise at her knowing this seemed to amuse her. "When ye've lived as long as I have, and served in as many households, few things escape yer ears. I may ken someone who can tell us more. If Miss McEvoy wouldna' mind lookin' after Miss Gage one afternoon."

Bree's face softened. "O' course."

Anderley observed this with a gentle smile, and I wondered if he was thinking of the future, of the possible children they might have, but perhaps I was being fanciful.

"I'm curious what Sir James Riddell might know about them as well," I suggested, adding to our growing list of people to be questioned. "I'd like to ask him about his remark about Lord Eldin turning in his grave at the idea of his collection being auctioned."

"A statement that is in direct opposition to the stipulations of his will," Gage noted.

"Or so Mr. Winstanley claimed," I cautioned. "Perhaps we should seek out Lord Eldin's solicitor to find out exactly what the will says?"

"Let's speak to Mr. Clerk first. If he confirms what the auctioneer told us, then it may not be necessary."

"And Mr. Clerk is the beneficiary?" Anderley asked, seeking clarification.

"Of his properties and much of his estate, yes," Gage confirmed. "But all Lord Eldin's brothers and sisters are supposed to share in the proceeds of the sale of his art collection." His voice dipped leadingly. "And we've been led to believe they're not all happy with the manner in which the auction is being conducted. Though it would be nice to confirm this with at least one of them besides William Clerk."

"From what I understand, most of them are scattered afield in various parts of Scotland," Jeffers intoned.

I hid a smile. Trust our all-knowing butler to be already versed in this information. However, my good humor was short-lived as I recalled what Mr. Rimmer had told me. "Mr. Winstanley's assistant mentioned to me that there is a dispute over the Adam brothers' architectural drawings. That some of

Lord Eldin's brothers and sisters are contesting their inclusion in the auction."

"Something else to discuss with Mr. Clerk, then. And it raises another point." Gage turned to Anderley. "I'd like you to look into the auctioneer's employees. Find out what you can about them."

His valet grinned, agreeing to this request without further question. But then again, the pair of them had been working together on inquiries for quite some time. Their trust in each other ran deep, making them able to often communicate without words.

However, Bree wasn't as willing to accede to this silently, and I couldn't blame her after what had happened during our inquiry in Cornwall the previous autumn. "Ye suspect one o' 'em's involved," Bree asserted, her eyes narrowed in suspicion.

Had Gage looked at me, I would have indulged in my own bit of silent communication, warning him not to disregard her concern. Fortunately, my husband held more respect for her than that. And perhaps he was also thinking of Cornwall and the danger he'd placed Anderley in.

"The method and timing of the sabotage have to make us wonder. Yes, it's possible Mr. Clerk is the one involved. And yes, someone might have broken into the house overnight. The security was lax enough, and the locks easily picked. But the auction employees had the greatest access to the house during the time the joist must have been tampered with, so they must be considered." His jaw hardened sternly as he turned to address Anderley. "However, I don't want you taking any risks. This auction house specializes in art, and Mr. Rimmer, at the least, knows who Mrs. Gage is and is an admirer of her work."

I flushed as the others turned to look at me.

"So it would be safe to say he might know we have a valet

who assists us in our endeavors," Gage continued, lowering his voice. "They're also all aware that the joist was tampered with, so tread with care."

Anderley had sobered in the face of the undercurrents flowing between him and Gage and him and Bree, and he dipped his head in agreement. "Of course." Once Gage had released him from his gaze, he turned to Bree, who still eyed him guardedly. Anderley's fingers twitched where they rested against the sofa cushion between them, and I could tell he wanted to touch her in reassurance, but he knew better than to attempt it in front of an audience.

"There's one other avenue I think we should explore," Gage posited, steepling his fingers before him. "I know you dismissed the possibility of the sabotage being done by a rival collector because even if they had no regard for human life, they wouldn't wish to see the art damaged," he told me. "But what of a rival auctioneer? Someone who is angry that a firm from Liverpool was given the contract and not them."

"Someone local?" I surmised.

"Yes."

I tilted my head, weighing the prospect. "If they were not great art lovers themselves, then yes, I could see that. If they were angry and vindictive and callous enough." I frowned. "Though I'm uncertain who those rival auctioneers might be."

Gage turned to the members of our staff in turn, in particular Jeffers and Mrs. Mackay, to see if they might know.

"Let me find oot," Bree stated, smoothing down her green skirt. "I can come up wi' a list o' local auctioneers. Shouldna be hard. And I'll see what I can discover aboot their reputations as weel."

"Add brokers to the list, too," I said, wondering if such an intermediary could also be involved. After all, there were some people who were less enamored by the mastery of the art itself than simply the act of possessing it, and those men usually hired brokers to amass their collections and do their dirty work. I'd encountered a few such men in my time as an artist. In particular, the broker of one rather unpleasant earl who was outraged I wouldn't undertake a portrait commission for him.

Bree's whisky brown gaze met mine in comprehension. "Aye."

"Then we all have our tasks," Gage declared, rising to his feet. The others filed out as he crossed to the sideboard, pouring himself a finger of whisky. He downed it in one swallow.

"Your arm still aches," I stated unequivocally.

"And you're still subsisting on almost no slumber," he challenged not unkindly.

I sighed. "I've done so many times before."

His tone gentled. "Yes, but not when your body is still recovering from a ten-foot fall."

"True." I turned toward the window, where flecks of rain were striking the glass. "But if I lie down now, I won't be able to sleep."

His hand stole into mine, recapturing my attention. "Too many thoughts spinning in your head."

I offered him a faint smile, for he knew me too well. "I'm going up to my art studio for a while."

When my head and heart were most muddled, art had always had the ability to help me find clarity. There was something about the way it freed my subconscious and yet focused it. Something about the scent of linseed oil, gesso, and turpentine soothed me—contradictory as that might seem. Each brushstroke was like a heartbeat, each rasp of bristles against the canvas notes of a symphony only I could hear.

Gage knew all this and didn't fight it. He simply pressed a kiss to my forehead and sent me on my way.

CHAPTER 11

Sergeant Maclean arrived bright and early the following morning while we were still breaking our fasts. I invited him to join us. Something, at first, he seemed reluctant to do. Until a rasher of bacon was set before him. Then he mumbled his thanks before applying himself to the meat and a couple of eggs. Gage's amused gaze met mine across the breakfast table, and I strove to hide my answering smile behind my cup of chocolate.

"If ye dinna mind me sayin' so," Maclean said after swallowing a drink of still-steaming coffee, "ye look much more the thing this morn, m'lady."

"Yes," I conceded with a light gasp of laughter as I set down my cup. "I can only imagine how peaked I still looked yesterday." I'd certainly felt it. "But I'm feeling much recovered today." Or at least my aches and twinges were more manageable.

I'd even allowed Bree to dress me in one of my more stylish plaid silk gowns with a white pelerine draped over the shoulders and upper gigot sleeves. Though I despised the massive sleeves that were so *en vogue*, I could not escape them entirely and thus insisted they not be quite so expansive, nor the sleeve supports constructed of buckram and wire and filled with soft feathers tied beneath them be so large. A wide carmine belt to match a shade in the plaid cinched in the silhouette at the waist before it expanded again in the full skirts. Considering the number of calls we intended to make that day, several of which were to fashionable people, it behooved me to look the part of my station.

Gage also appeared to be in better health and was impeccably tailored, as usual, in a coat of midnight blue superfine and a waistcoat of cerulean laced with silver. The color combination accented his pale winter blue eyes, making them appear even brighter than normal. They shimmered now with a mixture of regard and relief.

"I'm glad tae hear it," Maclean said as he tapped open his second egg before peeling it. "I took the liberty o' sendin' word tae Mr. Clerk that he should expect a call from us before nine."

"He does seem like the type of gentleman who dislikes surprises," Gage remarked as he sliced off a bite of sausage.

Maclean's lips quirked cynically. "O' course, that means he's had time tae prepare. But at least this way 'tis harder for him tae turn us away."

One could hope.

"And after Mr. Clerk?" I queried after taking another drink. "Where shall we go next? Do you know where Mr. Winstanley's employees are staying while they're in Edinburgh?"

Maclean named the White Horse Inn off Canongate. "But if ye're thinkin' o' the Fletcher lad, I already spoke tae him. Thought it was best tae do so before the other assistant could warn 'im, and they could corroborate stories."

I shouldn't have felt a pulse of irritation. It was Maclean's investigation, after all. He didn't need to seek our permission to speak to a witness or suspect, and he certainly had a valid point about the timing. But I felt a flicker of annoyance all the same.

However, Gage appeared entirely unperturbed, stabbing a bite of kippers as he asked, "And what did he have to say?"

"He confirmed his colleague's story. Seems they departed together the evenin' before and arrived together that morn, and they share a room. So unless they're in collusion or Mr. Rimmer slipped oot after Mr. Fletcher retired for the night, 'tis unlikely either o' 'em is the culprit."

"Could they be in collusion?"

Maclean scratched his chin, which sprouted dark stubble. "Aye, I suppose. Though 'twould indicate terrible plannin' on their part. Mr. Fletcher's face was bruised and battered, and 'twas obvious he was in some pain. And Mr. Rimmer barely escaped a similar fate."

I had to admit, that did make them drop to the bottom of my suspect list, especially since we were unaware of a motive for either of them to sabotage that joist.

"Ye're welcome tae call on 'im yerselves," he continued. "But keep in mind, he's probably back at work today. Said Mr. Winstanley ordered 'im tae take the day off yesterday because he kept havin' dizzy spells and needin' tae sit doon lest he drop somethin' valuable. Said as long as those had passed, he'd be expected back at Picardy Place."

This admission didn't color the auctioneer in quite so favorable a light, but I supposed he was scrambling to salvage the collection and move the auction to a different location. All the while, he was losing profits in added expenses. Ones that the client might not have been expected to cover. As such, he was relying greatly on his assistants.

Gage wiped his mouth with his serviette. "If you're satisfied with Fletcher's answers, then I have no further questions to put to him. At least for the moment."

Maclean nodded, but his gaze shifted to me in consideration as he chewed his last slice of bacon, and I could tell he had something else to say. My muscles tensed as I recalled how our falling-out the previous spring had begun much the same way. Perhaps he'd found out about Bonnie Brock paying me a visit two days prior. It was possible. Though I didn't think Maclean could possibly know the content of our conversation. Even so, such a discovery could cause complications to our reconciliation with the sergeant.

"Mr. Fletcher claimed his colleague is quite the admirer o' yer art," he finally stated, lifting his freshly filled cup of coffee by the brim, not the handle. "*Enamored* is, I believe, the word he used." His eyebrows arched over the cup as he took a drink.

I blushed at the implication, though I didn't think Maclean meant to imply anything untoward.

"Yes, Mr. Rimmer was quite . . ." Gage narrowed his eyes as if searching for the appropriate word ". . . *enthusiastic* when he made her acquaintance on the second day of the auction." Gage grinned at me. "With good reason."

Maclean scrutinized my flushed cheeks and then Gage's teasing expression before setting his cup down as he declared decisively, "If you're no' concerned by it, then neither am I." He pushed back from the table but hesitated before rising. "Shall we?"

We climbed into our carriage to set off toward the small abode we'd been informed that Mr. Clerk lived in near the Custom House. As the steps were set by our footman, Gage asked if Maclean had made any other inquiries the previous afternoon.

"Only aboot this Mr. Innes that Mrs. Gage and Mr.

Sullivan mentioned. Took most o' the afternoon to track down his location. I'd like tae pay him a visit."

Gage nodded, glancing at me in silent comradery. "We also wondered if you'd considered Lord Eldin's past as a motive. Perhaps something that occurred during his time as a judge."

Maclean crossed his arms, the gray fabric of his coat straining over his burly shoulders. "Ye mean like a criminal oot for revenge? Maybe someone recently released."

"Or a disgruntled plaintiff. One he didn't rule in favor of."

Maclean grunted. "'Tis worth considerin'." He turned his head to peer out the window at the sunshine peeking through the scattered cover of clouds and shining down on the trees beginning to bud in Queen Street Gardens. "I'll speak tae my superintendent. 'Twill likely require him tae intercede at the Court o' Session if we hope tae gain any information or access any o' their records."

Had I not been looking directly at a pair of horse chestnut trees abutting the five-foot-high rod iron fence surrounding the western garden, I was certain I would never have seen Bonnie Brock standing in the shadow of one of the trunks, watching our carriage pass by. Such was his stillness, the shades of his clothing blending with his surroundings, that it would have been easy to overlook him. At least, I hoped so. I cast a wary glance over Maclean's face, but he seemed lost in his own thoughts and all but oblivious to the world passing by outside the window. I could only be glad of that. Though I did wonder why Bonnie Brock was lurking so close to our home. He'd seen that I was well and delivered his warning. What more did he want?

It was a valid question. For Bonnie Brock kept a tally of favors, and if you were in his debt, he expected to be repaid. After the events of last spring, I thought we were even. He might have rescued us from the vaults, but we'd been there in the first place because of him. However, he *had* then sought out the men in the rival gang that had attacked us and recovered my mother's amethyst pendant, which they'd stolen from me. Perhaps he believed that placed me in his debt. I would argue not, given the fact the retrieval had only been secondary to his desire for retribution against those men, but that didn't mean he saw it the same way. He was nothing if not contrary.

Much like Bree. I knew she was concerned about Anderley venturing out in disguise, as he had the previous evening, searching out the pub where the auctioneer's employees congregated after hours. The same place they were lodging, as it turned out. The fact she'd adopted a breezy, indifferent attitude to his new escapade did not fool me. Not when I could sense the tension in her frame and hear how her words were clipped at the end.

Perhaps she was angry at me and Gage for taking on another murder inquiry, for asking Anderley to put himself in potential danger. It was a fair complaint considering how severely Anderley had been beaten by those smugglers in Cornwall. Though I didn't know how to resolve it. Gage and I weren't going to stop conducting inquiries. Not when justice was required and murderers needed to be stopped. Not when the newly established police forces in cities like Edinburgh and London still focused on preventing crime, not on investigating after the fact. I supposed we could always refuse to allow Anderley to be involved, but I knew he would not thank us or Bree for that. Furthermore, we *needed* him. He was a valuable asset.

Nonetheless, I still felt for Bree and hoped to find a way to draw her out.

As we neared the garden at Drummond Place, situated to the rear of the Custom House, which had formerly been the mansion Bellevue owned by the Marchioness of Titchfield,

Maclean leaned forward, lowering his voice as if to impart something important. "When we arrive, the pair o' ye go on in tae speak wi' Clerk. I've a few questions I'd like tae put tae his manservant." From the glint in his eyes, I suspected he was relishing this task.

I understood once we were ushered inside. Though Mr. Clerk was merely a court clerk, the butler who greeted us at the door was quite possibly the most supercilious I'd ever met. His nose was pointed so high up in the air that I could practically count the hairs in each nostril. Which I suspected outnumbered the ones still clinging to his scalp. When he spied Sergeant Maclean entering after us, his mouth contorted as if he'd eaten a crab apple.

Normally, a policeman would be expected to use the tradesman's entrance, something it was unlikely Maclean begrudged, as he was often involved with police matters in New Town and undoubtedly accustomed to this protocol. As such, I doubted this was the reason for his dislike of the manservant, even when he attempted to close the door in his face, coming up against the immovable block of Maclean's foot.

"He's with us," I told the butler, trying to smooth over matters. Only to be answered by a sniff and a withering eye cast over my person. One so disdainful that my back stiffened and I felt the temperature of my blood rise.

"We're here to see Mr. Clerk," Gage informed him in a voice that brooked no argument. Clearly, he'd not missed the butler's snub of his wife.

"He's expecting you. Or rather him," he droned with a sneer at Maclean. "I'll show you . . ."

"We'll show ourselves up, shall we?" Gage interrupted, pulling my pelisse from me and depositing it into the butler's arms, which already cradled our hats and gloves. Then he turned his back on the man, escorting me across the narrow and gloomy entrance hall toward the stairs.

"Aye, I've some questions just for ye," Maclean declared with a hint of menace, speaking over the butler's efforts to protest.

"Is this routine something the two of you have performed before?" I murmured to my husband as we mounted the steps.

His lips quirked. "No, but I recognized Maclean's intent. He needs the man off guard and rattled enough he might answer his questions honestly. Namely whether his employer was in residence when he said he was and not off tampering with the construction of his brother's home."

I peered back over my shoulder to see that Maclean had the fellow cornered with his arms still full of our outer garments. "I don't know about that, but he might be outraged enough to let something slip. At least, enough to indicate whether he's lying."

Once we'd reached the floor above, we turned our steps toward the open door at the front of the house. We'd decided that Mr. Clerk was most likely to have planned to receive us there, as the drawing room would be the most formal. However, his butler's remark about having not expected us but only Maclean made me second-guess this assumption. In any case, there was nothing for it but to try that room first, buying the sergeant more time.

The drawing room proved to be rather small compared with many in New Town, however the furnishings within were of excellent quality, with scrolls and embellishments and little carvings. The walls were papered in a floral-patterned silk and the drapes fashioned of a gossamer-like fabric of palest pink. It was not the type of decoration I'd anticipated for an old bachelor, but neither was the sight of Mr. Clerk lounging in a loose silk banyan, smoking a cigar.

His head was buried behind a newspaper, and though he didn't look up, he must have heard us enter. "I dinna appreciate bein' expected tae wait upon a policeman's convenience," he replied crisply after exhaling a puff of smoke toward the ceiling. "I'll give ye five minutes o' my time and no more." One leg was crossed over the other, and the foot jostled up and down—pale and shockingly bare.

"That's too bad," Gage intoned, finally startling Mr. Clerk into lowering his paper with a sharp rustle. "For it means we'll simply have to return until we get all the answers we seek."

He glared at Gage, his eyes all but disappearing beneath his heavy brow. Between that and a rather pugnacious nose and thick lips, he wouldn't be described as attractive, but he certainly wasn't unassuming.

"I'll no' be held responsible for my brother's insistence on that foolish auction," he declared, rising to his feet and setting the newspaper aside. He reached for the pewter dish on the table at his elbow, stubbing out his cigar, I supposed in deference to my presence. As a rule, gentlemen did not smoke in front of ladies. He disappeared briefly through a doorway that led into the adjacent room. In our town house, a type of small butler's pantry connected the drawing room to the library. I wondered if here it was the same. When he returned, the pewter dish and cigar were gone.

"Then you didn't wish to hold the auction like your brother had stipulated in his will?" Gage inquired as Mr. Clerk came to a stop behind the leather armchair he'd been seated in.

The query seemed to surprise him, for he scrutinized us both again in turn. "Nay. It should have been handled quietly and privately. No' this . . ." he waved his hand as if searching for the right word ". . . *spectacle* Winstanley has put on." His mouth screwed up in disgust. "If it is compensation ye seek, ye should talk to *him*."

Ah, now I understood his reaction to us, and I couldn't help asking, "Have many come demanding such?" For their injuries or loss of property.

He scowled. "Nay. But there's always a first."

And he'd been anticipating it. I wasn't sure whether this made him a better suspect or worse.

"That's not why we're here," Gage told him, persisting despite the skepticism etched across his features. "We'd heard contradictory rumors that Lord Eldin both stipulated the terms of the auction and the auctioneer to conduct it, and that he was rolling over in his grave to see his relatives auction off his collection."

Mr. Clerk scoffed.

"We wondered which it was."

"John always had tae have things his way. Even in death." His face screwed up in disgust. "As I said, this entire farce was his idea." He shook his head. "Nay, I would've handled it quite differently."

"With private bidders and such?" I replied, seeking to understand.

Mr. Clerk gestured toward the scroll-end settee on our right while he rounded the armchair to resume his seat. I noticed he'd donned a pair of embroidered slippers. "No need for this *pageant*. But John always did like to show off. No doubt he expected accolades for his collection, even though half o' it is scarcely more than rubbish. Scraps from treasures that *were* truly worth somethin'."

I had also noted that while some of the pictures and drawings and objects of virtu were of great value, others were barely more than detritus. Detritus from an ancient civilization, yes, but detritus all the same.

Gage lifted the tails of his coat before sitting beside me. "Were you aware of the terms of his will before he died?"

A humorless chuckle rumbled in Mr. Clerk's throat. "John left that surprise for after his death. Though I'd kent he'd hired a firm from Liverpool to assess his collection." He turned away, muttering under his breath. "Couldna' stop crowin' aboot its alleged worth."

"Were you aware that you were going to inherit his properties?" Gage asked.

Our host's gaze sharpened. "Aye, as I'm the next eldest. But I'd always planned tae sell the town house. I dinna need it." He gestured to the ceiling and walls, indicating his current home. "And neither do our other brothers and sisters."

"What about your nephews and nieces?" I interjected.

He sat back, clasping his hands over his lap. "Dinna have any. None o' us have married. We're determined bachelors and spinsters all."

I didn't know how to respond to this. Seven children and yet none had married. I wondered why and then acknowledged it was none of my business. At least, as long as it had no bearing on this investigation.

It was during this lull that Maclean appeared. We heard him before we saw him, even though I could tell he was trying to step lightly. He bowed his head to Mr. Clerk, who glowered at him before turning to Gage.

"Mr. Clerk has confirmed Mr. Winstanley's claim about Lord Eldin's will."

At these words, Mr. Clerk's neck stiffened as he eyed both men suspiciously and then me, recognizing that we were collaborating. "I see. Then I take it ye're aware that the joist was tampered wi'. Somethin' *I* canna be held responsible for."

"No' unless ye or someone ye hired did the tamperin'," Maclean replied.

CHAPTER 12

The sergeant stood at the opposite end of the tea table since Mr. Clerk had yet to offer him a seat. Something he was unlikely to do if he baited him.

"Why on earth would I do such a thing?" Mr. Clerk demanded. "I'm the one who's goin' tae have tae foot the bill tae repair it, for 'tis doubtful that reprehensible builder will be brought tae account. No' when the tamperin' is made public." His face had flushed bright red with fury. "And I canna even begin that process because the police need tae investigate further and Winstanley still needs tae move the collection tae another site before he can reconvene the auction. An act which is goin' tae cost me even *more* money, no doubt, as I dinna expect *Winstanley* . . ." he spoke the name witheringly ". . . will voluntarily cover the cost, even though 'tis *his* fault for packin' the rooms wi' *too many people*!"

What there was no doubt of was Mr. Clerk's sense of righteous anger over the entire affair. He'd not wanted the auction in the first place. He'd not wanted it held in his brother's—now *his*—home. And a great deal of headache and misfortune had befallen him because of everything that had happened.

Given all this, I couldn't believe he had anything to do with the tampering. There was simply no real benefit to him doing such a thing, not physically, emotionally, or financially.

However, Maclean still seemed to require convincing. "And where were ye the evenin' before the collapse occurred?"

"I was here. As I already told ye," Mr. Clerk snapped. "I departed Picardy Place aboot four o'clock and returned home. *Where I stayed* until the followin' morn when I departed for court."

Maclean nodded, for presumably this tracked with what he'd already been told. "And ye arrived there?"

Mr. Clerk ground his teeth. "Shortly before half past seven. I'm quite certain there are a number o' people who can vouch for that. Shall I list them?"

"That's no' necessary." Maclean crossed his arms and spread his legs as if settling in for a long stay. However, I was growing tired of craning my neck to look up at him. "The house's security. Mr. Winstanley says ye were in charge o' it."

"A fact he did not divulge to *me*."

"'Twas in the contract. I saw it."

Mr. Clerk glared at Maclean as if he was a pest he wished to squash, even though Maclean probably had at least three stones greater weight than him, all of it muscle. "My brother signed the contract, no' me." Which didn't explain why he hadn't read it, though I didn't expect him to answer that. "And I hired the two footmen as Winstanley suggested. He made no further recommendations." Mr. Clerk grasped the arms of his chair, leaning forward. "Though *I* was the one who insisted on lockin' the study. There were too many important things kept there. Fortunately, a great deal o' 'em were in the safe, which the collapse could no' have damaged."

"Important things such as?" Gage pressed.

Mr. Clerk's enraged stare swung toward him. "Documents mostly. My brother's . . . *memoirs*," he sneered. "I might o' moved them here, but I hadna decided what tae keep and what tae discard."

Gage and I shared a speaking look.

"The memoirs," he said. "May we read them?"

A muscle twitched in Mr. Clerk's jaw. "You may not."

"But they might tell us who would commit such an atrocious act," I argued.

"They won't." His voice was clipped and decisive. "They're mostly my brother's ramblings aboot his ain consequence and that benighted collection o' his."

"Still."

"Nay." He seemed immovable on this, but then his gaze flickered as he continued to meet my pleading one, and he heaved an aggrieved sigh. "But I'll take another look at them myself. If I can *get* tae them," he growled in Maclean's direction, as if the study's compromised structure was his fault. "And I'll let ye ken what I find."

It wasn't the answer I wanted. Would Mr. Clerk even know what to look for? Would he grasp its significance? Sometimes the smallest, most seemingly inconsequential piece of information could prove to be the linchpin to uncover the culprit. However, his offer seemed the best I could hope for, so I had no choice but to accept it with grace.

"We also understand there's some disagreement over the Adam brothers' architectural drawings," Gage broached.

"Because they werena John's tae dispose of," Mr. Clerk sniped, weariness beginning to overtake his temper. "When Mother bequeathed them tae him, 'twas wi' the stipulation that they'd remain in the family until such time as there was no one else to pass them tae."

"Yet he listed them as part of his collection to be auctioned in his will?"

"Aye." Mr. Clerk rubbed his forehead. "We've been searchin' for some sort o' documentary evidence from Mother to prove this, but so far we've had no luck."

"Could it be possible one of your siblings . . . ?" Gage began, but Mr. Clerk cut him off.

"Risked the lives o' hundreds o' people in some misguided attempt tae what?" He waved his hand again, as I was beginning to learn was his habit when he was searching for what to say. "Halt the auction? Give us more time tae find proof o' Mother's wishes?" He shook his head. "Nay. No one in my family is that callous. But if that doesna convince ye, none o' my brothers or sisters are even in Edinburgh. They've no' been here in several months."

Which didn't preclude the possibility they'd hired someone to do the sabotage for them, but I still thought it improbable. Not without Mr. Clerk being involved. And the longer we spoke to him, the more certain I became that he wasn't. So I tried a different tack.

"Who do *you* think did it?" I asked, curious what he'd say.

His mouth compressed into a thin line. "I'd like tae say that *vile* auctioneer." He heaved a sigh. "But I dinna think he did it. It simply doesna make sense that he'd risk his reputation like that. Beyond that, I honestly dinna ken." He turned his head toward the window overlooking London Street, where outside a carriage could be heard passing by. "John could sometimes rub others the wrong way." He scoffed at himself. "I dinna ken why I'm mincin' words. He *often* did. He was argumentative and fractious and contradictory. Father intended him for the Indian Civil Service, but John insisted on somethin' else. Apprenticed tae a Writer to the Signet before becomin' a member o' the Faculty o' Advocates himself and establishin' his own practice at the bar." He snorted. "No' that I can blame 'im. Arguin' cases 'twas a better fit for him than diplomacy."

"Did he ever mention someone from one of those past cases?" Gage queried.

"Nay. 'Twouldn't have been John's way."

"What of the Bannatyne Club?" I posited.

Mr. Clerk's face screwed up in distaste.

"Could his activities with them have some bearing on the matter?"

"I dinna see hoo," he muttered derisively. "Unless ye think one o' its members damaged the joist in a drunken haze."

This was clearly meant in sarcasm, and I found myself questioning his animosity toward the group. Did his disapproval merely stem from the club's antics, or was there a different motivation behind it?

Regardless, I could think of no further questions to put to the man and, after a glance at my husband and Maclean to see that they were also finished, began to rise to my feet. "Then we'll take no more of your time."

He nodded. "Send Tarvit up tae me when ye go," he requested, speaking of his butler, I supposed. Then his voice dipped wryly as he stared pointedly at Maclean. "Unless you've restrained him somewhere."

I wondered briefly if we might have gotten the manservant in trouble, but given how unpleasant he'd been, I struggled to feel much empathy for him. What I had been able to dredge up evaporated as soon as I saw his haughty face in the corridor. Obviously he'd been eavesdropping, though he would deny it if we dared to point it out. Given this, there was no need to relay Mr. Clerk's message.

He didn't follow us to the door. I understood why when Gage and I discovered our outer garments in a heap on the floor of the entry hall. I rolled my eyes at this childish bit of retaliation, plucking my russet-shaded pelisse from the pile.

"I'm afraid that's my fault," Maclean said. "I may've provoked the bumptious fellow beyond his endurance."

What exactly this meant, I wasn't sure, and the remorseless grin that stretched the sides of his lips—at least as much as possible given the number of punches to the jaw the sergeant had taken over the years—didn't make matters any clearer. Though Tarvit hadn't appeared like he'd been physically assaulted.

"As long as you got results," Gage replied, passing me my chapeau bonnet.

"Aye." Maclean glanced up the stairs. "Clerk didna leave the house. Least no' wi' his butler's knowledge. And scabs like him always ken who's comin' and goin'."

I didn't argue with this sentiment. Not after finding the man listening at the door to the drawing room.

"I don't think the answer lies with Clerk or any of the members of Lord Eldin's family," Gage murmured as he ushered me through the door.

"Aye," Maclean agreed somewhat begrudgingly, and I was glad to hear we were on the same page.

Mr. Innes lived in a slightly less respectable address along the South Back of the Canongate in Old Town. The area was becoming increasingly industrialized with coachworks, glassworks, and several breweries now sharing the same street his building stood on. Though far from the stately Georgian town houses of New Town, the structure was not without its own charms. The landlady to whom we applied to speak with Mr. Innes seemed to have a great love of plants, and her window boxes and small garden plot boasted a number of early spring blooms—camellias, anemones, crocuses, and hellebores.

The landlady herself was less colorful. Dressed in a dowdy gown which matched her gray eyes and faded hair, she seemed drained of almost all pigment. Though from her clear complexion and few wrinkles, I gauged she couldn't have been older than forty.

"Is Mr. Innes in some sort o' trouble?" she asked suspiciously as she led us into a small parlor filled with heavy furniture that had likely been purchased secondhand. It smelled of the flowers we'd passed outside, and peering around the room I spied a vase perched on a table near the window. "Because I canna have that sort livin' here."

"We merely wish tae speak tae Mr. Innes as a witness," Maclean assured her. "We believe he may've been standin' near the gentleman who was killed durin' the floor collapse at Picardy Place. He might've seen what struck the fellow."

"Oh," she replied, frowning up at him as if she wasn't sure she believed him, though the sergeant gazed back at her steadily. "I'll just go fetch him, then."

"Thank ye."

She nodded once, glancing at Gage and me distractedly before departing.

"That was kind," I told Maclean once she was out of earshot, grateful for his circumspection.

"Aye, weel I dinna wish tae make trouble for the man if there's no cause for it." He rolled the brim of his hat between his fingers and paced toward the window, leaning forward to peer out. I wondered if we were close to his home. I knew he lived east of Cowgate and High School Yards, where Surgeons' Square, lined with private anatomy schools, was located, but I'd never been to his abode. Though humbler than our home on Albyn Place, from what I knew of Mrs. Maclean, I'd always expected it was cozy and well run. However, I wasn't about to invite myself and intrude on their domesticity.

It wasn't long until we heard heavy footsteps clattering down the stairs. Mr. Innes appeared in the doorway, still straightening his collar after pulling on his coat. His clothing was neat and utilitarian and would have passed all but the most discerning of inspections. However, his unkempt medium brown hair still needed a trim, and his fingers were stained with ink. If he was ill at ease about our visit, he didn't show it.

"I'm Mr. Innes," he announced, scrutinizing us each in turn before focusing on Maclean in his gray coat denoting him a member of the city police. "Mrs. Stewart said ye had some questions aboot what happened durin' the collapse, but I'm afraid there's been a mistake. I wasna there."

"But ye ken the deceased?" Maclean asked, moving closer and resting his hands on his wide belt, to which his baton was strapped.

"Aye." His eyes dimmed with what appeared to be genuine sadness. "Alexander Smith was a good man. 'Tis a terrible loss. Especially for his family."

"And ye were at the second day o' the auction. What did ye bid on?"

"I wasna there tae bid. Wait." He looked at each of us in turn again, his brow creased with confusion. "What's this aboot?" His gaze began to skirt past me again, but then abruptly returned, recognition dawning followed swiftly by alarm. "Oh!"

"I can see ye recall the altercation her ladyship witnessed," Maclean said.

"I wouldna call it an altercation exactly," he protested.

I arched a single eyebrow in disbelief.

"Listen, I ken I lost my temper. And I owe ye a proper

apology for bumpin' intae ye as I was leavin'. I do heartily beg yer pardon for that," he declared, pressing a hand to his chest.

I nodded in acceptance, as our presence here wasn't about that.

"But I can explain."

Maclean held out his hand, granting him permission to do so.

He exhaled, scrubbing a hand down his face as he began to sink into the nearest chair. Realizing we were all still standing, he abruptly righted himself. "Please, have a seat?"

We all found a spot to perch, and Mr. Innes began again in a measured voice.

"I was angry because Lord Eldin had been blockin' my membership tae the Bannatyne Club for more than three years."

"Why?" I asked, having wondered this since I'd witnessed his row with Reverend Jamieson.

He exhaled another long breath, evidently not having expected to be interrupted. "Because . . . my father wrote a scathing editorial aboot his father's essay on naval tactics," he confessed in a monotone under his breath.

I turned to Gage, curious if he understood what he was referring to since his father had been an officer in the Royal Navy for many years. "I know the treatise to which he refers. My father has always spoken highly of it."

"I never said I *agreed* wi' my father," Mr. Innes countered. "I dinna ken enough aboot naval tactics tae express an opinion one way or the other. But that dinna matter to Lord Eldin. The relation was enough."

"But when Lord Eldin died, you thought perhaps the other members would see differently," I prompted.

"Aye! And I've been waitin' nearly ten months for 'em tae call a vote on the matter." He scraped a hand back through his messy hair again, tugging at the overgrown tresses. "I saw the notice aboot the auction in the paper and what a large turnout there was the first day, and I just . . . lost my temper. I'd been bidin' my time for *so long* wi'oot a single word. So I decided tae see if I could track doon any o' the members that second day and get an answer." His hand fell to his lap, and his shoulders slumped. "I realized almost immediately after I left that it'd been a mistake. That I'd let my frustration get the best o' me and I'd destroyed my chances."

"Why do you wish to join the Bannatyne Club so badly?" Gage asked, not managing to mask his bewildered disapproval.

"I ken their reputation," Mr. Innes admitted. "But they're first and foremost a publication society wi' the goal o' printin' works o' Scottish interest. I have a number o' rare works o' Scottish history I've curated that I'd like them tae publish."

Then his interest was serious and, judging from the number of ink splotches on his fingers and cuffs, part of his vocation.

"So ye blame Lord Eldin for yer failure tae be admitted?" Maclean stressed the point.

"Aye," Mr. Innes agreed. "I ken it was him for he confessed so tae my face." He sat taller as outrage began to build again, but then abruptly deflated. "But noo that he's dead, I suppose I canna blame him entirely. No matter what hold he may still have o'er the others."

"You think he still has a hold over some of the members?" This surprised me.

The only answer Mr. Innes gave was a shrug.

Maclean shifted forward as if preparing to rise. "Just tae be clear, Mr. Smith wasna a member?"

"Nay. He was only tryin' tae help calm me." He paused, looking from me and Gage to Sergeant Maclean in consideration. "But why the interest in my outburst? I thought the collapse was an accident."

"Merely tryin' tae clear up some loose ends," Maclean replied affably as he stood. "Thank ye for yer time."

"O' course," Mr. Innes mumbled, his expression still perplexed. We filed out the door and past the door opposite, which seemed to lead into the landlady's private sitting room. She sat watching us as she stitched something in her lap. Unlike Mr. Clerk's butler, it was obvious she'd not stooped to eavesdropping, but she was wary of us all the same. We each nodded to her in turn and departed the house.

CHAPTER 13

We parted ways with Maclean outside Mrs. Stewart's boardinghouse as he set out on foot to the police house on Old Stamp Office Close while we returned to Albyn Place. It was nearly time for luncheon, and Emma would soon be needing me.

While overall it had been a productive morning, it had not been an altogether satisfactory one. For while we'd seemed to eliminate some suspects, we were still no closer to figuring out who had actually caused the floor collapse. I hoped the members of our staff had had better luck in that regard.

"Anything to report about Mr. Smith?" I asked Jeffers upon our arrival as I removed my kid leather gloves and passed them to him.

"No, my lady. At least, only good things."

"Which is wonderful to hear, especially for his family," I answered with a sad smile, tugging on the ribbon of my bonnet. "But not for our purposes."

"Yes, my lady." He accepted my hat, setting the items on the petticoat table fashioned of warm wood and picking up a folder.

"What's this?" I asked as he passed it to me. Gage crowded closer to peer over my shoulder as I opened it. It was a list of names and addresses.

"One of Mr. Winstanley's assistants delivered it while you were out."

I realized it was the roster I'd requested of the people who had been sent the auction catalog. "Excellent. I shall have a look at this later," I said, passing it back to him so that I could remove my pelisse. "Have it taken up to our bedchamber."

Jeffers cleared his throat, indicating he had more to say. "I thought you should know, the young gentleman who delivered it seemed disappointed not to be able to speak to you."

I caught a glimpse of Gage's amused smile out of the corner of my eye and felt myself begin to flush.

"Mr. Rimmer is quite the admirer of Mrs. Gage's paintings," he said.

"I see," Jeffers replied, all seriousness. "But I believe this gentleman said his name was Fletcher."

My hands stilled at my pelisse's buttons as I turned to meet Gage's gaze. He was clearly wondering, as I was, why Mr. Fletcher had wished to speak to me. Was he an admirer as Mr. Rimmer was? He'd not said as much to Sergeant Maclean when he spoke with him, instead intimating that Mr. Rimmer was enamored of me, but that wasn't something a young gentleman would necessarily admit about themselves to a policeman. Or perhaps Mr. Fletcher had sought me out for a different reason. Perhaps there was something he'd not felt comfortable discussing with Maclean, who could be quite intimidating. There was really no way to know.

"Did he mention whether he intended to return?" I asked our butler.

"He didn't say."

I nodded absently, slipping the last button from its hole before passing my pelisse to Jeffers.

"It might mean nothing," Gage murmured to me as we climbed the stairs.

"Or it might mean a great deal," I countered. "We won't know until we speak to him."

But it would have to wait. We didn't have time to call upon the other assistant that day or the next. We'd made our excuses for the dinner parties and theater show we'd planned to attend the past three evenings—none of our hosts or companions requiring much explanation as we were still recovering from our ordeal—but I hated to bow out of that night's event.

The Inverleith Ball was held every year as a fundraiser for the Royal Botanic Garden Edinburgh. A few years earlier, a portion of the Inverleith House estate had been purchased by the botanic garden so that its collection of plants could be moved away from the filth and crowding at the center of the city. Our physician, Dr. Robert Graham, acted as the society's Regius Keeper, as well as serving as chair of botany at the University of Edinburgh and managing shifts at the Royal Infirmary of Edinburgh. He was a busy man and also one of the rare medical men who did not shun or dismiss me because of my scandalous role with my first husband's work in anatomy. Because of that, and his kindness, and the good the society's studies in botany did humanity, I wanted to attend in support.

However, the short drive north lulled me into slumber, and I woke with a start as we pulled up the long drive flanked by a variety of trees and shrubs, some more exotic than others. Bree had fussed over me while she helped me dress, warning me I would regret spending the entire afternoon in my art studio rather than taking a nap as she'd suggested. I feared she was right.

I reached up to fluff the curls Bree had painstakingly rolled at the sides of my head, fearful I'd flattened them by allowing my head to rest against Gage's shoulder.

He took my hand, smiling gently. "You look beautiful."

"You always say that," I contradicted, recalling numerous instances when I'd been covered in mud and gore, or drenched and limp with exhaustion, and he'd still called me thus.

"Because you are," he insisted, and I had to admit it was impossible not to feel a flutter of warmth and pleasure from the way he was looking at me. "But perhaps what you really need me to say is that you cut quite a dash."

My lips twitched at his use of slang. "As do you."

Indeed, he looked far too handsome in his evening attire, with his artlessly unruly golden hair tumbling over his brow.

"This gown." He reached out to lift aside the edges of my cream-colored wrap so that his gaze could brush up and down over my figure. "It's new."

"Alana insisted I order it," I confessed, tugging at my long white gloves nervously.

"It suits you," he declared. "And the sleeves . . ." he flicked the fabric lightly ". . . are not so wide that I cannot do this." By the roguish light in his eyes, I knew that he was about to kiss me, and I did absolutely nothing to stop it. Rather I basked in his attention for several delightful moments before he pulled back with a groan. "On second thought . . ." His eyes traveled over my shoulders and the decolletage revealed by the wide sloped neckline, leaving licks of heat wherever they lingered. "Perhaps I like it too much. Perhaps I want to keep you all to myself."

I laughed at his playful banter.

I had to admit, it was a lovely gown. Often my sister tried to convince me to order clothing that, while *en vogue*, was not to my taste in the least. But this gown I could appreciate, for it was a piece of art.

It was fashioned of a fabric of pale burnt umber with flowers and leaves in shades of goldenrod, blue-green, and maroon. However, the full skirt split in the front to reveal a cream ruffled petticoat, much like the open robes of the previous century. The short sleeves were banded in alternating strips of the floral fabric and then cream silk, with a ruffled trim around the neck and at the bottoms of the sleeves. I still had to wear a pad tied around each upper arm to help the whalebone-enforced sleeves maintain their shape, but it was less cumbersome than the padding required for daytime attire. A sapphire necklace Gage had given me for Hogmanay completed the look.

When our carriage reached the small portico entrance, a footman opened the coach door. Gage exited before me, reaching a hand back inside to help me descend. As on our last visit to Inverleith House, I was struck by the simplicity of its architecture. Georgian in design, the manor was all straight lines and symmetry. The charm of the property lay almost entirely in its grounds and gardens.

We joined the queue entering the building and divested ourselves of our outerwear before being greeted by our hosts. The Rocheids owned the manor and generously hosted the fundraiser every year to support the botanic garden that now shared the grounds. However, this year, I noted that Dr. Graham also stood with them. A nod to the ball's purpose, I supposed.

"Mr. and Mrs. Gage," he declared with delight. "I'm glad to see you both up and about. All is healing well, I trust."

"Yes," I replied with a glance at my husband, who didn't disagree.

"Good!" He rocked back on his heels, addressing Gage. "Though I'll drop by in a day or two to take a look at those stitches. But for now . . ." he grinned ". . . please enjoy yourselves."

We assured him we would.

An arch of stunning blooms—some of which I did not recognize—curved over the entrance to the ballroom, and swags and garlands of more flowers and greenery adorned the walls. We found more of the same in the drawing room, parlor, and to a lesser extent the dining room. Their heady scent filled the air.

"Good heavens," I exclaimed. "I hope they haven't emptied their new greenhouses."

The recently built structures had allowed the Royal Botanic Garden to add even more specimens to their collection.

"Have no fear, Kiera. I hear there's still plenty left," a familiar voice behind me drawled, and I turned to find myself face-to-face with Gage's half brother. Lord Henry Kerr's silvery gray eyes twinkled at my evident surprise.

"Henry!" I exclaimed, throwing my arms around him, heedless of those around us watching. "But when did you return to Edinburgh?" Though we'd known he would be arriving within the next fortnight, we'd had no idea it would be so soon.

"Just this morning," he replied as I released him. He turned to shake Gage's hand. "Couldn't miss my . . ." He paused, correcting himself. "Emma's birthday."

The truth about their relationship to each other wasn't widely known. In fact, Gage had been made aware of their kinship only last year. Their father had concealed Henry's existence from Gage, even threatening Henry and his mother, the Duchess of Bowmont, should they reveal the truth. It had been a large source of tension between Gage and his father, which had come to a head in August. Fortunately, much of it had since been resolved, though there would undoubtedly always be some moments of contention between them. Lord Gage was too critical and controlling, and prone to scorn when he didn't get his way. At least, with his sons and daughter-in-law. Thus far, his granddaughter could do no wrong.

However, the truth of Henry's real parentage was kept quiet. For one, he'd already been claimed by the Duke of Bowmont and had grown up happily in the bosom of the duke's large brood. Not that the duke was unaware of his wife's infidelity. The duke and duchess had both been rather notoriously unfaithful to each other once their heir and a spare were born. The duchess had given birth to three more sons and a daughter—all of whom had been sired by different men, though the duke had claimed them as his own. And the duke had fathered numerous side slips with his mistresses, whom he took care of, though they could not be claimed as legitimate.

Given all of this, Henry was understandably loyal to the family he'd been raised with. For all intents and purposes, the duke was his father, and he'd always shown him as much love and care as the rest of his children. So it had been agreed that it would be best for all for the truth to remain hidden. As such, publicly, Henry remained but a dear and trusted friend to us.

If I were honest, I was somewhat surprised more people had not already figured out their relation to each other. It was true, Henry had inherited his auburn hair from his mother, but the rest of his traits, including his tall, muscular physique, seemed to have come from his father. When Gage and Henry stood side by side, the similarities in their profiles—their strong jawlines, their high cheekbones, and the clefts in their chins—were even more pronounced. They both even sported an unruly twist of curls, which fell over their foreheads, but of course, that had become a common affectation of the age.

"Staying at Bowmont House?" Gage inquired as we turned to observe the dancers twirling about the floor in clouds of colorful silks and dark evening wear.

"Yes. Ned is there, too."

"Oh," I exclaimed with pleasure. I hadn't seen his brother, Lord Edward, since the previous January, when a number of rather unsavory secrets had been revealed, the least of them being Henry's parentage. "Bring him along to dinner one evening later this week."

"I will," he promised with a smile.

Edward was rather incorrigible and enjoyed bedeviling his brothers, especially the youngest, Henry. As Lord of Misrule at his parents' annual Twelfth Night party the previous year, he'd had full opportunity to display his touch for the dramatic. This could sometimes rub people the wrong way, but I rather liked him. At least his jests were never deliberately cruel. Something I couldn't say about everyone in society.

"I heard about what happened at the auction of Lord Eldin's art collection." Henry scrutinized us each in turn. "I'm relieved to see you're both unscathed."

"Relatively," I replied. "Gage has a few stitches in his arm."

Henry turned to him with a start. "Then . . . you were one of the people who fell through the floor?"

From the frown etched across my husband's brow, I could tell he wasn't pleased I'd mentioned his injury. "Yes. We both were."

Henry examined me in concern.

"I sent a letter to Sunlaws Castle, not wanting you to be worried if you received word of it. You must have departed before it arrived."

"How terrifying! But are you truly both unharmed? Except for the stitches."

"Only a few scrapes and bruises," I confirmed. My thoughts veered back to the moment the floor gave way and the cloud of choking dust that had enveloped me as I plunged downward. I blinked, trying to dislodge the memory of the debris from my vision, the horrified screams from my ears. I inhaled a tremulous breath. "But it's not an experience I care to ever repeat."

Henry did not speak, but I felt his hand steal briefly into mine, squeezing it in sympathy.

We watched the dancers for a moment and the shuffle of people in and out of the ballroom. A number of gentlemen were making their escape, undoubtedly bound for the gaming tables set up in the parlor or to indulge in the food laid out in the dining room. The spread was always impressive.

I tilted my head toward my brother-in-law in query. "How did you know we were at the auction?"

"I didn't. Not for certain. But it was an art auction, allegedly boasting a number of very fine paintings." His lips curled into a gentle smile. "Given that, I gave it even odds you might have been there."

I gave a breathless chuckle, liking that he knew me so well.

But as he turned back toward the assembly, his mood sobered, and he shook his head. "What a dreadful, dreadful accident."

"Yes," Gage murmured, but it was far from convincing, and I could only surmise that was on purpose. After all, Henry had helped us with several inquiries in the past.

In any case, he took the bait, eyeing his brother with dawning suspicion.

"Come see me tomorrow," Gage said.

Henry nodded, knowing better than to say more about the matter until we were in private. The latest set of dances had ended, and the next was about to begin. "No doubt Sebastian intended to claim your first waltz, but on the chance he failed to ask . . ." His eyes flashed impishly as he held his hand out to me.

I laughed, giving him my hand. "I would be delighted."

Gage rolled his eyes good-naturedly as Henry led me out onto the floor. The strains of Schubert floated over the assembly, and we fell comfortably into step, swirling around the room. I soon lost track of Gage along the periphery of the floor, enjoying the music and the colors and the floating sensation I always derived from such a dance.

As a younger woman, I'd always felt awkward and out of place at balls, not understanding the necessity for small talk or the boundaries which dictated it. Had I merely been allowed to focus on the movement of the dance, I might have found them far more tolerable, but that was not truly their purpose. Thankfully, now, as a more mature woman—a widow and bride again at just seven and twenty—I was allowed to do as I pleased. Dance if I wished or not. Converse if I chose or not. It was tremendously freeing. And altogether foolish that young, unwed ladies could not do the same.

"Tell me truly," Henry suddenly urged. "These stitches of Sebastian's. The laceration that required them. How bad is it?"

"Very minor," I assured him. "Though I understand why you're asking. I'm not sure he would have sent for a physician or a surgeon if it had not been for me. Even so, I had to insist upon him being examined as well." For even the smallest cut could become infected if not properly tended to.

"Stubborn," he said with a shake of his head.

"Yes. It runs in the family," I replied drolly.

Henry didn't even attempt to deny it.

"The duke has been keeping you busy," I remarked, as we'd not seen him in some months. He often handled delicate business matters for the Kerrs, as he was diligent and detail oriented.

"Yes. As well as some family friends."

He didn't elaborate, and I sensed he didn't wish me to pry. Which of course only made me want to do so more. But I obeyed his wishes, deciding this was neither the time nor place to probe anyway.

"Nell and Marsdale visited us in early March."

I perked up at this news, as he must have known I would. Each of his siblings, it seemed, had unique and scandalous tales or rumors attached to their name, and his sister Eleanor was no different. The events that had led to her second marriage to her childhood sweetheart—Lord Marsdale, who had once been an inveterate rogue but now seemed entirely smitten and devoted to her—were a tale for another time.

"They were supposed to stay for the entire month," he continued. "Even jested about surprising you by coming with me to Edinburgh. But Marsdale received word that his father had taken a turn for the worse."

The Duke of Norwich had suffered from illness for some time.

"He's outlasted the physician's expectations," I remarked, recalling that he had not been anticipated to live to see the year 1833.

"Yes." His lips quirked wryly. "Something that runs in *that* family."

I laughed, for I'd long observed that Marsdale enjoyed subverting others' expectations. Though that had recently changed.

"'Tis why they missed the Twelfth Night party this year," he continued once my laughter died away. "They didn't want to be in Scotland when Norwich was breathing his last in East Anglia. But when he lasted until March, they decided to risk it." His smile turned sad. "I'm not sure I've ever seen Marsdale more sober than the day they left."

"Because he might, as we speak, already be a duke. And no matter his irreverence and professed apathy, I think we both know that he acknowledges the gravity of the title and its responsibilities."

We were silent for the remainder of our set, lost in our own thoughts. When he escorted me back toward the periphery, Gage was nowhere to be seen, but the crowd had grown, making the space rather warm. I began to ply my fan, exchanging greetings with friends and acquaintances as we circulated. Michael and Caroline—Lord and Lady Dalmay—were also present, as well as her brother, Lord Damien, looking much less like the fop he'd affected to be the last time I'd seen him, and altogether happier for it.

Here and there, I heard rumbles of discussion about the floor collapse, and our hostess seemed to be making a point of informing everyone that it was fortunate their ballroom was located on the ground floor, or else they might have been forced to postpone the ball, as others had done while their home's construction was inspected. No doubt this was supposed to be reassuring, but it came across as almost gloating. A few people asked about my and Gage's brush with death. I would have preferred not to put it in such terms, but society was rather fond of hyperbole. However, most of the conversation was about far more mundane topics.

Except in the parlor where we found Gage. He was playing cards at one of the round tables that had been brought into the room for just such a purpose. Most of the men puffed at cigars and cheroots, filling the air with a light haze of smoke, while all of them nursed a glass of some sort of strong spirit. Gage's appeared to be whisky.

Normally, my husband eschewed the gaming room, knowing full well the bluster that went on. Unless there was information to be gained. I suspected that was why he was here now. When his gaze lifted to meet mine before darting to the player across the table to his right, I became certain of it.

CHAPTER 14

Judging from his smirk, Sir James Riddell possessed a good hand. Or perhaps he was merely bluffing. There was no way to tell just from a glance. But it was clear Gage hoped to extract some sort of information from him. Just as it was clear he wished me and Henry to leave before we foiled his efforts to do so.

Unfortunately, a fellow at one of the other tables hailed Henry as we moved to depart. "Oy! Lord Henry! Whendidyegethere?" Judging from his raised voice and slurred speech, the man had already been dipping too deep.

Henry cringed as his name was shouted again, the fellow waving him closer, refusing to be ignored.

"Go," I urged Henry. When he looked uncertain, I added, "I need to excuse myself for a moment anyway."

"You're sure?" he murmured.

"Yes." I peered over my shoulder, seeing the men at Gage's table beginning to take an interest in the disturbance. "Go!" I gave him a little push before moving toward the exit. Once in the corridor, I paused, undecided where I should go. I supposed I could venture to the lady's retiring room as I'd implied to Henry, but it was upstairs and not actually necessary at the moment. Surveying my surroundings, I realized with a start that this was nearly the exact spot where I'd met Lord Gage for the first time. It had been a rather memorable altercation given the ill opinion my father-in-law had already formed of me and his determination to set me in my place and separate me from his son. We had come a rather long way since then.

"Lady Darby."

I turned to see the man Mr. Innes had been arguing with hurrying toward me. Rather than evening wear, Reverend Jamieson wore his traditional black clergyman attire with the distinctively tied white cravat.

"I'm relieved tae see ye lookin' so hale and hearty," he declared with a compassionate smile. "I'd heard ye were one o' the people who suffered in the floor collapse, and I've been meanin' tae call on ye and yer husband, but then, aye . . ." he said with a sigh ". . . there are so many."

"And you were among the number?"

"Nay. The papers got that wrong."

My eyebrows arched in surprise.

"Though I stumbled comin' doon the stairs. That must be where the confusion came from." He waved this off as if it was inconsequential. "But I dinna suffer more than a bump tae my ole backside." He flashed a playful grin. "Fortunately, 'tis well padded."

I laughed.

He seemed pleased to have caused me such amusement, but then a furrow formed in his brow. "I only wish everyone had been so lucky."

I agreed, sobering. "Mr. Smith was a friend, was he not? I'm sorry for your loss."

"Thank ye, lass." His face pinched in pain, and for a moment I thought he might actually weep. "Alexander was a truly good man. And a friend tae all."

Though it felt somewhat callous, I couldn't ignore the opportunity he'd afforded me. "Including Mr. Innes?"

He exhaled a heavy breath. "Aye, even David Innes." Jamieson smiled sadly. "I'm afraid when ye witnessed our little altercation ye'd caught him on a bad day. I'll no' deny the man has a temper, tae be sure. And he had reason tae be angry on that occasion. Though I'm certain he bore neither Mr. Smith nor myself a grudge because o' it."

"Then it's true what he said. That Lord Eldin was preventing his membership to the Bannatyne Club?"

The reverend quietly scrutinized me, a slight frown tugging down the corners of his mouth, and I feared for a moment that I'd overstepped. That my interest was not only inappropriate but rude. These men were his friends, after all. I could detect the conflicting emotions flickering across his mobile features. "While he was alive? Aye," he admitted, and then surprised me by adding, "And since he's been dead?" He turned his head, peering down the corridor toward the people milling back and forth between the public rooms. "Aye, that, too."

I was about to ask how that was possible when he explained.

"Some o' the other Bannatyne members seem tae have taken up his cause, either unbidden or because he tasked them wi' it."

"Would he have done such a thing?" I asked after a pause.

"Aye." He sighed again. "Sadly, aye."

"Because of Innes's father?"

A spark of curiosity lit his eyes. "Ye ken aboot that, do ye?"

I didn't respond, trusting he would take my silence as confirmation.

"Unfortunately, Lord Eldin was the type tae bear a grudge." He shook his head. "Tae bear it into his grave and beyond. Though I trust the good Lord has set him straight aboot that noo. Too late tae change his actions, but there are those o' us left tryin' tae set it tae rights."

The intensity with which he spoke these words made me wonder whether he was talking about more than Mr. Innes's membership in the Bannatyne Club. But before I could even attempt to prod, we were interrupted.

"Jamieson, old fellow."

We both turned toward the sound of the voice, watching as a man hobbled forward with the aid of a cane. One leg appeared to be shorter than the other, either because he'd been born that way or it had been broken and had not healed properly. Whatever the case, it gave him an awkward rolling gait that I imagined must cause him pain from the improper alignment. Nevertheless, all his focus appeared to be on his friend.

"I heard ye were caught up in tha' terrible business at Lord Eldin's auction." He grasped Jamieson's hand, shaking it. "I'm glad tae see you're well. And 'twasn't a repeat o' what happened at Kirkcaldy. Ye must've feared the same. I ken Reverend Irving was a friend o' yers."

"His father-in-law, aye," Jamieson confirmed, his expression distressed.

"Even worse! For 'twas his parishioners who suffered the loss." The man shook his head. "'Twas a right sorry business."

I recalled that Reverend Irving had been the son-in-law of the clergyman who led the church at Kirkcaldy whose gallery had so tragically collapsed nearly five years ago and resulted in the deaths of so many people. A former resident, Irving's visit from London and intention to preach had been the reason for the larger than usual crowd for that evening service.

Given Jamieson's vocation and age, it was not surprising that he knew the clergymen involved. It would be foolish to think he knew every man of the cloth throughout Scotland, but I suspected he knew a great deal of them.

I spied a familiar figure emerging from the parlor where the gambling was taking place and decided to slip away while the two men were commiserating with one another before they recalled my presence. However, I nearly turned back when Jamieson's friend grumbled, "I thought they were supposed tae change the law so this never happened again." Only my realization that would almost certainly discourage rather than encourage them to say more kept me from doing so.

Instead, I followed Sir James Riddell as he ambled into the ballroom, almost colliding with him when he stopped abruptly just inside the entrance.

"Oh, pardon me," I exclaimed, deciding to use this stumble to my advantage when he turned to address me.

"No, pardon me," he pronounced with a smooth smile. "I should know better than to halt in doorways." He seemed quite content, even a little cocksure, making me think he'd walked away from the gaming room with more money in his pocket than when he'd entered. But it could have been an act, or a result of the whisky I could smell on his breath. He was now standing about a half step too close to me, even taking the crowded room into account.

"I saw your name mentioned in the newspaper. I'm glad to see you weren't severely injured," I remarked, borrowing the same approach Reverend Jamieson had used on me to broach a conversation. Given how soon Sir James had departed the gaming room after me, I doubted Gage had sufficient time to glean enough information from him—not in the midst of playing loo.

"And I you," he replied.

"What a terrifying experience that was," I reflected, not having to struggle to summon my emotions as I attempted to draw him out. Someone bumped me from behind, and Sir James grasped hold of my elbow, compelling me toward a bank of tall windows nearby which overlooked the gardens.

"It was certainly unpleasant."

The gardens were mostly in shadow except for the wide terrace which could be reached through the French doors farther along. I found myself wondering why the ball wasn't held later in the spring or early summer to take advantage of the lovely Royal Botanic Garden we were there to support. But I supposed a number of the largest donors were bound for London soon and the opening of Parliament and the new social season.

"They say it happened because of a faulty joist," I remarked, still searching the shadows. "That the builder used faulty materials." I turned to look at Sir James, speaking with care so as not to reveal the truth. "Yet Lord Eldin had the house built for his own use, didn't he? You knew him. Was he the type to miss such a thing? Or to hire employees who missed such things?"

A lively reel had just begun, entirely at odds with our conversation.

Sir James clasped his hands behind his back, still standing nearer than was proper, though this time I knew it was not the crowd forcing him to do so. I shuffled half a step away as he joined me in my scrutiny of what could be detected in the flickering light of the torches at the edge of the terrace. "I would like to say no." He sighed. "But I'm afraid I can't. Lord Eldin was . . ." He corrected himself. "Well, he had the typical arrogance of many of our breed that no one in our service would dare defy or cheat us."

I frowned. "But he was a Lord of Session."

"And you think that means he should have known better." He shrugged one of his shoulders. "I'll not argue that."

"Is that why you suggested he would be rolling over in his grave to see his collection sold off? Because he'd assumed his beneficiaries would keep it intact."

"Oh, no. He knew better than that. Made specifications in his will for how the collection should be handled. Even chose the auctioneer himself."

This seemed entirely contradictory to what he'd told me before, and I opened my mouth to say so when he continued.

"No, if he could see it, he'd be rolling over in his grave simply from the pain of watching it be dismantled. He loved that collection. More than he loved any person, I always thought."

I couldn't tell if Sir James had been deliberately misleading before or if he'd just spoken poorly. Whatever the case, if I were to point it out, I could already tell he was the type of man to adopt a condescending demeanor and insist the error in misunderstanding was mine. So instead, I swallowed my irritation, reminding myself this was at least added confirmation of what we'd already been informed about Lord Eldin's will.

However, Sir James seemed to view my momentary agitation as an opportunity to sidle closer to me yet again. It was all I could do to not stomp on the man's foot, but such an act in my thin dancing slippers would hurt me more than him. I couldn't decide whether his intent was to make me feel flustered and flattered, or if the roué was actually attempting something. Either way, I was having none of it.

"It's dreadful what happened to Mr. Smith," I said as I

moved a full step away, not bothering to conceal the fact I was putting distance between us.

However, Sir James only smiled, and I remembered too late how Lord Marsdale had once told me that some men delighted in the chase. That the pricklier I became, the more determined they would become. I was beginning to suspect Sir James was one of those men, which made me wish I'd chosen a different response in order to temper his interest. Though my even having to give such consideration to the matter infuriated me more. *He* was the one misbehaving, after all.

"Aye," he agreed rather indifferently as he turned to survey the other guests clustered about the ballroom. "But all things considered, it could've been worse."

"Not for Mr. Smith's family," I couldn't help but counter. His callous demeanor left much to be desired.

He didn't respond to this, and neither did he look chagrined. In fact, he seemed determined to simply ignore it, nodding to a passing acquaintance. I was about to excuse myself when he spoke again. "You should come to dinner one evening." He turned to look at me then, a challenge in his gaze.

I knew then that he was toying with me, playing one of the silly, frivolous games that members of society indulged in because they hadn't found anything better to do with their time, careless of whom they hurt—even themselves—so long as it alleviated their ennui. It was all I could do not to scoff out loud in disgust.

"My husband and I?" I retorted instead.

His response was a beat too long in coming. "Of course."

I couldn't help it. I rolled my eyes and walked away. I was relieved when a few steps across the room, I met with Gage.

"There you are," he murmured cheerfully. But after one look at my face, his brow pleated. "What is it?" He searched the space over my shoulder even as I shook my head.

"Can we go?" The evening had been somewhat ruined by Sir James's insinuations and the ache behind my eyes.

His gaze shifted abruptly back to me, assessing me. "If you wish."

I'd not spoken to even half the people I'd intended to, but I was suddenly too tired to even contemplate it. "I do."

He nodded once, pulling my arm through his as he guided me toward the door and down the corridor, navigating past all the wide skirts and equally wide sleeves. I spared a moment's thought for Henry and the fact we hadn't said goodbye, but he'd arrived without us and would undoubtedly come to call the following day. I could make my excuses then.

In short order, we were once again ensconced in our carriage, wrapped in our outer garments. For added warmth, Gage's arm was draped around me, cradling me close to his side. His clothes reeked of the tobacco the other gentlemen had been smoking, but if I leaned close enough, I could still smell the starch in his cravat and the spiciness of his cologne.

His fingers gently brushed the curls away from my temple. "Tell me, did your wanting to leave have anything to do with the smug look on Sir James Riddell's face?"

The carefully modulated tone of his voice and seeming lack of concern did not fool me. I knew perfectly well how protective Gage could be. So I lied.

"No. Though the man is quite coldhearted. He was entirely unmoved by Mr. Smith's demise, as if one death mattered little," I replied sharply, feeling hostility stir again. I knew I had to tell Gage something to explain my anger. Better this than Sir James's private dinner invitation.

I sighed heavily, rubbing my forehead. "I feel a megrim beginning. One that tells me that perhaps I'm not as recovered as I wish to be."

"Honestly, I'm not either," he admitted in chagrin. "Just the repetitive motion of laying down those cards aggravated my shoulder."

I pressed a consoling hand to his chest. "Something you were only doing in order to extract information from Sir James. But it didn't work, did it?"

"He was a far more focused player than I would have ever credited him as being. But the effort wasn't entirely wasted. He did speak to *you*."

I wasn't sure I wouldn't have preferred that Gage had extracted the information from Sir James himself, given his behavior.

"And I did overhear something interesting."

I peered up at him when he didn't continue, seeing he was still gnawing over the implication of whatever he'd heard.

"Apparently, several of the men were under the impression that the laws had been changed. Specifically, after that incident in Kirkcaldy. They were . . ." I straightened at this pronouncement, and he broke off. "You heard something similar?"

"I was speaking with Reverend Jamieson. The man who Mr. Innes quarreled with," I reminded him in case he'd forgotten. "And a gentleman who approached him implied much the same thing."

Gage gestured with his opposite hand. "Now, what exactly these laws were supposed to be changed to, and whether they were supposed to apply to private buildings as well as public, no one seemed to have the answer to."

"But it has made your mind start turning."

"What if this law—whatever it was meant to be—had something to do with Lord Eldin? No, he wasn't a lawmaker, but he *was* a Lord of Session. So maybe he heard a case related to the Kirkcaldy balcony collapse. Perhaps he issued some ruling that had bearing on the matter."

"Something that hindered the law change or prevented

justice in some way," I suggested, trying to follow his line of thinking.

He tipped his head to the side uncertainly. "I can't deduce any specifics at the moment, but I feel . . ." he frowned ". . . I feel it should be looked into."

"It shouldn't be hard. Much of it would be a matter of public record, wouldn't it? And we know the date of the Kirkcaldy incident was sometime in June of 1828." I bit my lip, recognizing a potential snag. "Lord Eldin also resigned from the bench in 1828, though I don't know which month. But at least that limits the period of potential overlap."

Gage didn't respond, but I could tell that was because he was already considering his next steps. It was unlike him to latch on to a theory so quickly and tenaciously, but in this case, I had to concede we had very little to go on in terms of motive and suspects. In truth, we seemed to be eliminating the ones we had faster than we were coming up with new ones. At least this information gave us another angle to pursue.

"What did Sir James have to say?" Gage asked, pulling me from my own ruminations. "I assume you broached the topic of his claims about Lord Eldin's desire for the auction being counter to his will."

I told him the implications Sir James had made, and the fact they'd tantamounted to our having misunderstood. Gage seemed to find this skeptical as well. "Though I did find it interesting that he suggested Lord Eldin loved his collection more than any person. It would seem to corroborate what Mr. Clerk told us about his brother."

All told, the information we'd gathered during the past few days had not allowed me to form a positive impression of Lord Eldin. He seemed rather arrogant, self-absorbed, and obsessed with his own consequence. But then, we'd spoken to only a handful of people—most of whom seemed to have some issue with the man. Maybe we would hear differently from others.

"What else did Sir James have to tell you?" The tone of Gage's voice was carefully modulated, but I wasn't fooled. I sensed he was still suspicious of my reaction to the man.

"Nothing more than I already said," I replied, feigning a yawn as I rested my head against his shoulder. "Well, he did invite us to dinner," I conceded, choosing my words with deliberate nonchalance. "But I declined. I can think of much better ways to spend an evening." I snuggled closer.

Gage took the hint. "Is that so?"

"Hmmm," I hummed as his fingers traced a trail down the line of my jaw. It didn't diminish my headache, but it made me feel better, nonetheless. Especially when he cupped my chin and tipped my head up toward his so that our mouths could meet. It was naught but a shallow kiss of lips. He didn't attempt to deepen it. But I felt my blood stir regardless.

I thought perhaps Gage would take it further once we'd retired, but when we returned home, Jeffers indicated that Anderley was waiting for Gage in the morning room.

His valet met him in the doorway, conferring with him in a low voice. He was dressed in the same serviceable but unfashionable attire he'd worn the previous evening when he'd ventured out to attempt to ingratiate himself with Mr. Winstanley's employees. It was obvious from their intent whispering that he'd uncovered something.

When Gage returned to my side, I expected him to explain, but he merely pressed a kiss to my brow. "Anderley has someone he needs me to speak to. I'll explain in the morning. Don't wait up."

Then he was off, returning to the morning room and then out the French doors, which I heard close with a click, to the garden and the mews beyond. Whether they were setting off on foot and didn't want to be observed from the front or they intended to halt Joe before he unhitched the horses from our coach, I didn't know, but apparently, I was unwelcome.

I stifled a grunt of aggravation, wishing they'd at least shared where they were going. It would certainly have eased my mind.

Or perhaps not. I supposed it depended on the destination.

I turned to look at Jeffers, who had been waiting patiently for me to hand him my wrap, but I'd already decided it was too chilly inside the house to do so. Not until I'd reached the warmth of my bedchamber. "Did Anderley tell you anything?"

"I'm afraid not, my lady."

I studied him a moment, trying to decide if he would tell me if he had. His steady gaze gave nothing away, but our butler was nothing if not loyal. It was doubtful he would keep something from me or Gage. If by chance I was wrong, I decided I would instead be glad he knew something about where they'd gone. Better him than no one.

"All quiet here?"

"Yes, nothing to report."

I nodded, understanding his answer was twofold. Nothing unusual had occurred while Gage and I were gone, and he also had nothing new to report about Mr. Smith. I'd not expected he would.

The wall sconces cast a warm glow over the woodwork and forest green carpet which tracked across the entry and up the middle of the stairs. It was a sight which always made me feel cheered and secure, for it meant I was home. Perhaps it was that sense of well-being which gave me the impetus to speak. All I knew was that the words were out of my mouth before I'd fully anticipated saying them.

"I have someone else I want you to look into."

If Jeffers was surprised by this request, he didn't show it. Nor did he react to the name I spoke.

"Sir James Riddell."

There was something cold and calculating about the baronet, and I was determined to find out if that had made him someone's target.

CHAPTER 15

Bree was waiting for me when I reached our bedchamber. Though I'd thought I'd done well to conceal my headache and fatigue, she took one look at me and pronounced, "Aye, ye look fagged tae death, m'lady. Come. Let's get ye oot o' this gown and intae somethin' more comfortable."

She made quick work of the shawl and necklace, setting them on the dressing table, before unfastening my overskirt and draping it over a chair. "Ye've a megrim, havena ye?" she asked as she began on the small buttons which marched down the back of my bodice.

I paused in removing my gloves, startled she'd noticed, though I should have known better. Bree noticed everything.

"Ye've a little furrow between yer brows," she explained. "Gets that way when a headache's brewin'."

Thus far she'd shown remarkable restraint in not reminding me that she'd warned me just such a thing would happen if I didn't rest earlier that afternoon. However, I didn't expect that to last. Not unless I diverted her.

"Yes, well, I suppose I also get that little furrow when my husband does something to vex me," I pronounced, tossing my gloves down next to the shawl.

"What's he done noo?" Her tone was wry, and her concentration fixed on my buttons, so I couldn't tell if she was merely humoring me. I plowed on regardless, with my hands propped on my hips.

"Oh, Anderley was waiting for him when we returned, and they've gone off somewhere to speak to someone."

Bree's hands stilled, and I suddenly realized that in my annoyance I'd not considered how this statement might affect her, too.

"He didna tell ye where?"

"No," I replied more calmly.

"I'd ken he'd gone oot earlier, but no' that he'd returned." She resumed her work on the buttons. "I s'pose at least they're together." She harrumphed. "That's somethin'."

My bodice loosened, she helped me remove it and the sleeve supports before turning her attention to my underskirt and petticoats.

"Perhaps they'll return with answers that will resolve this inquiry," I ventured. "Then neither of them will need to take further risks."

"Until the next inquiry."

Her words were like a bucket of ice water, for she was right. There was always another investigation, always someone with a problem to be solved, be it theft or blackmail or murder. I'd known that when I wed Gage. I'd even relished it—the ability to help people. To put to good use the knowledge I'd reluctantly accrued during the darkest period of my life. Yet I also had my art. If another inquiry never came our way, I could be quite content without it.

However, Gage was not the same. His restlessness and agitation over the last four months, not to mention the incident with him hanging out the nursery window, had made that clear. The normal occupations of a gentleman simply weren't enough for him. And while I knew he loved us, I wasn't naïve enough to think that Emma and I and whatever other children we might be blessed with could fill his every need, just as they couldn't fill mine.

It would be flippant to suggest he simply find another occupation—a safe and normal one—politics or business investments or patronage of the arts. For it wasn't just about a means to pass the time. Gage needed to feel purposeful, and he enjoyed the challenge. I'd accepted that, and even embraced it.

But I would be lying if I didn't admit there were times now when I wondered if it could be different. Wondered what a life without fraught investigations and death and danger might look like. Wondered whether we gave enough consideration to the way the life we'd chosen to lead affected those around us.

For as long as Gage continued conducting inquiries, Anderley would insist on working alongside him. His valet was nothing if not loyal, and just as engrossed in the purpose and challenge of their investigations. Yet, if his fidelity was forever to Gage, could it ever be fully given to Bree? But on the flip side, did Bree have the right to ask him to change, to give up the role he so relished and found meaningful in order to appease her fears?

I didn't have the answers to these questions. I didn't know how to resolve this conflict between Bree and Anderley. Nor did I know how to reassure her when Anderley took these risks at our impetus.

And what of her own? I knew that Bree also enjoyed helping us with our inquiries. That she'd taken risks as well, though not as often as Anderley. How was it possible to define which risks were acceptable and which were not? Where was the line when so often we had little control or even awareness of the danger until it was too late?

Now my head was truly pounding, but fortunately, in short order, I found myself tucked in bed with Bree standing at the end of it, my undergarments and a petticoat with a small tear gathered in her arms for laundering and mending. "I'll return wi' that headache powder," she assured me. "Just try tae rest. As ye should've this afternoon," she added under her breath as she turned to go.

When the door closed behind her, all I could do was groan resignedly, for I'd known it was coming.

Lord Moncrieff. Mr. George Thomson. Mr. James Macdonell, W.S. Mrs. Keay of Snaigo. Mr. Robert Dwear. Dr. Maclagan, George Street.

I sighed, continuing to read through the list of names the auctioneer had supplied of those who had received catalogs and invitations to the auction of Lord Eldin's collection. Most of the ones that caught my eye did so only because I'd read in the newspapers that they'd been injured—or in Mr. Alexander Smith's case, killed—or else I'd interacted with them. The rest were but a muddle of mostly Scottish and English surnames, some attached to people I'd met or heard of elsewhere, some I'd never encountered in my life. In any case, I was nearing the end of the list and starting to think this had been an utter waste of time.

Not that anyone other than me was wasting it.

Gage had returned in the wee hours of the morning, still reeking of smoke and alcohol as he climbed into bed. That, more than anything, had told me where he and Anderley had spent the remainder of their evening. Though given the number of public houses scattered throughout Edinburgh, it didn't narrow it down considerably.

I had been resting rather lightly when he joined me in bed and had considered ordering him to go take a cold hip bath. But then he'd reached for me, speaking words of affection to me in a whisky-deepened voice as his clever mouth and fingers had found the places I was most sensitive. He had always been difficult to resist, even in such a state. Given the pleasant results and how deeply I'd slept afterward, I could hardly complain.

Though I was a little irked that he was still abed at nearly eleven while I was sitting here scouring this list.

Stifling another sigh, I flipped to the last page and began reading the names scrawled there in a relatively neat hand. Once again, none of the names leapt out at me. Yet I was left with a vague sense of uneasiness. At first, I tried to brush it off as merely a consequence of my irritation, but as I lowered the page, the feeling lingered. It was akin to the nagging sensation one felt when you were certain you'd forgotten something—something important—but couldn't quite recall what. I lifted the pages again, gently riffling through them, hoping something would jog my memory, but they were just names. Names that, for the most part, were meaningless.

I stared up at the painting of Philipa and Earl Grey the cat hanging above the fireplace, searching for inspiration. The house was mostly silent, but for the occasional creak. Being at the back of the house in the library, I couldn't hear the traffic passing in the street outside. The servant quarters were two floors below, making the comfortable domestic sounds of them at work and chattering together all but undetectable. Occasionally I heard Emma squeal or fuss and Mrs. Mackay's answering chatter, but even they were mostly quiet.

I'd almost resolved to set the list aside as well as my conundrum when I heard the sound of the front door knocker. Jeffers's measured tread crossed the floor to answer the summons while I pondered who it might be. At this hour, it was probably a close friend or relative, though there was also the possibility it was a delivery. But those usually went to the tradesmen's entrance.

The thought suddenly struck me as being profound, though I didn't know why. I wrangled with it even as I could hear Jeffers had admitted a caller. A male one, from the sound of their voice.

Then, like a bolt of lightning, I realized what was troubling me. Gathering up the list, I flipped through it again more doggedly. So preoccupied was I that I barely spared my caller a glance as Jeffers opened the door to admit them.

"Lord Henry Kerr, my lady."

"Henry," I exclaimed. "Come look through this list for me. Tell me if I've missed my name."

To Henry's credit, he didn't even bat an eyelash at this strange request but crossed the room to sit beside me on the sofa. He took up the pile I'd already discarded on the cushion as I continued to scour the other pages. "Just yours or Sebastian's, too?"

"Either."

"Tea, my lady?" Jeffers intoned, watching us shuffle papers.

"Yes, please," I replied without looking up.

Several moments passed with only the rustle of paper and the ticking of the clock. I finished my read through, setting the remainder of the list on the sofa between me and Henry, and waited for him to finish. However, I was already certain neither my name nor Gage's was there. I'd read through its entirety painstakingly the first time, intent on not missing anything. My second and third look were merely forlorn hopes.

I turned as Henry lowered the last page, shaking his head. "It's not here." He was clearly perplexed and trying to decipher from my expression what troubled me. "Is it supposed to be?"

"It's a list from the auctioneer of everyone who received invitations and a catalog of the auction," I explained, still puzzling through the ramifications of this discovery.

"And you received one," he deduced.

I nodded, staring down at the papers still clasped in his hands. "But I'm not on the list. I can't decide if that means something."

Henry paused to consider the matter. "Well, this is a copy, isn't it? So maybe they left you off the list to save themselves time and effort because you already knew you'd received one."

"Yes, I suppose that makes sense," I conceded, though I wasn't convinced. I wondered what Mr. Fletcher had wished to speak to me about when he delivered the list. Could it have had something to do with my name not being on it?

"Or maybe someone else received the invitation initially and passed it on to you, believing you would find the art being auctioned to be of interest."

I frowned. "But then why didn't they include a note telling me so? Why send it to me anonymously?"

"Hmm, yes." His brow puckered. "That is odd."

"And potentially suspicious."

I'd not considered the possibility before, but now that I'd voiced it, I had to wonder. Had *I* been the target?

Anyone who knew me in the slightest would know I would find such an invitation almost irresistible, especially after seeing the catalog of pictures up for auction. Had someone tried to lure me there deliberately? But why? To what end? Sabotaging the joist and causing the floor to collapse under nearly one hundred people in order to kill just one was as reckless and faulty in logic with me as the intended victim as it was for all the other lone individuals we'd considered. If that had been the goal in truth, then the culprit's motivation would have to be so strong, their anger or desire for revenge so great, that they could ignore the potential for other victims. Yet I couldn't think of anyone who would be that determined to kill me.

Unless I was merely the means to hurt someone else.

After all, Gage had enemies. My father-in-law, too. And if last year had proved anything, I was a vulnerability for Bonnie Brock as well. Could a rival gang have done this to lash out at him? It seemed far-fetched, but then we'd encountered our share of bizarre schemes.

Whatever the case, the entire notion was unsettling in the extreme. And not something I could share with Henry, no matter how much affection I held for him as my brother-in-law. He had a different mind-set anyway.

"Perhaps, but it seems more likely they purposely left you off the list," he tried to reassure me.

"I'm sure you're right," I said, wishing I could believe that.

"We could pay a visit to the auctioneer and ask."

"Yes, that would be the most sensible step."

"Kiera?"

When he didn't continue speaking, I turned to look at him, finding him watching me. His gaze dipped briefly to where I'd begun to pleat my skirt in agitation before returning to my face. "You don't have to agree with me. If you think something's wrong, I'll listen."

I considered ignoring him, but this was Henry. He wanted to solve everyone's problems, not just because he was supposed to, but because he cared. I couldn't just rebuff his attempt to help. "The trouble is . . ." I pressed a hand to my forehead. "I don't know what I think. Or rather . . . I think too much." I shook my head. "Does that even make sense?"

"I think so."

He was trying to understand. He genuinely was. But I knew what I needed most, and Henry couldn't give it to me.

"I appreciate you listening to me, and I'm . . . I'm not trying to be rude," I said, knowing that whatever I said, it was undoubtedly going to come out wrong. "But I . . . will you excuse me?"

His face registered surprise. "Of course."

I nodded and pushed to my feet, worrying I actually *had* offended him. "I'll . . . have Jeffers inform Sebastian you're here," I whirled back to tell him.

"Thank you?"

I thought I detected a hint of a question mark at the end, but I didn't pause to consider it, instead hurrying from the room. Jeffers was approaching with the tea tray. "Please have Mr. Gage informed that Lord Henry is waiting for him in the library," I told him, knowing he would send Anderley to do it.

Then I fled up the stairs to my studio.

How long I'd been standing in front of the canvas, I didn't know, but it had obviously been for some time, as exhaustion had begun to penetrate the veil of my absorption. When it came to my art, I had always been that way. Unable to stop myself from becoming fully immersed and all but deaf, blind, and dumb to the rest of the world. Those who loved me had long accepted this about me, and our staff had been trained how to handle my artistic distraction. They knew not to disturb me unless necessary, and to leave only food that wouldn't grow cold or turn rotten as it sat unnoticed and untasted on the table beside the door for perhaps hours.

Of course, now that I had a daughter, I couldn't ignore her.

I wouldn't. Though I did wonder what would happen as she grew older. If she would understand.

I reached up to rub my forehead tiredly, vaguely recalling that I'd paused to nurse and play with her for a short time around midday. However, I could tell the sun was now close to setting, for the light filtering through the eastern-facing window was leaching away. Soon there wouldn't be enough natural light to work by.

Slowly, reality began to penetrate my consciousness. The floor collapse. The inquiry. The list. Henry. Gage. Then, as if summoned by my thought, the door opened a crack and my husband peered in. He knew better than to knock. If I was absorbed in my painting, I would never hear it.

"You're back with us," he said in response to my meeting his gaze. Opening the door wider, he stepped through it before closing it after him. "I suspected the fading daylight would rouse you if nothing else."

"And you've risen for the day," I retorted, though there was no heat to it. I was as yet too tired and unfocused, but I recalled my earlier irritation.

"Hours ago," he replied unruffled. "I did come to see you earlier. Even tried to speak to you. But you were preoccupied with that portrait . . ." his eyes flicked toward it ". . . so I let you be."

"I'm sorry . . . ," I began to apologize, lifting my hand to rub my forehead again, but Gage halted me.

"There's no need for that, Kiera," he protested gently, extracting the paintbrush from my fingers and dropping it into the jar of linseed oil at my elbow. "I fully understand how your mind works and that you can't help it. I accepted it long ago." He turned to look at the portrait again. "Especially when the result is this." He didn't speak for a long moment, and I felt anxiety stir within me.

"You like it?" I asked hesitantly.

"Like it? Kiera, it's magnificent!"

I didn't know about that, but I had done my best to capture the flower seller we had seen outside St. Giles' Cathedral some weeks past. The woman had lost many of her teeth, and her skin was rough like parchment, but the joy in her face as she bounced a small child on her hip who must have been her granddaughter or great-granddaughter had been infectious. I'd drawn the toddler as well, including her dimples and dirt-streaked cheeks, her mouth thrown open in laughter to reveal she had as few teeth as her grandmother.

"How did you remember all this from memory?" Gage wanted to know. "I was there, too, remember, and I wouldn't have recalled half of these details if you'd asked me to, though I do now that I see them again."

I shrugged one shoulder. "I don't know. I just did."

The look in Gage's eyes was tender, telling me I'd said something artless, though I didn't know what. He picked up a cloth from the table scattered with my supplies and gripped my chin. "Let me have a look at you. You've as many paint smudges on your face as that child has dirt smudges." He began dabbing at my forehead.

"It might be easier just to let me do it."

"We'll see," he replied vaguely, preoccupied with his ministrations.

Meanwhile, I was becoming conscious of how close he was to me and how near his face was to mine. "I'll get paint on your clothes," I protested weakly.

"I'll be careful."

I fell silent, allowing him to concentrate, but other thoughts began to intrude. "Is Henry still here?" I asked softly. "I'm afraid I was rather rude to him earlier."

"You weren't," he assured me. "Though he did express

concern. Said you were unsettled by the absence of your name from Winstanley's list."

"Among other things." It wasn't only the conspicuous absence of my name that had bothered me.

"We'll talk to the auctioneer. Find out why you're missing."

"Then you're *not* concerned?" I couldn't help but be surprised by his sangfroid.

His gaze shifted from the spot on my cheekbone where he was dabbing to meet mine. "Of course I am. But there's no use in speculating what it means until we have more information. Besides..." He pulled the cloth away from my face. "We have a much better suspect."

"Who?"

A small pleat formed in his brow as he scrutinized my features. "I'm afraid I couldn't get it all."

I tugged the cloth from his fingers and brushed this concern aside in annoyance before demanding, "Who?"

"Mr. Sullivan," he finally replied.

"The auburn-haired fellow who works for Mr. Winstanley?" I asked in clarification. "The one who was monitoring the small adjoining parlor where the coins and other trinkets were displayed?"

"The very one. Anderley discovered he has a connection to someone here in Edinburgh. A cousin." His eyebrows arched leadingly. "Who works for a rival auctioneer."

"Well, that's suspicious." Setting aside the cloth, I surveyed my table scattered with supplies as I considered the ramifications. Picking up a palette knife, I began scraping the remnants of paint from my palette into a container I would discard later. "I suppose that's where you went with Anderley last night."

"Yes, darling. I'm sorry I couldn't tell you more then. Anderley feared that the man he'd convinced to speak with me to share what he knew wouldn't wait long, so time was of the essence."

I wondered if Bree or Jeffers or even Henry had told him of my annoyance with him, or whether I was simply that transparent. "And what did the man tell you?" I asked, dropping the palette knife into the jar of linseed oil and dipping the edge of the cloth into the liquid to begin wiping the remnants of paint from the board.

"That he'd witnessed Mr. Sullivan making multiple visits to his cousin while he was at work, and that he'd even seen him speaking to the owner."

I glanced at Gage, who stood with his arms crossed, watching me. I could sense his barely restrained energy. "I presume that means you wish to question him."

"Already have. Anderley, Henry, and I tracked him down and cornered him today."

I didn't react to this, having already begun to suspect it, for it explained his flush of accomplishment.

"He denies any wrongdoing, of course. And we couldn't ask Maclean to arrest him based solely on his associations, but he's going to have his men keep an eye on him."

I set aside the palette and began cleaning my brushes and laying them out to dry. "I presume you also intend to confront this rival auctioneer."

"Brade Cranston." He supplied the name before confirming my supposition. "Tomorrow. I'd like to shake him to see what falls out."

"I'd like to come with you."

Gage agreed. "Then we can speak with Mr. Winstanley about his list."

I paused in wiping one of my brushes, peering closely at the bristles to see that a few of them were beginning to look frayed and would need attention. "Does he know about Mr. Sullivan's connection to a rival?"

"Not from us. Not yet."

But he would have to be told eventually, and it could cost Mr. Sullivan his position. I could tell that this had already occurred to Gage, and he was not unaffected by it. After all, if Mr. Sullivan proved to be innocent of any involvement with the floor collapse, if he'd committed no crime, then it would be unfair for him to be dismissed. After all, being related to someone who worked for a rival was not illegal. However, we also were not responsible for Mr. Winstanley's reaction or his consequent actions, regardless of whether we'd supplied the information that led to them.

Having finished with the brushes, I wiped my hands. "Has Anderley spoken to Bree about Brade Cranston? After all, it was her task to research rival auctioneers. Perhaps she's learned something that might help us when we question him tomorrow." I reached behind me to begin untying the apron I wore over my dress, but my husband found the strings first.

"I'll remind him of that," he assured me as I pulled the apron over my head and hung it on its peg by the door. I turned, expecting Gage to be behind me, but he was still standing before the portrait of the flower seller.

Conflicting emotions stirred in my breast. Pride and pleasure, naturally, that he found the portrait so arresting. But also doubt and something akin to panic, for watching someone examine a piece of my art always left me with the sensation of being exposed. It was something I'd never grown accustomed to. Perhaps because my first art exhibition at my father's house in London had been such a disaster.

I supposed it wasn't as dire as all that, for I had acquired a number of portrait commissions based on the merit I'd shown.

However, I still recalled the disparaging remarks some of the members of society had whispered about me, belittling my efforts and aspirations, labeling me as unnatural even then. Their words had pricked like thorns. Even now the memory of them had the power to make my skin sting like tiny insects were biting me.

That exhibition had also brought me to the attention of Sir Anthony Darby. I suspected it was then and there that he'd decided to pursue my hand in marriage so that he could put my artistic abilities to use for his anatomy textbook. Given this, was it really any wonder that I was struggling with mixed emotions about my second exhibition?

"It truly is astonishing, Kiera," Gage murmured, before gesturing to the other canvases scattered about the room, some still drying on easels and others carefully stacked in the corners or on top of the special shelves Gage had built for me. "They all are." He turned to look at me. "Are you finished, then? Is the collection ready to show?"

"Not quite," I prevaricated, my chest feeling tight. "I still have a few final touches I need to add. And I thought I might paint one more."

"Kiera," he said softly, but I spoke over him.

"Do you remember those boys we saw racing turtles near the Meadows?"

"Kiera."

"The littlest of the lot, he seemed so serious, yet he had such a cherubic air about him."

"Kiera." He grasped my hands, cutting off my chatter. His smile as he gazed down at me was gentle. "You're stalling."

I dipped my head rather than acknowledge this.

But he wouldn't let me hide. Using two fingers, he tipped my chin upward so that I was forced to look at him. "You do still wish to exhibit them, don't you?"

"Yes," I replied after a few moments of hesitation. "It's why I painted them. To cast a light on those that the world, that society largely chooses to ignore. To force them to see, truly see the people all around us. Not just their plight and squalor, but their humanity. The spark that connects us all as God's children, no matter who we are. The beauty of each of us." Seeing the slight curl at the corner of Gage's lips, I faltered. "I . . . I know beauty perhaps seems the wrong word, but . . ." I searched for the right words to make him understand. "Art is not just about beauty. It is about revealing truth. Of capturing more than what is capable of being detected with the naked eye. And there is *beauty* in that truth."

Hearing the passion in my voice, I flushed, shaking my head. "Maybe I'm not making sense."

"You are," he assured me, his voice warm with affection. "You are."

My rapid pulse steadied under his regard, only to stutter when he continued. "But you can't reveal that truth if you never exhibit the paintings."

I knew he was right, and yet the idea of doing so still terrified me.

Something Gage could tell. "Just think on it," he told me.

I nodded, for that was an easy promise to make. I'd already been thinking about it for months, and there was little chance of my stopping now.

CHAPTER 16

Brade Cranston Auctioneers turned out to be a conglomeration of two names, not one, each belonging to one of the founders of the firm. Mr. Brade had since passed from this mortal coil without issue, bequeathing his half of the business to his partner, Mr. Cranston, so long as his name was not removed from the firm's title. Or so the chatty fellow who had met with Gage and Anderley had claimed. He'd also claimed that Mr. Cranston had threatened to dissolve the company and start a new one just to spite the man. Except then he would have been thirty thousand pounds poorer.

Standing across from Mr. Cranston now, I could well believe the chatty fellow's allegations. Though nearly sixty, he might have passed as a man ten years younger, and a handsome one, too. That is, if not for the ugly sneer curling his lip and twisting his features into the approximation of one of the ragged, snarling figures Hieronymus Bosch had painted in his work *Christ Carrying the Cross*.

Thus far he'd done very little but glare at us, allowing Gage to do much of the talking while Anderley and I looked on. The warehouse in which we stood bustled with activity, though the employees gave us a wide berth while still eyeing us curiously. I didn't know what types of items Brade Cranston normally handled, but there were crates of all sizes—some as small as an ormolu clock and others as large as a grand pianoforte.

"Noo, just why would I tell ye anythin'?" Mr. Cranston retorted once Gage explained in a roundabout way the reason for our presence. His voice dripped with scorn. "Ye're no' the police. Ye're no' even Scottish."

"No," my husband replied evenly. "But if you won't speak to us, we can arrange for you to speak to the city police. Sergeant Maclean and his men would be only too happy to pay you a visit."

As threats went, it was quite skillfully done. Mr. Cranston would not want the police descending on his business, for that might draw unwelcome attention and suspicion to his doorstep, potentially damaging his reputation. However, Mr. Cranston proved to be a tougher nut to crack than anticipated.

"That's Winstanley's plan, is it?" he demanded, grinding his teeth. "Ruin me, too?"

"No one is trying to ruin anyone." Gage's voice had grown terse. "But we are trying to ascertain all the particulars surrounding the calamity. Now, do you know a man by the name of Sullivan? We've been told his cousin works here."

"No' that I can recall," he prevaricated. "And I dinna keep track o' my employees' associations. No' as long as they dinna interfere wi' their work."

"Are you sure?" Gage pressed, which made the muscle in Mr. Cranston's jaw twitch. "Because a witness saw you speaking with him."

"Hoo should I ken who this *witness* . . ." he spat the word ". . . saw me speakin' tae. I speak tae a lot o' men in the course o' my day. I dinna ken all their names."

Questioning him further would be a waste of time. Mr. Cranston had already revealed what we needed to know. He had a temper. A terrible one if the almost carmine hue of his flushed cheeks was any indication. He was wary, even though we'd not told him of the sabotage. And he definitely harbored animosity toward Mr. Winstanley. Whether that would lead him to engage someone to sabotage the floor of Lord Eldin's Picardy Place home, I couldn't say, but it wasn't outside the realm of possibility. As such, we should send Sergeant Maclean to speak to him. If nothing else, the fact he was a policeman might convince Mr. Cranston to talk just so they would leave his property.

However, Gage hadn't come to the same conclusion yet. That, or he thought goading him with more queries would provoke him into disclosing something incriminating. Meanwhile, I was forced to focus on taking deep, calming breaths as I struggled against the urge to turn and flee. Though I'd improved considerably since the days of my first marriage, angry men still made my heart race and my skin prickle with anxiety. The more livid they became—and Mr. Cranston was certainly livid—the more difficult it became to stand my ground. It was times like these that I despaired of ever being totally free of Sir Anthony and the pain and abuse he'd caused me, for my body responded without conscious thought. It was a reflex I simply couldn't control.

In my peripheral vision, I noticed Anderley moving a step closer to me so that he stood just beyond my left shoulder. I thought perhaps he'd noticed my distress and was trying to offer me support by letting me know he was there to protect my back and flank. But then I caught the flicker of movement between the stacks of crates almost directly behind Mr. Cranston which must have drawn Anderley's attention. I didn't have to look twice to recognize that the woman with strawberry blond hair was Bree.

At first, I feared she'd come there to warn us of some trouble. My thoughts immediately flew to my daughter. But then I realized that there was no haste to her movements, no sense of urgency. In fact, she seemed deep in conversation.

She wore a smart fawn brown ensemble as she strolled with a short, scruffy man she appeared to be questioning. It was clear she'd not seen us yet. As they disappeared behind a stack of crates, Anderley twitched, shifting his feet as if he intended to follow them. When the movement drew Mr. Cranston's eye, he stopped, standing stiffly at my side.

Mr. Cranston studied him suspiciously before his sour gaze transferred to me, narrowing in even greater dislike. Gage evidently sensed something was amiss, and when Bree and the other fellow emerged from behind the crates, he was at a better angle to see them. His eyes flared wide before he managed to mask his reaction.

"I have nothin' else to say," Mr. Cranston snarled, though he obviously did, as he continued his diatribe. "'Tis Lord Eldin's fault he hired such a ramshackle lot. Brade Cranston would never have allowed such a shameful thing tae happen."

"Are you suggesting it's Mr. Winstanley's fault the building joist was faulty?" I couldn't stop myself from asking, even though it drew Mr. Cranston's scornful attention back my way.

"I would have known better than tae hold the auction at such an address."

Considering the fact Picardy Place, while not one of the most exclusive addresses in Edinburgh, was still part of the graceful Georgian New Town, this statement made little sense. Especially since he, along with the general public, was still being led to believe the collapse was an accident caused by defective lumber and construction methods.

Unless he knew differently.

Some of the other men laboring in the warehouse were now taking notice of Bree, who had paused with the fellow escorting her to talk to a younger man. Anderley's stance was stiff, his hands clenched into fists at his side. Which was more than Mr. Cranston could ignore. Glancing over his shoulder, he spied the young woman speaking to his employees at about the same time Bree looked up and saw us. She was too far away to tell for sure, but she seemed to blanch.

"Hey! You canna be here!" Mr. Cranston yelled, moving toward her until Gage's words brought him up short.

"She's with us."

If looks could have flayed a person alive, Mr. Cranston's surely would have done so. "Leave my warehouse. And take yer women wi' ye."

There was nothing for it but to comply, no matter how unpleasant the man was and how much I could tell Gage would have liked to put him in his place. It was obvious Cranston believed we'd tasked Bree to charm information from his workers while we distracted him. It was difficult to counter the assumption when the truth was almost no better.

Anderley set off across the warehouse toward Bree first, his spine rigid with anger. Gage swiftly followed, either eager to head off their confrontation or because he wasn't sure he could restrain his tongue in front of Mr. Cranston any longer. Having been unprepared for their hasty retreat, I hastened to catch up. But before I could take even two steps, a hand shot out to grip my arm, halting me.

"A word, m'lady."

I was so shocked by Mr. Cranston's audacity in grabbing

me that I struggled to form the words for a proper setdown. By the time I had, he'd released me.

"I've heard the rumors yer puttin' together yer own exhibition." His eyes glittered sharply, though I couldn't deduce what his intent was. "And I ken Winstanley's assistant's been cozyin' up tae ye. Dinna be taken in by him. He'll no' be taken seriously."

For a moment, I thought he was going to propose that he broker the exhibit, though it was an odd way to go about it, especially after the way he'd just treated us. As such, I was opening my mouth to deliver a scathing rebuttal when a nasty smirk transformed his face.

"Anyone who's reputable kens such an exhibition is a waste o' time. No' tae mention the outlay o' capital." He scoffed. "No one respectable would willingly risk their reputation on such tomfoolery."

I felt as if I'd been punched in the gut. It was all I could do not to either cast up my accounts all over his shoes—which I supposed would have served him right—or burst into tears. Mortified enough, I hurried away, his nasty laugh ringing in my ears.

I wished I could have served him a blistering retort. Surely a more poised, socially confident person would have. The trouble was, part of me worried he was right. That any art dealer worth their salt would find my portraits meaningless and absurd. I had to swallow hard, lest I truly lose the contents of my stomach.

Gage glanced at me in concern as I drew even with and then passed him, Anderley, and Bree, anxious to escape the confines of the warehouse and reach the relative safety of our carriage. I didn't even wait for my husband to help me but accepted our footman Peter's assistance climbing into the conveyance. Bree clambered in after me, sitting opposite me, which forced the two men to share the same leg space across from each other. Normally, we would have staggered out of consideration of their long legs, but it was clear from Bree's scowl that neither she nor I cared about such niceties at the moment.

"What were you thinking?" Anderley demanded of her once the door to the carriage was shut. "To venture to such a place, *by yourself*, with no one the wiser."

It was apparent, at least to me, that his chief concern was her safety. Though one could be forgiven for being unclear about that when faced with his furious glare and righteous tone. Bree seemed to miss it, keeping her arms crossed tightly over her chest and her head turned away to glare out the window.

"I'm afraid I must agree, Miss McEvoy," Gage interjected more calmly, though his voice was still taut with displeasure. "You potentially placed yourself in a dangerous situation, and I cannot abide that. Not while you're living in my household, under my protection."

"Not to mention the fact you bungled our interrogation of Cranston," Anderley muttered, removing his hat and raking his hand back through his dark hair. "He'll not be speaking to us again anytime soon."

Through all these proceedings, I'd been observing them with my peripheral vision, keeping my gaze angled toward the window like Bree. My stomach still roiled from Mr. Cranston's words, and I wanted nothing more than to retreat to somewhere quiet to stew over them for a time. But I couldn't sit idly by and allow the men to continue to berate Bree. Not when they were being rather dense about their own portion of the blame. And hypocritical, to boot.

"I thought you were going to ask Anderley to speak to Bree

about your discoveries and our intentions for this morning," I reminded Gage. Otherwise, I would have done so myself.

Both men fell silent, and out of the corner of my eye, I saw Bree's eyes flick toward me.

"I did," Gage stated shortly. "Did you not?"

Anderley's delay in response spoke volumes. "I tried."

"When?" Bree snapped, speaking for the first time.

"After you finished dressing Mrs. Gage for dinner."

"In the servants' stair?" she bit out.

"Yes. You brushed past me. Said you were too busy."

"I had a paint stain tae remove from m'lady's skirt before it set. Ye should have told me what ye wanted."

"I tried," he argued.

"Nay, ye asked if I had a minute. I thought ye wanted . . ." She broke off before finishing that statement, color cresting her cheeks. Anderley appeared equally flustered. "All ye had tae do was tell me what 'twas aboot," she rallied. "I would've listened." Her eyes narrowed. "And I would've shared what *I'd* learned! After all, researchin' rival auctioneers was *my* task."

"Is that why you were there today?" I asked her. "You learned something that made Brade Cranston a likely suspect."

"Aye. I'd heard the firm wasna doin' so well. That the owner was furious Thomas Winstanley and Sons got the job and had been blatherin' aboot it ever since the floor collapse. That he had a vicious temper."

"Yet you decided to venture into his warehouse?" Anderley inquired incredulously. "Alone."

She shrugged. "'Tis no more than *you* do."

"It's not the same thing!" Anderley shouted, losing his temper for the first time in my presence.

But Bree was unmoved. "I fail tae see the difference."

"Well, I do, Miss McEvoy," Gage interrupted before Anderley could counter. "For one, Anderley is a man. And as such, he's afforded the protections of being that sex. I'm not saying it's fair or it's right," he added in response to her irritated scowl. "But it is true. He can go places you cannot without being harassed and barely even noticed."

Bree couldn't counter this. Sadly, no female could.

"And Anderley also has the benefit of experience. He's been doing this for far longer. So he knows his limits." Gage quirked an ironic brow at his valet. "Most of the time."

Anderley's lips pursed in displeasure.

"That doesn't mean he never runs into a spot of trouble, like in Cornwall." Gage's voice had gentled, clearly realizing that Bree would be thinking of Anderley arriving on the doorstep beaten and bloodied during that investigation. "But for the most part the protections we put in place prevent such things from happening. For example, I always know where he is." Gage's voice had sharpened again with this statement. I simply couldn't let it stand.

"Now, that's not strictly true."

Gage's head snapped around to look at me.

"Is it?"

His eyes flashed with annoyance. "Once again, I'll remind you, we have experience that neither of you do."

"Which gives you the right to not follow your own rules?" I charged calmly. Or at least more calmly than the others had thus far managed.

"If you're speaking of the other evening . . ." He huffed an aggravated sigh. "Then yes, you're right. I should have at least informed you of our intended destination. As we will *all* do in the future." His voice was firm, brooking no arguments as he looked at each of us in turn. "No one goes anywhere without informing someone in our household of their destination. Is that clear?"

"Of course, dear," I replied, earning myself a scowl.

Bree begrudgingly nodded before returning her glare to the view outside the window.

Anderley also nodded, a quick jerk of the head, but I could tell some silent communication passed between him and my husband. The type that indicated the matter was not so cut and dried. While I understood that inquiries sometimes led one to unexpected places and that having to report one's every movement could prove to be a severe hindrance, it seemed rather obstinate and inconsiderate to already be searching for the loophole.

Upon our return home, I lied and told Bree I had a rip in my hem. She followed me up to my bedchamber, but before she could fetch the sewing supplies, I grasped her hand, stopping her. Her expression was tight and her eyes hard, and it was all I could do not to embrace her.

"I apologize. I shouldn't have relied on Anderley. I should have told you myself what their intentions were and asked if you'd uncovered anything." I pressed one of my hands to my forehead. "The truth is, once I mentioned it to Gage, it slipped my mind. I've been too distracted of late."

Her gaze softened. "Aye, weel, you've had a great deal on yer mind. This inquiry, Emma's birthday, yer art exhibition . . ." Her voice trailed away as if she had something more to say. I looked at her quizzically, but she merely shook her head, as if she'd thought better of it.

She began to turn toward the dressing table, and I halted her. "There's no tear. I simply wanted a moment to speak with you in private."

Judging from her guarded expression, she was aware I wasn't just being kind.

"I appreciate the initiative you were taking. I truly do." I bit my lip. "But I also suspect you were intent on proving a point to Anderley."

She arched her chin as a pale pink wash of color suffused her freckled face.

"I'm not chastising you. It was high time Anderley had a taste of the worry he routinely inflicts upon you."

A furrow formed in her brow, and she opened her mouth as if to argue, perhaps not liking my choice of words. I held up a hand, forestalling her.

"But I'm asking you not to do so again. To hare off into a potentially . . . *fraught* situation." I refused to use the word *dangerous*, for there was no real proof Bree had been in danger earlier. "Without anyone knowing where you are. If something were to happen to you . . ." My voice broke, and I swallowed before continuing earnestly. "Well, Bree, let's just say I would be terribly upset."

She blinked at me as if she was also battling strong emotions.

"Will you do that for me?" I asked.

She nodded, and this time I trusted in her agreement rather than the forced compliance Gage had extracted from her in the coach. "I didna mean tae worry ye."

"I know," I assured her. "Now." I perched carefully on the dressing table bench. "Tell me everything else you've learned about the local auctioneers you think might be pertinent."

CHAPTER 17

Gage and I arrived at Picardy Place to find Mr. Winstanley in something of a sulk. Apparently, he'd been informed by one official or another that he could not remove Lord Eldin's collection to another location until permission had been granted.

"And with the ongoing investigation, that could take some time," Mr. Rimmer informed us as he led us toward the back room where the auctioneer was snapping at someone.

Which meant that all of this was costing Mr. Winstanley considerably more time and money than anticipated, not to mention aggravation.

"Add to that the fact that one of his employees has not shown up for work today, and . . ." Mr. Rimmer shrugged as if to say, *This is what you get.*

"Allow me to guess," Gage murmured wryly. "It was Mr. Sullivan."

Mr. Rimmer turned to him, consternation causing the corners of his eyes to crinkle. "How did you know?"

Gage didn't answer, his expression now less than inviting. When Mr. Rimmer looked at me, I pretended not to see, recognizing Gage's silence was intentional.

"Mr. Winstanley," Mr. Rimmer said as we entered the room cluttered with even more objects.

The auctioneer swiveled his head toward his assistant, appearing as if he were about to berate him as he had been the other man standing before him. However, upon catching sight of us, he changed his whinge. "Don't tell me you've come to deliver more edicts. Now, see here, I have a business to run."

"We are aware," Gage replied firmly. "And as we understand it, you are now down one employee."

Mr. Winstanley's gaze flicked toward Mr. Rimmer, sharp with displeasure. "Yes."

"I would like to speak with your other employees about Mr. Sullivan."

"Why?" The auctioneer's eyes had narrowed, clearly suspecting something.

Gage hesitated, considering how much to reveal. But given the fact the man in question had likely absconded after being confronted by Gage and Anderley the day before, there was little need to shelter him from his employer's reaction anymore.

"Mr. Sullivan has a cousin who works for Brade Cranston."

There was no need for Gage to say more, as Mr. Winstanley's face actually flushed purple with rage. I worried for a moment that he might give himself an apoplexy.

"That contemptible knave has been trying to cause trouble for me at every turn simply because Lord Eldin chose my firm to handle his collection and not his. But he didn't trust the blackguard, and neither do I." He narrowed his eyes to slits. "Oh, I should have known he was behind this. Is Sullivan the person who tampered with the joist? Is he the cause of my suffering? Why, I'll wring his . . ."

"We don't yet know that Mr. Sullivan, or Mr. Cranston for that matter, are culpable of anything," Gage said, cutting him off. "Merely that they are figures of interest. Which is why I would like to speak with your employees again."

Judging from Mr. Winstanley's expression, he'd already decided they were guilty of something, but he ordered Mr. Rimmer to round up the other men in the entry hall. Mr. Rimmer hurried to do this while the other man looked on. His face was battered and bruised, and his left hand bandaged, and I realized now that this must be the other assistant, Mr. Fletcher. He was older than Mr. Rimmer by some years, and taller, too, and his sandy hair was trimmed shorter than most gentlemen favored. Close enough to reveal a round, shilling-sized red mole on the left side of his head. His gray eyes were hooded, which accounted for some of my difficulty in reading his expression. At turns, he appeared drowsy, bored, and calculating, but I didn't know if any of those were accurate.

"We have one more matter to discuss with you," Gage said.

Mr. Winstanley appeared wary of whatever he was about to say. I supposed we couldn't blame him for that. He gestured for Gage to continue.

"The copy of the invitation list that your assistant delivered." He nodded at the other man, evidently having also deduced he was Mr. Fletcher. "Was Mrs. Gage's name deliberately left off of it?"

The auctioneer frowned while Mr. Fletcher's face remained impassive. "I don't understand the question."

"Mrs. Gage received an invitation and a catalog, but her name was not included on the copy of the invitation list you gave us to review."

Mr. Winstanley continued to look confused.

"We simply wondered if you'd left her name off because we obviously knew she received one," Gage attempted again to explain, exasperation fraying the edges of his voice.

"Mrs. Gage shouldn't have received an invitation," Mr. Winstanley retorted. "She wasn't on the list."

My stomach dipped.

Gage appeared taken aback. "You didn't send her an invitation and catalog?"

"No." He almost seemed appalled by the notion. "But she received one?"

My husband turned to me, so I answered. "Yes. A week ago. The day before the start of the auction."

"We mailed the invitations and catalogs weeks ago," Mr. Winstanley replied defensively.

"I did wonder at its late arrival," I admitted.

"Yet you received one?" The auctioneer appeared genuinely baffled.

"Yes."

"But how?"

I shook my head, conceding I didn't know. And that not knowing troubled me. Greatly.

"Perhaps Mr. Rimmer sent it," Mr. Fletcher suggested, speaking for the first time.

Mr. Winstanley whirled to look at him. "Why would he do such a thing?"

"He's a great admirer o' her paintings. She's practically all he speaks of."

This remark and the avid look in Mr. Fletcher's eyes seemed to make all of us uncomfortable, not just me. According to Maclean, Mr. Fletcher had implied Mr. Rimmer was obsessed with me, and that seemed to be what he was doing now, though his words were slightly more polite.

"Wants to broker the art exhibit she's working on," he added.

This was no more than I'd already suspected, but to hear Mr. Fletcher refer to it in such a tone made it sound sordid. I clasped my hands before me, struggling not to react.

Mr. Winstanley was not so circumspect. "Did you send Mrs. Gage an invitation and a catalog?" he barked at Mr. Rimmer as he returned to the room.

Mr. Rimmer stumbled to a stop, his eyes widening in the face of his employer's anger. "To the auction?" he stammered. "No." His gaze darted between us all. "Was I meant to?" He frowned. "But wait. You had a catalog," he said to me. "I recall you referring to it. Did someone lend it to you?"

"Then you didn't send it to her?" the auctioneer persisted.

"No," Mr. Rimmer replied vociferously, evidently deducing that was what his employer was charging him with. "I didn't."

But Mr. Winstanley and Mr. Fletcher still looked suspicious.

"Then how else could she have received one?" Gage wanted to know, planting his hands on his hips.

No one seemed to have a ready answer, until Mr. Rimmer waded in again, his dark eyes leery. "I suppose it's possible someone who received it decided to forward it to Lady Darby. Her interest in art *is* well known."

"But why wouldn't they have included a note?" I queried in a small voice.

"I . . . I don't know, my lady. Perhaps they forgot?"

It was a weak response, to be sure, but at least he was sensitive to my distress. Mr. Winstanley seemed more concerned with how this new development affected him and his staff, and the manner in which Mr. Fletcher was eyeing Mr. Rimmer communicated he didn't believe his denials.

For my part, I didn't know what to think. And after being confronted by Mr. Cranston's cruel assertions, I was feeling rather vulnerable. I found myself inching closer to Gage, anxious for the reassurance of his presence.

Unfortunately, my husband was preoccupied with advancing the inquiry. "Maybe you would take some time then, Mr. Rimmer, to consider from the invitation list who that might have been."

The assistant was plainly surprised by the request. "I can try."

But Gage was barely listening. "If you'll excuse me," he declared as he strode out of the room, no doubt off to interrogate the other employees, leaving me staring awkwardly at the three men. Mr. Winstanley had turned away, muttering to himself while Mr. Fletcher wore a smirk. Only Mr. Rimmer seemed inclined to speak, but I didn't want to have to feign equanimity. Not when I could sense my composure eroding as we spoke.

Instead, I smiled tightly and fled, like the coward I clearly still was.

"They're all too intimidated by Mr. Winstanley," Gage groused as we rumbled over the cobblestone streets the short distance to our door. "And anxious not to lose their jobs."

"They are far from home," I pointed out, my gaze fastened out the window. It was raining again—big, fat droplets that seemed to find their way under hats and over collars, rolling down one's neck and leaving an icy trail.

"That, or someone else has convinced them to remain silent," Gage mused, as he'd been doing since we left Picardy Place. I wasn't even sure he'd heard me. He seemed to be doing a remarkable job of recapping his interview with the auctioneer's staff without my help, even though I'd witnessed nearly the entire thing, albeit hovering in the background.

I was almost relieved to escape the confines of the carriage and my husband when we reached our door, though I waited patiently for the step to be lowered and an umbrella to be brought forth. But once inside, Gage still wasn't finished.

"Jeffers, collect Anderley, Miss McEvoy, and Mrs. Mackay and have them join us in the library. We need to confer."

"Mrs. Mackay isn't here, sir," Jeffers reminded him while I stood dripping all over the rug, trying to manage the buttons of my pelisse while I shivered from the sudden chill in the air. "She's gathering information on the Bannatyne Club, as requested."

Which meant Emma had been left in Bree's charge.

"I'd forgotten. Well, then, carry on," he stated with a wave of his hand. "We'll convene later."

I'd finally managed to slip free the last button, and Gage removed the garment from my shoulders and passed it to the butler.

"Come, my dear. Let's get you somewhere warm."

It was some relief to discover he wasn't completely oblivious to my state of being, and I reveled in the heat generated by his large body as I crowded close to his side as he ushered me up the stairs and into the library. However, once I was deposited in front of the roaring fire, he left me there and moved toward his desk, where the correspondence Jeffers had informed him had arrived was waiting for him. I lifted my hands toward the blaze, trying not to feel like a discarded waif. At the same time, I knew I was being ridiculous. Naturally, Gage was absorbed with the inquiry. All I needed to do was speak up and tell him I was troubled, and he would attend to me. I knew this, and yet the words stuck in my throat, stifled by my own insecurities.

"You've a letter here as well," Gage remarked even as I heard him slitting open a piece of his own correspondence.

I turned to meet him as he crossed the space toward me, already reading the contents of his missive. A furrow marred his brow as I accepted my letter from him. I allowed my gaze to drift over the handwriting. "Is that from your father?"

"Yes," he said absently, remaining where he was as he continued to read.

"Is anything wrong?" I ventured at the risk of pestering him while he was still immersed in the note.

"Hmm?"

"It's simply that you seem . . . perturbed."

His gaze flickered toward me before returning to the paper. "Father is informing me there's been a delay with some of the stonework at the dower house."

"But didn't you already correspond with Mr. Watkins about that last week?" As steward of Lord Gage's Warwickshire estate, Bevington Park, Mr. Watkins had been tasked with supervising the refurbishment of the dower house while we were in Edinburgh and Lord Gage was in London.

"I did. And Father has undoubtedly confused the man, for he directed Watkins to do the exact opposite of what I instructed him."

I grimaced. "I'm sure he's just trying to help."

"No, he's just trying to control the situation. Like he always does."

I couldn't dispute this, for it was true. Though in this case it might be a mixture of both.

I sank onto the sofa as I broke the seal of my letter, recognizing my brother's nearly illegible scrawl. Trevor had never been a lengthy correspondent, and this missive was no exception. In any case, I would see him soon enough.

"From Trevor?" Gage asked as I refolded it.

"Yes. To let me know he'll be traveling up from Blakelaw House on Saturday."

"You must be anxious to see him," he remarked, still perusing his own missive.

I nodded. It had been nearly three months since we'd spent Christmas and Hogmanay at my childhood home, Blakelaw House, which was now Trevor's estate. While my brother and sister and I had always been close, we'd never spent our lives in each other's pockets—ever moving in and out of each other's spheres with ease. But in that moment, I felt tears bite at the back of my eyes and a distinct yearning to see my brother again. For all the aggravation he'd caused me as a big brother, I couldn't deny that I'd always felt safe and protected, and perhaps most importantly, accepted by him. Losing our mother at such young ages had formed a strong bond between us, and that uncomplicated alliance was something I found myself craving.

Blinking furiously, I rose to my feet and crossed toward the window, gazing out at the rain that still fell in buckets. It ran in rivulets toward the mews and formed puddles on the lawn. One could even smell the dampness in the air, seeping through the glass. I hugged my arms tightly around me against the chill.

A movement near the carriage house grabbed my attention, and for a moment I wondered if we were receiving another unorthodox call from Bonnie Brock. Then I spied Joe, our coachman. He was fidgeting with the door that led into the garden and speaking to someone over his shoulder, likely the carpenter. I recalled now that there had been a complaint about the door leaking when it rained.

While I wasn't precisely disappointed to discover it wasn't Bonnie Brock, it did make me pause to question where the rogue had gotten to the past few days. Normally during the course of our inquiries here in Edinburgh, he seemed to be perpetually underfoot at the most inopportune times. I knew he had seen Maclean in our carriage on the day I'd spotted him watching us from Queen Street Gardens, but I'd not seen him since. Which wasn't to say he wasn't still about. He'd simply not made himself known. But I had some questions for him. Questions that I began to wonder if he was reluctant to answer.

There was a rap on the door, and Gage called out for them to enter.

"Mrs. Mackay has returned, sir," Jeffers entered to say. "But she asked me to inform you that Miss Gage has already awakened from her nap."

"Tell her to bring her with her," I told him before Gage could reply.

Jeffers nodded before departing while Gage scrutinized me from where he now stood next to his desk.

"Are you certain? As much as I love my daughter, I know how distracting she can be."

"I'm certain," I replied, turning back toward the window. Suddenly the act of holding my daughter was what I wanted most of all.

Not that Emma wished to be held for long. Not when there was a new chamber to be explored.

We moved the low tea table in front of the hearth to block it and set Emma down on the Axminster rug, sprinkling it with a few of her toys—including her ragdoll Rosie—so that she could roam. And roam she did. She'd become quite the quick crawler and had even begun to pull herself up to standing. Mrs. Mackay assured us it wouldn't be long before she was walking.

Emma's presence also had the unanticipated but welcome effect of mitigating some of the tension in the room, particularly between Bree and Anderley. It was clear they hadn't yet reconciled after this morning's quarrel. Perhaps it was too soon. After all, they had both been greatly riled. I hoped they wouldn't leave it too long and let feelings continue to fester.

"Since ye seem tae have been waitin' for me, shall I start?" Mrs. Mackay asked, drawing Emma's attention, who grinned broadly at her nanny. "I'm afraid I havena much tae report. No' yet. But I must tell ye, after speakin' wi' a few members o' Lord Thomson's staff . . ." she shook her head ". . . I dinna think we're goin' tae find our answers wi' the Bannatyne Club."

Lord Thomson had served as the club's vice president since its inception, and its president since Sir Walter Scott's death six months ago.

"Go on," Gage urged, smiling at our daughter as she turned to look at him.

"Accordin' tae them, while the members can, indeed, sometimes get touzie—'specially after a drink or two—'tis nay more than the average Scotsman. And they said Lord Eldin was no worse than the others. That none o' 'em seemed to have any catterbatter wi' him."

I normally heard the Scots word *touzie* spoken in relation to a person's disheveled hair, but I supposed I could infer its meaning in this context. However, *catterbatter* was certainly new.

"No *obvious* disputes anyway," Gage remarked helpfully.

"Aye," she agreed as Emma pulled herself up on the sofa cushion between her nanny and Bree. "I've one more old acquaintance I can ask, but 'tis all."

Gage nodded before turning to Bree. "We're already aware of some of the information Miss McEvoy uncovered." This was a diplomatic way of phrasing things. "But were there any other rival auctioneers you believe we should take a closer look at?"

Bree shook her head. She and I had already discussed the matter earlier and decided that nothing she'd found out about the others was enough to raise suspicions.

Jeffers cleared his throat, and attention shifted to him. "I have not learned anything that would alter our belief that Mr. Smith was not the intended victim. However . . ." The arch of his eyebrows as he turned to me seemed to contain a world of meaning. "Sir James Riddell is proving more complicated. I'll have a more complete report for you tomorrow or the following day."

Gage glanced between us in confusion, and I realized I hadn't told him that I'd asked Jeffers to find out what he could about the cad.

"Very good," I told Jeffers, deciding his statement was both explanation and justification enough for what I'd asked of him.

My husband seemed to realize this as well, though the look he fastened on me promised there would be questions later. Questions about what had prompted me to ask our butler to investigate Sir James.

"Then that leaves Mr. Sullivan and his connections at Brade Cranston Auctioneers as our most promising suspects." Gage sat back in his chair, crossing one leg over the other, watching Emma as she crawled across the floor toward the fireplace, where a loud snap had drawn her interest. Being nearest to the hearth, I also watched her closely, ready to nab her if she attempted to go around or underneath the table blocking her path. "I'd hoped one of Winstanley's other employees might be able to tell me something useful," Gage continued. "Especially after Mr. Sullivan didn't appear for work today. But they proved to be determinedly closemouthed."

Emma had reached the tea table, pulling herself up so that she could bang her hands against the top. I could see her scrutinizing the flickering flames, her little legs wobbling with the effort to remain upright, but she remained where she was for the moment.

"You've seen them interact in the evening away from their employer's influence," Gage said, presumably to Anderley. "Do they genuinely seem so loyal to one another?"

There was a pause as the valet considered the question. "I suppose so. At least, on the surface. But Sullivan was the newest of them. If they were going to break ranks to tell tales about anyone, it would be him."

"Then perhaps you should continue your acquaintance with them."

"What if Sullivan warned the others about him?" I cautioned.

"I suppose it's possible," Gage conceded. "But not likely. Either way, be careful," he told Anderley.

Out of the corner of my eye, I saw Bree's lips purse with displeasure, and I couldn't say that I blamed her. For all their talk of precautions, they didn't seem to be taking enough for either of our liking.

"What of the other employees? Have you noticed anything suspicious about them?" I asked, curious what his impressions of them were away from Picardy Place.

"Most of them seem to be exactly who they say they are, and eager to return home. Several of them have families in Liverpool."

I glanced at him swiftly, sensing the *but*.

"But the two assistants—Fletcher and Rimmer. They both seem to be hiding something."

"What makes you say that?" I asked as Emma dropped down onto her bottom.

"Their speech and mannerisms. Neither of them is entirely comfortable with the others. And I don't think it's merely because the others report to them."

I trusted Anderley's instincts. Both because he was sharp and because I'd sensed something similar. But that didn't mean their secrets had anything to do with the floor collapse. They could be related to something different. At least, I tried to tell myself that.

"We have another potential problem," Gage declared, and I wished I could turn my head to see what he was thinking, but Emma was now leaning down, peering under the table. She was quite intelligent, and I had no doubt she was pondering whether she could get to the pretty flickering flames by crawling underneath it. The question was whether she would recognize the heat coming from it quickly enough to deter her.

I slid to the edge of the sofa, ready to spring into action if needed while Gage explained what we'd discovered about my name not being on the invitation list.

"If not this Mr. Rimmer, could it've been someone else from the auction house who sent m'lady the catalog?" Bree asked in concern.

"It's possible," Gage replied. "Though the three likeliest to do so denied sending her one."

Emma scooted her little body underneath the wood just as I dropped to my knees from behind, grabbing her about the waist to stop her. She protested—loudly—but I held fast, pulling her out and lifting her into my arms as I gently scolded her. "No, Emma. The fire will hurt you. No."

She arched her back, continuing to express her displeasure, but I kept my arms tight around her as I sat back down on the sofa. "I know the fire is fascinating, but you can't touch it." I grasped her little hand, holding it out toward the flames, though of course not near enough to actually harm her, and then recoiling it as I exclaimed, "Ouch!" She quieted, watching me with wide eyes as I did this twice more and then pressed kisses to her cheek and temple just below her cap, her golden curls tickling my nose.

Anderley reached down to snag her doll Rosie from the rug, offering it to her. She tipped her head back to look at him almost upside down, and he smiled uncertainly. Though never unkind, the valet didn't generally seem to know how to behave with children, and in that moment, I found his awkwardness endearing. Perhaps because I was the one who was so often awkward.

Emma seemed to agree, smiling back at him as she accepted the doll. I sat her upright so that she could better see the handsome, dark-haired fellow next to her.

"The likeliest solution," Gage said, picking up the threads of our conversation, "is that someone who received an invitation from Winstanley and Sons then forwarded it to Mrs. Gage because they knew she would be interested, but failed to include a note explaining."

"Failed tae or deliberately wished tae mislead her," Bree warned.

"That's the question, isn't it?" Gage agreed, sounding far more uneasy than he had at Picardy Place. "Did any of the names on the invitation list strike you as someone who would do such a thing, either well intentioned or not?"

"Not at first glance," I said. "But I'll take another look. I intended to anyway."

His eyes glinted with strong emotions, and I could easily guess where his thoughts had gone looking at me holding Emma. None of us wanted to face the same sort of danger we had found ourselves in last November in Cornwall. "I don't want to jump to any conclusions. Not when the idea of you being lured there as the target seems pretty implausible. But then many of our theories have seemed implausible. So I'd rather you not leave the house without an escort of some kind. Even to walk to your sister's house."

"That seems sensible," I concurred, knowing it would ease his mind and mine.

Emma cooed as if to say she assented as well, and we all chuckled. One thing was clear. She was following in her father's footsteps. A natural mediator, if ever I saw one. But everything else seemed as murky as Nor Loch.

CHAPTER 18

Several hours the following morning were devoted to final preparations for Emma's birthday celebration in a little over a week's time. Considering my lack of skills as a hostess and my sister's delight in planning soirees of every variety, I had asked for her assistance. Alana was a countess, after all, and she had ample experience in such things. She also had four children and had thus arranged quite a number of fetes for wee ones.

Of course, asking Alana to assist with anything meant that sooner or later she took control. It wasn't that she intended to run roughshod over me—her little sister. She simply couldn't seem to help it. It was just her way. And while there were times when Alana's managing could be quite vexing, in this case, it was actually the reason I'd asked her. For she was so incredibly competent at those sorts of things, and I was not. Besides, I knew it would make her happy.

As such, I didn't say much as Alana reviewed plans for

Emma's day with Jeffers; Mrs. Baxter, the housekeeper; and our cook, Mrs. Grady. By and large, I didn't care what food was served or the types of flowers or decorations, as long as they were delicious and lovely and smelled sweet. Emma was too little to have many preferences. However, I did insist that Mrs. Grady make some of her lemon cakes, for we'd discovered that Emma enjoyed them as much as I did, her mouth puckering with humorous delight. Though I knew it would be difficult to find so many of the ingredients at this time of the year.

At one point, Gage stepped into the drawing room to greet Alana, but just as quickly he departed. A few moments later, I saw him outside the window, riding off on his chestnut gelding, Titus, with Anderley trailing behind on another steed. I knew they were intent on finding out more information about Mr. Sullivan and Brade Cranston Auctioneers, and they intended to confer with Sergeant Maclean. Part of me wished I was joining them, but another part of me was glad that I couldn't.

Though I couldn't explain it, my instincts told me we were looking in the wrong direction. Yes, Sullivan and Cranston were viable suspects, but the scenario in which they were the villains was far from satisfactory. There were, as yet, too many unknowns, and I couldn't help but think that we were missing too many pieces of the puzzle to form a clear picture. I just didn't think that evidence was going to come from Sullivan or Cranston.

However, I would be the first to admit I could be wrong. As such, it behooved us to continue that line of inquiry. At the least, it gave my husband something to do while we waited. After sitting idle for so long, he was rather like a child with a new toy. I only hoped he didn't become too consumed by it.

"Dearest," Alana said, pulling me from my woolgathering

after she'd dismissed the staff. "Are you sure everything is to your liking?"

"Oh, yes," I assured her. "It's going to be lovely." I leaned forward to squeeze her hand. "I truly must thank you again. I could never have done this without you."

She gazed at me quizzically, and I rushed into speech before she questioned me about my evident distraction.

"Did I tell you Trevor is arriving late tomorrow?"

She nodded. "He wrote to me as well. But are you sure you wish him to stay here? We have plenty of room at Cromarty House."

"Yes, I do. I'm looking forward to it." I gave her a teasing smile. "Why? Are you afraid we'll spend all our time gossiping about you?"

She arched her chin, gathering up her effects. "I know what you do when I'm not around."

I gasped, reaching for her hand again. "That's not true! Please, don't tell me you think that. I was only teasing."

I saw then the impish glint in her deep lapis-lazuli blue eyes and smacked her arm.

She laughed. "Just be sure to bring Trevor to Sunday dinner or his other nieces and wee Jamie will be quite upset with you."

"I will," I promised as she pressed a kiss to my cheek and swept from the room in a cloud of French perfume.

I listened as she conferred with Jeffers while she collected her outer garments and then heard the door close as she departed. I had no pressing plans for the day other than dinner that evening with Henry and Lord Edward, and normally I would have retreated to my art studio to immerse myself in painting, but something held me immobile. While I knew it was ridiculous to place any stock in Cranston's words, I couldn't seem to stop myself from hearing them over and over again in my mind.

No one respectable would willingly risk their reputation on such tomfoolery.

Every time I thought of them, the pit which seemed to have replaced my stomach yawned wider. It was enough to make me want to avoid the one place that had always been my sanctuary. For I knew from experience that if I stood before an easel concerned about what someone else thought, the results at the end of my paintbrush would be dull and lifeless and distorted. It was better to stay away until the sting of his insults had faded and I had a more even perspective of the matter.

My hands tightened reflexively in my lap as anxiety flooded me at the thought that might never happen. I forced myself to breathe deeply—once, twice, three times. It would. *It would.* Until then, I simply needed to occupy myself. Which was easier said than done. I spent time with Emma and enjoyed a leisurely luncheon. I even picked up my dusty viola and played for a time. However, when I'd tried and failed for the fourth time to read the same page of the novel I'd previously been enjoying, I decided what I truly needed was physical exertion.

Since Anderley was out with Gage and our footman Peter was busy assisting Mrs. Baxter, I sent for Bree, urging her to fetch her bonnet. "We'll only venture as far as Queen Street Gardens," I told Jeffers as he helped me into my hazelnut-shaded redingote, lest Gage return and begin to worry.

"Very good, my lady," he intoned, passing me the key which would gain us access through the gate.

Unfortunately, Bree didn't seem as pleased by the prospect of a brisk stroll through the private gardens as I was. She trailed behind me, as most maids did their mistresses, maintaining a short distance between us. I tolerated this until we were through the gate and into the garden's westernmost segment.

"You needn't lag behind me," I told her. "In fact, I prefer you not."

"'Tis only proper."

I brushed away this protest with my fingers, refusing to move forward until she stood at least close enough that she was just behind my shoulder. Tipping my head back, I enjoyed the way the trees swayed in the wind. It was a lovely early spring day, if a trifle blustery, and the elm, lime, horse chestnut, and laurel trees which lined the paths had all begun to bud. The maroon ribbons of my bonnet trailing below my chin waved in the breeze as if greeting passersby.

The deeper we strolled toward the center of the garden, the more the sounds of the city outside its perimeter began to fade, so that soon we were surrounded by naught but birdsong, softly sighing branches, and the crunch of the gravel beneath our feet. The flowers had begun to emerge from their winter rest, opening their petals toward the sunlight. Inhaling their gentle fragrances, I could feel my shoulders lower and relax and the knot in my diaphragm loosen. This was precisely what I'd needed.

"See now. Isn't this lovely?" I remarked to Bree.

"Aye. The perfect day for a stroll."

I started at the sound of the deep, but familiar, burr answering mine, and then turned to scowl at Bonnie Brock as he moved in step with me. A glance over my shoulder showed me that Bree had dropped behind, eyeing the scoundrel beside me with disfavor.

"And I suppose you've been waiting for me," I retorted, disliking his habit of sneaking up on me, though admittedly it had been some time since he'd done so. "I've been wondering when you would turn up again."

"Ye missed me, then," he quipped with a roguish grin.

"I knew it was too much to hope we were rid of you."

"Aww, noo. Dinna be cross wi' me just because I was right." His gold-green eyes flashed. "I saw ye wi' Mean Maclean."

"Yes, you were right," I conceded with a sigh. "And, as I know you're already aware, we are investigating."

We were approaching the crescent-shaped shrubbery fashioned of holly and yew at the center of the western garden, the sun striking us more fully as the taller trees failed to arch overhead. A broad expanse of lawn adjoined it to the north and to the south, gently sloping up toward the streets bordering the garden. I found myself wondering, as I had in the past, whether he'd picked the lock at the gate or simply scaled the five-foot-high rod iron fence to gain entrance. Either possibility would be straightforward for a man with Bonnie Brock's penchants and abilities.

"I ken ye also discovered ye were no' on the guest list."

I turned to him in surprise, even though I knew it would please him. "How on earth did you find that out?"

He shrugged. "Little goes on in this city wi'oot me kennin' aboot it."

I narrowed my eyes in displeasure at this answer, but in all honesty, I'd known better than to expect a legitimate response. Bonnie Brock would always keep his methods and sources close to the vest unless revealing them was necessary. "I suppose that means you won't tell me how you learned the floor collapse wasn't an accident either."

He maintained an innocent expression—or as innocent as the criminal was capable of—provoking me to roll my eyes.

"Obviously, you have an informant among the police or working with the auctioneer. Probably both," I conceded.

He neither confirmed nor denied this as we circulated the crescent-shaped shrubbery. I noted that the garden was all but deserted except for Bree's brooding presence behind us. While this was fortunate in the sense that no one would be reporting on my scandalous stroll with the roguish outlaw who had set many a lady's heart fluttering when he was depicted in the various plays adapted from *The King of Grassmarket*, the infamous book written about him the previous year, it was also slightly suspicious. I knew that I'd seen and heard other people in the gardens when Bree and I first arrived. Was that where Stump and Locke—Bonnie Brock's perpetual shadows—were at? Were they keeping other pedestrians at bay?

Another, perhaps wiser, woman might have felt unnerved by this thought. But after the events of last year, I firmly believed that Bonnie Brock would never harm me. Though one peek over my shoulder at Bree told me she wasn't as convinced.

"I also ken that yer husband's valet has been spendin' a great deal o' time at the White Horse, and I dinna think he's there for the ale and oysters."

I didn't know whether he'd marked my glance in my maid's direction and was saying this for her benefit or mine, but I knew she would be listening closely now.

"And I'm no' the only one who's noticed."

I turned to scrutinize his face and he nodded, confirming my worries.

"Ye might warn him o' that."

We would, but it would be far more helpful if he wasn't speaking in such oblique terms.

"Who noticed?" I pressed.

But his answer was as vague as his warning. "The auctioneer employees he's meant tae be cozyin' up tae, for one."

"And?"

I wanted to growl when he refused to elaborate further, all but ignoring my query. Though I was grateful when he prevented me from blundering into a pile of unpleasantness left by some animal.

"The auctioneer's assistant. The tall one wi' the injured hand and the nasty sneer."

"Mr. Fletcher?" I asked, trying to understand if this related to his warning.

He shrugged in dismissal. "What'ere his name is. He's been talkin' a lot aboot the other lad's fascination wi' ye."

"Mr. Rimmer."

"Raggin' him somethin' fierce."

An uncomfortable sensation filled my chest at the thought of Mr. Rimmer being belittled because of me, because he appreciated my art. It reopened the well of misgiving Cranston's derogatory comments had created.

Bonnie Brock scoffed. "As if he's no' just as fascinated."

This remark was not in the least what I'd expected to hear, and it took me a moment to grasp the implication. I frowned in confusion.

"Best be wary o' him."

"Rimmer?"

He scowled. "Nay. Fletcher. At least Rimmer has good taste."

Though it shouldn't have had such a profound effect, this artless aside warmed me from inside. Probably because it *was* so guileless.

"But this Fletcher, he's usin' these taunts tae mask somethin'. Whether that's his own culpability or simply somethin' he kens but hasna shared, I dinna ken. But my money's on him bein' the one tae watch."

His expression had taken on a rather ferocious cast, making the ridge of scar tissue running along his crooked nose stand out white against his angry flush and inspiring a sudden pulse of empathy for Mr. Fletcher. No doubt if Bonnie Brock was warning me about him, then his men would be tailing him. A fact I found reassuring. There were already too many people to keep track of in this inquiry.

I thought again of how Mr. Fletcher had asked to speak with me when he dropped off the invitation list and I had not been home. He'd not renewed the attempt when we'd met him at Picardy Place the previous day, though there had been the opportunity. Had he intended to say something about Mr. Rimmer's interest in me, or was there something else he'd wanted to tell me? Or, as Bonnie Brock suspected, was he fascinated by me, too?

I found it hard to believe that I was that intriguing to so many men. Yes, I was a female portrait artist, and there were few enough of us, but that did not inevitably make me a figure of fascination. Bonnie Brock must be misreading the situation.

"I can tell ye think I'm wrong?" he challenged, coming to a sudden stop. The hard glint in his eyes was now directed at me.

It was slightly unnerving to discover he could interpret my reactions so well.

"Not wrong. Just . . . mistaken."

The eyebrow he arched at me communicated his failure to see the difference between the two. "Mistaken or no', be careful." A shadow passed over us as the clouds overhead blocked the sun. "I ken I dinna have tae remind ye that the closer ye get tae the truth, the more danger you'll be in." He didn't wait for a response, instead striking out across the broad sweep of lawn toward Queen Street without looking back.

"He's no' wrong aboot that, m'lady," Bree said as she moved to my side.

I inhaled a sharp breath of acknowledgment, watching Bonnie Brock disappear over the terraced edge, and then turned my steps toward home. "He's not wrong about some of the other things he mentioned either." We strolled in silence for a moment before broaching the topic that I suspected was uppermost in her thoughts. "We'll have to warn Anderley."

"If he'll listen," she grumbled.

I turned to her in surprise. "I know that Anderley can sometimes be a trifle . . ." I searched for a diplomatic term. "Stubborn. But he's not foolish."

"Aye, but will he consider Bonnie Brock's warnin' tae be legitimate? Will Mr. Gage?"

She had a valid point. In the past, Gage had been reluctant to trust Bonnie Brock's words. However, after he'd saved us from the vaults last year, and after his assertions several days ago about the floor collapse being no accident had proved to be true, I didn't think my husband would require much persuasion to heed the rogue's plea of caution.

"This time, I think he will," I said. "I know the last thing Mr. Gage wants is a repeat of what happened to Anderley in Cornwall."

Bree didn't respond at first, and I wondered if she was reliving the moment Anderley had appeared on the doorstep of Roscarrock House battered and bloody. I almost regretted mentioning it. However, her next observation suggested her thoughts had gone elsewhere.

"I dinna like Bonnie Brock," she stated. "He's a knave and a bully and a blackguard. And I've never approved o' yer collaboratin' wi' him."

This was the first time I'd heard her express such an opinion, and I was caught off guard.

"But I canna deny he's done ye a good turn a time or two. You and Mr. Gage. And . . ." Her mouth clamped into a thin line almost as if she was reconsidering saying something. "If this warnin' proves tae be a timely one, I'll thank him heartily for it."

"I had no idea that's how you felt," I admitted as we approached the gate.

She brushed a stray strawberry blond curl back from her face. "Aye, weel, 'tis no' my job to make yer life and yer choices harder. As yer maid, ye dinna have to listen to me anyway. Many a mistress would simply tell me tae shut my gob."

"But that's not the relationship we have," I countered. "It never has been."

"Nay, but that doesna mean I have the same freedoms ye do. And I have tae mind that. Just as Anderley has to mind it, though he'd prefer no' tae think o' the future and merely live in the present."

I felt a little like Bree was speaking in riddles, but I thought I deduced her point. I might in some ways treat her as more of an equal, but she wasn't. She was my lady's maid. She was paid to care for me and my clothes, to wait on me hand and foot, if I asked her to, because she was beholden to me for her livelihood. Even her relationship with Anderley was in many ways subject to our whims, for if we chose to, we could separate them, either temporarily or permanently. Not that we would. But we could.

In fact, everything in their respective worlds was currently subject to us. It didn't matter that we were for the most part understanding and largely avoided meddling in their personal lives. Or rather, it did. But that didn't change the truth of the matter.

It was similar to the way that everything in my life was subject to Gage. According to the law, as his wife, I was entirely beholden to him. My wealth, my body, my well-being, even our children were all his to control. Or they could be, if he chose to ignore my wishes.

When she complained of Anderley not thinking of the future, it would be easy to assume she was voicing frustration at his failure to assess the seriousness of their relationship. But after considering her remarks in this new light, I began to wonder if it was the opposite. If Anderley was the one who was pushing for something more permanent—for marriage—and *Bree* was balking. Because her life would not only be beholden to us, but to Anderley.

It was something I could empathize with, and not a decision to be made lightly. After all, I'd turned down Gage's first offer of marriage because I'd been terrified of placing my life in the hands of another man after enduring the cruelty of my first husband. It had taken a great deal of love and a tremendous leap of faith on my part, even knowing Gage was nothing like Sir Anthony. So I could not fault Bree for hesitating, especially while there were so many unresolved issues between her and Anderley.

CHAPTER 19

Bree was just affixing the clasp of my mother's amethyst pendant, putting the finishing touches on my attire for the evening, when we heard Gage and Anderley bustling about in the adjoining chamber. I'd begun to wonder what was keeping them and if my husband would even have time to change before dinner. Bree's gaze met mine in the mirror as Gage's frazzled-sounding voice carried through the wall and then the door to the corridor was heard opening and shutting with a resounding click.

"Perhaps you should see if Anderley is in need of assistance," I suggested as his footsteps hurried down the corridor toward the stairs.

She nodded, exiting as I stood and brushed my hand over the cornflower blue silk bodice of my dinner dress. Swiveling to the left and then the right, I examined my reflection, liking the way the color of the gown made my eyes sparkle. It was a relatively simple design, trimmed with white accents across the shoulders and along the skirt. The sleeves—while still puffed—were slimmer and more manageable.

Crossing the room to the door leading into the adjoining chamber, I rapped once before entering. Gage looked up with a scowl, and while his reaction was not all a wife would hope for from her husband, the remaining sight of him was.

"My, my, what have we here," I cooed, closing the door behind me and leaning back against the frame to better appreciate his bare torso. Almost daily rides as well as bouts of fencing and other strenuous activities had given him a marvelous physique. One that, I admitted, I found endlessly fascinating, from an artist's perspective as well as a wife's.

"Whatever you have to say, you'd best make it quick," he griped. "Anderley will be returning with water soon so that I can wash, and you'll embarrass him if he finds you here ogling me." The slight quirk at the corner of his mouth told me he wasn't as vexed as he seemed.

"Oh, your valet isn't so shy," I retorted, pushing away from the door to saunter forward. "Besides, don't you have a kiss for your wife?"

His pale blue eyes suddenly looked anything but icy as they leisurely slid over my frame, leaving licks of heat wherever they touched. "Not if you don't want that gown hopelessly rumpled."

I found myself wishing for a fan to cool my flushed cheeks.

"Stop looking at me like that," he ground out. "Or I'll do something that *will* embarrass Anderley."

I lowered my gaze but then couldn't resist baiting him by raising it again to murmur, "We could always lock the door."

When he moved a step toward me, I held up my hands before me, laughing. For we both knew we didn't have time for what we truly wished to do. Henry and Lord Edward would be arriving within a quarter of an hour.

"What detained you?" I asked, knowing this would divert him. "I expected you home hours ago."

"Sullivan," he practically growled.

I arched my eyebrows in query.

"He led us on a wild-goose chase. Knew what he was doing, too. Wasted nearly our entire afternoon."

I grimaced. "How infuriating." No wonder he'd been in such a foul mood. What I had to share was not going to make it better.

He scraped a hand back through his hair, making the muscles in his broad shoulders stand out in sharp relief and momentarily distracting me. "What of you? How was your day? Did you finish the preparations for Emma's birthday?"

"Yes."

"That's good." He began opening drawers in the clothespress and pulling out various items he needed.

"Bree also went with me for a stroll."

"It was a lovely day. I'm glad you weren't cooped up inside for all of it."

"And we ran into Bonnie Brock."

At this, he nearly slammed his fingers in a drawer as he turned to glower at me.

"I didn't know he was going to be in Queen Street Gardens waiting for me," I argued.

"Obviously we need tighter security measures," he muttered to himself as he crossed the room toward the bed, where some of his other clothing items were already laid out.

"He wanted to warn us that Anderley's presence at the White Horse has been noted." When he turned to look at me, I arched my eyebrows in emphasis. "By Winstanley's employees and others."

"What others?"

I gave him a withering look. "This is Bonnie Brock we're talking about. Do you honestly think he specified?"

"Of course not," he said with a sigh, but then nodded after only a few moments' consideration. "I'll order Anderley to steer clear."

I exhaled in relief, glad that I didn't have to convince him of Bonnie Brock's trustworthiness.

"What else did he have to say?" he asked as I was turning to leave.

"He thinks Mr. Fletcher should bear greater scrutiny. That he's masking something."

"I would have to say I agree."

"You do?"

He flashed me a self-deprecating smile. "Surprised? I suppose there's a first time for everything. Even agreeing with Kincaid."

Before I could reply, the sound of voices in the corridor alerted us to Anderley's return. Gage shooed me toward the connecting door with exaggerated motions that told me he was just as aware of how ridiculous the notion was that his valet would be shocked by my presence. Nevertheless, I complied, laughing as I went.

The laughter continued over dinner, as I'd known it must. Lord Edward Kerr was nothing if not a wag, forever jesting and making light of things that perhaps should not be made light of. But he did it with such charm, such insouciance, that he was able to get away with it. This, among other things, made him a popular dinner companion. Of course, his being a duke's son also helped, though it was all but openly acknowledged that, like Henry, the man who sired him was not actually the duke.

I knew that Henry was fond of Ned, as he called him. And

Ned was fond of and protective of Henry, who was seven years his junior. That was all that was needed to endear him to me, despite his sometimes devilish antics.

By the time we retired to the drawing room, my side actually ached from laughing so much. Since I was the only lady present, the men had declined to take their port in the dining room and had instead joined me with their postprandial drinks. I had also chosen to forgo tea in favor of a glass of sherry.

Henry passed this to me as he sat beside me on the walnut settee upholstered in daffodil silk. "Sebastian tells me there's a bit of a brangle over how you received an invitation to the auction. That you were right to be concerned."

"What's this?" Lord Edward demanded to know, sinking into one of the adjoining giltwood armchairs.

Gage briefly explained the situation as he poured himself a glass of whisky.

"How mysterious," Lord Edward exclaimed before taking a drink. His eyes widened as he appeared to savor the age. "Is this from Cromarty's distillery?"

Gage nodded, having taken his own sip.

"I shall have to beg a bottle or two from him," he proclaimed, downing another finger of the amber liquid. "But back to Kiera's problem."

"I don't know that it *is* a problem," I demurred. "But it's certainly a question I'd like answered."

"Did you have a chance today to look over the guest list to see if there's anyone you think might have forwarded their invitation to you?" Gage asked.

"I did. And I suppose there are a few names that are possibilities. I'll write to them and ask. But I don't really expect any of them to admit to it."

"Maybe it was just someone making mischief?" Henry suggested, endeavoring to ease my mind.

"If that's the case, then perhaps I should have you and your brother glance over the list. For the only one on it who I know enough about to consider them capable of such a thing is Sir James Riddell. Yet I hadn't made his acquaintance until the first day we attended the auction."

"Sir James Riddell, hmm?" Lord Edward ruminated. There was a tone to his voice that was less than complimentary.

"You know him?" I inquired.

"We've met," he replied somewhat obliquely, rolling his glass between his fingers and studying the way it caught the light. "But I would say it's more that I know *of* him."

"And what do you *know*?" Gage asked, catching on to his dramatics.

Lord Edward flashed a smile at him before abruptly sobering. "Word is his men were rather brutal when they cleared two clachans on his land."

Gage crossed one leg over the other knee, settling deeper into the matching giltwood armchair. "What's a clachan?"

"A small village of mostly tiny cottages owned by farmers or fishermen," Henry replied. "They're dotted all over the Highlands." He frowned. "Or they were."

"Many landowners have forced the inhabitants to leave so that they can use their land for grazing sheep and other livestock," I supplied. "Though some have been more kind and accommodating about it than others."

Lord Edward scoffed. "Well, 'kind and accommodating' is not how Sir James's tenants would describe him. When they wouldn't vacate quickly enough for his liking, allegedly, his men shot some of their dogs and goats and drove away their livestock. And when that wasn't enough, Sir James had their roofs removed. In the middle of winter, mind you." He leaned forward, his expression grim. "But the worst of it was when his men seized a simpleminded woman who refused to depart and locked her in her cottage. Bricked her in from the outside and wouldn't let her out—or let anyone bring her food—until she agreed to vacate."

"That's barbaric," I exclaimed, and I could tell Henry and Gage agreed. Their shock and disgust were evident.

Lord Edward sat back, brandishing his glass. "If anyone was the intended victim of that floor collapse, I'd put Sir James forward as a good candidate. That is, if any of his former tenants had a mind for revenge and found their way to Edinburgh."

It was worth considering.

"I have to wonder," Henry began after some rumination. "If Sir James is capable of such cruelty, are there others he's mistreated?"

"It's a rational question." Gage's gaze met mine, and I knew he was thinking of Jeffers and how I'd asked him to uncover what he could about Sir James. We'd yet to hear his report.

"One we definitely need to ask him," I said. And wasn't that going to be a pleasant conversation.

"Well, wear your dowdiest dress," Lord Edward advised after taking another drink of his whisky. "He has an eye for the ladies." He dipped his head to indicate my attire. "If you arrive in a gown with that neckline, you'll be addressing the top of his head."

I flushed at this remark, and Henry glowered quellingly at his brother. However, I realized Lord Edward meant well, even if he was a trifle too forthright, and I knew better than to be discomfited by his notice of my attributes, such as they were. Lord Edward was not interested in me—or any woman, for that matter. Gage seemed to be aware of this, too, for his displeasure was all directed at me, undoubtedly seeing this as confirmation that I'd misled him about Sir James's behavior at the Inverleith Ball. Particularly considering the decolletage of my ball gown that evening had been lower than the one I wore now.

"Marvelous color, by the way," Lord Edward added casually. "It brings out your eyes." Then his own dark gaze flashed with mischievous intent. "I quite see why some have called them 'witch bright.' It gives them an excuse for falling under your spell."

Henry groaned, tossing a pillow at him. "Terrible, Ned. Simply terrible."

I shook my head, but upon hearing Lord Edward's ringing laughter I couldn't withhold a smile.

"She's certainly bewitched me," Gage quipped, joining in.

Henry searched to the left and then right. "Where's another pillow?"

At this, we all broke into peals of laughter.

However, we weren't laughing the next morning when we sat down with Sir James Riddell at his Abercromby Place home. It was located just three blocks away, on the north side of Queen Street Gardens, so we'd elected to walk despite the slight drizzle in the air. Per Lord Edward's suggestion, I wore a rose-printed morning dress with a high neckline—one that went all the way up to my chin—and a scalloped pelerine that did much to hide the shape of my figure. Gage had taken one look at me when I appeared at the breakfast table and nearly choked on his bite of sausage.

"Taking Lord Edward seriously, are we?" he rasped after his coughing fit. "Or is there something else I should know about your desire to escape Riddell's presence at the Inverleith Ball?"

I'd been able to successfully divert him from asking this sort of question the previous evening after Henry and Lord Edward departed, but I should have known my garments would invite comment. Fortunately, with our staff bustling in and out, I was able to defer the query again with a simple, "No."

Though seated in Sir James's drawing room, with Gage eyeing the man with thinly disguised disfavor, I wondered if perhaps I should have told him something. At least then he wouldn't be picturing whatever it was he was imagining.

"Is your wife not in Edinburgh with you?" Gage inquired with a slight bite that Sir James didn't seem to notice. Or perhaps he simply didn't care.

He leaned back, crossing one knee over the other as he draped his arm along the back of the camelback sofa. "No, no. She's at our estate in Strontian. Prefers it there."

I was not acquainted with Lady Riddell, but I did know that Strontian lay in the far northwest of Argyllshire, near the Sea of the Hebrides. Having spent a winter at Philip's castle in the northern Highlands along the part of the sea called the Minch, I knew just how cold Strontian must be in winter and how frigid the winds must blow. As such, Lady Riddell was either a heartier soul than I'd imagined or the other compensations of living there—perhaps the absence of her husband—far outweighed the inconveniences of the climate.

"Now, how may I help you?" he asked, presenting himself as the ever-gracious host.

I turned to Gage, allowing him to do the talking despite his vexed demeanor, for the matter was delicate. The possibility of Sir James having been the intended target must be explored, but without revealing there was anything suspicious about the events at Picardy Place.

"It's come to our attention that someone may be here in Edinburgh intending to do you harm."

"Really?" Sir James's eyebrows arched, though he looked only mildly interested. Perhaps this was a common occurrence for him—people wishing him harm.

"Someone who wants revenge for the ruthlessness used when you had those clachans cleared from your land."

An annoyed pleat formed in his brow. "That was nearly five years ago. It seems rather silly to think they would be coming after me now. Not to mention highly unlikely any of them have made their way to Edinburgh."

His failure to even attempt to refute the claims of brutality and otherwise callous disregard for the matter and the people impacted seemed to affect Gage much the same way it did me. At first stunning us into silence and then igniting our tempers.

"You don't deny the charges, then?" Gage demanded.

"Of ruthlessness? Why would I? It was my land they were living on and doing very little of good with. It was more profitable being used by the sheep." He held up his hands as if to ward off our growing anger, but his tone of weary indifference did nothing to help. "I know some of my men got a trifle out of hand. That incident with the half-witted woman was unfortunate. But it was her own fault for refusing to leave when given ample warning."

It was no more than I'd heard from any number of Scottish landowners. Philip was forever bemoaning the brutal treatment some Scots had received at the hands of their fellow countrymen. Lairds who should have cared more for their people than lining their own pockets. Nevertheless, that didn't make Sir James's words any easier to endure.

"As I said, that was five years ago," he drawled. "So what does it have to do with now?" He arched an eyebrow quizzically. "Unless this is because of the floor collapse in Picardy Place. Like the roof collapses."

"The ones *your* men caused," Gage pointed out.

I pressed a hand to Gage's arm in warning, for there was a distinctive glint in Sir James's eye that suggested he saw more than we wished him to.

His full lips pursed as he scrutinized us both. "I thought the floor collapse was deemed an accident."

"It was," Gage replied. "We merely wished to warn you of the rumors and ask if there's anyone in particular you would be wary of."

"No," Sir James said, sounding unconvinced, though he didn't press us further.

Much as I wished there was something else we could question the man about to draw him out, Jeffers hadn't uncovered anything else distinctly untoward. Not unless you counted Sir James's penchant for taking lovers, but many gentlemen did so. As such, we had no choice but to excuse ourselves, lest we give away the game. Continuing this ruse was becoming a tremendous headache and a hindrance to our investigation.

Once back on the street, I could restrain myself no longer. "Deplorable! He expressed absolutely no remorse for his or his men's actions. Blaming those people for not wanting to leave their home. A home their family had probably lived in for generations."

Gage patted my hand where it rested against his arm. "I know, darling. I was no more impressed than you are." His mouth flattened into a grim line. "But even though I dislike the fellow. *Intensely.* That doesn't make him the intended target."

He turned his head to look at me as we waited at a corner for a carriage to pass by. "His arguments were valid. Five years is a long time to wait for revenge unless there's another impetus, and we haven't discovered one. And while it's not impossible that one of the people he ejected made his way to Edinburgh, it is unlikely."

With Gage's assistance, I leapt over the puddle left between the cobblestones and the pavement as we crossed the street. "Then I suppose we're back to Sullivan and Cranston."

I glanced toward the leafy bower of Queen Street Gardens across Heriot Row. "Unless it's me."

His pale blue eyes met mine.

"Unless I was the intended target."

He clutched my arm tighter, as if doing so would ward off the possibility.

We were quiet for some time. I suppose each of us was lost in our thoughts. Though I rather wished he would distract me from mine. I turned to peer down the next cross street and happened to see a pair of men carrying a stack of planks. The sight of the building materials jogged my memory.

"What of the research you wanted to do on building laws?" I asked, reminding him of what he'd said in the carriage on our way home from the Inverleith Ball. He'd seemed so keen on it being the key to solving the mystery. But that had been before he'd returned home to hear what Anderley had learned about Mr. Sullivan. I supposed that had diverted his interest.

"Perhaps you should ask Henry to look into it," I said. "He's rather good at those sorts of things."

"An excellent suggestion," Gage pronounced, gazing at me in approval. "I'll pay him a call this afternoon."

CHAPTER 20

"Trevor!" I exclaimed when he appeared in the door of the nursery, nearly oversetting Emma, who had pulled herself up on the rocking horse.

A glimpse at the window showed me that the sun was still streaming through the glass. "I didn't expect you for at least another two hours," I said, struggling to my feet. "You must have made good time."

Trevor enfolded me in his arms, and I smiled as his warmth and familiar scent mixed with that of his horse from the long day's ride engulfed me. "I couldn't sleep. So I set off a bit earlier than anticipated. Plus, for once, the roads weren't a complete stew."

He pulled back, and we examined each other. There was no mistaking our resemblance. Not when he boasted the same unique coloring we'd all inherited from our mother, though his chestnut hair was the lightest and his lapis-lazuli blue eyes the darkest. However, his skeletal structure came from our father. Now that he was grown, when I saw his broad shoulders and trim figure from behind, for a fleeting moment I always thought he was Father, and it was rather bittersweet to realize he was not.

Despite the difficulties he'd gotten himself into over the past few years, Trevor had always been a generally happy and healthy person, but standing before me now, he practically radiated with it. I knew that his hard work and shrewd estate management had allowed him to recoup his losses and nearly set to rights all his financial difficulties faster than anticipated. He'd even been able to make some sound initial investments in the new steam locomotives he was so keen on, being certain they would revolutionize Britain. He'd also managed to convince Gage and Philip to join him. While these were all achievements that he should be proud of—indeed, *I* was proud of him—I could tell there was something more behind his radiant smile.

He touched the fading bruise on my cheek. "Looks like you were telling the truth when you said you survived your tumble with just a few bumps and scrapes."

Calling it a tumble was quite an understatement, but I appreciated his trying to make light of the matter.

"Would I lie to you?" I countered.

His eyebrows arched in gentle scolding. "To keep me from worrying? Yes." He lowered his gaze to a spot behind me. "But where is this niece of mine who is growing up much too quickly?" Dropping to his haunches so that he was more at Emma's level, he grinned. "Soon enough you'll be attending balls and giving your father gray hair."

Emma watched him with wide eyes, an uncertain smile hovering at the corner of her lips.

"Don't remind me or you'll give me a fit of the vapors," I said as I sank onto my knees beside her, offering her my hand.

Taking it, she moved one shaky step toward me before launching herself at my chest. I brushed her golden curls back from her forehead as she tilted her head to peer shyly at her uncle.

"You've never had a fit of vapors in your life," Trevor argued.

"Yes, well, if anyone was to give me one, I imagine it would be my child."

He chuckled. "And where did this handsome steed come from?" He clapped his hand onto the seat of the rocking horse, apparently having noticed the large bow tied around its neck.

"Her grandfather." It had been waiting in the entry hall for us earlier when we'd returned from Abercromby Place.

"I see. Your first pony." He leaned forward to croon to Emma. "Lord Gage has excellent taste in horseflesh."

She cooed back, making both of us chuckle.

"I see you agree. And I hear you've got him wrapped around your little finger." He darted a twinkling look up at me. "Your father is reputed to be the charming one, but I think your mother has her own type of magic to bring such a wily ogre around to her side."

I shook my head at his nonsense. "Tell me all the news from Blakelaw House. Did Crabtree's catarrh ever clear up?" Our longtime butler had been struggling with an excess of mucus over the winter.

We sat contentedly on the nursery floor as Trevor informed me of the state of affairs at his estate and the comings and goings in the village of Elwick. Meanwhile, Emma snuggled into my shoulder and drifted off to sleep. My brother was the first to notice it, falling silent as he nodded toward his niece with an adoring smile. With his help, I managed to climb to my feet without tripping over my skirts and laid her in her cradle.

"A new tenant has leased Twizel Hall with an eye to purchase," he stated as I softly closed the door to the nursery.

I threaded my arm through his as we began to descend the stairs, attuned enough to my brother's tone of voice to recognize this was important, and not just because the estate in the neighboring village had sat dormant for some years. Not a decade earlier, the large Gothic Revival manor had hosted lavish country house parties that were the talk of the parish and much farther afield. But since its owner's death, it had sat empty except for a steward and a few seasonal laborers.

"Jeremiah Birnam. It's doubtful, but you may have heard of him. He owns a number of highly profitable mills. Made a fortune from them. And now he's heavily investing in steam locomotives."

"Along with acquiring an estate."

Though I'd spoken in a neutral tone, there was a question in Trevor's eyes when he looked down at me. "Yes."

It was a common tale. Wealth was no longer restricted to those of land and privilege. The new industrialists were acquiring fortunes at a staggering pace and eager to purchase the trappings of an aristocratic life.

"His interest in locomotives must give you something to talk about."

"Yes." His reply was again hesitant.

Suspecting I knew where this was headed, I waited to say anything more until we reached the drawing room. Jeffers stood just outside the door, and I instructed him to bring tea. "And tell Mrs. Mackay that Emma is napping."

He bowed his head before departing.

I gestured for Trevor to sit in one of the giltwood armchairs while I settled comfortably on the sofa, arranging my skirts. "And does Mr. Birnam have a family?"

I looked up to find him watching me with fond exasperation, having realized I'd guessed his secret. "Yes."

"A daughter?"

"Yes."

I bit back a smile. "I imagine she's quite lovely."

"Give it up, Kiera," he demanded. "Who told you?"

"No one."

He narrowed his eyes playfully.

"Truly," I said with a laugh. "I simply know you too well."

He sank back with a resigned grunt, as if to say, *We'll see.*

"What's her name?"

"Matilda." The way he said her name and the tenderness in his eyes told me this was not a passing fancy.

"And does Miss Birnam return your regard?"

A light flush crested his cheeks. "I think so. No. I *know* so," he revised before rattling off an extensive list of her attributes. He was clearly smitten.

I knew I must be grinning like an idiot, but I just couldn't withhold my joy for him. "And her father? Is he amenable?"

Some of Trevor's eagerness faded. "I have no title, and he knows my wealth and estate are small."

"But surely those aren't his only considerations," I protested, knowing full well that in the marriages among our class they were, and that a man with enough wealth—self-made or not—might be eager for the same.

"Fortunately, no. He wants his daughter to be happy." His voice turned wry. "And fortunately, I do have two influential brothers-in-law with powerful connections."

I frowned. "You are an excellent catch on your own. Any woman would be lucky to have you."

"Thank you, Kiera. Though I do believe you're a trifle biased." He sighed, tipping his head back to look up at the ornamental ceiling. "I can't blame Birnam for wanting to secure the best future for his daughter. And frankly, if emphasizing my connections convinces him to accept my suit, then I will use whatever tools I have at my disposal."

"Then you *have* asked?"

"Not yet . . ."

He broke off as Jeffers entered, setting the tea tray on the table.

"Why not yet?" I prodded as the butler left, picking up the teapot to pour for my brother.

"I wanted to be sure. And . . . I suppose I wanted your opinion."

I paused to look up at him in confusion. "But I haven't met her." I straightened, setting the teapot down. "Or is she coming to Edinburgh?"

Trevor smiled. "I suppose what I wanted your opinion about was her father." He held up a hand. "And before you say it, I know you haven't met him either. But what is your opinion of the fact that, well . . . he's in trade?"

"But you're not marrying Miss Birnam's father?"

His expression turned long-suffering, and I realized I was being rather thickheaded. "Right. Of course. You might not be marrying Mr. Birnam, but he will still be an important part of your life."

"Hasn't Lord Gage affected your marriage?"

I huffed a laugh as I nodded. "Both for the good and the bad. Which was nothing less than I expected." I tilted my head. "Actually, I expected more bad. Mercifully, I was wrong." I spoke earnestly. "But whatever the possibility, I still would have married Sebastian. Ten times over."

Trevor's gaze was soft with memories. No doubt recalling how I'd turned down Gage's first proposal and how he'd been the one to convince me that a life with Gage was far preferable to a life without him.

"Only you know how you feel about Miss Birnam. But if it's the same as what I feel for Sebastian. The same as what Alana feels for Philip. If you believe she's worthy of your regard." I lifted my hands. "Then I don't think you need to hear anything from me. Though I can't wait to meet her."

I knew my brother. I knew his heart. He had grown tremendously in the past few years in wisdom and fortitude. But his heart had always been kind and true. I trusted him if he said he'd met the woman who was right for him.

But his voice was still tinged with uncertainty. "And the fact that her father is in trade? That doesn't bother you?"

I shook my head at the absurdity. "Trevor. My first husband was a surgeon. Yes, he'd been made a baronet by the king. But he certainly wasn't a gentleman born." I paused. "Though I hope Mr. Birnam doesn't hold my past against you."

"Not since you're now the daughter-in-law of one of the king's most trusted advisers."

"Oh, well, that's good." My brow furrowed. "I suppose." I reached for the creamer, adding a splash to his tea before I passed the cup to him. "Does it bother *you* that Mr. Birnam is in trade?"

"No. Not really."

"Then why . . . ?" I inhaled, grasping the genuine source of his concern. "Alana."

He grimaced as he lowered his teacup after taking a drink. "She is far more particular about such things."

And as a countess, our older sister did have a far higher rank than either of us, making the differences between her and a tradesman potentially far greater.

I inhaled the fragrant blend of the tea deeply as I poured my own cup. "I suppose all you can do is talk to her. Explain the situation to her as you have me. All Alana truly wants is your happiness." I offered him a smile. "And know that whatever the outcome, you have my support."

"Thank you, Kiera."

As I stirred cream and sugar into my cup, I did spare a

moment to wonder if Trevor might be moving too hastily. After all, he'd not mentioned Miss Birnam at Hogmanay four months ago. How long had they been acquainted? How much time had he actually spent with her? For the sake of caution, I felt I should offer one more piece of advice.

"You might also have a word with Philip and Sebastian. As you pointed out, they have powerful—and useful—connections. They might know things about Mr. Birnam that you don't. Things that could ease your mind."

Or trouble it. We would confront that if it became necessary.

"I will," he agreed, taking one last sip of his tea before setting it aside and rubbing his hands together gleefully. "Now, tell me what treats I may anticipate for Emma's celebratory tea. Is Mrs. Grady making some of her lemon cakes?"

Our stroll to church the following morning was heralded by bright sunshine and warmer temperatures. So glorious was it that I couldn't begrudge Trevor and Gage for their desire to go riding after luncheon. I even considered joining them, except that Emma had required my attention and if they'd delayed their departure for me, then we would all be in a rush upon our return to bathe and change for dinner at Cromarty House. As such, I waved them on, and once I'd settled Emma, I sat down again with the list of people invited to the auction, hoping inspiration might strike.

And it did, in a fashion.

I was scouring the third page, trying to recall if I'd ever been introduced to anyone called Marjoribanks or if the names had simply all begun to run together in my mind, when Jeffers cleared his throat lightly, drawing my attention. So consumed was I with my task that I'd not even heard him enter.

"My lady, there is a Mr. Rimmer requesting to speak with

you. He informed me he'd forgotten his calling cards." This was evidently a major strike against the man in the butler's book, for his mouth pursed in disapproval. "He seems rather... agitated."

I pondered what that might mean. Whether he was concerned about my reaction to Mr. Fletcher accusing him of sending me the catalog. Perhaps he'd feared that his counterpart's continued remarks on the matter had reached my ears. Or maybe he'd uncovered something of pertinence. A connection between me and a collector that I'd missed. After all, Gage had asked him to check the invitation list as well.

"Shall I send him away?" Jeffers queried when I sat immobile for too long.

"No, send him up. But... linger nearby."

As Jeffers had alluded to, Mr. Rimmer was definitely troubled. His complexion was pale, his movements tense, and he barely seemed able to sit in the chair I'd indicated, instead perching anxiously on the edge. "I see you're looking at the list," he said in response to my asking if there was something I could help him with.

"Yes," I said with a sigh. "But I'm afraid I haven't had any luck figuring out who sent me the catalog and invitation." When he didn't respond, I prompted him. "What of you?"

"It was me!" The words burst from his mouth before I'd finished speaking. He closed his eyes, as if afraid of my reaction. "I'm terribly sorry I lied, but I simply couldn't admit it in front of Mr. Winstanley. Not when Fletcher was portraying it in the most dreadful light."

He opened his eyes warily, and when I didn't speak, hastened to explain further. "I *am* an admirer of your portraits, but I am *not* obsessed." His face hardened. "Or whatever vile word Fletcher is trying to tarnish me with." He leaned forward, extending his hands in pleading. "I just wanted to meet you. And I knew that you would appreciate some of the pictures in Lord Eldin's collection. So I figured there would be no harm in sending you the catalog to be sure you were aware of the auction." He shook his head. "I had no idea that the floor would collapse. That someone would *sabotage* it. Believe me, had I known, I would never have sent you the invite." His chest heaved with each breath as his words ran out. Or almost. "Please. You must believe me."

"I do," I admitted. His response was too real to be feigned, and I'd never sensed any malice from him during our previous interactions.

His shoulders dipped and his head bowed low in relief, his dark curls concealing his face. "Thank you."

"But why did you want to meet me?" I asked, probing carefully for holes in his story. Just because I believed him didn't mean I wasn't leery of his interest in me.

He straightened in surprise. "Because you're brilliant. Your portraits . . . they're so evocative, transcendent even." He gestured with his hands as he spoke each adjective. "It's like you can *see* into the heart of a person and somehow reflect what you find there in their eyes and their faces, in their bodies."

I blushed upon hearing his praise, warmth filling my chest. For I was not immune to the effects of flattery, particularly when it seemed so genuinely given.

"And . . ." He shrunk into himself again sheepishly. "I heard about the exhibition you're preparing. *The Faces of the Forgotten*." He spoke the title as if it was decided and not something I was still wrestling with.

Which only made me wonder how on earth he'd learned it in the first place. I'd spoken of the title to only a select number of people. Though I supposed it was possible one of them had mentioned it to someone else and then it had spread from there. Such gossip was practically endemic among society.

And it was certainly no secret I was working on a private exhibition. That juicy bit of tittle-tattle had begun spreading the moment I mentioned it to a countess whose portrait commission I'd refused.

"I hoped I might have a chance to convince you to allow me to arrange it," Mr. Rimmer continued. "Either on behalf of Mr. Winstanley or . . . or myself."

I understood his self-consciousness now. He was young but ambitious. Mr. Winstanley's other employees might be content to work under him and his sons for the rest of their lives, but Mr. Rimmer had grander plans. Perhaps that was why Mr. Fletcher disliked him and was so eager to take him down a peg. To spoil his aspirations.

However, those current aspirations seemed somewhat flawed to me. Or misrepresented.

"But you haven't even seen the paintings?" I objected.

"I don't need to," he startled me by interjecting. His gaze was direct. "I know what you're capable of, my lady. And since these paintings are of your own impetus, not simply to appease some vain aristocrat . . ." He flashed a coy smile. "I know they must be striking."

I wanted to believe him, to believe Gage, but Mr. Cranston's words continued to reel in the back of my head. "It likely won't prove profitable," I cautioned him. "The exhibit is more of a social statement. One that is bound to be controversial among some."

He stared back at me as if I'd suddenly sprouted a second head. "But that's precisely why it *will* be profitable. Society absolutely cannot resist a furor." He leaned forward as if sharing a secret. "Or wanting to own a piece of it."

Then Mr. Cranston was wrong? His cruel words were just a taunt? Or was Mr. Rimmer the one misleading me? I pressed my fingers to my temple, wishing I knew my own mind.

"You won't tell Mr. Winstanley what I've done, will you?" Mr. Rimmer asked, growing fretful again. He obviously feared losing his position. Something that was bound to happen if the auctioneer learned he'd lied.

"No," I said, not wanting him to be penalized. If Mr. Fletcher hadn't used such provocative terms, I believed he would have been more truthful, so the other assistant was as much to blame. "But thank you for telling me. As for the other . . . I'll think about it." That was all I could promise.

But Mr. Rimmer still grinned as if I'd handed him the moon and the stars.

CHAPTER 21

"Then you're at a standstill," Philip pronounced, settling deeper into the green brocade wingback chair in which he lounged, his hands clasped across his abdomen. The hour growing late, his Scottish brogue, which had been educated out of him—as all good noblemen learned to speak the King's English—had crept into his deep voice around the edges. I suspected the second glass of whisky now sitting empty on the table at his elbow had also contributed.

Much as it had contributed to *all* our contentment as we lounged in the lavish drawing room of Cromarty House on Charlotte Square. Though full stomachs and the conviviality of family also had a great deal to do with it.

As expected, dinner had been both delicious and boisterous, as the children had been allowed to join us. Even Emma, who was learning to feed herself. She'd managed to get about half of the food we'd given her into her mouth versus her lap. Her cousins had found her messy eating to be quite entertaining. Though wee Jamie, who was just a year older, hardly did better.

After the meal had come a lively round of hobbyhorse. Alana and I couldn't decide whose antics were more high-spirited—the children's or the gentlemen's. They certainly egged each other on. Philipa, who was *almost* eight; Greer, who was *almost* four; and Jamie, who was *almost* two—or so they reminded us—had chosen Gage, Philip, and Trevor as their mounts respectively, and they were all determined not to lose. Or if they did, to do so in spectacularly hilarious fashion. Emma, meanwhile, jogged along at a more decorous pace on my or Alana's lap, alternately clapping and laughing, or staring wide-eyed at the others' uproarious behavior. The only person missing from our fun was my ten-year-old nephew, Malcolm, who was still away at school.

When the races had finished, Philip and Alana's children were hustled off to bed, while the men—thoroughly fatigued from their efforts—sought refreshment from the decanters on the sideboard. I had taken Emma into the adjoining parlor to tend to her, and once she'd fallen asleep, I'd laid her in a nest of blankets and pillows on the settee. Leaving the door cracked so that we could hear her if she woke, I'd rejoined the others in the drawing room.

Gage had saved me a place beside him on the spring green fainting couch, and I nestled close to his side, stealing a sip of his whisky. Our discussion seemed to naturally turn to the floor collapse at the auction and then our investigation. Sergeant Maclean had wanted us to keep quiet about the sabotage, and he hadn't given us permission to share the matter with my family, but Gage and I knew that they could be trusted. Just as we knew that sometimes fresh eyes could provide a fresh perspective.

It hadn't taken long to review what we had uncovered so far

and the various potential suspects, most of whom we'd already ruled out. This had led to Philip's emphatic observation, which summarized our current circumstances. We were at a standstill.

"Though I must say that I'm relieved to hear you weren't lured there under false pretenses," Alana stated, eyeing me almost in scolding. "Or at least, not false pretenses which would make you the . . . the target."

My sister had reconciled with my desire to continue assisting Gage with his inquiries, even though they sometimes put us in danger, but I didn't think she would ever truly approve. As such, I'd known what her reaction would be to the discovery of my being left off the invitation list. Still, I'd hoped my revelation that Mr. Rimmer had been the one to send me the catalog would mitigate her disapproval. Gage had been glad of it, albeit a bit less forgiving of his deception.

"Even so, it seems to me a dubious ploy," Trevor declared, leaning back in his matching wing chair and stretching his legs out to prop his feet on the edge of the tea table. This earned him a scowl from Alana.

"Yes," Philip agreed. "If anyone wished ill of Kiera, or Mr. Smith, or Sir James Riddell, or any of the hundreds of other individuals who were expected to attend the auction, tampering with a joist in the hopes that it would collapse at the exact right moment and kill the exact right person frankly sounds ridiculous."

"That's what we've been struggling with," Gage admitted, smoothing his hand up and down my arm. "It *does* seem ridiculous. Which is why we've turned to other potential motives, like a rival auctioneer intent on ruining Winstanley."

"And I understand you have some corroborating evidence which might bear that out, but once again, it seems a trifle ridiculous to imagine this Mr. Cranston would embark on such an overly complicated plot in order to hurt his rival's business," Philip ruminated. "If he had a man working for Winstanley, as you propose he did, couldn't he have simply had him disrupt matters in far easier and more guaranteed ways."

"Like tampering with paperwork or delaying shipments? Those sorts of things?" I asked.

My brother-in-law pointed at me. "Precisely. It seems a large leap to go straight to causing a floor to collapse when enough of those small, nearly innocuous acts of sabotage could do the trick without the potential for loss of life and criminal consequences if he was caught."

"He has a point," I told Gage, grateful that Philip had put into words what had been bothering me about his focus on Sullivan and Cranston, though I'd known Gage wasn't going to like hearing it.

He was scowling, but in frustration rather than anger. "Then what *is* a motive that makes sense?"

"You mentioned the possibility of it being an act of revenge against Lord Eldin's memory," Alana reminded him.

Trevor shook his head, his brown hair flopping over his forehead. "Yes, but the logic behind that isn't much better. Not unless the attack against his memory, his reputation is clear. And it's not."

I could sense my husband growing restless. He was deeply invested in this inquiry for a number of reasons. It was the first inquiry Sergeant Maclean had trusted him with since the awkwardness that had arisen the previous spring. It was the first inquiry of any magnitude or depth that he'd been tasked with since our time in Cornwall five months prior. And since we'd both been victims of the floor collapse, he also had a personal connection to it. Because of those reasons and perhaps more, he wanted fervently to solve this. But I feared that his eagerness to do so was blinding him to things he normally wouldn't miss and making him hold on to things he shouldn't.

I tugged gently on his expertly tied cravat. "What of your supposition that it has to do with the building laws? You overheard those men at the Inverleith Ball who seemed to think they'd been changed after the incident at Kirkcaldy, and you wondered if Lord Eldin, acting as a Lord of Session, might have been involved."

"That Eldin somehow delayed or prevented or overall hindered that from happening—at least in the eyes of the culprit—and so the saboteur sought to make a rather emphatic point about the law's faultiness." Philip's dark eyebrows arched. "Yes, I could see that. At least the severity would befit the act. Dozens of people lost their lives at Kirkcaldy."

"Did you speak to Henry about researching those laws?" I pressed Gage.

He tossed back the remainder of his whisky, grimacing as it burned its way down his throat. "I did. Though Henry warned me it might take some time to discover if Lord Eldin was involved, and then even more time to find a connection to the men who might have gained access to the town house." Which left Gage with nothing to do, unless he dug through records with his brother. But tedious paperwork had never been his forte.

"Do any of you happen to remember any legal proceedings related to it?" I asked Philip, Alana, and Trevor. "It would have occurred sometime in the summer or autumn of 1828."

Philip tilted his head in thought, the silver which had begun to show at his temples catching the light. "We stayed in London late that summer, if I recall. Parliamentary business. And then . . ." He broke off and I wondered why.

Until I remembered.

"And then Father died," Alana said.

A stunted silence fell over the room.

I closed my eyes, ashamed and embarrassed that I'd forgotten. "Yes, of course."

Gage's arm tightened around me, offering comfort. For he knew that in 1828 I'd still been married to Sir Anthony, and every moment of my life had been consumed with simply surviving. That my first husband had not even let me return home when my father died was merely another indication of his determination to keep me firmly under his thumb in all things.

"I don't think any of us were paying much attention to any legal matters pertaining to local building that year," Trevor said.

His eyes were kind when I opened mine to look at him, as were Alana's. But I still felt abashed that I could have forgotten the importance of that year as our last parent slipped away. Even as awful and sometimes terrifying as my life with Sir Anthony had been, even with the near constant state of vigilance I'd had to maintain, lest I be caught unawares, making the punishment that befell me all the worse for my not being prepared for it. That all these years later it still diverted my attention from the place it properly should have been—remembering the passing of my father—unsettled me.

But it also made me wonder.

I frowned at the pattern of the Aubusson rug, trying to grapple with the inkling I'd suddenly had and drag it to the surface. To turn it over and examine it and make it coherent.

"What if the floor collapse wasn't the objective?" I murmured, still uncertain of exactly what I was trying to say but hoping it would become clearer. "What if it was the diversion?"

I looked up to find the others staring at me with varying degrees of puzzlement.

Trevor lowered his feet, sitting more upright. "You mean, what if their real aim wasn't to cause injury by damaging that joist?"

I nodded slowly. "Maybe they didn't even intend to cause an actual collapse. Maybe they purely wanted to compromise the structure enough that it would tremble or groan or what have you. Enough to cause the building to be evacuated." Maybe they'd thought it would be safer than starting a fire or any of the other methods they might have chosen.

"In order to do what?" Gage replied.

"I don't know," I admitted, tapping my chin. I suggested the first thing that came to mind. "Perhaps to take something."

"But Winstanley's employees checked the collection's inventory, and so did you."

"Yes, but much of it was packed up, making it difficult for me to say for certain," I argued.

"Even so, nothing has been reported missing."

"What of the rest of the house?" Alana had propped her elbow on the back of the sofa, cradling her head in her hand. "Did they check to be sure nothing had been taken that wasn't part of the auction?"

"Or what of the guests?" Trevor proposed. "Maybe something was stolen from one or more of them. They might not have even noticed it in the tumult."

I turned to meet Gage's gaze, having to admit that either was a possibility.

"Then perhaps theft *is* your answer." Philip drummed his fingers together where they rested in his lap. "A successful diversion, indeed."

"But that also means they've had more than a week to cover their tracks." Gage heaved an exasperated sigh. "We'll have to pay another visit to Picardy Place tomorrow."

But I wondered if Mr. Winstanley or his staff had paid enough attention to the other contents of Lord Eldin's town house to recognize if something was missing. Perhaps Mr. Clerk was more familiar with his brother's possessions—particularly the items in the study he'd insisted remain locked—but even that seemed doubtful. Though presumably, if an item *had* been taken, it must be valuable. Or else why go to so much trouble to steal it?

That was the question, indeed.

The following day when we returned to Picardy Place, it turned out we weren't the only ones with questions. We caught sight of Sergeant Maclean striding down the pavement from the opposite direction.

Having reached the door seconds before us, he waited to enter. "Winstanley summoned ye, too?" he asked.

Gage and I exchanged a bewildered look.

"No," Gage replied. "Mrs. Gage had a possible epiphany. But before we tell you, why did Mr. Winstanley summon you?"

Maclean held the door open for us. "He didna say except that it was urgent."

Stepping inside, we were immediately assailed by the sound of raised voices. The auctioneer was clearly furious and venting that fury on at least one of his employees. And one of those employees was yelling back.

Gage pressed his hand to mine where it rested on his arm, perhaps wondering, as I did, if Mr. Winstanley had learned Mr. Rimmer had lied to him about sending me the auction catalog.

Hurrying across the entry hall, we were momentarily forestalled by the appearance of two men carrying a large canvas between them. They were transferring it from the morning room to the dining room, all the while casting skittish glances toward the stairs from which the shouting was coming. Catching sight of us, they stumbled to a stop, but Maclean shooed them on. Once they'd passed, we could see the constable guarding the entry off the corridor to the collapsed study. The corners of his eyes were creased in consternation, but he merely shook his head to our questioning looks.

"You should have checked everything yourselves," Winstanley was shouting. "That's what I pay you for."

"There wasna time!" a voice yelled back. "*You* were the one who insisted we hurry. That the collection be preserved lest the entire benighted floor collapse."

I deduced it must be Mr. Fletcher arguing with the auctioneer, not Mr. Rimmer. Though his accent sounded slightly different. Indeed, when we rounded the landing in the middle of the stairs, we could see the older assistant nearly standing nose to nose with his employer while Mr. Rimmer hung back.

"There was a great deal of uncertainty as to how stable the house was," Mr. Rimmer offered more tentatively. "It made sense to secure the items first and then check them more thoroughly later."

"But I asked *you* to inspect and secure them," Winstanley retorted, his face red and his spectacles nearly sliding from his nose. "Then leave the carrying and lifting to the lumpers."

This was rather a derogatory way to speak of his other employees, particularly within their hearing, showing just how riled he was. Though the answer as to why he was so riled still wasn't clear.

Mr. Rimmer caught sight of us first, his eyes widening even as Mr. Fletcher snapped back. "There *was* no time for inspection. And *I* was injured."

Mr. Winstanley whirled to face us, taking in my and Gage's presence before focusing on Maclean. "Finally! It took you long enough to get here."

The sergeant's only reaction to this unjustified criticism was his dry response. "Ye said 'twas urgent."

Mr. Fletcher's lips quirked, clearly appreciating this bit of wit, though the hard glint in his eyes never faded. I remembered how Bonnie Brock had warned me that he was the one to watch.

The auctioneer sniffed. "You need to arrest Mr. Sullivan."

"I see," Maclean replied calmly, resting his meaty hands on the belt to which his baton was strapped. "And why should I do that?"

"Because he's stolen something. Or rather, several somethings." He seemed reluctant to share this, and I had an unsettling feeling why.

My eyes met Gage's in silent apprehension.

Unaware of our suspicions, Maclean was growing impatient. "And what are these *somethings*?"

Mr. Winstanley's already thin lips nearly disappeared as he struggled to make the revelation. "Several rare coins."

CHAPTER 22

A moment of silence followed this pronouncement, such was our surprise. In my case, it was startlement that I'd been correct about the floor collapse possibly being a diversion. In Sergeant Maclean's, it was incredulity followed by anger.

"You said you'd taken inventory and nothin' was missin'," he charged.

"We did," Mr. Winstanley snapped. "But after I learned that Mr. Sullivan's cousin works for Brade Cranston and that he'd been seen consulting with the knave, I ordered them to check the collection again. That's when I discovered that my assistants . . ." he turned his head to scowl at the men ". . . had not done quite the thorough job I'd believed."

Mr. Rimmer appeared somewhat abashed, though from the glint in his eye I suspected it was more from mortification at being reprimanded in front of others. Mr. Fletcher, on the other hand, was still openly defiant, his nostrils flaring in resentment, though he didn't speak.

"Apparently, Sullivan helped check the coins and other miscellaneous articles of virtu in the back parlor," Mr. Winstanley continued in a sharp voice. "And while the appropriate number of items were accounted for, their *quality* was not inspected."

"Meaning?" Gage prodded. I could tell he was growing irritated at the auctioneer's failure to state things plainly.

He stiffened, his chin lifting as if someone was holding a knife to his throat. "Some of Lord Eldin's most valuable coins were replaced with counterfeits."

My husband and Maclean both turned to me, I supposed expecting me to take the reins of the questioning. While it was true I had some experience in uncovering art forgeries, those were of paintings, not coins. I knew next to nothing about that.

"You're confident they weren't counterfeit before?" I queried. "When you initially put the collection on display."

Mr. Winstanley recoiled. "Absolutely not." Despite his taking offense, I knew enough of his firm's workings and his personnel to suspect *he* couldn't actually state this fact with any certainty. Not when it had been one of his assistants who possessed the expertise to evaluate them.

As such, I turned to Mr. Rimmer and Mr. Fletcher to hear their answers, risking insulting the auctioneer further. A flash of dark amusement lit Mr. Fletcher's eyes as he turned to his colleague, Mr. Rimmer, who appeared momentarily nonplussed.

"I . . ." His gaze flicked toward his employer nervously. "I'm quite confident they were authentic when I placed them in the case. Since they were among the rarest and most valuable, I took considerable time assessing them."

I nodded, trusting *this* answer. "Where were they displayed?"

Mr. Rimmer led us into the back parlor which adjoined the room where the auction had taken place. The display cases were still arranged about the room, but one near the wall opposite the rear drawing room now had a smaller wooden glass-fronted case sitting on top of it. It was toward this that he pointed.

"Here. This smaller case—or rather one very much like it—contained the four coins in question, and it was placed inside this larger locked case."

I recalled seeing it on the second day of the auction before Mr. Innes distracted me.

"Then the thief somehow got into the locked cabinet, extracted the entire smaller case, and replaced it with a similar case containing the counterfeits?" I summarized, gazing down at the imitations nestled in silky fabric. To my untrained eye, they appeared legitimate, but I knew that meant nothing. The average person had no hope of identifying even a mediocrely forged painting, while I could often detect them within seconds.

"That's what we suspect," Mr. Rimmer replied.

"It wouldn't be hard," Gage ruminated. "This smaller case would fit under a coat or within the folds of a skirt if carried carefully."

"Which is also how they probably smuggled the counterfeit coins and case *into* the auction," I said.

"Sullivan must have swapped them during the chaos of the floor collapse," Mr. Winstanley stated with utmost conviction. "When no one's attention was on the coins, but rather the calamity unfolding."

It was no less than I'd surmised the evening before when I'd speculated the floor collapse might have been a diversion, drawing everyone's attention away from the real target. But there was a problem with this theory given the new information that had come to light.

"Perhaps," I conceded. "But Mr. Sullivan worked here. He might have accessed the case at any time. Why would he go to the trouble of breaking into the house to damage the joist to cause the floor to collapse just so he had a diversion to steal the coins?" I shook my head. "It's unnecessarily convoluted and fraught with complications."

"Yes, but if it had happened at any other time, I would have known it was one of my employees," Mr. Winstanley retorted.

"*If* it was noticed." I glanced at Mr. Rimmer. "After all, I doubt you had your employees inspect the inventory every day. Not once it was situated inside the locked cases. And you must have had other people entering the house from time to time. Mr. Clerk. The footmen he hired. Various tradesmen."

Mr. Winstanley sneered, acknowledging this point.

"Even if it did happen as you said, during the floor collapse, any number of other people might have taken advantage of the situation. A bidder, a guest, someone who simply walked in off the street. After all, I don't recall anyone checking invitations or barring people entrance. The auction was open to all." I also recalled how Maclean had told us that a carpenter strolling by had heard the screams from inside when the floor collapsed and had walked in without anyone taking notice, offering his assistance to break down the doors. Of course, the likelihood of a random thief from off the street choosing that moment to nab something was even slimmer than Sullivan's potential guilt.

"How did they access the locked case?" Gage asked. "Obviously it wasn't broken."

Or someone would have noticed sooner.

"They must have picked it," Mr. Fletcher remarked, speaking up for the first time since we'd interrupted his shouting match with Mr. Winstanley. "Either that or they had a key," he added with a sly glance toward his employer, stirring the pot.

"If they picked it, then they were a dab hand at it," Maclean remarked gruffly. "No' just anyone would be able tae open it quickly. 'Specially wi' such an uproar aroond 'em, and the potential o' bein' caught at any moment." His gaze lifted to meet mine, and I could tell we were both thinking of the specialized criminals in Bonnie Brock's employ—chief among them being lockpicks. Though they couldn't all work for him. There must be a fair number within the city who did not.

"I don't think picking the lock was even necessary." Gage had leaned down to examine the mechanism and the wood surrounding it and now straightened. "I've seen these cabinets before. They're fairly popular." He turned to look at Maclean and then Mr. Winstanley. "And if you have a key to one of them, they can often open others."

Mr. Winstanley stiffened.

"You mean the keys aren't tailored specifically to each case?" I asked for clarification.

Gage's countenance was grim. "Not like they should be."

"Then anyone wi' a key tae a similar cabinet might o' gained access," Maclean grumbled.

"In theory."

"Well, I didn't know that," the auctioneer growled. "I use similar cases in Liverpool, and the man who lent these to me said they were the most secure of their kind."

"Obviously he lied," Mr. Fletcher interjected unhelpfully, earning him a ferocious scowl from his employer. That is until he added, "Maybe he should be the one held accountable for the theft."

Then Mr. Winstanley's sour expression transformed to one of speculation. "Excellent point."

Mr. Rimmer observed all of this with a frown.

"Has anything else been found to be missing or . . . replaced?" I asked him, hoping to direct them back to matters more pertinent to our investigation.

"No." His dark gaze flickered toward Mr. Winstanley. "But we still have some inventory to examine."

Gage had moved along the cases, scrutinizing the contents of the adjoining ones. "What were the coins that were taken?"

Mr. Rimmer named a silver Roman coin and three Greek ones—one of Athens, another of Massenae, and a third.

"Will you write that down for me, along with a description of each. And make a copy for Sergeant Maclean," Gage added, peering over his shoulder at the policeman.

As Mr. Rimmer hurried off to do this, Maclean insisted on calling together Mr. Winstanley's other employees and questioning them on the matter. Most of them swore they knew nothing about it, and little enough about Mr. Sullivan, who was a relatively recent hire. However, Mr. King—the older clerk who had worked faithfully for the auctioneer for thirty-three years—insisted that Mr. Sullivan was at his side, helping to guide to safety those bidders still standing on the portion of the floor that had not collapsed in the rear drawing room.

"Then ye're prepared to testify that at no point followin' the collapse was Mr. Sullivan no' wi'in yer sight?" Maclean pressed.

"Well, not in the immediate aftermath," Mr. King said. "There was too much debris." It still coated every surface in a fine layer despite dusters having obviously been swiped across the room's contents and a broom taken to the floor—probably several times in the past few days. "But it was no more than a minute or two before I reached him standing in that doorway." He pointed toward the opposite wall.

"Leaving this room all but unattended," Mr. Winstanley griped.

Mr. King frowned. "Yes, I suppose. But at the time, it was more important to see to the guests. He ushered most of them farther into this room, urging calm and patience until it was safe for them to descend the staircase."

If this was true—and I had no reason to doubt Mr. King—then Mr. Sullivan had behaved admirably. For he'd helped prevent the panic which had proved so calamitous at Kirkcaldy when those frantic to escape had trampled some and suffocated others in the crush.

"Wouldn't you have had to pass through this door yourself to get out?" I asked Mr. Winstanley in confusion. It would have been the only method of exodus left to those in the back portion of the rear drawing room. The other two doors into that chamber opened directly onto the section of the floor that had collapsed. "But you didn't see Mr. Sullivan?"

The auctioneer reared back in affront. "I was quite disoriented. I very nearly fell into the chasm myself, and I was choking on the debris."

Except that Mr. King, at the clerk's table, had been closer to the collapse. Nevertheless, I knew that people responded to traumatic events differently. What seemed logical or even endurable to some was beyond the ability or ken for another, and very often there was no rhyme or reason to it. I'd seen the frailest women exhibit extraordinary courage while the burliest of men had crumbled. Based on his reaction, it was safe to assume Mr. Winstanley had not reacted valiantly, but that didn't mean he had done anything wrong. It merely meant he was human.

Mr. Rimmer returned soon enough with the lists, and we prepared to leave. But Mr. Winstanley wasn't satisfied.

"What are you going to do?" he demanded. "Surely you're not going to just ignore the possibility that Mr. Sullivan committed such a crime?"

"We dinna have evidence tae prove that he did. However..." Maclean held up his hand to halt the auctioneer's next objection. "I am goin' tae take him intae custody for questionin'. And I may keep him there until this is all sorted oot." He turned to the other employees, his jaw hardening. "So if any o' ye ken where he is, or where he's likely gone, noo would be a good time tae tell me. For if I find oot later that ye ken and didna say anything..." he cracked his knuckles "... I'll arrest ye for obstruction."

Judging from several of their pale countenances, they believed him, but no one spoke up with information to share. Not even Mr. Fletcher, who seemed the least intimidated. In fact, to my nuanced eye, he appeared rather defiant. Or maybe I merely wanted him to seem that way, for I'd developed a disliking for the fellow. One he seemed to share if the surly glare he directed at me just before we departed was any indication.

"Do you truly mean to arrest Sullivan?" Gage asked once we were back on the street.

"Aye. 'Twill least help us ken where he is." Maclean's voice dipped. "And keep anyone else from gettin' tae him."

"You expect trouble?" Gage asked in surprise as we began to stroll west.

"Ye canna deny he'd make an excellent scapegoat."

"Especially if he turned up dead," I finished for him.

Maclean's sharp gaze shifted to me. "Aye."

The octagonal corner turrets of St. Paul's Chapel rose before us as we crossed Broughton Street and paused next to the rod iron rail which separated the churchyard from the pavement. The large ornate windows gleamed in the late morning sun.

"What was this epiphany ye wanted to tell me aboot?" the sergeant asked.

Gage huffed a humorless laugh. "Precisely what just occurred."

Maclean's eyebrows ruffled in puzzlement.

"I wondered if perhaps the floor collapse had been intended as a distraction," I explained in a low voice, conscious of those promenading past. "If the culprit even *meant* for the collapse to happen, but rather that creaks and rumbles and other indications of instability might evacuate the house and afford them some sort of opportunity."

"For theft."

"Yes." I tipped my head back to peer up at the pierced parapets and crocketed finials adorning the chapel. A light breeze buffeted the ribbons of my bonnet and carried with it the scent of honeysuckle and damp earth. "Though I didn't suspect any items were stolen from the collection. I believed Mr. Winstanley when he said his inventory was correct. I thought perhaps something else from the house was taken. Or that a pickpocket of sorts had been at work amidst the alarmed crowd." I dropped my eyes to Maclean, who was studying me with interest. "Has anyone who was there reported anything missing?"

"Not anyone who didna fall through the floor. And presumably their lost valuables are at the police house or still waitin' tae be found."

"Mr. Winstanley seemed quite convinced the thief was Sullivan," Gage said, tapping his walking stick lightly against the rail. So deep did he seem to be in contemplation that I wasn't certain he was even aware he was doing it. "But I must say, Kiera's arguments against that probability are rather difficult to surmount."

I couldn't tell if he was happy about this or not. After all, he'd been very determined in his pursuit of Mr. Sullivan. Even allowing himself to be dragged on a wild-goose chase. I didn't expect him to give him up as a suspect so easily.

"If the collapse and the theft are related, then it seems more likely that someone who was not employed by Thomas Winstanley and Sons was involved, either solely or in collusion with Sullivan or another member of the staff," Gage continued. "Because they would need the auction and the collapse to gain access to the objects they wished to steal."

"What of the footmen Mr. Clerk hired?" I asked Maclean, knowing he'd been looking into them.

"They would be a neat solution, wouldna they?" he conceded, removing his hat to scratch the side of his head. "But I've spoken wi' 'em both and dinna think they're involved. They simply dinna have the stink o' criminal on 'em." He snorted. "Plus their landlady is a fair dragon, and a nosy one tae boot. She swore the lads were in their room at the time any tamperin' could o' taken place, and I believed her."

"Speaking of landladies," I murmured, a thought occurring to me. "I wonder if Mr. Innes's landlady is equally as nosy. After all, the coin room is where the incident between him and Reverend Jamieson occurred. And I've since discovered from the reverend that several of the members of the Bannatyne Club intend to continue blocking his membership even in the absence of Lord Eldin."

Maclean's eyebrows arched in surprise and then lowered. "And ye think that might o' driven him tae steal those coins?"

"I don't know." I nodded politely to a passing couple before continuing. "But it gives us an excuse to speak with him again. He claimed he wasn't at the auction on the third day, but he never told us where he was."

Maclean rubbed his chin in thought. "Do ye have time noo?"

"Yes," Gage told him after consulting his pocket watch. "But let's take our carriage. We'll get there quicker." He offered me his arm so we could resume our stroll westward, but I paused before taking it to look behind me.

There were any number of people watching us, either directly or surreptitiously out of the corner of their eyes. After all, my husband was quite attractive, and we were relatively well known due to our exploits. Add in the hulking presence of Maclean in his policeman's gray coat, and we were all but guaranteed to draw attention. However, I couldn't halt the sensation that we were being observed by someone with particular intent—and not necessarily a pleasant one.

The simplest answer was to assume it was Bonnie Brock or one of his lackeys. I knew he was still keeping an eye on us and our movements, and that he was keeping abreast of the inquiry, whether because of us or for his own benefit. Likely both. It was rare that his acts of kindness didn't also have ulterior motives.

Nevertheless, I wasn't convinced it was the rogue or his men. But neither was I convinced it wasn't just my imagination.

So when Gage turned to me with a query in his eyes, I forced a smile and grasped his arm firmly with my own, determined to turn my thoughts to something more productive.

CHAPTER 23

"I told ye before, I wasna even there," Mr. Innes protested, the temper I'd witnessed on the second day of the auction flaring. "So hoo could I have stolen somethin'?"

A pair of men strolling among the gravestones deeper into Canongate Kirkyard turned at the sound of his raised voice. I found myself wondering if he would have spoken thusly if we'd called upon him at his rooms along the South Back of the Canongate, alarming Mrs. Stewart, his landlady. If so, it was fortunate for him that we'd spotted him striding down Canongate with a portfolio tucked beneath his arm. He'd clearly not been happy to see us, but he'd allowed us to coax him into the kirkyard rather than stand in the midst of the busy street.

"Where were ye, then?" Maclean replied unruffled. "Ye never did say."

Mr. Innes scowled. "I was meetin' wi' my editor, if ye must ken. 'Tis no' secret. I write for *Blackwood's*." A popular magazine in Edinburgh and elsewhere.

That would be easy enough to verify, and I could tell from the sergeant's nod that he was satisfied with the answer as well.

The gentle breeze from earlier had increased, the wind blustering through the gaps in the buildings and sending the remnants of the dried leaves from the previous autumn scuttling across the kirkyard between the gravestones. One particularly strong gust nearly blew the hats from the men's heads and tugged at my bonnet, fastened under my chin with ribbon.

"What was it that went missin'?" Mr. Innes inquired.

"We're no' at liberty tae say," Maclean answered.

He frowned. "Weel, it must be valuable if the police are involved." His hooded gaze shifted to us. "As weel as Mr. and Mrs. Gage."

"Did the Bannatyne Club ever call their special meeting?" I asked, deciding to be direct with him.

"Nay," he grumbled. "'Twas postponed. *Again*."

"But you expect them to approve your membership?"

Mr. Innes glanced distractedly toward a plinth erected as some sort of monument. "Honestly?" He heaved a sigh. "Nay."

His awareness of this surprised me. "You don't?"

"Reverend Jamieson came tae call on me some days ago. Told me that a number o' the members were still determined tae uphold Lord Eldin's obstruction o' my membership." His mouth twisted with contempt. "That they intended tae use the excuse that since they'd published some o' Eldin's father's drawings, that havin' me as a member would be some sort o' conflict o' interest."

"Did your father write poor reviews of those as well?" Gage asked.

"Nay." Mr. Innes scoffed. "'Tis all rubbish." His shoulders drooped as he glowered at the wall behind us, separating the church from the road. "But there's naught more that can be done."

I remembered what he'd told us about why he wanted to join the Bannatyne Club in the first place. "Do you truly need them? Couldn't you simply print the tracts yourself?"

"It costs money. Money I dinna have." He lifted his hand to secure his hat as another gust of wind blew past us, billowing my skirts. A more hopeful light entered his eyes. "But Reverend Jamieson said he might be able tae find a way tae help me wi' that."

"How?" Gage asked, clutching the brim of his own hat.

He shrugged. "A sponsor perhaps. He dinna say. But we made plans tae meet next week."

Maybe that was what Jamieson had meant when he'd said that there were those who were left who were trying to set things to rights. It had struck me as being significant to him at the time, but I hadn't understood why. Maybe this was the answer.

As Mr. Innes departed, the three of us huddled near the wall next to the lych-gate, hoping it would block some of the wind.

I could tell from Gage's stony silence and the look in his pale blue eyes that he was turning something over in his head. When he looked up to find me studying him, he finally dared to voice it.

"I know you spoke with Reverend Jamieson at the Inverleith Ball, but I think we should pay him a visit. He seems to intersect with a number of the people and organizations and events in question, and I'd like to find out what else he can tell us." He frowned. "It also might behoove us to learn a bit more about him."

"You suspect something?" I deduced.

"No." He paused. "Maybe." He shook his head. "Let's just find out more."

So we made plans to meet Sergeant Maclean at Jamieson's

address in George Square on the south side of the city the following afternoon before parting—Maclean on foot and us in our coach.

But we didn't make it far when the door was unceremoniously yanked open at about the same time we heard a shout from Peter, our footman. A man hurtled into the carriage before Joe, the coachman, could set off again. Even without the advantage of sight, I could have guessed who would be insolent enough to attempt such a stunt. True to form, Bonnie Brock grinned remorselessly back at our scowls.

Peter soon appeared in the doorway, looking frazzled.

"Be at ease, Peter," Gage told him, never removing his gaze from our guest, whom he eyed with disfavor. "Apparently, Mr. Kincaid wishes to beg a lift."

"Sir?"

"Tell Joe to carry on."

"Aye, sir."

The door was shut, a word was shouted to Joe, and the carriage rocked lightly as Peter climbed back onto his perch. Then we were off again at the sedate pace town travel required.

"What do you want, Kincaid?" Gage demanded of our guest when he didn't speak but simply lounged deeper into the plush squabs.

"Who says I want somethin'," he replied idly. "Maybe I saw ye passin' and desired a moment o' yer company."

Gage's expression communicated what he thought of this nonsense. "Mrs. Gage, perhaps. But not me."

"True enough." He tipped his hat back so we could better see the mischief in his gold-green eyes, and I realized this might have been the first time I'd seen him wear anything on his head. Normally he went without. But I supposed if you were trying to blend in—or at least not stand out among the general populace—some sort of hat was necessary.

"Word is," he continued, "there's been a theft."

"Wouldn't be your handiwork, by chance, would it?" Gage replied, pouncing on the opening he'd provided.

"No' my style. And no' profitable enough," Bonnie Brock replied, not bothering to hide his complicity in other such crimes. Of course, I also had cause to know, for we'd worked together on one special robbery in the past. "Does it relate tae the floor collapse?"

"We don't know," I said, earning a frown from Gage, I supposed for sharing information. But Bonnie Brock was not part of this. If anything, he'd been helpful, cautioning us that the collapse wasn't an accident, warning us that Anderley had been identified. "But it's suggestive."

Bonnie Brock nodded, slumping to one side so that his fine linen shirt gaped open at the throat to reveal a chest sprinkled with hair. "I've no' seen the cabinet the coins were stored in, but the back door is no' difficult to pick. A green lad could probably do it if he'd enough nerve."

Gage arched a single eyebrow. "And how would you know that?"

"Professional curiosity." He shrugged one shoulder, widening the gap in his shirt even farther. Something I was quite certain he was aware of, for he darted a glance at me as if to see if I was looking. But while he possessed the muscular stature I'd already anticipated—given my close encounters with him in the past and the way his trousers always molded to his legs, especially when he was seated in such a gauche position as now—I was not about to give him the satisfaction of letting him know I'd noticed. In any case, Gage's physique was far more impressive.

"And how do you know it was coins that were taken?" I inquired.

He feigned a weary sigh. "Must we really go over this every

time? My sources are my own. Noo . . ." He straightened. "Bein' the obliging lad I am, I'll ask aroond tae see if anyone kens who did the job. That is, if 'twas done by professionals." He sounded doubtful that it had been.

"And what's *that* going to cost us?" I well knew his penchant for keeping a tally.

Bonnie Brock merely flashed me a grin as he leaned forward to peer out the carriage window.

Before he could alight, I made the decision that if we were in for a penny, we might as well be in for a pound. "Then if we're already going to be in your debt, how about you find out whatever you can about Mr. Fletcher as well? After all, you've suggested he's the one to watch."

I was aware I'd essentially thrown down a gauntlet, and I fully anticipated the rogue wouldn't be able to stop himself from picking it up. The glint in his eye told me I was right. And that I just might regret it.

"Done."

With this, he reached up to rap on the roof of the carriage and had descended before I could lift a hand to halt him.

Once we continued to roll forward again, crossing North Bridge Street, I turned to find my husband scrutinizing me.

"You're playing with fire, Kiera."

I batted this concern away. "Oh, Bonnie Brock will never hurt me."

"It's not him hurting you that I'm afraid of."

I whipped my head back around to look at him, but he was facing the opposite window.

I had steeled myself to return to my art studio the following morning, knowing that later in the week as we approached Emma's birthday, I would have a harder time getting away.

But this time I was foiled not by my own doubts and misgivings, but by Mr. Clerk.

Lord Eldin's brother arrived unexpectedly on our doorstep in the midmorning. He seemed agitated as he was shown into the drawing room where Gage, Trevor, and I were gathered. His footsteps faltered for a moment at the sight of my brother, but he swiftly recovered. Given his troubled expression, I thought perhaps he'd learned of the missing coins from his brother's collection, but the leather-bound book he clutched in his hands soon made me suspect differently.

The usual cordialities having been exchanged, he sank into the giltwood chair I indicated, seeming to need a moment to gather himself. "I told ye I would take a look at my brother's memoirs," he declared after a deep breath. "And I think I've found somethin'."

"You were able to access the safe?" I asked in some surprise, for this was the first I'd heard that anyone had been able to return to the study after the engineers had declared the remainder of the ceiling too unstable.

"Nay." He flushed somewhat sheepishly. "But I realized I'd never returned this." He lifted the book in illustration. "It was still in my home. Now, see here . . ." He flipped open the book to a page he'd marked before passing it to Gage.

"He makes reference tae a trip tae Kirkcaldy he took in July o' 1828. I'm no' sure if ye're aware, but there was a terrible calamity there in June o' that year when their church balcony collapsed."

"Yes, we're aware," I said, anxious for him to continue.

"Aye. Weel . . ." He nodded toward the pages Gage was now scouring. "He mentions a visit he paid tae that congregation and hoo he spoke tae a number o' the people afflicted, reassurin' them somethin' would be done."

I arched my neck, wishing I could read the handwriting from where I perched. "When you say he reassured them that something would be done, do you mean to alleviate their suffering and financial difficulties, or to prevent something like the collapse from happening again?"

"He didna say." Mr. Clerk's voice turned wry. "He was more concerned wi' boastin' about his own graciousness in consolin' 'em." He clasped his hands tightly in his lap. "It only caught my eye because o' the similarity between both events, wi' them involvin' floors collapsin', though one was a balcony, and the recent correlation made in the press. So maybe it's much ado, but I thought I should mention it."

"Do you know if your brother ever actually did anything about it? Either alleviating their suffering or preventing a collapse from happening again?" Gage asked, looking up from the page. He allowed his thumb to riffle the later pages of the memoir. "Did he boast about it in another entry?"

"Nay. And I *did* look." Two pleats formed between his eyes. "Which makes me think he didna."

My husband turned to look at me and then Trevor. This was Lord Eldin's connection to Kirkcaldy, then. He'd made a speech or simply paid some calls on the parishioners and promised them aid. Now, this didn't mean that it was the motive behind what happened at Picardy Place, but it was definitely something which required greater scrutiny.

"I dinna ken if this information is o' any use tae ye," Mr. Clerk said. "But I thought ye should ken."

We thanked him as he pushed to his feet, saying he needed to return to his duties at the courthouse. Though we asked to be able to keep the memoir, he insisted on taking it with him, so we had to let it go. Even so, it hadn't contained many details that could help us in tracing who was aware of Lord Eldin's remarks. He'd not listed any names or addresses or any other identifying factors about the people of Kirkcaldy except the minister and a town official. I supposed he'd deemed the rest to be inconsequential.

Gage sat staring at the doorway through which Mr. Clerk had departed, drumming his fingers agitatedly against his lap. Seeing the deep furrow in his brow, I knew he was thinking of his inkling that what had happened at Kirkcaldy was key to the solution of who had tampered with the joist at Picardy Place, and his allowing himself to be diverted by Anderley's discoveries about Mr. Sullivan.

"You couldn't have known," I began to say, but he shook his head, cutting me off.

"Perhaps I should see how I might be able to assist Henry with his research." He pushed to his feet, striding from the room before I could stop him.

"Let him go, Kiera," Trevor said, earning a scowl from me, but he was unmoved. "Besides, I need you to play guide. Or rather, to completely forget I'm with you once you become absorbed in one of the paintings at the Royal Institution."

This shocked me into speechlessness, but only temporarily. "You want to visit the Royal Institution?"

"Yes, I've heard the building is a marvel of engineering. I read that since it's situated on ground that the Nor Loch used to cover, two thousand piles had to be driven into the foundations to make them stable."

An amused smile curled my lips. "So you want to see the building, not the art or antiquities it holds?"

"Yes, but we can go inside, if you wish," he offered. "I'll be just as happy studying its interior."

I had to admit it wasn't a bad way to spend part of a day. And since everyone else seemed to be focused on uncovering the information we needed and our interview with Reverend Jamieson had been postponed to the following day, there was nothing to stop me from enjoying myself and my brother's company. Given the fact Lord Eldin's collection contained art and antiquities, I could consider it research.

CHAPTER 24

Reverend Jamieson lived in a tidy abode in George Square at the southern edge of the city near the Meadows. The square had been developed in the mid-eighteenth century, prior to the creation of New Town, and had catered to more prosperous citizens who wished to escape the overcrowding of Old Town. The Georgian terraced houses were handsome, but rather more modest than those in New Town to the north.

Before his retirement three years prior, Jamieson had ministered to a church on Nicolson Street nearby. Having asked around about the cleric, we'd learned that he was a Fellow of the Royal Society of Edinburgh as well as the Society of Antiquaries of Scotland—a group with which we'd tangled before. He was also the author of a number of works, several of them being important to Scottish history and the Scottish language. As such, his membership in the Bannatyne Club made sense, as did his sympathy toward Mr. Innes.

"'Tis no' fair. I'll state that plain." He leaned back in his worn but evidently comfortable chair, its legs creaking. "I went round many a time wi' Lord Eldin aboot it. Mr. Innes *shouldna be held* accountable for his father's actions." He shook his head. "But Eldin wouldna budge."

"And now his friends in the club won't."

He looked up at me where I perched on the striped sofa between Gage and Maclean. "Aye. 'Tis a sorry business. 'Specially considerin' the aim o' the society is tae promote Scottish culture, be it literature, language, history, or poetry. Mr. Innes's tracts would o' been worthy additions tae the canon."

"He said you might be able to help him find funding," Gage said, his eyes roaming the room, which was neat and orderly except for the stacks of books beside Jamieson's chair and along one wall.

A sheet was draped over something in the corner, and when I heard twittering, I realized it was a birdcage. Which seemed fitting given the bird-patterned wallpaper and delicate bird figurines perched on several of the surfaces. I wondered if it was the reverend or his wife who was so interested in our feathered friends.

Jamieson nodded, folding his hands in front of him. "I've a number o' connections I've made over the years. Seems only right I should help him hooever I can since the Bannatyne Club willna."

"Maybe so. But not everyone would willingly go to such lengths," Gage prodded further.

However, Jamieson did not take the bait, brushing the matter aside as if it were of no consequence. Except I'd noticed how white his knuckles were and I sensed the shiftiness of his eyes was not entirely due to modesty.

"Then ye and Mr. Innes have made up since yer tiff at the auction," Maclean stated bluntly.

"Oh, aye," he responded almost in relief, making it clear

the incident with Innes was not his source of anxiety. "He apologized. Told me he wished he could've done the same wi' Mr. Smith." He shook his head. "'Tis a sad, sad business."

I thought back over the things that had been said, trying to identify precisely what had caused his conscience to flinch, and believed I knew what it was.

"Seeing things set right is important to you, isn't it?"

Jamieson regarded me quietly, his neck and shoulders exhibiting tension. "Shouldna it be important tae all o' us?" he countered.

"Perhaps," I answered evenly. "But it isn't. Not to everyone. Not to some of your friends."

"We all have our faults, our blind spots. The beam in our eye."

Obviously, he was referring to Matthew 7:3–5, which began, "And why beholdest thou the mote that is in thy brother's eye, but considerest not the beam that is in thine own eye?" Reciting it in my head, I couldn't help but react to the word *beam*, as a joist and a beam were much the same. I noted that Gage and Maclean also showed sharpened interest.

Whether Jamieson had actually intended anything by this, I couldn't tell, but he was struggling to mask the fact he was ill at ease.

"And Lord Eldin's tendency to hold his family's, his *own* consequence above others' was his beam?" I persisted.

"'Pride goeth before destruction' for many o' us, m'lady," he replied, quoting again, this time from Proverbs.

"'And an haughty spirit before a fall,'" I finished for him, suspecting he was lumping me into the category of the prideful.

"Just so."

I couldn't prove it, but as I locked eyes with Reverend Jamieson, I suddenly felt certain he was behind the theft, and *possibly* the tampering with the joist. The latter was more difficult to believe, unless he had an accomplice. But his reasoning for the theft seemed plain. There was no contention in his gaze, only firm resolve tinged with strain, and so I decided to test this theory and his obedience to the tenets of his faith.

"Did you steal the coins from Lord Eldin's collection to fund Mr. Innes's publications?"

Gage and Maclean's shock at my asking this outright was obvious, but Jamieson's reaction was far more interesting. Though he visibly flinched, he didn't grow angry or defensive. Instead, he began to rise from his chair, relying heavily on the leverage he gained from pushing on the arms. "My dear lady, do ye truly think me capable o' such a thing?"

Watching him hobble several steps toward the door before his gait smoothed out told me that if he had been behind the joist being sabotaged, he must have had an accomplice. Perhaps Mr. Sullivan, who had thus far eluded Maclean and remained at large.

Before we could protest, he'd disappeared into the corridor, leaving us to stare after him. For several moments, none of us moved, all wondering if he would return, I supposed. When he didn't, Gage and I both turned to Maclean.

He gestured emphatically toward the doorway. "He's a reverend and a respected member o' the community. Wi'oot proof, I canna do anythin'."

"And his failure to answer?" Gage rejoined.

"People will argue that a man of his position *shouldn't* have answered a question like that. That it's below his dignity," I said, knowing full well the stakes against us.

Gage grumbled under his breath, being less accustomed to butting up against the restrictions so often thrown in the way of the less powerful.

A maid appeared in the doorway. The same timid woman

who had admitted us. Having no justification for remaining, there was nothing for it but to allow her to usher us out. Though that didn't stop Gage from peering into the open doorways we passed on our way. At one, he hissed, compelling me to backtrack several steps to see what he was motioning toward.

It was a cabinet similar to the type which displayed the coins of Lord Eldin's collection. Something he pointed out to Maclean as soon as we returned to the pavement and the door was shut behind us.

"If he has a similar cabinet, then he must have a similar key to open the lock."

Maclean scowled. "Aye, but I looked intae that cabinet, and 'tis remarkably popular. There's probably a hundred or more households throughoot Edinburgh and the surroundin' area that boast 'em. 'Tis no' distinctive enough tae implicate 'im."

"Perhaps not alone but added together!" Gage was growing agitated and drawing stares from those gathered in the square opposite.

I pressed a hand to his arm in an attempt to calm him. "Perhaps we should continue this discussion inside the carriage . . ."

"A case, an unanswered question, and yer wife's uncanny intuition dinna make a compellin' argument," Maclean interrupted.

I stiffened at his use of the word *uncanny* for anything that smacked of the slur *unnatural* raised my hackles. After all, I'd been slandered with the term more times than I could count, and it was still a sore spot for me. However, it was more important to maintain my composure and calm their tempers. "Gentlemen," I scolded firmly. "If you will please . . ."

"Do *not* call Mrs. Gage uncanny," Gage snapped.

Maclean's jaw worked and his hands balled into fists. "I meant no offense. But ye have to admit her intuition is almost supernatural. Like the second sight."

Being half Scottish myself, I recognized that this wasn't meant as an insult. Many Scots, even the dourest of Presbyterians, gave credence to the existence of abilities and creatures beyond their knowledge.

But as an honor-bound, exceedingly rational Englishman, Gage could not grasp this. "No offense! Well, you've just given us one."

I gripped his arm, insisting, "No, he hasn't."

Neither of them was listening to me, instead leaning toward each other as their sniping escalated. I'd had enough. Turning on my heel, I strode away, quickly approaching the corner with Charles Street and turning left. Whether they'd noticed my departure yet or not, I didn't know, but I was determined to walk home if this was the bickering I was to be subjected to.

Gage was so intent on solving this inquiry that he was becoming almost unbearable. After all, Sergeant Maclean hadn't countered with any arguments that I wouldn't also have raised. My theory that Reverend Jamieson was guilty of some part of the crimes committed at Picardy Place was, taken together, just that—a theory. We needed to prove it. That was how the law worked. Gage knew this. He knew this even better than me. And yet at the smallest provocation, he'd lost his head.

I veered left, cutting across the grounds of the Lying-In Hospital, and then up Park Street toward the triangle of streets including Teviot Row. The Charity Workhouse and, beyond it, Heriot's Hospital were to my left, while Greyfriars Kirk loomed before me. It wasn't the most genteel of areas, with unmentionable things running through the gutters, but in broad daylight with ample traffic moving north and south, it was safe enough.

Or so I thought.

I'd paused at the edge of the pavement, waiting for a large, speeding mail coach to pass before I crossed the street, when a hand suddenly planted itself between my shoulder blades and thrust me out onto the cobblestones.

I stumbled, nearly falling to my knees on the uneven surface. At the same time, I was conscious of the horses bearing down on me. I could hear the shouts of those behind me and the shrieks of the steeds as the coachman must have pulled on their reins. Everything seemed to move like quicksand as I frantically attempted to reverse my course, to scramble out of the horses' path. I swore I could feel their hot breath upon my face as I braced for impact.

Then a body slammed into mine, once again from behind. But this time it propelled me up onto the pavement and directly into the mass of people standing there gawking. We landed with a thud, and the air was driven from me by the person landing atop me.

For a moment, I could do nothing but struggle to draw breath. Then the sights and sounds of a dozen people gazing down at me, all talking at once, crashed into me. Gage was the closest, his body being the one that had knocked the breath out of me. But considering the fact he'd saved my life I could forgive him for that.

I blinked up at him as he peppered me with questions between scolds. "Kiera, are you hurt? Can you speak? What were you thinking? Tell me what hurts. Why did you take off like that? Did you trip?"

Several of the people standing over us were offering their own opinions as to what happened, varying from intoxication to broken mortar to madness. I ignored them all, allowing Gage to help me into a seated position.

"I . . . I didn't trip," I finally managed to gasp. "Someone . . . pushed me."

Gage frowned in concern. "You're certain?"

Even now, I could feel the firm hand at the center of my back. "Yes!"

"Did anyone see anythin'?" a deep burr demanded behind me, and I realized Sergeant Maclean was also there. "Who was standin' behind her ladyship?"

The rate of the bystanders' speculation increased at the mention of my title, and I inwardly winced. We were only a short distance from the Grassmarket, where Burke and Hare had once plied their murderous trade. And where I had nearly been ripped to shreds by an angry mob aware of my macabre reputation from the work I'd done with my late anatomist husband. It wouldn't take these people long to figure out just which lady I was.

"I saw a tall lad run off that way just after she fell," one woman claimed, pointing east into a warren of streets and closes. Others agreed, but when Maclean asked for a description, they all differed, bickering among themselves as to who was correct. Then a man suggested he'd seen an older gentleman abscond to the south, but the woman next to him argued that he was only middle-aged. Though I could follow only about half of what was being said, so thick were their accents or so scrambled was my brain.

Amid the chaos, Gage helped me to my feet, dusting me off and adjusting my aventurine merino skirts. "Does anything hurt? Can you walk?"

My hip ached as I took a few tentative steps forward, but I didn't think I'd suffered anything serious. "I'm well enough," I assured him, cringing as I noticed the unmentionable substance on my sleeve.

Gage did his best to clean it off with his handkerchief, helping me to our carriage, which Joe had drawn up nearby.

After settling me inside, he paused to confer with Maclean. In spite of my rattled composure, I noticed they were both using more congenial voices. I supposed that was something.

By the time my husband clambered into the carriage beside me, I'd closed my eyes. I heard him rap on the ceiling to signal Joe to drive on and a few moments later draw breath to speak.

"It was your and Maclean's fault," I bit out before he could resume reproving me for setting off on my own.

When he didn't speak, I opened my eyes to find his lips pressed tightly together as if he was holding in an outburst.

"You were butting horns like a couple of rams. In the middle of the street," I emphasized.

He glared at me a moment longer and then abruptly deflated. "You're right."

"Why were you being so fractious? I realize you've been at loose ends lately. That it's important to you to solve this inquiry. But your leaps from one theory to another, pouncing at them with all the subtlety of a . . . a . . . an American buffalo are illogical."

He flinched. "That bad?"

However, I could not find the humor in the situation, closing my eyes again with a huff.

Gage's hands stole into mine. "I know, Kiera. You're right." He squeezed my fingers, coaxing me to look at him. "I have been rather too keen and erratic." His gaze dipped. "I suppose I feel I have something to prove."

I frowned. "But, darling, you've already successfully unraveled dozens if not hundreds of inquiries. What on earth could you need to prove?"

He ignored this question, peering down at me with wild eyes. "Had I known someone would intend you harm, that my words would drive you straight into danger, I would have nailed my own lips shut."

"Sebastian, what nonsense," I said not unkindly, extracting one of my hands to lift it to his face. "Of course you couldn't have known. Had *I* known, I would never have stridden off on my own." I arched my chin toward the box seat outside the carriage where our coachman sat. "I would have simply climbed into the carriage and ordered Joe to drive off."

"Why didn't you?"

"I didn't think of it," I grumbled, shifting in my seat as the ache in my hip twinged. "But back to this other nonsense you spouted." I glared at him, letting him know I refused to be diverted again. "Why do you have something to prove?"

He flushed, and his pale blue eyes clouded with some sort of memory, but when I arched my eyebrows to encourage him, he turned away, tossing his hat into the opposite seat. "You're right. It's nonsense."

But it clearly wasn't. Not when his body was as rigid as a pole and his gaze would no longer meet mine.

I thought back over the last few months, recalling his growing restlessness, his determined efforts to be useful. He'd taken on inquiries he normally would have referred to others and sought out answers to questions about his various properties that he usually would have left to his various staff. He'd even prepared canvases for me despite the fact the gesso mixture I used was highly noxious. I'd noticed he'd not volunteered to do that again. But clearly there was something I'd missed.

"Sebastian," I began gently. "Why are you an inquiry agent?"

He turned to me in surprise. "What do you mean?"

"I mean, why do you undertake inquiries, particularly when they're not personal to you?" I wasn't certain it was something I'd ever asked him before. I knew his mother's murder had a profound effect on him, especially since her slow poisoning had happened right under his nose as a child. And I knew his father's decision to become a gentleman inquiry agent had put him on the road to his current occupation. But I didn't think I'd ever spoken to him about it. I'd merely assumed I knew the reasons why. "You're a wealthy gentleman who could spend your days in leisure, but you don't. Why?"

His brow furrowed. "You think I should?"

I glared at him in mild reproof. "I'm not asking you what I think. I'm asking why *you* do it."

The lines at the corners of his eyes told me he was still confused, but he considered the matter, fumbling at first over his words. "I suppose it's because I like unraveling the enigma, and bringing murderers to justice, and attaining answers for those whose loved ones have been wronged." His brow lowered, and his tone deepened with earnestness. "I . . . I like knowing I've been helpful to others. That I've done something worthwhile." His lips twisted. "That I haven't just passively allowed things to happen or taken up space as a pampered aristocrat good for nothing but his money."

I began to understand, for I heard the voice of someone from his past in those remarks. Someone whose spiteful words I'd not realized had sunk so deep.

"So you do it because it makes you useful?" I clarified.

"Yes," he agreed, as if glad I'd put it in succinct terms.

"Because if you're not useful, then why would anyone love you?"

When he blanched and it felt as if all the air had been drawn from the carriage, I knew I'd plucked at the heart of his fear. As painful as the words were to utter, as awful as it was to watch how they transformed my beloved's face, I had to continue.

"You were useful to your mother, comforting and cheering her through her long years of illness. You became useful to your father when you joined him as an inquiry agent, taking on some of his investigations." Though some semblance of self-preservation had remained when he'd fled London rather than wed the young lady his father had chosen for him, which would only have dragged him even deeper into the snare of approbation.

I inhaled a ragged breath, persisting. "You proved useful to your relatives at Langstone Manor when we uncovered the truth of what was going on there two years ago. And you showed yourself to be useful to Rika and her brothers as you fought alongside them in the Greeks' struggle for independence. That is, until you refused to take part in the massacre at Tripolitsa. Then she cast you aside and revealed her true colors. That her affection was conditional on your usefulness."

I hated speaking of Rika, of thinking of how Gage had once loved her and sought to marry her. But I would invoke her specter if necessary—and considering he'd just quoted her words from nearly twelve years ago, it was necessary—in order to help him grapple with this lie he was telling himself. For she was the one who had accused him of passively allowing things to happen and taking up space as a pampered aristocrat good for nothing but his money. She was the one who had put that into his head.

However, the worst was yet to be spoken.

"And you are without a doubt useful to me. Helping me prove my innocence of murder. Saving me from drowning and stabbing and being crushed to death. Salvaging my reputation. Giving me your protection. Always having to be the hero—for everyone—not just me."

Gage's expression was stark, the plains of his face haggard. Unable to bear it any longer, I yanked the gloves from my hands, determined to have nothing between his skin and mine as I cradled his jaw. "But while I appreciate all of that . . ." I shook my head, my voice falling to just above a whisper ". . . it's not why I love you."

His eyes ached with unspoken doubt.

"I love you because you're you. And that love isn't contingent on you being useful." I pressed my forehead to his. "I'm sure it was the same for your mother and even your father, though in the past he's been abominable at showing it."

The corners of his lips quirked at my feeble attempt at a jest, though pain and uncertainty still clouded his gaze when I lifted my head so that I could see him.

"All your friends and family—they don't love you because they *need* you." I brushed my thumbs over his jawline, feeling the rasp of stubble just beginning to grow. "I don't know when you started believing that was true, but it's not. They simply love *you*." I put all my heart into my next words. "As do I."

He pulled me to him, pressing his lips to mine, though they soon slid along my cheek as he buried his face in my shoulder. His muscles remained rigid for a few moments longer before finally relaxing as he gave a long sigh.

"These inquiries we conduct," I said into his hair. "They do not make you worthy. You already are. And you don't need to prove *anything* to *anyone*," I added vehemently, gripping the back of his neck with my hand and urging him to look at me. "You do not always have to be the hero. Understood?"

This time when he kissed me, his mouth did not slide away. This time when the kiss deepened, I felt the connection that had always been between us strengthen and intensify, a bulwark against the rest of the world, whatever it wreaked.

CHAPTER 25

Over the next few days, while Gage seemed calmer and less prone to vacillate between suspects and theories, there was still tension in the air. I suspected much of it had to do with the feeling we nearly had all the facts we needed to solve both the sabotage and the theft—whether they were related or not—and yet we couldn't quite put them together in a cohesive order, let alone prove any of our suspicions.

Reverend Jamieson seemed to be involved, as well as at least one of the auctioneer's employees, but whether it was Sullivan, Fletcher, Rimmer, or one of the others was still up for debate. That there was some connection to the collapse of the church balcony at Kirkcaldy appeared credible, but beyond the entry Lord Eldin had made in his memoir documenting his visit to the town, there didn't seem to be any other record of a connection. At least, none that Henry could find, and I trusted his thoroughness.

Mr. Sullivan remained elusive, though Sergeant Maclean was confident he would be apprehended. It was only a matter of time. Then maybe he could be persuaded to provide us with some answers.

I considered sending for Mr. Rimmer and asking him to keep an eye on his cohort Mr. Fletcher, or to at least report any strange doings. Bonnie Brock had promised to find out what he could about the surly assistant, but we'd yet to hear from the rogue. In any case, a note from Maclean made me question the wisdom of trusting Rimmer. For the sergeant had discovered that Rimmer and Fletcher had both been absent from Picardy Place, allegedly running errands, at the time I'd been pushed in front of the mail coach. As such, I couldn't be certain either man could be trusted, though there was every chance that neither of them was the culprit.

Given the suddenness and unexpectedness of the attack, Gage had insisted that neither me, Bree, nor Mrs. Mackay set out on foot without a male escort. I could hardly argue with him. Especially with Trevor in residence, eager to accompany me when Gage and Anderley were elsewhere. Anyway, I rarely had time to venture far, for Emma's birthday was drawing near and there was much to do about the house to get ready for the party.

When there wasn't, I found myself standing at the door to my studio, or one rainy afternoon, actually entering it. But I didn't pick up a brush or even remove my apron from the wall peg. Because Gage had been right. The portraits were finished. All that remained was for them to be shown. Yet still I shied away from the prospect. The very thought of exposing them to other people's eyes, to their criticism, made my heart race and my palms sweat. So I locked the door and stayed away.

Then the morning of the thirty-first dawned, and I realized that perhaps the main source of tension over the past few days, at least within me, had been the anticipation of this date. It was the anniversary of the day we'd been ambushed and tossed into the depths of the vaults where I'd gone into labor. Where we'd been left to die.

Gage and I had endured many frightening moments since embarking on our inquiries together, but that had been the most terrifying by far. Worse, it caused me to feel conflicted about the date. For while it had been perhaps the worst day of my life, it had bled into the next day, which had been one of the happiest, for Emma was born. I disliked this contradiction, wanting only to experience joy, but there was so much more within me.

Unsure how to confront it all, I instead opted for avoidance.

It being a Sunday, we attended church service at St. George's and then ate dinner at Philip and Alana's for a smaller celebration of wee Jamie's second birthday. Traditionally, while first birthdays and other important milestones were celebrated with some panache, other birthdays passed more quietly, but no one wanted Jamie to feel overlooked. A number of additional family members who had come to town to celebrate Emma's birthday were also there, including my friend Charlotte and her husband—my cousin Rye. It was a joyous reunion, for I'd not seen them since their last visit to Edinburgh from their nearby estate some months prior.

However, the afternoon passed all too quickly, and since Emma had failed to nap, it was decided that we should return home so that she could get plenty of rest before the next day. I'd hoped then that Gage, Trevor, and I might spend a quiet evening at home. Trevor had yet to tell me how Alana had reacted to his telling her about his courtship of Matilda Birnam, but from the pinched speculation I'd seen on her face several times that afternoon when she looked at him, I guessed it hadn't been entirely welcomed. Or perhaps Alana was merely worried it was all progressing too swiftly.

Regrettably, at least for my plans, there was a letter waiting for my husband when we returned home. Mr. Sullivan had been apprehended, and Sergeant Maclean wanted Gage to join him at the police house off Old Stamp Office Close for his interrogation. I knew better than to ask to accompany him. Gage would never willingly allow me to visit the police house and, truth be told, I didn't wish to. The short amount of time I'd spent at the Bow Street Magistrates' Court in London when I'd been accused of several crimes following the discovery that I'd sketched anatomical drawings for my late husband was more than enough time in a police house for me.

Nevertheless, the afternoon was waning into evening, and with the memory of what had happened a year ago so fresh in my mind, I was not about to let him leave alone. Gage resisted at first when I insisted he take both Trevor and Anderley with him. I didn't know if Gage had forgotten the significance of the day's date or he was unruffled by the remembrance, but my genuine distress seemed to convince him. In truth, I was very near tears when even my adamance seemed unable to budge him. Gathering me close, he pressed a kiss to my temple and promised solemnly to return as soon as possible.

I watched through the window as the three men departed in our carriage before closing the sage green damask drapes to shut out the encroaching night. Of course, that left me in greater gloom. At least, until Jeffers entered to light the lamps. I turned to watch him, my hands crossed before me, as I tried to still my agitated mind.

"Can I get you anything, m'lady?" Jeffers asked as he straightened. There was kindness in his eyes.

I wondered if I should feel embarrassed that my apprehension was so transparent, but then decided that was senseless. "No. Thank you."

He nodded and departed, leaving me to my restless thoughts. However, I soon discovered he'd done what he could to help without even saying so. Having grown tired of pacing the drawing room, I began to wander from room to room and found that Jeffers had lit nearly every lamp and wall sconce, forcing back the darkness. His thoughtfulness made tears threaten yet again.

The staff largely left me to my own devices, even Bree, perhaps sensing this was not something they could grapple with for me. This sensation of being at rather tattered and loose ends would not abate from their company and, in fact, having them underfoot might only spark my fragile temper. I knew well the temptation to vent fury when the other emotions one was feeling were far more uncomfortable. So I paced, sitting down briefly in the morning room to try to politely eat some part of the small repast Mrs. Grady had prepared for me, though sadly I sent most of it back to the kitchen untouched.

I noticed a light mist had begun to gather when I peered out the French doors into the garden; gauzy tendrils snaked through the grasses and flower beds. I hoped the men would return before it thickened. If they were delayed and didn't return in a timely manner, I feared the little I'd consumed wouldn't stay put for long.

Then the haze shifted and a figure appeared, moving toward the house. It didn't take me long to recognize him. In some strange way, I believed I'd actually been expecting him, given the date and the role he'd played in the events surrounding it. In any case, my already taxed system barely wondered at his appearance.

Bonnie Brock's pace slowed as he caught sight of me watching him. What he was thinking, I couldn't tell. His expression was more inscrutable than usual. Or perhaps such minute observations were beyond my abilities at the moment.

I didn't wait for him to knock but opened the door to allow him to slip inside. I knew he was no danger to me or those within. If anything, he would *prevent* harm from coming to us.

His brown greatcoat and his tawny hair were damp from the mist. "I ken Gage and his valet and yer brother are at the police house. That Maclean nabbed the auctioneer employee he's been searchin' for."

"And so you decided now was a good time to pay me a call?" I surmised ironically, not in the least surprised that he was aware of all our comings and goings.

His gaze scoured mine. "I thought maybe you'd welcome the distraction."

I blinked rapidly in the face of this compassion, feeling tears bite at the back of my eyes yet again. Seeing this, he took a step toward me, but I turned away, peering out into the garden as I blinked furiously, refusing to release the emotion threatening to strangle me.

"I also have information," he said.

This, at least, was something I could focus on without losing my composure, and I gestured impatiently for him to continue.

"Whoever stole those coins, 'twasn't any o' the normal tradesmen."

This was no more than confirmation of what we already suspected, but it was good to have corroboration that a . . . *tradesman*, as he'd called professional lockpicks, wasn't involved.

"I've also discovered somethin' interestin' aboot Mr. Fletcher."

I knew Bonnie Brock well enough to recognize that tone. Whatever he had to tell me would be interesting, indeed, but he intended to reel it out piece by piece, making me work to drag it out of him. It was a rather annoying habit which provoked me to scowl at him, letting him know I was not in the mood to humor him.

He flashed me a smile. "Apparently, Mr. Fletcher has made friends wi' a rather obligin' barmaid at the White Horse." He crossed his arms, leaning his shoulder against the doorframe. "A rather obligin' barmaid, indeed . . ."

I scrunched up my nose at this reference, for I understood what he was implying.

"For she told Locke . . ." one of Bonnie Brock's henchmen ". . . that on the night before the floor collapse, Mr. Fletcher convinced her tae dose Mr. Rimmer's drink wi' some sort o' tincture."

I started.

"Aye," he said, letting me know I'd heard correctly. "From her description, 'twas probably laudanum."

"Mr. Fletcher and Mr. Rimmer share quarters," I murmured, recalling that Rimmer had said so.

"Aye. The lovely maid thought she was givin' the lad a sleepin' draught so that she and Fletcher could carry on undisturbed. She was still quite miffed that instead Mr. Fletcher left the White Horse and didna return 'til the wee hours o' the mornin'."

My eyes had widened to saucers, and I clasped my hands over my mouth.

"The maid thought he was visitin' another lass, but I believe you and I ken better."

"It was Fletcher," I exclaimed, lowering my hands. "He must have returned to Picardy Place with Mr. Rimmer's keys, tampered with the joist, and went back to the inn, with Mr. Rimmer none the wiser because he was drugged." I turned toward the door as if to find Gage, only remembering too late that he wasn't home.

"The maid said he returned wi' an injury as well. A cut tae his hand she had tae bandage for him."

Mr. Rimmer had mentioned that Fletcher had injured his hand the day before the collapse, that it had become infected when he'd fallen. Or perhaps it simply hadn't been tended correctly. After all, a barmaid was not a doctor. Either way, it seemed evident he'd sliced his hand while tampering with the joist. During the auction, he'd hidden it beneath the gloves he'd worn to move the paintings about.

"Yer husband's man might o' found all this oot eventually, had he no' been so obviously English. And no' gone soft." His brogue dripped with insinuation. "Courtin' yer maid, isn't he?"

I elected to ignore this query in favor of one more important. "But why?" I asked, baffled by Fletcher's reasoning. "He killed an innocent man and injured dozens of others. And it might have been much worse. But to what end?"

"I dinna ken the why. You'll have tae figure that one oot on yer own. What I do care aboot is that he's likely the one who tried to harm ye by pushin' ye in front o' that carriage."

I looked up, suddenly alerted by the tone of his voice, and the fact he was now standing much closer to me. I could smell the damp of his wool coat, feel the warmth radiating off him, see the gold flecks in his eyes.

"And nay one harms what's mine."

Instinctively I took a step back, only to come up against the cool glass of the door. "I'm not yours," I protested, my pulse suddenly pounding.

He arched an arrogant eyebrow as if to say, *Ye are if I say ye are*, and crowded closer, his intent clear. "Noo, aboot my favor."

My heart rose into my throat as his mouth lowered toward mine, but I turned my head at the last, so that his lips brushed across my cheek.

This wasn't the first time Bonnie Brock had tried to kiss

me, but it was his first attempt since my marriage to Gage. Gage had tried to warn me, but I'd ignored him, believing Bonnie Brock wouldn't dare try such a thing. Evidently, I was wrong.

"Ye made a bargain, lass," he growled in warning, his breath gusting hot in my ear and his bristles lightly abrading my skin. The indolence from before was gone, leaving only a man bent on what he wanted.

Memories of my marriage to Sir Anthony flooded through me, reminding me of the enjoyment he'd gotten out of turning on me when I'd least expected it and backing me into a corner. He'd fed off any reaction, be it shock, resistance, or fear.

I inhaled a shaky breath, trying to clear my thoughts, to focus on the obvious. That this was not my first husband. For one, he smelled better, and the plains of his body were hard where Sir Anthony's had been soft. But the recognition that Bonnie Brock could be as much a threat to me as anyone made my limbs tremble and threaten to give way.

I'd known this man was a dangerous criminal. I'd known it, and yet I'd deceived myself into thinking I could trust him. That he meant no harm.

I inhaled again, compelling the fog of panic to recede, refusing to lose sight of what I knew to be true, despite the seeming proof to the contrary. Bonnie Brock could be trusted. I simply had to prove it—to myself and possibly even to him.

I pushed out with my hands where they were trapped against his chest, creating some distance between us. "I'm not going to kiss you," I told him plainly once our eyes met.

His jaw was hard, his eyes determined, so I hastened to continue before he could argue how I owed him the token of his choosing.

"But I have something better for you."

He looked disbelieving but allowed me to continue.

"You're going to have to let me fetch it."

His eyes narrowed mistrustfully. "I've seen yer pistol, ye bloodthirsty wench."

"It's not my pistol. It's . . . a gift." I searched his expression for any sign of weakening. "Please, will you let me go get it?"

I could feel the restraint vibrating through him, the sharpness of his desire, and for a moment I feared I'd miscalculated again. But then he stepped back abruptly. I edged past him, worried he would change his mind, and hurried down the corridor toward the staircase.

As I ascended, I spared a moment to wonder where all the staff had gone. I was surprised none of them had heard us talking or stumbled across our altercation and intervened. But then I realized they must all be at dinner in the servants' hall. All but Joe, Peter, and Anderley, who had gone with Gage, and Mrs. Mackay, who would be eating in her own room while Emma slept.

I panted slightly when I reached the top floor—unaccustomed to climbing three flights of stairs at such a speed—and hastened toward my studio. Unlocking the door, I tumbled into the darkened chamber. Jeffers knew better than to leave a lantern unattended in here. Carefully skirting the contents of the room, I crossed to the window and yanked open the curtains. Moonlight flooded the space, allowing me to pick through the canvases leaning against the interior wall. Three back, I found the one I was searching for.

Pulling it out, I cast one last critical eye over it before deciding there was no time to second-guess myself. I'd already decided I would never exhibit it, and I knew I would never hang it in any of our homes. Gage would never have stood for it had I even tried. So rather than let it languish in a corner of my studio, this seemed a better choice.

Locking the studio door, I returned down the stairs to the

morning room, finding Bonnie Brock waiting impatiently for me. He stood facing the French doors, his hands planted almost defiantly on his hips, but upon my appearance, he rounded, almost as if he'd not believed my assertion that I'd not gone to get my pistol. His gaze dipped to the canvas I held in confusion.

"I . . . I want you to have this." I advanced toward him, suddenly feeling unsure of myself. Perhaps he wouldn't like it. Perhaps he would be insulted. "You may do whatever you wish with it." With this statement, I turned the canvas so that he could see it, holding it out to him.

He accepted it hesitantly, scrutinizing the image depicted.

It was a portrait of him and his sister, Maggie. Painted almost exactly where he was standing now, illuminated by moonlight. She was tucked against his side, her head resting on his shoulder trustingly though a single tear lingered in the crevice beside her nose. His face was turned to look down at her, quiet affection writ in his eyes and the sharp angles of his face, but also regret and determination.

I had called it *A Reconciliation*. And it had captured precisely that. A moment in time that happened over a year ago now, but that had lingered with me long after.

Several minutes passed without Bonnie Brock saying anything. At first, I'd studied his features, trying to discern his reaction, but I'd soon abandoned the effort, for it felt too invasive. Instead, I took up his previous stance in front of the French doors, attempting to gauge whether the mist had deepened or remained the same. I was still trying to decide when he joined me, his shoulder brushing mine, the portrait still held before him, but lower.

"Thank ye," he said.

I nodded, not unaffected by the gravity of his tone.

It was the subdued tenor of his demeanor that allowed me

to dare to voice a question I would normally have never risked. "Isn't there a better way forward?"

Than running the largest criminal enterprise in Edinburgh. Than committing theft, extortion, smuggling, body snatching, assault, and murder, as well as any number of petty crimes I might not be aware of.

"Nay," he stated confidently, but with little satisfaction. "No' kennin' who would take my place. I canna quit nor leave." His shoulders straightened. "Too many people rely on me." He shook his head. "I canna fold."

I fully appreciated then what a trap he'd constructed for himself. Yes, he'd committed terrible acts to get where he was. He continued to commit them. But his power also protected a great deal of people who could not protect themselves. It was why so much of the city was content to live under his thumb. He had his own code of honor, and as long as you played by it, you were secure. Which was more than they could say about the law of the land, which often catered to the wealthy and titled at the expense of the masses.

If Bonnie Brock were suddenly to disappear, the vacuum created would result in chaos and carnage, certainly for those closest to him. The very thought was actually quite frightening. I couldn't guarantee even we would be safe.

I turned to him, offering him my hand, telling him it was time to go. "Give Maggie my regards."

He took it, squeezing gently. "Aye."

Then lest I start to think he'd become too tame, he yanked me toward him, planting a smacking kiss on my cheek. Before I could retaliate, he released me, slipping through the French door and out into the night.

I turned to scowl through the glass at him, his laughter reverberating back to me as he strode away. His shadows,

Stump and Locke, were no doubt waiting for him by the carriage house. There was no telling what they would think upon hearing it.

As he disappeared into the mist, a smile cracked the corner of my lips, too, before being quickly suppressed.

CHAPTER 26

At some point during the evening, I realized I couldn't continue pacing the house indefinitely, or visiting the nursery to look in on Emma every quarter hour. She was safe. She was sleeping peacefully with Mrs. Mackay just steps away. My fretting was not helping anyone, especially me, and might very well wake her.

So I retired to my bedchamber and rang for Bree. Changing into my nightclothes might not make me less anxious, but at least I would be more comfortable. Plus the act of my maid brushing and braiding my hair had always had a rather soothing effect on me.

Bree was quiet as she worked, her fingers gliding through my tresses with practiced ease as she smoothed and separated and weaved. I closed my eyes, allowing myself to be lulled by her ministrations and the silence except for the shush of the strands of my hair rubbing against each other and the soft tick of the clock. I'd begun to feel some of my anxiety dissolving and wondered if I might be able to seek the oblivion of sleep after all before Gage returned. Until Bree spoke.

"Was he correct? Did I hinder the investigation? Would Anderley have uncovered what he learned aboot Fletcher sooner wi'oot me?"

My eyes popped open to stare at her fretful countenance in the mirror. It took me a moment to grasp that *he* referred to Bonnie Brock.

"You were listening in the corridor."

"Aye." Her gaze flicked up to meet mine, hesitant at first and then more resolute. "Wanted tae be sure he didna mean ye harm."

I didn't scold her. Not when I was grateful for her concern for me. Though she must have returned to the servants' quarters soon after Bonnie Brock had made his remark about Anderley going soft. Otherwise, I knew Bree would never have stood idly by while the rogue tried to force me to kiss him. She was more likely to have fetched a pistol or a knife and threatened to make garters of his guts. That was something I would have liked to see.

Her mouth pleated as she resumed braiding my hair, and I realized she'd taken my silence for agreement with Bonnie Brock's sentiment.

"No, Bree," I said. "He wasn't correct."

But doubt still lingered in her eyes.

"For one, we already know Anderley's presence at the White Horse was drawing unwelcome speculation," I reminded her. "For another, if he hadn't become suspicious, there's no guarantee the maid would have shared anything with him."

Her skepticism was tangible, and I had to concede that Anderley's charm and good looks had proved to be rather potent forces in the past. Regardless, this was not my most important point.

"But even if he could have . . . *coaxed* the information from her." I chose my words with care. "Doesn't mean he should have."

Bree frowned. "But the inquiry . . . ?"

"Uncovering the truth, finding justice for those who have been wronged is important, but not at the expense of wronging the innocent in the pursuit of that truth. And misleading that maid would have been wrong."

She finished tying the ribbon securing my second braid, and I turned on the bench to grab her hands, forcing her to look at me.

"Anderley might still have gotten the information from her without crossing a line that would be unfair to her and unfaithful to you. He knows this now, and I believe he's all the better for it. I'm sure his conscience rests easier."

When she would have pulled away, I prevented her, deciding to once again break my and Gage's rule not to interfere in our staff's personal lives. Truth be told, I was abominable at following it. Anyway, Bree was the one to raise the subject. Or so I excused myself.

"I thought his altered behavior was what you wanted. His failure to adapt his flirtatious ways was one of the reasons you decided to return to merely being friends a year ago, but I thought you'd reconciled the matter since then. Am I wrong?"

"Ye're right. We did."

"Then why are you questioning it now? Is it just because of what Bonnie Brock said?"

She backed away, and this time I let her. Turning toward the bed, she picked up my orchid pink dress, running her fingers lightly over the jonquil stitching as if she was examining it for damage. "It . . . it's no' just that. It's . . ." She couldn't seem to find the words to explain, and the longer she remained silent, the more concerned I became.

"You both seem to care deeply for the other," I broached softly, trying to help her.

She nodded. "Aye, we do. That's no' the problem." She frowned fiercely. "Or perhaps it is."

"I don't understand," I admitted when she failed to elaborate.

She lowered the dress, staring at the wall above the head of our bed. "I canna see a future for us." Her voice was tight with anguish. "No' one where we're both happy."

I still didn't comprehend. "Because of your positions?" I tried to guess. "As long as it didn't adversely affect your work, we would keep . . ."

"But it would," she interrupted vehemently, turning toward me. "There's no way tae avoid it."

"But nothing would truly change. You would still hold the same positions and help us with our inquiries." I flushed lightly. "Nothing except that you and Anderley would share chambers."

"And when a bairn comes along?" she demanded almost angrily.

Realization slowly began to trickle through me.

"I canna perform my duties and take care o' a bairn. I realize ye might be unconventional, m'lady . . ." she shook her head ". . . but ye're no' impractical. I would have tae resign." She gazed down again at the dress clutched in her hands, her voice growing increasingly forlorn. "We'd rent a cottage in Warwickshire near yer estate or rooms here in Edinburgh, where I would remain while Anderley continued tae travel wi' ye, pursuin' yer inquiries. That, or he'd resign as well and be forced tae find other work. But I dinna see him wantin' tae leave Mr. Gage's employ, and I would never ask it o' him."

I could tell now that she'd been stewing over this for quite some time, and I felt a sense of shame that I'd not recognized the difficulties earlier. Having a child had certainly created logistical considerations for me, but as a wealthy gentlewoman, I could hire whatever staff was needed and pay for anything I desired to minimize any complications. I could pursue my art, and conduct inquiries, and travel wherever Gage went as long as certain members of our staff came with us. The greatest potential barrier came from my husband, who could forbid me from doing any or all of those things and I would have no legal recourse to fight him. Fortunately, Gage did not exercise such an authority over me. Our marriage was a partnership. But the fact of the matter remained that lawfully he still could.

While I didn't expect Anderley to be dissimilar, his and Bree's situation was much different. They were not wealthy. They were dependent on their wages for their living. When children came along, as of course they would—there was no effective way to prevent it, and I knew Bree wanted them eventually anyway—she would have no choice but to resign her position to take care of them. They couldn't afford a nanny or a governess like people of my and Gage's station could, and offering Bree to use ours was simply not done. Not only because it was unorthodox and frowned upon by many, but because it very likely might cause a revolt among the staff, who, if possible, were even more conscious of social class and rank than those who employed them. Even *our* staff.

"And I take it you don't wish to remain behind?" I asked carefully, recognizing that her dissatisfaction stemmed from this.

"Would *you*?" she challenged, misunderstanding me.

"No. No, I wouldn't."

This seemed to appease her, for her irritation softened into gloom. "I like bein' yer maid." She arched her chin. "I like the satisfaction o' kennin' I sent ye tae a ball or soiree lookin' like a duchess, even if ye are no' one." She smoothed her hand over the silk of the gown draped over her arm. "I like travelin' tae new places and seein' new things. And I like helpin' wi' the inquiries, o' makin' a difference, even if 'tis just a small one." Her gaze when it lifted to mine was unspeakably sad. "I would miss ye, and wee Emma, and Mrs. Mackay, and all the others. I'm just no' ready to give all that up."

I offered her an empathetic smile. "Have you explained this to Anderley?"

She stiffened in frustration. "Aye, but he doesna understand. Or maybe he simply doesna *want* tae. All he seems tae hear when I try tae make him see the matter from my perspective is that our bein' wed isna enough tae make me happy. Which is easy for him tae say. Nothin' would change for him. He can carry on as he has. I'm the only one whose life would be totally upended."

It was no wonder she'd been so conflicted these past few weeks and months. All these things had been stirring in her mind, with no immediate solution in sight. And she'd largely been facing them alone since Anderley seemed unable to see the matter objectively from her point of view.

"I'm sorry, Bree," I told her, wishing there was something more I could do.

"'Tisn't yer fault," she said, brushing a stray strand of her strawberry blond hair out of her eyes as she began to gather up my other discarded garments.

"No, but I wish I'd realized sooner what a conundrum you're in. I wish I knew the solution."

She turned to face me and sighed, offering me a smile of comfort. "I ken ye do, m'lady. 'Tis why I havena said anythin'. 'Tis my problem. Weel, mine and Anderley's. And you've enough tae contend wi'. I dinna want ye takin' on this burden, too."

"You're never a burden, Bree," I assured her, but I could tell she didn't believe me.

"Aye, weel, dinna sit up frettin'. Anderley and Mr. St. Mawr willna let anythin' happen tae Mr. Gage. Worryin' will only give ye boils."

I wondered if this was another dubious piece of folklore she'd picked up from her family in Kirkcudbright, but then she paused in the doorway to cast a teasing smile over her shoulder, telling me it was all in jest.

When Gage returned with the others about half an hour later, he found me seated sideways on the robin's-egg blue settee before the hearth, gazing up at the portrait I'd painted of him before we wed. The one which had, in many ways, prompted his proposal. Or at least given him the courage to make it. A portrait of infant Emma hung on the adjoining wall.

"Apologies for the delay, darling," he declared as he came bustling in, bending over to press a kiss to my brow. He plopped down into the chair opposite, tugging at his cravat as he toed off his shoes. "It took longer than anticipated to convince Sullivan to talk, but once he understood the seriousness of the potential charges being leveled against him, he was happy to point the finger of blame at someone else."

After hearing what Bonnie Brock had uncovered about Fletcher, I could only turn to Gage in bewilderment. Unless he was going to tell me Sullivan acted as his accomplice.

He tossed the cravat aside and began shrugging out of his frock coat. "He claims he was paid to look the other way. That the third day of the auction, once the bidding started, he was supposed to stand near the doorway leading to the rear drawing room with his back to the room."

He was speaking of the theft then, not the collapse.

"Who paid him?" I asked, adjusting the indigo dressing gown over my lace-trimmed nightdress.

"He wasn't given the man's name, or the reason why he was to look the other way . . ."

I scoffed. "Though he must have guessed it."

Gage nodded, draping his coat over the back of his chair as he began to unbutton his slate gray waistcoat. "But he followed the man. Said he wanted some leverage in case the police came looking for him."

"Smart man." I tilted my head. "And where did this man he followed go?"

He arched his eyebrows. "George Square."

And we knew exactly who lived there. "Reverend Jamieson." I wondered for a moment if he or Sullivan had been behind me being pushed in front of the carriage. If Bonnie Brock had been wrong about that part of it. After all, the incident had occurred after we'd just spoken to the reverend. But surely Gage had questioned Sullivan about it.

"That's why we were delayed," Gage continued to explain. "We went to question Jamieson again, but he wasn't home. In fact, he's left the city."

"How convenient."

The twist of his lips told me he'd caught the wry tone of my voice. "Maclean is having his men keep watch in case he returns, but for the moment, he's beyond our reach."

"Then Brade Cranston, the rival auctioneer, isn't involved?" I asked for clarification as Gage tossed his waistcoat over his frock coat. It slid to the floor.

"Not that Sullivan admitted to."

I thought back to the nasty comments Mr. Cranston had made, almost wishing we had a reason to see him locked up. "And the floor collapse?"

"He swears he knew nothing about that. Though he voiced his suspicions that one of Mr. Winstanley's assistants was involved."

"It was Fletcher," I pronounced gravely.

"Is that your intuition speaking, or has Kincaid swayed you?" he teased with a grin as he finished unbuttoning his cuffs and then looked down to start on the buttons running down the front of his shirt.

"That's based on what Bonnie Brock told me tonight."

Gage's head jerked upright, his golden hair falling in his eyes. "Kincaid was here?"

I explained about Bonnie Brock's visit and what he'd told me about Fletcher while Gage listened raptly. Gage's stormy expression lightened as he became caught up in what the maid at the White Horse had revealed. Though I was certain it would change in an instant if I told him about Bonnie Brock's attempt to kiss me.

"Then it must be Fletcher," Gage declared, rising to his feet to pace the small space behind his chair. He scraped a hand through his hair, pushing it from his face, though it did little good, for it flopped back over his brow. "But why?"

"That's the same thing I asked. And Bonnie Brock reminded me that's for us to find out."

Gage paused to glower at me, though I knew it was really directed at the infamous rogue. "And how much more quickly might Anderley have uncovered this if we'd not listened to Kincaid's warning to steer clear of the White Horse."

I scowled, thinking of the conversation I'd just had with Bree. "Unless he was right, and Anderley continuing to venture there *would* have placed him in danger. Would you really have wanted to take such a risk?"

He looked as if he was about to argue, but then sighed, shaking his head. "No. No, I wouldn't." He sank into the chair again. "But the man is a menace, Kiera!" he growled.

It was obvious he was speaking about Bonnie Brock.

"He has absolutely no regard for boundaries!"

I bit my lip, lest I give away how accurate this accusation was. Revealing so would only endanger Gage's life, for I knew he would feel honor bound to do something about Bonnie Brock's behavior toward me.

"Could you not have turned him away?"

It was my turn to scowl.

"No, I suppose not," he conceded. "After all, Kincaid does what Kincaid wants. And he did provide us with some invaluable information," he admitted begrudgingly before fuming silently for a few seconds. "Then what's our next step? Obviously, Maclean needs to be told." He grimaced. "Though he's not going to like the source."

I shrugged, pulling my knees up toward my chest and wrapping my arms around them. "So don't tell him who we learned it from. Or let him believe it was Anderley. I'm sure it won't be difficult for him to locate this barmaid at the White Horse and have her corroborate it."

"Perhaps you're right." He began to reach for his shoes. "I suppose I'll have to . . ."

"Not tonight," I snapped.

He halted, turning to me in surprise.

I tightened my arms, lest he notice their trembling. "The sergeant will, no doubt, already be home with his family." I swallowed. "Tomorrow morning is soon enough. Before Emma's party."

"You're right." His eyes were soft as he searched my face, looking for something.

I wanted to ask if he'd forgotten what had happened on this date. How one year ago we would have already been huddled together in the vaults, counting the minutes until the light from our only lantern went out, terrified as my labor pains increased. But then he asked a rather astute question. One that let me know he wasn't quite so oblivious.

"Have you looked in on her?"

I inhaled past the tightness in my chest. "Not in the last hour," I confessed.

He rose to his stockinged feet, holding his hand out to me. Taking it automatically, I allowed him to pull me up. Then hand in hand we stole upstairs to the nursery. There was no light showing underneath Mrs. Mackay's adjoining chamber door, so we moved stealthily so as not to wake her or Emma.

Our daughter lay on her back, her hands resting on either side of her head, palms open. Her face was turned slightly toward us, resting in sweet repose. She had contrived to remove her cap, as she often did at night, and her golden curls lay rumpled against the white sheets. It was much the same position I'd found her in an hour earlier, and my heart constricted and flooded with warmth, as it always did at the sight of her. It took everything within me to restrain myself from bending closer to smell her sweet baby scent or reaching out to touch the tender curve of her cheek. I had to content myself with the sight of her slumbering, with the soft sigh of her exhale.

It was the last that caused tears to overflow my eyes and a sob to gather in my throat. I must have made some sound of distress, for Gage pulled me away from her cradle and out of the nursery, closing the door quietly behind us. Then he gathered me close as I finally gave way to the tears that had been threatening all evening. He guided me back to our bedchamber.

"How . . . how can something so wonderful also make me so . . . so sad?" I blubbered into his shirt once we had returned to the warmth of our room.

"The memory of Emma's birthday?"

"Yes. No." I hiccupped, swiping at my cheeks. "That, and the fact that soon she'll no longer be a baby, and she won't need me. And before we can even blink, she'll be grown and married and living with her husband and having her own babies."

Gage passed me his handkerchief, his eyes lit with gentle amusement. "Slow down, Kiera. I think you might be rushing things just a little."

"Don't laugh at me," I protested, pushing away from him.

But he gathered me close again. "I'm not. Well, yes, I am. But only because you're being a tad ridiculous."

I glared up at him.

He grimaced. "I'm not making this any better, am I?"

I let my huff answer for me.

"The thing is." He brushed the wisps of hair that had already escaped my braid back from my face. "Our daughter is always going to need you. Even when she's grown and has her own babies. She'll just need you in a different way."

I sniffed, searching his pale blue eyes for reassurance. "How can you be sure?"

"Well, don't you still need your mother? Don't you wish she was here?"

I dabbed at my eyes, thinking of all the times in the past year and more when I'd wished—sometimes desperately—that my mother had been there. To give me advice. To console me. To coo over her newest granddaughter.

"Do you miss your mother?" I asked, though I already knew the answer.

His expression dimmed. "Every day."

I offered him a watery smile of commiseration.

"But even though I will never stop wishing she was with me, in most instances, I already know what she would say."

"Like what?" I asked.

He cupped the side of my jaw with one hand. "That I married the right woman. That she's glad I've reconciled with Father. That she adores her little namesake."

I blinked as more tears threatened.

"Just as I imagine you know what your mother would say." He gazed intently at me. "That she loves you. That you're a wonderful mother." His eyes twinkled. "That surely you must have married the most perfect specimen of all mankind."

I made a noise between a giggle and a sob. "Is that so?"

"You shouldn't argue with your mother."

I laughed more genuinely and then leaned forward to press a kiss to the hollow of his throat. "I suppose not."

"And you know what else she would say." He pulled back, lowering his chin so that I looked him in the eye. "That you should exhibit your art, and any naysayers be damned."

The nerves I'd been suppressing fluttered in my stomach. "She would never use such coarse language."

His expression turned mildly chastising. "Don't try to divert from the point, Kiera." He raised his hands to grasp my shoulders. "It's time."

I swallowed the lump in my throat, but I still couldn't speak. Not in the face of his earnestness, his belief in me.

"Maybe others will never see the world as you do. Not exactly. But that doesn't mean you shouldn't try to show them. At the very least, it will open a few of their eyes, just like you've opened mine. And isn't that what you said you want? For us all to no longer turn away blindly?"

It was no more than I'd already been thinking. Especially after giving Bonnie Brock the portrait I'd painted of him and his sister, and after seeing his reaction to it. It was then that I'd finally accepted that the gift I'd been given was meant to be shared. That if I believed that art was about the beauty found in truth, then hiding it away was not only selfish, but a form of repression, of dishonesty, of lies.

To leave those paintings I'd worked so hard on gathering dust in the corner of my art studio, to never bring them into the light of day, was too nauseating to contemplate. It was like denying all the people I'd depicted the right to have their truth known and told. It was being complicit in society's determination to look away.

However, the acceptance of what I must do did not remove the fear. The words stuck in my throat so that all I could do was nod and whisper. "Yes. Let's do it."

He seemed surprised at first that I'd agreed so easily, but then he smiled. "Truly?"

"Yes."

His lips captured mine. "Then you must let us all help. And if we can't find a suitable exhibition space, we'll host it ourselves."

"Yes." I arched up on my toes to kiss him again. "But there's nothing to be done about it tonight."

A reprieve, albeit temporary, before I had to screw up my courage entirely.

My mouth met his again, longer this time, as I towed him toward the bed. "And if we must pass this night, I would prefer it be in your arms in the warmth of our bed rather than continuing to remember last year."

He followed me down onto the mattress, his hard body covering me as his lips trailed over my cheek to my earlobe and then down my neck. His voice was a deep caress. "Then let's make a far more pleasurable memory to replace it."

And we did.

CHAPTER 27

My daughter's first birthday was everything that I'd hoped it would be. At breakfast, we celebrated with Trevor and our staff, almost all of whom were as enamored with Emma as everyone else. Mrs. Grady made tall stacks of fluffy bannocks, which everyone—especially Emma—enjoyed with creamy butter and jam. There was much laughter and merriment, and our daughter loved the spinning top that the staff gifted her. Though she couldn't make it spin on her own yet, I imagined it wouldn't be long before she figured it out. Or before Mrs. Mackay made certain she did.

Then Emma was whisked off to the nursery for a bath, and the rest of the staff set to preparing for her birthday tea. While I supervised, Gage and Trevor dashed off to inform Sergeant Maclean of our discovery about Mr. Fletcher. Or rather, Bonnie Brock's discovery, but I knew Gage would do all in his power to leave the criminal out of the discussion. However, not before I noted him conferring in hushed tones with Bree and Anderley while I directed Jeffers on the placement of some of the furniture. I wondered what it could be about, but it was over before I could venture closer to ask. From that moment on, I was busy answering one question or another, moving from room to room.

When Alana arrived an hour before the party, she found me still in my morning gown and promptly took over, shooing me off to my bedchamber to change. Even then, I was still peppered with queries at times relayed through the door. By the time I made my way up to the nursery a quarter of an hour before the guests were supposed to arrive, Mrs. Mackay was already dressing a still-sleepy Emma in her white-satin-and-gauze dress festooned with periwinkle ribbons and bows that matched the color of my gown.

"Ye dinna want tae sleep the day away," the nanny cajoled her. "No' this day." Catching sight of me, she proclaimed cheerily, "Didna want tae wake from her nap, but nay worries. Soon as she hears those cousins o' hers, she'll perk up."

I suspected she was right. In any case, I rather welcomed a few minutes of extra snuggles before the excitement of the tea began. Gage was waiting for us when I made my way downstairs with Emma's face buried in my neck, her fingers idly playing with the amethyst pendant draped around my neck. It made me feel that in some way my mother—Emma's grandmother—was with us in spirit.

He was smiling that private little smile he reserved only for me as I neared the bottom. However, there seemed to be an extra element to it. Something that made me suspicious.

He must have sensed this, for he leaned down to speak with Emma. "Feeling a little shy, are we?"

"Sleepy." My gaze flicked toward the dining room, where I heard voices.

"Charlotte and Rye are here with the children, as well as Henry and your cousin Jock."

My lips quirked. "I suppose that accounts for the loud crowing." Jock was always ready with a jest.

Gage shook his head, though laughter was lurking at the corners of his mouth. "Don't ask."

We turned toward the front door as Jeffers opened it to admit more well-wishers. This time it was Philip and the children. True to Mrs. Mackay's prediction, Emma looked up at the sound of wee Jamie chattering away in his own peculiar toddler tongue. She turned to grin at him as he removed his coat, dropping it onto the floor in his haste to greet her. I could only laugh at the pair of them, which drew a weary smile from Philip, who had snatched the coat from the floor as Jeffers was helping his eldest daughter, Philipa, out of her pelisse. Greer soon appeared at my side as well, reaching up to take Emma's hand as she cooed to her.

"Let's all retire to the dining room, shall we?" I told them just as Alana stepped into the corridor to greet her brood. "I hear there are sweets."

This raised a cheer from Jamie and Greer, though Philipa was attempting to appear more dignified. I touched the sleeve of her gown. "You look lovely," I told her, earning a smile from her. "Quite grown-up. I can't believe you're going to be eight years old in just a few short weeks."

"Don't remind me," Alana said wistfully, tucking an errant hair behind her daughter's ear.

Philipa flushed and hurried after her brother and sister.

Alana shook her head before sharing a tender look with her husband. Then she turned to Emma with a bright smile as she held her arms out toward her. "May I hold the birthday girl?"

I looked to Emma to see if she was awake enough now to be passed about, and she willingly went to my sister.

I looped my arm through Gage's, leaning my head against his shoulder as we followed them into the dining room. It was a brief moment of connection before we separated to greet our guests and immerse ourselves in the celebration. Mrs. Grady had truly outdone herself, making platters piled high with delicious sandwiches, scones, and various sweets, including her lemon cakes, which were all washed down with pots of tea and pitchers of lemonade. Alana had arranged games for the children in the morning room while the food was cleared away, and then I helped Emma to open her gifts. They ranged from dolls and windmills and hobbyhorses to a toy drum, courtesy of Trevor. He'd smiled unabashedly at us once Emma had figured out how to use the stick to beat it and make a loud sound.

Jamie had instantly been captivated, asking his uncle to get him one. All of us were amused by the alarm that lit Philip's and Alana's eyes at the prospect.

"Sorry, old chap," Trevor told Jamie between chuckles. "But maybe a fife."

This would be no kinder to their household's eardrums, but I supposed he was less likely to be tempted to bash things he shouldn't with it as opposed to a drumstick.

My favorite gift was from Alana, who'd had the flower for Emma's birth month—a white daisy—pressed and framed, along with an inscription of her full name, just like she'd done for each of her own children on their first birthdays. Alana had even included a few short lines of verse she'd written just for her niece. Upon reading it, I'd had to sniff back tears.

When the gifts were finished, I'd believed the party was all but over, but Gage had another trick up his sleeve. He murmured to Alana, asking her to mind Emma, who was playing with her new toys along with her guests. Then he beckoned me out to the corridor.

"What is it?" I asked in confusion. "Did Maclean send word about Mr. Fletcher?" We'd not had a chance yet to discuss Maclean's reaction to what he'd told him this morning.

"No, no. This isn't about the inquiry." He pulled me a short distance away from the door, wrapping his arms around my waist as he gazed down at me with a warm smile. "Are you feeling brave?"

I blinked at him uncertainly. "I don't know what you mean."

"You will."

Nerves began to flutter in my stomach at this rather cryptic remark, especially when he glanced over his shoulder toward the corridor outside the morning room. Mrs. Mackay and Bree stood waiting, but they began to move toward us at his nod. Then he gripped my hand and urged me back to the dining room entrance.

"If I could have your attention, please," he announced, waiting for the room to fall silent except wee Jamie, who was banging sharply on the drum as he sat in Trevor's lap. Judging from his expression, he regretted his gift choice. "We have a bit of a surprise for you, if you'll follow me. The children can remain here."

He pulled my arm through the crook of his, guiding me toward the stairs.

"What surprise?" I asked as we ascended.

"You'll see," he responded again with maddening ambiguity.

"Sebastian," I murmured with a rising sense of dread. "What have you done?"

Given our conversation before retiring, I had an unsettling feeling about what awaited us. For a moment, as we veered toward the drawing room and not the stairs leading to the upper levels and my art studio, I thought perhaps I'd been wrong. But then I caught a glimpse of the contents of the drawing room and was unable to stifle a gasp.

He turned to me as I gazed in panic at the sight of all the portraits intended for my exhibit arrayed about the chamber. It was far from ideal, as I possessed only four easels, but the other portraits had been carefully propped on sofas and chairs and any surface which could safely support them. Furniture from the neighboring library had also been dragged into the room and put to such use. This, then, must have been what he'd been whispering to Bree and Anderley about.

Gage grasped my hands, pivoting me so that he could see into my face. "Trust your friends and family, Kiera. Trust *me*," he pleaded.

Part of me wanted to rage at him, for he'd really given me no choice in the matter *but* to trust him. But another part of me was afraid if I opened my mouth, I might be sick all over my shoes. So I remained silent, standing stiffly to the side of the door while the others filed in.

At first, I was too apprehensive to look at their faces, frightened of what I might see. They might lie and tell me they were good, but they could never conceal the truth from my eyes. I would know it the second I read their expressions.

But wasn't that what I needed to know—no matter how painful? Wasn't it better to see the truth in my loved ones' faces first before the portraits were exposed to strangers? Before it was too late to halt the entire thing?

In the end, it was my cousin Morven's soft exclamation that gave me the courage to look up. I knew that sound. I knew it was one of revelation and astonishment. And I knew she was seeing what I'd hoped she would in the painting she was examining. The sweetness of the Irish mother's relationship with her child, the bone weariness of each of her plodding footsteps along the road, the flickering hope in her eyes that life would one day be easier for her little one.

As my gaze swept around the room, I saw similar expressions of absorption and connection with the subjects of the portraits, and the terror that had gripped me nearly in a stranglehold began to abate, replaced by a mixture of wonder, profound relief, and overwhelming gratitude. I squeezed Gage's hand where he still gripped mine and peered up at him to see his eyes were shining with triumph and not a small amount of smugness. I let him have it.

In any case, I had questions to answer and love and praise to receive. Each word and stunned shake of the head and embrace was a precious balm to my artist's soul. Even Alana, who was so much more concerned with class expectations, only had good things to say. But then, she had always supported my art. It was my involvement with murderous inquiries she struggled with. They each pledged their help in arranging the exhibition and spreading the word to make it a success. Philip even confessed he intended to share the matter with his fellow Whigs, as they were planning to leave for London in a week's time, following Easter Sunday.

It was more than I could have hoped for, and I had Gage to thank for forcing it upon me. As much as I wanted to be angry at him for that, I simply couldn't. Not when I knew he'd only had my best interests at heart. Had it been anyone else, I never would have tolerated it, but he knew me, and he knew the people who loved me well enough to understand that this was the safe push I needed. I might have arrived at the realization that I couldn't leave the paintings gathering dust. I might have told my husband this, but he'd known I would continue to drag my heels for months if not years, despite my art being ready, if he didn't force my hand. Given that, it seemed best to forgive him for his high-handed interference. Best to forgive and express my appreciation. I made certain to do so appropriately that night.

• • •

With the excitement of Emma's birthday over, we settled our minds back to the inquiry. Sergeant Maclean had sent word that evening that Mr. Fletcher hadn't been seen in two days at either Picardy Place or the White Horse, where he was lodging, and no one seemed to know where he'd gone. The barmaid Bonnie Brock's associate had spoken with had confirmed her story with Maclean, but denied having said anything to Mr. Fletcher that might have led him to believe his secrets were no longer safe. Whether this was a lie or Mr. Fletcher had become leery for a different reason was beside the point. He was missing and potentially dangerous to those who were aware of his guilt.

As such, Gage reiterated the necessity of none of us venturing out alone when we gathered in the library the morning after the soiree. This time, Trevor had joined our number, as well as Henry. All told, we were a party of seven, plus Mrs. Mackay, who was in the nursery with Emma but would be informed of our discussion later. Yet our larger numbers meant nothing when Mr. Fletcher had stealth on his side and several days' lead in planning his next move.

"Are we all in agreement that we can eliminate most of our other suspects?" Gage asked after recapitulating what we'd recently learned. "Innes and Clerk and Brade Cranston?"

"What about Sullivan?" Anderley asked. His face was drawn and pinched, making me wonder how much he'd slept the previous night.

Gage's gaze shifted to meet mine. "While Mr. Sullivan had a hand to play in the theft of those coins, I think we can eliminate him from the sabotage of Lord Eldin's town house. His actions the day of the collapse speak for themselves, and his elusiveness following your discovery of his cousin's employment at Brade Cranston can easily be explained by his fear of being caught for the bribe he took."

"What of Reverend Jamieson?" Jeffers inquired, his posture as impeccable as always, even seated on one of the sofas. "You seem convinced he was behind the theft, and Mr. Sullivan appears to have confirmed it, but what of the collapse?"

"I honestly don't know," I confessed when no one else leapt in to voice their opinion. I turned to frown at the overcast sky outside the windows. "The trouble is, we still don't understand the motive behind the sabotage of that joist, why someone would do such a thing and risk so many lives. Until we do, it's difficult to say whether Mr. Fletcher was working alone or with an accomplice. If he was the head of the operation or he cut the beam at someone else's behest. Someone like Jamieson."

Bree lowered the stitching she'd brought with her. "But wasna Mr. Fletcher injured in the collapse? Wouldna he have done whatever he could tae steer clear o' the room if he ken the floor was goin' tae give way?"

"Yes, but if he didn't show up to work that day, he must have known suspicion would fall on him," Anderley pointed out. "Perhaps he thought he could switch tasks with another employee but then was unable. Or maybe he thought he would have enough notice of the pending collapse to escape before it happened."

"He *was* one of the people standing closest to the entrance to the front drawing room." Gage shook his head. "But I don't think we'll be able to answer that for sure until we talk to Mr. Fletcher himself." He leaned forward, motioning decisively with his hands. "But the motive . . . I think it must have something to do with the building itself. With past collapses like at Kirkcaldy."

"There have been a number of articles and editorials in the newspapers debating current building practices and the laws around them, and speculating as to whether there are other such calamities just waiting to happen," Henry chimed in to say.

Trevor bumped me with his knee as he lifted it to rest his ankle over the opposite leg. "There's been a scramble to have buildings inspected to ensure they're secure."

"A scramble here in New Town at the private residences of the wealthy." Anderley's voice was forbidding. "But what about the public buildings? Particularly those in the older parts of the city. And what of the tenements?"

It was a justifiable question, with unsettling implications. One that none of us held the answer to.

"Have you read the *Edinburgh Evening Courant*, by chance?" Henry asked Anderley in curiosity.

"No?" he replied, a query in his voice.

"There was a letter to the editor published there just a few days ago. It asked much the same question, and suggested we'd learned the wrong lesson from all of this. That it will happen again, with perhaps even more devastating consequences, if the law isn't changed and enforced."

This was a sentiment I could agree with, but the grave look on Henry's face made it clear there was more.

"The writer even went so far as to reference Easter Sunday, when all the churches will be packed with worshipers."

My gaze flew to Gage, wondering if he found this as pointed and chilling as I did.

"What was the writer's name?" he asked his half brother.

"I'll try to find the article again to check," Henry replied. "But if my recollection is correct, it was a concerned citizen or some such code for anonymous."

Henry could look, but I trusted his memory was correct. The very fact that the writer hadn't wanted to include his real name made me all the more uneasy. We needed to find Fletcher by Sunday. We needed to uncover everyone behind the sabotage and why they'd done it.

Gage ran his index finger over his lips, glaring unseeing at the floor before him. "Mr. Clerk did find an entry in his brother's memoir that described a visit he made to Kirkcaldy soon after the collapse. He apparently made some sort of grand declaration that he would ensure something was done. But neither Lord Henry nor I have been able to find any reference to Lord Eldin actually doing anything to help Kirkcaldy or change the law. He seems to have just been spouting proclamations."

"Which could be our connection to Lord Eldin's former town house, except what do Fletcher and Jamieson have to do with Kirkcaldy?" Trevor turned to Gage. "You said Fletcher was from Liverpool?"

"All of Winstanley's employees purportedly were." He nodded toward his valet. "But of course, Anderley uncovered that wasn't actually the case with Sullivan. So who's to say that another of them might not also have lied?"

This stirred a vague recollection in me. One I couldn't immediately place. So I brushed it aside in favor of sharing a fact I knew was relevant.

"Reverend Jamieson knew the minister at Kirkcaldy. I heard him discussing it with another fellow at the Inverleith Ball. He was familiar with the congregation there."

Trevor lowered his leg and slid toward the edge of his seat. "Then we need to speak to Jamieson."

"He's still missing," I reminded him.

"Or so his staff claimed." Gage turned to Jeffers. "But a staff loyal to their employer might prevaricate on his behalf. Even to the police."

It wasn't a question, but Jeffers answered regardless. "Especially to the police."

Gage nodded, recognizing this as a statement of loyalty to

us as well as confirmation of Gage's inference. Not that there was ever any doubt. "So he might be hiding under our very noses."

"I could speak to his staff," Anderley offered. Then his gaze flicked toward Bree. "Miss McEvoy and I could."

Gage considered this, but then shook his head. "No, I think I have a better idea. If Lord Henry and Mr. St. Mawr were to show up on his doorstep, he's less likely to be suspicious."

"And the staff will be, too," Jeffers interjected. "If the police have asked after the reverend, the staff will already be on guard to anyone asking questions of them."

"But what pretense would we give for wishing to see him?" Henry asked with an uncertain glance at Trevor.

"Tell him that you're scholars interested in the Scottish language," I suggested. "That you . . . read his *Etymological Dictionary of the Scottish Language* and wished to meet the author . . . to compliment him on his publication."

"I suppose that could work," Trevor said.

"But what if he starts asking us questions?" Henry protested. "I'm no lexicographer."

Gage pushed to his feet, moving toward one of the bookshelves closest to the hearth. "You need only stall him a few minutes," he explained, running his fingers along the spines of the books. "If you are willingly admitted to the house, then we shall take that as an admission of his being at home. We'll be close by, watching, and will force our way inside, if necessary. You only need to keep him talking and prevent him from leaving the room." His finger stopped, apparently finding what he was searching for, as he pulled a book from the shelf. "If it makes you feel better, you can brush up on Jamieson's work beforehand."

He passed the hefty tome to Henry, who flipped it over to reveal it was the etymological dictionary in question.

Henry briefly flipped through some of the pages. "I would prefer to have at least a few hours to prepare."

Sinking back into his seat, Gage yielded to this. "I'll need to speak with Maclean to arrange matters anyway."

"I would also like to have a word with Mr. Rimmer," I informed him. "Though I'm sure the police have spoken with him, he might have withheld something he knows, either purposely, or because he doesn't realize he knows it."

"And you think he'll tell you?"

"Yes."

Gage didn't question my perhaps unfounded assertion. "Then let's put our plans into motion."

CHAPTER 28

When we informed Maclean of our suspicions about Reverend Jamieson, he was more inclined to break down his door, brush the servants aside, and drag the minister out by his collar. We convinced him that might not be the best method of convincing him to talk, and that it would almost certainly result in outrage from the public given Jamieson's status. As his temper cooled, he conceded that our plan was more circumspect and logical, and promised to arrange for its implementation.

In the meantime, Gage and I paid a visit to Picardy Place in search of Mr. Rimmer. We found two carts pulled up out front, monitored by their drivers and a policeman, and Mr. Winstanley and his employees in a flurry of activity inside. It seemed they'd finally been given permission to move the collection to safer premises, and the auctioneer was making the most of the clearing in the clouds to transport what he could.

Winstanley's spectacles were askew and his cravat was

rumpled, revealing how frazzled he was. I imagined the loss of two employees—one of them being one of the assistants on whom he so heavily relied—had made matters much more difficult. As such, I didn't take it personally when he rounded on us after having instructed several of his men on what to carry out next.

"What do you want?"

"A word with Mr. Rimmer," Gage replied calmly.

"Must it be *now*?" he demanded.

"I'm afraid so."

He heaved an exasperated sigh, before flinging his arm toward the door leading to the servants' staircase. "He's supposed to be locating a tarpaulin or canvas. And he's taking his good time doing so."

I turned to Gage to see if this statement concerned him as much as it did me. Mr. Rimmer might simply have been enjoying a reprieve from his irascible employer, but I feared there might be a different reason for his prolonged absence.

"Stay behind me," Gage murmured as he pushed open the door, proving he shared my unease.

As the noises from above receded, we paused partway down the steps, listening for any sounds from below. I heard a faint drip of water coming from somewhere, but otherwise it was silent save for the periodic creak of the floor above. As we continued, I had to remind myself that the building had been inspected and was secure. That the creaks and groans we heard were normal.

When we neared the bottom, I wasn't as surprised as maybe I should have been when Gage reached beneath his coat and extracted the pistol he'd tucked into the waistband of his trousers. Perhaps because I was also carrying a gun in the reticule dangling from my wrist. Given Fletcher's and Jamieson's unconfirmed whereabouts and the previous attack on me, I'd decided it would be best to take my Hewson percussion pistol with us.

The corridor was silent as we inched our way down it, listening for any indication of occupation. If Mr. Rimmer was searching for a tarpaulin or canvas, he was doing so remarkably quietly. We peered into vacant rooms lit dimly by the light from the corridor and shrouded windows high on the walls, but nothing seemed disturbed. Gage moved with far more confidence than I did, but then I remembered that he'd been here before with Maclean searching for ladders and checking the locks. I'd never ventured belowstairs, though it appeared to be laid out much like the servants' quarters in our town house.

He stumbled to a stop as we rounded a corner, and I soon realized why. There was a stack of folded canvas lying on the floor, but no sign of Mr. Rimmer. That haphazard pile made me anxious for Rimmer's safety, for if he'd been gathering supplies as instructed, why had he stopped?

We found our answer inside the scullery. Mr. Rimmer lay crumpled on the floor, the back of his head matted with blood.

I sank onto my knees beside him. "Mr. Rimmer," I gasped, touching his shoulder, which was still warm. Pressing my fingers to the underside of his jaw, I felt for a pulse. When I found it, I exhaled in relief, nodding to Gage, who looked on. "He's alive."

But I didn't know for how long. It depended on how serious his head injury was, and there was no way to tell that just from the quantity of blood coating his hair and pooling onto the floor. Head wounds always bled rather alarmingly.

I glanced about me for something to stanch the bleeding. "Those towels," I said, catching sight of a stack near the sink. "Pass them to me."

Gage fetched them and then helped me to press them to the wound as I rolled Mr. Rimmer over to his back.

"We should send for a physician or . . . or a surgeon," I vacillated, uncertain which was the appropriate medical man for the job.

Gage jumped to his feet, but then hesitated. "Do you have your pistol?"

"Yes. Now go."

His footsteps swiftly receded down the corridor, and I cautiously examined Mr. Rimmer for further injury, all the while speaking to him and trying to coax him awake. "Mr. Rimmer, please. Who did this to you? Was it Mr. Fletcher?"

He seemed the logical choice. After all, he would know the layout of the house. But why had he returned? And why had he attacked Mr. Rimmer? Did he think his former colleague knew something that could implicate him, or perhaps foil whatever his future plans were? If so, that would be valuable information, indeed. And it made it all the more imperative we find out.

"Mr. Rimmer, please, wake up," I begged.

But his eyelashes didn't even flicker.

Mr. Winstanley returned with Gage, looking genuinely distraught at the sight of his assistant. He lingered as a surgeon who happened to live in the next block over arrived to examine Mr. Rimmer. The young man didn't wake through the entire process of examining the wound and checking him for other injuries. But while the surgeon couldn't promise Mr. Rimmer would recover, he found his reflexes and general health to be a hopeful sign. However, he would require constant supervision and care until he awakened and regained complete control of his faculties.

Mr. Rimmer remained insensible as the surgeon snipped the hair around his laceration and then carefully applied sutures.

"I . . . I suppose I can hire someone to nurse him," Mr.

Winstanley turned away to stammer to me and Gage, clearly still shaken. "Yes, I shall have to. Though the White Horse is not the most conducive quarters for such a thing."

No, a busy coaching inn was no place for a man to recover, and the hospital would only expose him to further disease.

"Have him brought to our house on Albyn Place," I urged, trusting Gage would not argue. "We can care for him there."

"Oh, but we couldn't impose in such a way," Mr. Winstanley protested, clearly shocked by the offer.

"It's not an imposition," I insisted, though Gage's expression suggested otherwise. "The truth is, he may know something critical to our inquiry. He and Mr. Fletcher shared lodgings, did they not?" I watched as Gage's brow smoothed and the same realization I'd already come to lit his eyes. "Then he might know something that could help us lead to his apprehension. Why else would Mr. Fletcher risk coming here to attack him?"

Mr. Winstanley's eyes widened with alarm. "You think Mr. Fletcher did this? Then . . . are we all in danger?"

"Not if you don't know anything." My gaze slid to meet my husband's and then back. "But we need to make sure Mr. Rimmer is secure so that Mr. Fletcher doesn't try again." And so that when—*if*—Mr. Rimmer woke, we could probe him about what he knew.

At the White Horse, he would be an easy target, either unconscious or too weak to defend himself should Mr. Fletcher decide to ensure he remained silent forever. At least, at our house, he had a chance of recovering.

"If you're certain you wish to do this?" Mr. Winstanley looked to Gage to confirm. "Then I would be much obliged." The anguish in his eyes was genuine when he turned once more toward poor Mr. Rimmer. "He is not one of my sons, but I still care for him like one."

The matter decided, I dashed off a missive to warn our staff to prepare the second guest chamber and gave one of the lads who were lingering to watch the goods loaded into the carts out front a coin to deliver it. The surgeon instructed me and Gage in the care Mr. Rimmer should be given while several of Mr. Winstanley's men carried the still-unconscious assistant out through the garden to the mews, where our coach was now waiting. As we rumbled slowly away from the vacant carriage house toward the tunnel which would lead out to Broughton Street, Mr. Rimmer's body jostling lightly from side to side where he lay across the squabs opposite us, Gage took my hand.

"You do realize that by taking Rimmer home, we might also be provoking Fletcher to come after us?"

I did, but that did not make hearing the words or the grim tone in which they were spoken any less unsettling, particularly knowing our helpless daughter slumbered in the nursery.

I swallowed past the tightness in my throat. "We shall simply have to remain vigilant."

And pray we didn't come to regret it.

"Here they come," I murmured as Trevor and Henry came striding down the pavement.

From my and Gage's perch on a bench partially concealed by surrounding shrubs, we could see Reverend Jamieson's arched doorway and that of his neighbor to the right, as well as periodic stretches of the pavement. Trevor and Henry disappeared behind some of the vegetation blocking our view before appearing again. Even to my knowing eyes, they looked like two ambling gentlemen at ease. Trevor even swung a walking stick jauntily at his side as if he'd not a care in the world, though I knew he was perturbed—about this venture *and* our sister's reaction to his courtship of a tradesman's daughter.

Alana had not been as enthused about his interest in Miss Matilda Birnam as I had been. However, she'd not voiced outright disapproval, but rather had advised caution. When Trevor had told me not three-quarters of an hour earlier about her suggestion that he introduce Miss Birnam to us before he decided anything, I'd agreed it wasn't a terrible idea. This had drawn some of the irritation he'd been directing at our sister onto me. Though when I proposed that we should invite the Birnams to the house party Gage and I had discussed hosting at Bevington Park in June or July, he'd been pacified slightly. Enough that, hopefully, he wouldn't botch this ploy.

That same confidence couldn't be applied to Henry, who tugged repeatedly at his collar as they waited for someone to answer their knock.

As Jamieson's front door opened, I instinctively shrank backward, coming up against the resistance of the back of the bench. The same maid who had admitted us the week before listened briefly to Trevor and Henry before telling them I knew not what and retreating into the house.

My shoulders slumped. "Perhaps he's not at home, after all."

"Just wait," Gage urged, seeing that Henry and Trevor were not departing, but rather stood waiting by the door.

The maid must have gone to confer with someone, which might very well indicate Jamieson actually was at home. Or it might mean that Trevor and Henry were a breed she hadn't been instructed how to respond to. Perhaps she was fetching a senior servant or even the mistress of the house to see to them. Had we known what she'd told them, we might have had a better idea. Trevor's continuing to swing his walking stick and Henry's tugging once more at his collar told us almost nothing.

I tried to remain cautiously hopeful, but enough time passed that I'd begun to slide into disappointment. Then the maid returned, ushering them inside.

My heart climbed into my throat despite the stern reminder I gave myself that this was also not confirmation that Jamieson was home. Trevor and Henry might have been invited in to speak with Mrs. Jamieson or someone else. However, I clung tenaciously to hope all the same that our suspicions had been correct and they were sitting down with the reverend even now.

I watched the front windows avidly, for we'd instructed them, if they were taken to either of the front rooms and given the chance, to signal us somehow. But none of the curtains even twitched, so we remained where we were, with Gage eyeing his pocket watch. We'd decided that if they remained inside for longer than three minutes that would be our indication that they'd likely been received by Jamieson himself.

I couldn't tear my gaze away from the windows, lest I miss their signal, so I had to trust that Gage was minding the time passing, though it felt like triple the number of minutes had passed before he suddenly snapped the pocket watch shut and urged me to my feet. This, too, was Maclean and his men's signal, and as we approached the front door, I noted several men fanning out from their own positions where they'd been idling—some in everyday clothes and others in their distinctive gray greatcoats. Maclean met us at the door.

When Gage tried the handle, he found it unlocked, allowing us to stride inside unimpeded. However, the sound must have alerted the maid, for she appeared in the corridor from a door on the right. Her eyes widened in alarm, but before she could utter a sound, Gage silenced her with a look and a nod toward Maclean, who loomed over my shoulder. Gage opened his mouth as if to ask her where they were, but I squeezed his arm to halt him. I could hear voices coming from a room above, so I pointed up the stairs. He nodded, and then with silent feet we quickly ascended.

In the upper corridor, we encountered another maid. This

one emitted a startled squeak before we could stop her, quieting the tenor voice of the man who'd been speaking in the back room. Not wishing to completely waste the element of surprise, Gage strode over and pushed open the door.

Though I'd not anticipated violence from the man of God, a part of me had still feared I was wrong. That we'd sent my brother and brother-in-law into a potentially lethal situation. After all, we didn't yet know the extent of Jamieson's role in the events that transpired on the third day of the auction of Lord Eldin's collection. Whether he'd callously risked the lives of nearly one hundred people and killed a friend all in the quest of some goal. If he'd been capable of that, would his conscience even balk at taking the lives of two nosy gentlemen?

But when Gage opened the door, I could see that both Trevor and Henry were sitting unharmed in two ladder-back chairs while Reverend Jamieson was propped upright in a bed. Rather than react with anger or alarm at the sight of us, he gave a sigh of weary resignation and even grinned with fleeting amusement.

"Pride, my besettin' sin, has ousted me. And rightly so, for me thinkin' I knew better than everyone else. Come in. Come in," he urged when we hesitated in the doorway, still grappling with the sight of him in bed and his response to our presence. A wet cough rumbled up from his chest as he even tried to jest. "Dinna be shy."

I supposed that answered our question as to if he was truly ill, though the redness of his nose and the dark circles around his eyes had given some indication that he'd not been in bed at three o'clock in the afternoon for no reason. Even dressed respectfully in a plaid dressing gown and cap, it was obvious he'd only recently pulled himself together to receive his visitors.

"I s'pose, then, that ye're no' really admirers o' my dictionary?"

he said good-naturedly to Henry and Trevor as they rose from their chairs.

Henry flushed and then frowned, though Trevor merely shrugged.

"Weel, I've been put in my place," Jamieson added, his voice rattling.

"Why did you refuse to receive Sergeant Maclean when he called to speak to you?" Gage queried in bewilderment. "Why did you tell your staff to *lie* about your whereabouts to the police?"

He heaved another sigh. "My wife warned me I shouldna have done that."

"Then why did you?" Gage pressed with Maclean standing at his shoulder, giving Jamieson no quarter.

"Because I didna want to answer the questions ye wished to put to me. 'Specially no' in this condition." Jamieson gestured to himself, indicating his nearly prone position in bed.

"Ye ken I've arrested Mr. Sullivan?" Maclean asked, unmoved by his honesty.

"Aye, and I need tae set that straight," he said grimly. "Mr. Sullivan is guilty o' nothin' more than bein' too trustin'."

Maclean's eyes narrowed. "Then ye didna bribe him tae leave the coin room unattended?"

"Ye must have misunderstood. 'Twas merely a contribution tae help wi' his poor mother's medicine and doctor bills. She's been verra ill these past few months."

"And after ye gave him this . . . contribution, he just happened tae look the other way while ye stole four ancient coins?" Maclean's voice dripped with sarcasm.

"That strains credibility, Reverend," Gage added.

"Stole?" Jamieson repeated, struggling to stifle a cough. "Why, that's preposterous. I would never . . ." He broke off, turning aside to cough into a handkerchief.

It didn't escape my notice that he was doing everything possible not to tell a direct lie, even possibly forcing himself to cough.

"Come now, Reverend Jamieson," Gage countered, turning on his charm. "We know it must have been you, and that you almost certainly did it for Mr. Innes's benefit. To fund the publication of his texts. It was Lord Eldin's fault he'd been denied membership to the Bannatyne Club, and so it only seemed fitting that he should be the one to help him, even in an indirect way." His lips curled into a coaxing smile. "Why, I imagine you even planned to inform the auctioneer—anonymously, of course—that the coins you swapped out for the real ones were fake before they ever went up for bidding. Because you had no intention of harming anyone else. Just to put a small dent in Lord Eldin's reputation in aid of setting a wrong to right."

I recognized he was using the words I'd told him Jamieson had spoken to me at the Inverleith Ball. The ones that had struck me as being significant, for it turned out they revealed his motive.

However, Jamieson simply turned his head toward the other wall. "I dinna ken what ye're talkin' aboot."

Gage looked to each of us, clearly undecided whether to continue to try to cajole the reverend or cede the field to one of us. I knew Maclean's intimidation tactics would never work. Nor did I think I could stomach them, especially while Jamieson was ill. But I also knew we could not leave here without information. Not when we suspected Fletcher had plans for further violence.

"Reverend, please," I leaned forward to plead. "This is far more serious than a few missing coins." I glanced sideways at Maclean, hoping he wouldn't be angry at me for what I was about to do. "The floor collapse. It wasn't an accident. Someone deliberately sabotaged that joist so that it would break under the stress of all those people in the rear drawing room standing on it for the auction."

Jamieson turned back toward us, a slowly dawning horror transforming his face.

"We know that Matthew Fletcher, an employee of Thomas Winstanley and Sons, performed the actual act of sabotage. What we don't know is if he was working alone or at someone else's behest." I fell silent, allowing Jamieson to work out the implication.

Which he did, with admirable speed. "Ye think *I* was part o' it?" His eyes were wide in his ashen face. "Nay! I could never . . . Nay!" he spluttered. "That ye should even suspect it o' me." He began to cough, shaking his head.

I lifted my hands in a helpless gesture. "How can we not when you won't be straightforward with us?"

CHAPTER 29

This seemed to finally penetrate through the haze of Jamieson's obstinance. His head sank back onto his pillows and he closed his eyes, a flush of color tinging his cheeks. "The clothing press." He indicated the piece of furniture near the foot of his bed. "Top drawer. Under the cravats."

Trevor was closest, so he reached out to comply. He rummaged for but a second before removing a wooden framed case. Turning it toward us, he revealed the four coins still nestled inside.

"'Twas as ye said," he told Gage. "I never meant tae do any livin' person harm. Only tae help Innes. But 'tis still wrong." He shook his head. "I was only foolin' myself tae think otherwise." Then his bright gaze shifted to meet mine and then Maclean's. "But I had nothin' tae do wi' the collapse. I'll place my hand on the Bible and swear it."

I believed him, regardless of any swearing. Especially since, for once, he'd given us a direct answer.

"I'd switched the coins and 'twas movin' toward the stairs when it happened." He grimaced, closing his eyes. "Thought for a moment 'twas the wrath o' God upon me. That would o' been better than the truth."

Having no interest in hearing him castigate himself, I pressed him on another point. "But you *do* know something?"

His eyes opened to stare at me intently.

"Something pertinent."

"Ye're quite the perceptive one. I'd heard that aboot ye."

I wasn't sure if this was meant as a compliment or criticism, but he continued before I had much time to contemplate it.

"Aye. I recognized this Mr. Fletcher. He was one o' the auctioneer's assistants? Short, light brown hair? A mole on the side o' his head?" He touched a spot above his left ear.

"Yes."

"He's from Fife. Or he used tae be. Five years ago."

"Let me guess? Kirkcaldy."

His expression was grim. "Four o' his cousins—all young women—were killed in the aftermath o' the collapse o' the church balcony."

I pressed my hands to my mouth to try to stifle my horror. Jamieson saw it anyway.

"Aye. Heartbreaking. Left the mother o' three o' the girls destitute. Reliant on charity and whatever other family members could send her."

"Like a nephew," Henry suggested with an arch of his eyebrows.

I supposed at least we now knew Mr. Fletcher's probable motive, heartbreaking as it was. Mr. Rimmer had indicated that Fletcher had worked for Winstanley for five years, so he must have moved to Liverpool soon after the tragedy. I wondered if he'd been sending money back to his aunt, as Henry had guessed. Perhaps he'd even planned to journey on to

Kirkcaldy to visit her after the auction in Edinburgh was over. It was just a few hours' north.

What had he thought when he'd discovered the auction was for Lord Eldin? Had he recognized his name? Or had the realization not dawned until he saw the portrait of him hanging in the study? He must have heard Lord Eldin make all his empty proclamations. He must have been furious that nothing had been done to help his aunt. That nothing had been done to prevent it all from happening again to someone else. And so he'd sought to have his revenge and make his point.

But it hadn't worked. Not as he'd hoped. The connection to Kirkcaldy had been noted. Efforts had been made to secure the private residences of the wealthy. But no one was focused on public buildings or the housing of those less affluent. The current laws and practices weren't being debated by those who could effect change. The world was moving on again. What might he do to stop that?

"Did Mr. Fletcher realize you'd recognized him?" Gage asked Reverend Jamieson.

Jamieson's voice rasped as he responded. "I . . . I dinna think so."

Gage turned to Maclean even as he pressed Jamieson. "But you don't know for certain?"

"Nay." He observed the men's silent communication. "Is that a cause for concern?"

"He's already injured, and possibly killed, another man tae keep him from talkin'," Maclean told him. "So we shouldna take any chances. No' while Fletcher is still missin'."

Jamieson sat up in alarm. "My wife. She's gone tae visit one o' our granddaughters."

"I'll see that she makes it home safely," Maclean assured him. "And I'll leave two officers here tae make sure ye're no' disturbed." His gaze sharpened. "And that ye dinna try to leave. Least no' until it can be determined what charges you'll be facin' for the theft o' these," he added, taking the case containing the stolen coins from Trevor.

The reverend didn't attempt to argue, perhaps still being too alarmed by the notion of Fletcher attacking him or his wife. I didn't know whether that was the cause of his most recent bout of coughing or the amount of talking he'd been doing. Either way, I waited until he'd quieted and reclined back against his pillows again before asking one last question.

"We believe that Mr. Fletcher is planning another act of sabotage. And we have some reason to suspect it may be at a church on Easter Sunday."

Jamieson blanched as white as his sheets. "Good Lord in heaven!"

"Do you have any idea which one he might choose?"

He appeared to consider the question but then shook his head at the futility. "There must be more than fifty churches in Edinburgh alone. No' to mention the surroundin' villages. How could I ken?"

And how were we going to inspect and warn them all? It was a monumental task.

"Well, if you think of something, even the smallest hint, please send word," I urged.

"I will," he promised. "And . . . I apologize for the trouble I've caused. The delay. Had I ken . . ." He grimaced. "Weel, I'm sorry."

Gage, Trevor, Henry, and I all departed, crossing over to the park at the center of George Square. There we all waited in uneasy silence for Maclean to issue instructions to his men and join us. The sun had decided to emerge from the clouds, and I squinted into it toward the dark slate rooftops. The brightness of the sun's rays partially blinded me, so much so that while I knew there were chimneys and dormer windows—I could even detect their outlines—I couldn't actually see them. Much like Fletcher's next move.

"Do you believe him?" Gage asked as Maclean joined us, looking thoroughly disgruntled and ready to tussle if someone gave him the least provocation. It was clear Gage was talking about Jamieson.

Maclean glanced over his shoulder toward the reverend's home, and then rolled one meaty shoulder. "Aye." His sharp gaze returned to Gage. "Same as you."

"Then presumably Mr. Fletcher is working alone," Henry ventured.

Maclean grunted, his eyes still directed pointedly at Gage. "Hoo certain are ye that Fletcher intends to cause some sort o' structural collapse on Easter Sunday?"

"Not certain at all," Gage conceded. "But somehow he knew we'd become aware of his drugging Mr. Rimmer and slipping out of the White Horse on the night before the floor collapse, and he took flight rather than risk being questioned. He might have then fled to anywhere, but instead he remained in Edinburgh and even sought out Mr. Rimmer and ended up attacking him to keep him silent."

"Are we certain that was Mr. Fletcher?" Henry queried, perhaps feeling the need for someone to point out the potential flaws in our reasoning.

"No, but it wouldn't be the first attack he's made on someone." Gage's gaze shifted to look at me. "If it wasn't Jamieson who pushed Kiera in front of that carriage, then it stands to reason that it was Fletcher, presumably as we were getting too close to the truth." He leaned forward. "And consider that no one else seems to have a motive to have harmed Mr. Rimmer. And no one else was in the right place to have done it."

"At least, no one that we know of," I admitted, crossing my arms as I tried to ignore the uneasiness Gage's words had caused by reminding me of Fletcher's attempt on my life. "But hopefully Mr. Rimmer will awaken soon and be able to confirm our suspicions, *and* tell us what Mr. Fletcher was so intent that we not learn from him."

"Ye presume it's tae do wi' a second target." Maclean spread his greatcoat aside, planting his hands on his hips. "And because o' that letter tae the editor o' the *Evening Courant*, that it's tae be some sort o' church on Sunday?"

Gage began to grow defensive. "It's all we have to go on, and something I should hate to ignore and then be wrong about, considering the consequences."

I grasped hold of Gage's arm. "We also now better understand his reasoning in the first place. Why he sabotaged that joist at Lord Eldin's former town house." I shook my head. "But his goal wasn't achieved. He risked everything to gain revenge and force changes, and neither happened. Now that he's been discovered . . ."

"What does he have to lose by causing another collapse?" Trevor finished for me.

I nodded solemnly. "Especially if he believes the end justifies the means." That it was simply a necessary evil that others might be killed or injured in the pursuit of progress and justice. "I don't believe he *can* stop. Not until he either achieves his goal or he's apprehended."

"His conscience won't let him," Henry added in agreement, his auburn hair appearing even redder in the sunlight.

"Aye, that's all weel and good, but it's no' somethin' I can take tae my superiors," Maclean grumbled. "They'll expect proof, and we have none. No' that he's goin' tae sabotage a church."

"What if I go with you," Gage offered. "Perhaps I can persuade them."

Maclean looked doubtful. "Sure and ye can try, but I'm afraid they're no' so imaginative."

"You don't think they'll warn the churches?" I asked in alarm.

"No' officially. They'll no' want tae create panic. Especially no' across more than fifty churches on perhaps the busiest Sunday o' the year. And dinna forget, they've no' given us permission tae share the truth o' what happened at Picardy Place." One of his eyebrows arched in mild chastisement at my rogue decision to tell Reverend Jamieson, though it had worked to our advantage. "As far as the public is concerned, 'twas an accident. So any word o' caution would be phrased along those same lines, and it's likely tae be dismissed by those who believe their buildings tae be o' solid construction."

I'd not considered this complication. One that was growing increasingly restrictive and hazardous. After all, forewarned was forearmed. In truth, it was playing into Fletcher's hands. For if another collapse did occur, the public would instantly assume it was an accident. And if the authorities then tried to backtrack and claim the incident at Picardy Place was sabotage, many would fail to believe them, seeing this as a ploy to stifle alarm.

"Have you searched his belongings?" Trevor asked, earning a glower from Maclean.

"Aye, the little he left behind. Gives no indication o' what he plans or where he went. My men will continue tae canvass the city, searchin' for Fletcher. Maybe we'll get lucky." The tick in his jaw communicated he didn't believe this. "Are ye comin'?" he demanded of Gage as he turned to leave.

Gage looked at me, and I urged him to follow. "Go. Trevor and Henry will see me home safely."

He nodded, trotting after the sergeant while the rest of us retreated to the carriage, bound for Albyn Place.

How is he?" I asked Bree softly.

She was seated in a shaft of sunlight streaming through the window of our second guest chamber, mending a hem while Mr. Rimmer lay unmoving on the bed nearby. A bandage was wrapped around his head, and he'd been changed into one of Gage's nightshirts.

"No alteration since he arrived, I'm afraid," she replied in a normal voice, reminding me the goal was for him to wake, so speaking quietly was decidedly unnecessary.

I gazed down at his closed eyes and pale countenance, battling a rising sense of urgency. Reminding myself it was only Tuesday, that we had five more days until Easter, did little to help. "We need to know what Mr. Fletcher was so anxious about you discovering."

This plea was met by silence and an empathetic smile when I turned toward Bree with a long sigh.

"Do you need a break?" I asked her.

"Nay. I'll let ye ken as soon as he starts tae come aroond."

I appreciated her confidence in this, but I was feeling far less optimistic. Poor Mr. Rimmer.

I went up to the nursery to look in on Emma, spending some time snuggling and playing with her. As always, her smiles and babbles soothed me, and even her tears, as she accidentally smacked herself in the forehead with one of her drumsticks, served to distract me. At least temporarily.

When I returned to the library, it was to discover that Anderley had joined Trevor and Henry there, and they were conferring about what we should do. From the sounds of what I'd heard coming down the corridor, the valet was proposing he return to the White Horse to try to glean more information from the staff and regulars, and Fletcher's former coworkers. I couldn't say I disagreed with his proposal, though the manner in which he fell silent as I entered suggested he thought I would.

"That's not a bad idea," I told him, deciding it would be a

foolish waste of time to pretend I hadn't heard. "Though you should ask Gage what he thinks when he returns. I already know he's going to insist you take someone with you."

"I could go," Trevor offered.

I suffered a tremor of uneasiness at the thought of either of them venturing to a place we'd been warned away from. But the reason for that warning no longer boarded there, and finding Fletcher was of tantamount importance. If only he was in custody, we could all breathe easier.

I settled on the vacant end of one of the sofas, resting my elbow on the arm as I reached up to massage my temples.

"How's Mr. Rimmer?" Henry asked.

"Sadly, no better."

"It may take some time," he consoled. "Why, I remember when my brother John took a hard knock to the head during a tussle on the stone stairs with Traquair." Their eldest brother and the duke's heir. "We were all terrified he might not wake, but after a day and a half, he roused with little lasting damage other than a mild headache."

"Truly?"

"Truly," he confirmed, but then his face fell. However, I suspected this had more to do with the location of his brother now than that long ago event. For John was living in exile, having been hustled out of the country after it had been uncovered that he'd killed a man. The circumstances were complicated, and given the fact he was a duke's son, it had been doubtful that John would have been convicted. But he'd chosen exile anyway over possible incarceration, not to mention the scandal the trial would have caused. At the time, Gage and I had been extremely displeased with the duke's entire family, including Henry, who had been tasked with escorting his brother to parts unknown. Truth be told, it was still irksome.

But that did not inhibit me from feeling empathy for Henry. I knew he missed his brother and that John's actions had grieved him greatly.

I was also grateful for his attempt to cheer me. Perhaps Rimmer would wake up. Perhaps he would have the answer to Fletcher's whereabouts or at least which church he intended to target. We just had to be patient.

CHAPTER 30

That patience all but evaporated when Gage returned home that evening. He was in a rare fury, for which I could not blame him, though it unsettled me, as anger in any man tended to do.

"What do you mean they're not going to do anything?" I asked as Gage stormed back and forth across the drawing room, where Trevor, Henry, and I had settled after dinner to await his return.

"It was just as Maclean predicted. There is no proof that Fletcher intends to target a church, and they have no desire to see 'ridiculous rumors' spread and potentially create panic." It was clear he was quoting one of the officials. "They also categorically refused to inform the public that the collapse at Picardy Place had not been accidental."

"Fools!" Trevor proclaimed, speaking for all of us.

"They actually berated Sergeant Maclean for not having

already located Matthew Fletcher and ordered him to do so immediately. Because *that* would resolve the matter."

I crossed my arms over my chest and huffed. "As if we don't know that. As if the sergeant hasn't been *trying* to." It was enough to make *my* temper spike.

"Maclean must have been livid," Henry ventured.

"He wasn't happy, that's for sure," Gage quipped.

"Then we'll simply have to take the matter into our own hands." Trevor's brow had furrowed with determination. "*We* can warn the churches."

"Except we've been forbidden to tell them the truth about the Picardy Place collapse. And they've threatened to take legal action if we disobey."

"But what can they really do to us?" I demanded. "When there are potentially lives hanging in the balance."

Gage ceased his pacing and turned to look at me. "It's that word *potentially* which troubles me most. For without proof, we may have little defense."

"Then . . ." I spread my hands wide ". . . you want us to do nothing?"

"I didn't say that. Only that we should exhaust all other possibilities before we do something that could land us in jail."

"Such as?"

"There's nothing precluding us from visiting the churches throughout the city and asking a few questions to see if anyone suspicious has been lurking around. From inspecting what is visible of their construction."

"But you heard Jamieson," Trevor protested. "There are more than fifty churches in Edinburgh."

"Then we'll have to try to narrow down the list." Gage moved to sit in the vacant giltwood chair. "I take it Mr. Rimmer remains unconscious."

"Yes," I said.

He slumped deeper into the chair. "Then until he awakens, we'll simply have to try to follow his tracks and see if we can determine whatever he discovered that provoked Fletcher into attacking him."

"Speaking of that, Anderley had a suggestion." I told him about Anderley's proposal that he and Trevor return to the White Horse.

Gage nodded, perking up a bit. "It's a good plan. Would you be willing to go tonight?" he asked Trevor.

"The sooner the better," Trevor agreed.

"Then go inform Anderley. I'm sure Jeffers knows where he's got to."

"Perhaps you might take Shep as well," I interjected, knowing my brother's own valet was loyal. If nothing else, three men would be better than two should matters turn ugly.

Sensing my worry, Trevor nodded before heading off to find both valets.

Henry watched them go before asking his half brother, "What can I do?"

"Make a list of all the churches in the Edinburgh area. Presbyterian, Episcopal, United Secessionist, Methodist, Baptist, Unitarian, the entire lot." He waved his hand in an all-encompassing gesture. "If they will worship on Sunday, include them."

Henry agreed, departing as well. Which made the next recommendation I was about to make a little less awkward.

"I hesitate to propose this . . ." I paused when Gage shifted his hand which had cradled his forehead so that he could better see me. "But sooner or later we're going to run out of time and . . ."

"You want to ask Kincaid for help."

His calm tone of voice surprised me, but I knew not to mistake it for acceptance. "Yes."

He glowered for a moment at the rug and then exhaled a long breath. "I suppose we don't have any choice. Kincaid does have an admirable system of informants throughout the city. If anyone can locate Fletcher, it's probably him. Or at least he might be able to discover which churches he's been lurking about, for Fletcher would have to do reconnaissance as he selects his target." His gaze shifted to me. "But how will you contact him?"

"One of the street lads who run messages will know how to find him," I replied, rising to go to the writing desk in the corner before my husband changed his mind. I spared a moment to worry that Bonnie Brock would misconstrue my message, but I would simply have to make the severity of the matter as plain as possible. After all, the populace he looked after in Old Town was in just as much danger of being harmed as the wealthier denizens of Edinburgh in New Town if Mr. Fletcher's plan was carried out to fruition. It served a number of his interests to stop him. That should be enough to keep him focused on the danger.

Three days passed with little development. Despite the police and Bonnie Brock's informants scouring the city for Mr. Fletcher, he remained undetected. It was enough to make me wonder if he actually *had* left Edinburgh, if we were searching for a man who was long gone. But the tightness in my chest and the sense of dread did not ease. He might have gone, but he would be back. I didn't want to be so certain of it, but I was.

None of Fletcher's former colleagues or the staff at the White Horse had been able to tell us anything we didn't already know. The clergy at the churches we'd been able to visit had proved equally unhelpful, and in some cases more suspicious of us for asking questions. It was beyond frustrating, particularly when a simple explanation of the truth by the authorities might have loosened their lips considerably. We had to content ourselves with issuing a general word of caution.

We'd spent hours debating one church over another as the potential target, trying to consider the matter from Fletcher's perspective, but it was difficult to know which criteria he might have weighed higher than another. Certainly, ease and accessibility must have played a factor, but would they rate highest? What about the denomination? Would he target one over another? What about the social class of the majority of the congregants? A church with more wealthy and powerful attendees might have a greater impact on those who could effect change most easily, but a large lower-class congregation would inspire more outrage, which could prove equally effective if the newspapers smelled fresh ink.

Would the church have some connection to Lord Eldin, or would he believe that was too obvious? Would he target a roof, a galley, a floor? Which buildings contained these likely targets? When did he intend to complete the sabotage? Was it already done and merely waiting for the weight of Sunday's Easter worshipers to bring it crashing down?

We didn't have the answers to any of these questions, and time was almost out.

Good Friday eve, Gage, Trevor, Henry, and I were all seated once again in our drawing room, our moods as bleak and solemn as any believer's might have been upon marking the remembrance of Jesus's crucifixion, except ours was also troubled by a more immediate threat. I felt exhausted from debating possibilities and had nearly run dry of hope of foiling Fletcher. I could tell the others felt much the same. I'd even begun to turn my prayers toward begging the Lord for events to prove me wrong. For Fletcher to not have plans to sabotage a church.

Then Jeffers appeared in the doorway. I was instantly

forewarned to some development by the alertness of his posture. "My lady, you have a visitor."

This was not precisely what I'd been expecting, rather wishing Mr. Rimmer had woken instead, but I soon rallied to this prospect, for I deduced who it was. I turned to Gage, seeing that he'd guessed as well.

"Show him up," Gage surprised me by directing Jeffers. I knew how he felt about Bonnie Brock being in our home, but I supposed it was rather ridiculous to all troop downstairs to the garden just to hear what he'd come to say. Besides, the greater number of people present might dissuade Bonnie Brock from tweaking Gage's nose and behaving inappropriately.

I should have known better.

"No' goin' tae send for tea," he mocked after Jeffers announced him and turned to depart.

If he'd hoped to ruffle our butler's feathers, he was going to be sorely disappointed. In fact, if it had not been below his dignity, I suspect Jeffers would have turned and cast him a withering glare.

"I thought something stronger would be more to your taste," I retorted crisply, annoyed by the taunt and anxious to move past his japes and gibes to hear what he'd actually come to say. I pushed to my feet to move toward the sideboard, hoping that would hurry the discussion along, when he stopped me.

"Nay. I'll say what I've come to say and then I'll go."

I halted abruptly, turning to him in surprise.

"I dinna want tae be the cause o' more anxiety."

The look in his eyes was soft with concern, and I realized I hadn't done a very good job of hiding my impatience.

Neither did Gage when he cleared his throat pointedly, pulling Bonnie Brock's gaze away from mine. "Go on."

Bonnie Brock's brow ruffled with annoyance, but then

smoothed as he turned back to me. "I havena found Fletcher," he pronounced solemnly.

My shoulders slumped as I sank back down on the sofa.

"But that's tellin' in and o' itself."

"What do you mean?" Henry asked, shifting in his chair so that he could better see the rogue.

"If he was hidin' anywhere in Auld Reekie . . ." he used one of the long-standing nicknames for the city of Edinburgh ". . . I would o' heard aboot it by noo. Which means either he's no' here. *Or* . . ." his jaw hardened ". . . he's lyin' low somewhere north o' the city where my hold isna so strong."

For Bonnie Brock to verbally admit such, especially in front of these men, was unexpected, making his supposition all the more credible.

"He may yet show himself or return tae the city. If so, we'll be watchin' and I'll alert ye immediately." He nodded to me and began to turn to go, but Gage stopped him.

"If your men spot him, ask them to detain him."

This request appeared to shock all of us, including Bonnie Brock, though his reaction was as carefully controlled as the rest of him.

Gage scowled. "We have less than thirty-six hours before Easter worshipers begin filling their churches. If Fletcher is spotted, I don't want him slipping away before the police or one of us can get to him. Better to have him restrained than free to continue his plans." His voice turned wry as he glared at Bonnie Brock. "Though I would prefer he arrive to the authorities all in one piece."

Bonnie Brock easily agreed, though the ruthless twist to his lips gave me pause. "But nay promises."

Once again, I expected Gage to argue, but he merely tipped his head. "Fair enough."

With that, Bonnie Brock slipped from the room and was

presumably met by Jeffers, who escorted him out. I knew our butler well enough to realize he'd been posted nearby, waiting for the rogue to depart. Jeffers trusted him even less than we did.

"Was that wise?" Henry questioned.

Gage tossed back the last of his whisky. "Maybe not. But whatever trimming Fletcher might receive, I trust it won't go too far." His eyes cut to me. "Not when Kincaid wishes to stay in Kiera's good graces."

I frowned at this remark, but Gage only arched his eyebrows.

"Then if Fletcher is north of the city—north of *here*—do we shift our search there?" Henry asked, changing the subject.

Gage sighed. "I suppose, given the time restraints, it gives us a smaller portion of the city to focus on tomorrow."

The last day before Easter.

My stomach cramped with dread.

"M'lady."

I attempted to roll away from the annoying hiss in my ear, but something restrained me, pulling me back.

"M'lady!"

I blinked open my eyes, staring up at Bree in the darkness. Though, it wasn't complete, I realized. There was a single lit candle resting on the table beside my bed.

"Mr. Rimmer. He's awake," she explained, looking from me to Gage, who had also stirred. "Ye must come quickly."

Alertness shot through my veins as I recalled the events of the past few weeks and our worry over Mr. Rimmer's continued unconsciousness. Our desperate desire to speak with him.

Bree hurried from the room, leaving the candle behind. Obviously, she'd noticed Gage's bare chest and, not unfoundedly, realized he might not be wearing any nightclothes. I ignored his fumbling to don a pair of trousers and reached for my dressing gown. A few moments later, we were hurrying down the corridor with the candle toward the open door of the second guest chamber.

Bree sat next to his bed, talking to him. At the sight of us, she rose to cede me the chair. "He's muzzy," she cautioned. "But I think he kens where he is and why."

We'd been warned that when he awoke he might be confused, but over time his mental faculties and any gaps in his memory should improve.

"Mr. Rimmer," I gasped, sitting down and leaning forward to reach for the hand that lay closest to me. "Do you know who I am?"

He stared up at me through pain-filled eyes. "Lady Darby," he said faintly.

"Yes," I replied, relieved to hear his brain wasn't completely jumbled. "We found you belowstairs at Picardy Place," I explained, glancing over my shoulder to indicate Gage. "You'd been struck over the head. Do you know who did this to you?"

"Fletcher," he croaked and then broke off, smacking his lips. I noticed how dry they were and nodded to Bree, who was already moving to pour water into a cup as he continued. "He . . . came . . . to talk . . . to me."

"About the sabotage?" I guessed.

"About . . ." his brow tightened ". . . spyin' on him."

His voice cracked at the end, and I urged him to drink some of the water Bree was offering to him. Gage stepped forward to elevate his head and shoulders while Bree held the cup to his lips. After a few sips, Gage lowered Mr. Rimmer back against the pillows.

He was breathing heavily from the effort but managed to wheeze. "Thank you."

I gave him a few moments to recover before prompting. "Mr. Fletcher thought you were spying on him?"

"Yes." He tried to shake his head, but stopped, grimacing in pain. "But I wasn't. Just . . . happened . . . to see . . . his notes. Our papers . . . got switched."

Gage's gaze met mine.

"What notes?" When Mr. Rimmer hesitated, I leaned forward again to grip his hand. "Please, Mr. Rimmer. This could be important."

He was obviously confused, but he continued nonetheless. "On Adam brothers buildings. Ones they'd designed. I didn't understand why . . . he was so upset . . . I'd seen it."

The Adam brothers, of course! The famed architects had been Lord Eldin's uncles. It made perfect sense he would target one of their churches if he was so bent on revenge. On damaging the family's reputation.

"Was there one in particular you saw?" I pressed, noting he was growing weary. His head would still require time to heal, and I hated to hound him so, but we were running out of time. "Perhaps a church here in Edinburgh?"

"I . . . I don't remember."

Gage and I both tried asking him several more questions, but he either didn't know or was too tired and confused to answer them. Regardless, the Adam brothers' connection was something we could work with. So after insisting Mr. Rimmer take a few more sips of water with Gage and Bree's assistance, we allowed him to fall back asleep, leaving him to Bree's competent care. Our physician was due the following morning to look in on the patient, and I deemed that to be soon enough to ensure he was recovering normally.

Neither Gage nor I bothered to dress as we hurried downstairs to the library, too anxious to scour the inventory of information Henry had compiled on local churches. I believed I recalled him listing the architects. Gage lit more candles while I sat at the long table, dividing the pages into two stacks.

When Trevor stumbled in, rubbing his eyes and demanding to know what on earth we were doing, I divided the pages again. Once we'd explained Mr. Rimmer's revelation, he sat down at the table with no more grumbling, diving into the task alongside us.

A short time later, I was startled when a hand reached over my shoulder to set a cup of tea before me. I peered blearily up at Jeffers, trying to decide if he was truly there or I'd conjured him with my silent wish for something warm and invigorating in the cold library. Trevor had stoked up the fire in the hearth, but there was still a decided chill in the room.

"Miss McEvoy rang down to the kitchens for something for Mr. Rimmer," he said. "She explained the situation."

Despite the fact Gage, Trevor, and I were dressed in nightclothes and wrappers—or in Gage's case, a hodgepodge of random apparel—Jeffers was as immaculately attired as always. I would have believed he'd slept that way but for the lack of wrinkles.

Lifting the cup of steaming brew to take a sip, I returned to the inventory with renewed vigor and was soon rewarded for my efforts. I discovered two churches in Edinburgh with a connection to one of the Adam brothers. Both of which were rather disconcertingly close to home.

After finishing reviewing the other listings in my stack, I sat stewing over the two buildings I'd stumbled across which met our criteria and tried not to worry that Henry's inventory was incomplete. Or that we might be wrong about Fletcher targeting a church. All we could do was work with the information that had been given to us. The clues we'd uncovered thus far all seemed to point to this.

Gage was next to finish, straightening with a long sigh and

a shake of his head when he found me watching him. His gaze dipped to the two pages I'd pulled from the stack, but I held up a finger and nodded to Trevor. Jeffers approached to refill my tea, and I sat cradling the warm cup between my two hands to warm them. Finally, Trevor looked up, grunting in disappointment, but his eyes swiftly lit with interest when he found us observing him in evident impatience.

"St. George's Church in Charlotte Square," I stated, a chill running down my spine as I gestured to one of the papers on the table before me. For that was where we usually attended along with Alana and her family. "And St. George's Chapel in York Place." Which stood just a few short blocks east, between us and Lord Eldin's town house on Picardy Place.

"Good God!" Gage exclaimed, for we'd attended there upon occasion as well. Both having been raised in the Anglican church, we probably rightly should have attended St. George's Chapel more often. But I'd taken to attending St. George's Church in Charlotte Square, which was Presbyterian, with Alana and Philip when I lived with them, and so more often we worshiped with them there. Particularly since we resided in Edinburgh for only a few months each year.

"But see here, Robert Adam created the original design for St. George's in Charlotte Square, but it was then redesigned by Robert Reid based off the originals." I turned to the second page. "However, St. George's Chapel in York Place was exclusively designed by Robert's younger brother, James Adam. Which, to me, makes it the more likely target from what we know about Fletcher."

Both men were silent for a few moments, reading over Henry's notes and considering my conclusions. "Yes, that makes sense," Trevor conceded. "But . . . what if you're wrong?"

There was no need to elaborate. I was aware of the

consequences. But what could we do but make the most logical leap of deduction?

Gage seemed to understand this as well. "We might be wrong about all of it. But we've run out of time and options." He pushed to his feet. "With enough men, we should be able to monitor both buildings and hope Fletcher comes slinking out of the shadows for us to catch him."

"Regardless, we are forbidding Alana and her family from attending Easter service tomorrow morning unless Fletcher is caught," Trevor informed me stridently as Gage crossed the room toward the door.

"Agreed," I said, thinking I might just resort to standing before the door and barring *anyone* entrance if Fletcher remained elusive. "Gage, where are you going?"

"To warn Maclean."

I glanced at the clock. "At a quarter to four in the morning?"

"He'll want to know immediately." He paused to speak over his shoulder. "I'll take Anderley with me."

Before I could say anything more, he was gone, presumably headed upstairs to change into more appropriate attire. I bit my bottom lip, trying to decide whether to go after him and voice the question hovering at the back of my throat.

Trevor seemed to already deduce it, turning it back on me. "Shouldn't you send word to Kincaid?"

With Gage gone for who knew how long, and Trevor's evident approval, I decided to take matters into my own hands, moving toward Gage's desk. "Yes. Yes, I should."

CHAPTER 31

I should have known better than to ask Gage if I could help keep watch at one of the churches. After what had occurred a year ago and in Cornwall just five months past, he was determined to keep me and Emma safe. Given the number of men who would be present at each St. George's, I wasn't truly needed.

Gage and Anderley would be positioned inside St. George's Chapel in York Place, with Sergeant Maclean and a handful of men concealed around the perimeter outside. Meanwhile, Henry and his brother Lord Edward were secreted inside St. George's Church in Charlotte Square with another handful of policemen on the exterior. At an even farther distance, Bonnie Brock had promised to keep his men to the shadows nearby, ready to apprehend Fletcher if the others failed to nab him.

Considering the dozens of men involved, I was beginning to grow more concerned that Fletcher would realize his plan had been uncovered and slip away before he was seen. Of course, there was also the ever-present worry that he'd already done his sabotage and scampered off to parts unknown. The men would be searching for any such evidence, but there was also the chance the damage would not be so obvious. I tried to block that fear from my thoughts, but I was no more successful at that than I was in ordering myself not to worry about Gage and the others as the hour grew later and later.

Trevor had remained behind to guard me and Emma. I had no illusions that he was merely there for company. In any case, he was little better than I was at concealing his anxiety. At one point, we began pacing the drawing room in opposite directions, crossing each other with each pass by the tea table. Had I not been so consumed with nerves, I might have found it amusing.

Finally, I could take no more. "I'm going to look in on Emma," I told my brother, not even waiting for a response before I strode from the room.

I found Emma sleeping serenely with Mrs. Mackay seated nearby, knitting. She offered me an empathetic smile. It didn't require a great leap in deduction to recognize that she'd also been tasked to play guard. In this case, I decided I couldn't fault my husband for doing so. It certainly made me breathe easier to know our daughter was under vigilant supervision.

Before returning to the drawing room, I decided to look in on Mr. Rimmer as well. He had woken several times during the day—the doctor had told us his fatigue was entirely normal—but he had nothing of use to add to what he'd already told us. His mind was still muzzy, as Bree called it, so there was no telling if he knew more and he couldn't recall, or if he'd genuinely recounted everything he could.

A quick peek through the door showed he was sleeping again, more peacefully than before it seemed. Bree had shifted the chair closer to the warmth of the hearth, where she could read by the light of the fire. She looked up as I opened the door, shaking her head in answer to my unspoken question to indicate there was nothing to report.

I nodded dejectedly, realizing I'd actually hoped there would be. Anything to end this interminable uncertainty.

As I was descending the stairs, I thought I heard a noise and paused, listening. When it didn't happen again, I continued, only to hear it again—louder this time. It sounded rather like a faint click. As I continued down the stairs, the click became more pronounced, but it came at random intervals. Inching forward, I realized it was coming from the library and wondered if Trevor had moved into that room, or if perhaps Gage had returned.

I briefly thought of the incident several weeks earlier when I'd been drawn to the nursery by another odd sound, only to discover my husband dangling out the window. For a moment, I pondered whether I'd begun to hallucinate, but then I heard the sound again. This noise was very different from the loud thwack of the fireplace poker striking the stone façade, but it was definitely coming from inside the library.

I pushed the door wider, peering inside the lit chamber, but there was no one inside and for a moment, at least, the clicking seemed to have stopped. I was about to turn to leave when I heard it again. A sharp clack. When it happened a second time, I recognized it was coming from outside the window. Without hesitation, I hurried toward it, thinking it must be Bonnie Brock trying to signal me.

I was just steps away when I realized this made little sense. He wouldn't throw rocks at the wall and window. He would simply rap on the French doors until someone answered or stroll right in.

I skidded to a halt, seeing my own reflection in the glass, for the drapes had yet to be drawn, and some instinct suddenly made me reverse course. Less than a second later, the window shattered, sending glass shards spraying in every direction. Because I had just turned aside, they mostly struck the back of my gown, ricocheting off the thick wool of my unfashionable garment, but my shoulder collided with the wall next to the window sharply.

My brother came hurrying through the door to the library a few moments later, finding me still pressed against the wall, panting heavily at my narrow escape. "Kiera," he exclaimed in alarm.

"Stop!" I ordered. "Someone just shot at me through the window."

He followed my gaze toward the ceiling, where the bullet was now lodged.

"They may still be out there."

Trevor slowly made his way closer, giving the sight line of the window a wide berth. "Are you injured?"

"I . . . I don't think so," I stammered, turning my back to him. "But you might check me for glass."

Jeffers and Bree soon appeared in the doorway.

"The garden," I told the butler.

He retreated and Bree advanced into the room, circling widely to where I stood. Trevor allowed her to take over the task of removing glass shards from my hair, while he inched toward the window, glass crunching beneath his feet. When he inched his head too far out for my comfort, I opened my mouth to caution him again when he spoke over me.

"They've got him!"

"Who?"

"I don't know."

I moved over beside him, gazing down into the shadowed garden where I could just make out a few shapes in the darkness. Two of the men were restraining another, who appeared to be Fletcher, for I heard him curse foully. They were tying him up with some sort of rope, and not gently. A fourth man looked on, and when he glanced up, I realized it was Bonnie Brock.

He touched his forelock with a rather exaggerated flourish and then melted away into the shadows. His men soon followed, leaving Fletcher trussed up on the damp grass. Not two minutes later, Gage appeared, followed by Anderley and Maclean.

My husband took one look at Fletcher and his pistol laid in the grass beside him and then up at me standing before the broken window and darted toward the French doors. A minute later, I was in his arms.

"He spotted one of the men," Gage explained with a shake of his head a short time later when we'd all gathered in the drawing room. Maclean had led Fletcher off to jail while the men stationed at the church in Charlotte Square were apprised of the situation. Henry and Lord Edward had arrived at our door soon after.

"He ran and we took off in pursuit. But he already had a significant lead, given Anderley . . ." he nodded to his valet ". . . and I were inside the chapel." Gage looked down at me where I sat close to his side with his arm draped around my shoulders. "He must have realized we were the ones to figure out his plans, and he undoubtedly already knew we were harboring Mr. Rimmer, so he came here." His eyes were shadowed with a regret I wanted to wipe away, for none of this was his fault.

"I was returning to the drawing room after looking in on Emma and Mr. Rimmer when I heard a strange clicking sound," I said, explaining my part in the matter. "Fletcher must have been throwing pebbles at the window to draw someone's attention, and I was too foolish to realize that it meant trouble until it was almost too late."

"At least, you *did* realize it," Trevor said. "I didn't grasp a thing was wrong until I heard the glass shatter."

"He'd fired a bullet through the window," I clarified. "Presumably content to hit whoever approached to discover what the disturbance was."

Henry's eyes widened at the horror of it. "Fletcher must be unhinged. I'm glad you arrived in time to catch him before he got away," he told Gage, who grimaced, confusing Henry. "You didn't? Then who . . ."

"Kincaid," Gage stated flatly.

Henry sat back, looking as if he would like to swallow his own tongue. Lord Edward, in the meantime, was watching us all avidly, as if this was a great show. I arched a single eyebrow at him, telling him he was rather transparent.

"I know I should be grateful to the man for he's saved us several times," Gage said. "Except I can't help but feel he does it to irk me as much as anything else."

"Oh, undoubtedly," I told him, reaching up with my hand to tug playfully on his cravat.

He narrowed his eyes at me and then, heedless of everyone present, suddenly pressed a fierce kiss to my temple. One that let me know just how deeply affected he still was by it all. I knew that Gage struggled with the knowledge that he could never guarantee my safety, no matter the precautions he took, specifically when we were conducting an inquiry.

"Fletcher must've been the person who pushed ye in front o' that carriage, too," Bree proposed. She was sitting close to Anderley's side on the other sofa—their differences still unresolved, but for the moment they seemed to be at peace with one another.

"More than likely," Gage replied. "He must have witnessed

my altercation with Maclean outside Jamieson's house and saw Kiera stride away. I can only assume he decided that attacking Kiera would convince us to give up the investigation or at least serve as a distraction."

"So the threat is passed?" Trevor wanted to know. "You're certain he hadn't already done any damage?"

"Yes. Judging from the tools found in his bag, he planned to do it tonight, and neither Anderley nor I noticed any indication that the structure had been tampered with. We've also informed the church leaders of Fletcher's attempt and apprehension, so that they can do a more thorough search of the building themselves. Meanwhile, Maclean will hopefully be able to extract more details from Fletcher himself, but we already have more than enough, especially considering his shooting at Kiera, to keep him locked up."

The room seemed to exhale a collective sigh of relief, perhaps each of us acknowledging for the first time the extent of the strain we'd been under.

"And now we can focus on more pleasant matters." Gage squeezed my shoulders. "Such as Kiera's art exhibition."

I flushed lightly.

"Speaking of which . . ." Henry leaned forward. "Father . . . the duke . . ." he corrected, realizing there might be some confusion at the term *father* among the people gathered ". . . wishes to host the exhibit at Bowmont House."

"Truly?" I murmured as Henry smiled.

"Mother is agreed," Lord Edward added. "They both said they would be delighted to."

I turned to Gage, recognizing there were still some feelings of resentment toward them for the manner in which they'd interfered during our investigation at Sunlaws Castle in January 1832. I didn't wish to upset him, but sponsorship by a duke and duchess, particularly ones as scandalous as the Duke and

Duchess of Bowmont, was certain to draw eyes. And eyes were what I needed if my portraits were to make an impact.

"I think it's a splendid idea," Gage replied.

And so it was that in just a few weeks' time, *The Faces of the Forgotten* was exhibited to a crush of guests at Bowmont House. I hired a fully recovered Mr. Rimmer to help me display them to maximum effect in the ballroom. The exhibition did not escape its critics, but then, I'd expected them. But by and large, the reaction was positive, and more than half the paintings had sold before the night ended. Demands for portrait commissions once again increased, though I continued to decline them all. I had a number of portraits intended for friends and family I'd put off as I finished *The Faces of the Forgotten* and then I had another series of paintings in mind I wanted to work on.

In any case, our lives were too full the next few months for me to spend much time painting. Even when we returned to Bevington Park in early June, we were too busy supervising the final stages of the renovations to the dower house that was to be our home and planning the house party we intended to host with Gage's father for me to pick up a paintbrush as often as I liked. When the date of the party finally arrived, I had high hopes of finally enjoying a few weeks of relaxation, but murder had a way of dashing such hopes. Even worse, it threatened to dash my brother's future happiness.

HISTORICAL NOTE

When I was brainstorming plot ideas for the thirteenth Lady Darby Mystery, I stumbled across a historical incident I simply knew I had to utilize. On March 16, 1833, the floor collapsed in the midst of the third day of the auction of John Clerk's (Lord Eldin's) collection of pictures, sending eighty to one hundred people plummeting to the story below. In my quest to learn more about this, I was able to obtain a copy of the real auction catalog as well as multiple newspaper articles describing the incident. These enabled me to portray the calamity as close to accurately as possible. I even found diagrams of the rooms at 16 Picardy Place before and after the collapse which had been created by a witness.

The one notable exception between my portrayal in the book and reality is the fact the collapse was almost certainly accidental. It was caused exclusively by the use of subpar materials and building methods rather than tampering and sabotage. But when I read about this extraordinary event, immediately the question sparked: "What if?" What if it wasn't an accident? What if someone helped it along? And so the genesis of the plot began.

Several of the characters in the story are also actual historical figures, including Lord Eldin; Thomas Winstanley, the auctioneer; William Clerk; Sir James Riddell; Alexander Smith, the only casualty; and Reverend Jamieson. Though many of the included attributes and anecdotes about these men were pulled from the historical record, others have been made up or interpreted in order to make the characters fully formed individuals. In particular, I would like to note that I've taken a bit of creative license with Reverend Jamieson. To the best of my knowledge, Jamieson never stole anything in his life, least of all four valuable ancient coins, even if it was for a good cause. In fact, Jamieson actually fell through the floor during the collapse, making such an act of larceny impossible. I changed this detail purely for the purposes of my plot.

The gallery collapse at the church in Kirkcaldy on June 15, 1828, was also a real historical incident. One which was referenced in the newspaper articles about the floor collapse at the auction of Lord Eldin's collection. In terms of loss of life and bodily injury, Kirkcaldy was the far greater tragedy. Though if the people at the auction had panicked, there undoubtedly would have been more casualties. The cooler heads that prevailed during that calamity saved many lives, as did the quick thinking of the passing carpenter who heard the cries for help and intervened.

ACKNOWLEDGMENTS

Books are rarely, if ever, created in a vanilla-scented vacuum while the muse sits on your shoulder and whispers sweet nothings into your ear. No, they're created on a deadline, with children and chaos reigning over the household, and your muse (if one exists) hog-tied to a chair in one corner of your brain trying to ignore the squirrels having a rave in another corner. At least, that's how it works for me. As such, there are always numerous people to thank for making the act of getting words on the page possible. First and foremost, my husband—chief child and squirrel wrangler. Thank you for your never-ending love and support, and for always having my back. I love you!

My daughters—chief chaos creators and the best children a mother could ask for. Thank you for your love and enthusiasm and snuggles and goofy grins!

My agent, Kevan Lyon—my fiercest advocate. Thank you for your wisdom and guidance!

My editor, Michelle Vega—who helps me get my muse back on track. Thank you for loving to edit Lady Darby as much as I love writing her and for always making my books better!

The incredible team at Berkley, including but not limited to Annie Odders, Elisha Katz, Kaila Mundell-Hill, and Larry Rostant. Thank you for your always stellar efforts!

My friends and family for all of their devotion and encouragement, especially my parents, siblings, in-laws, cousins, and Mom's Group. For all the times you lend a hand, listen to me grumble, pray with me, make me laugh, or keep me sane—thank you!

And God, for making all this possible, and for holding me close through every hurdle and triumph.

Photo by Shanon Aycock

Anna Lee Huber is the award-winning and *USA Today* bestselling author of the Lady Darby Mysteries, the Verity Kent Mysteries, and the historical fiction title *Sisters of Fortune: A Novel of the Titanic*. She is a summa cum laude graduate of Lipscomb University in Nashville, Tennessee, where she majored in music and minored in psychology. She currently resides in Indiana with her family and is hard at work on her next novel.

VISIT ANNA LEE HUBER ONLINE

AnnaLeeHuber.com

Ready to find
your next great read?

Let us help.

Visit prh.com/nextread

Penguin
Random
House